One of our most distinguished and successful novelists, Catherine Gavin was born in Aberdeen and went on into academic life, politics and journalism. In 1944, after the Liberation of Paris, she was accredited to Supreme Headquarters, Allied Expeditionary Force, and for the next nine months alternated between combat reporting and covering the complex political situation in Paris. She was present at the German surrender at Rheims in May 1945, and was later decorated with the 1939–45 Star and the France and Germany Star. She is the author of such acclaimed novels as *Madeleine, Traitors' Gate, A Light Woman* and *The Glory Road*.

D1325178

By the same author

Fiction

The Sunset Dream
A Light Woman
The Glory Road

The French Resistance

Traitors' Gate
None Dare Call it Treason
How Sleep the Brave

World War One

The Devil in Harbour
The Snow Mountain
Give Me the Daggers
The House of War

The Second Empire Quartet

The Fortress
The Moon into Blood
The Cactus and the Crown
Madeleine

Biography and Politics

Liberated France
Edward the Seventh
Britain and France
Louis Philippe

CATHERINE GAVIN

A Dawn of Splendour

This edition published 1994 by
Diamond Books
77–85 Fulham Palace Road
Hammersmith, London W6 8JB

Published in paperback by Grafton Books 1990

First published in Great Britain by
Grafton Books 1989

Printed and bound in Great Britain

Set in Palatino

A Dawn of Splendour

Part One

1793

1

I have come to the end of all things.

The woman in the tumbril taking her through the streets of Paris to the guillotine had no recollection of using those words. She had spoken them after the Revolutionary Tribunal found her guilty of intelligence with the enemy, but that was yesterday. Today was a cold grey morning in October 1793, and her arrival at the end of all things could be counted in a matter of minutes.

Daughter of an empress, widow of a king, Marie Antoinette was deaf to the yells of "Death to the Widow Capet! Death to the Austrian!" from the gloating mob which followed her progress to death. She ignored the renegade priest who sat beside her as she ignored the executioner at her back. He had already cut her grey hair into jagged ends in readiness for the blade, and tied her hands behind her back. The writhing hands were her only movement, for Marie Antoinette needed, in the last hour of her life, to arrange the skirt of the shabby white dress which would be her shroud. Before the end of all things there was the final humiliation of an issue of blood from her body, spreading and staining every breadth of her dress.

The ribald jailers had seen the blood when they dragged her from her pallet bed in the Conciergerie, and laughed at her entreaties for some cloth, any cloth, to hide her condition. Only the high walls of the tumbril and the bodies of the priest and the executioner gave her some protection from the eyes of the street crowd. The people at the open windows and on the rooftops of the Rue St Honoré saw it all, and jeered.

The mob pressed closer to the tumbril and began to scuffle with the National Guard lining the causeway. A girl called Marie Fontaine freed herself from the crush by scrambling up the steps of St Roch's church to the portico, where an artist was recording for posterity the dumb despair of the woman who had been queen. She was near enough to see how his quick incisive strokes depicted the gaunt face, the double lines of suffering which dragged at her mouth and the cropped hair beneath her white cap. Marie's first thought was "He's making her look like a man!"

Then she saw the blood-stained dress and knew that the prisoner was certainly a woman, and sickened at the sight. Marie Fontaine felt as if her own body's privacy had been invaded. She closed her eyes, and in the darkness was aware of running steps and the shouts of the crowd moving on to join the throng round the guillotine. When she looked again the steps of St Roch were almost empty and Marie hastened to go. A lingering nausea made her clutch at the railing, but only for a moment. She was living through the Terror, protected from its worst excesses, but she knew better than to show any pity at the death ride of the woman who had once been queen. The few who glanced her way saw a composed face and a steady step as Marie Fontaine crossed the Rue St Honoré and went towards her home.

She was a tall girl of nineteen, with dark blue eyes set in a face too pale for beauty. The pallor was the result of hunger, for the Republic like the monarchy before it had brought famine to Paris. Marie's best asset was her hair, which she wore loose and falling to her shoulders. It was an unusual shade of blond, too dark for flaxen and too light for chestnut; on it she wore, slightly askew, the red cap of liberty. The shabby grey shawl above her black dress was adorned with the tricolore cockade, blue and red for the city of Paris with a white stripe between for the old flag of France with the lilies, which King Louis XVI himself had been forced to wear. The same colours were repeated on a sign saying 'National Property' nailed to the gate of the mansion next to her own modest home.

The great house belonged to the Noailles family, distinguished for centuries in the history of France. One of the daughters of the present generation had married the Marquis de La Fayette, who at nineteen had held the rank of major-general in the Continental Army, fighting with the Americans in their revolutionary war against England. He had protected the king and queen when another revolution broke over France. Marie Fontaine as a child had been the playmate of the La Fayette children, for Anastasie, Virginie and George-Washington were about her own age. It was her delight to be invited into the great house, to peep at the treasures of the Golden Salon and romp in the gardens laid out in the style of Le Nôtre. Now the Noailles family was scattered far and wide for the crime of being *aristos*, aristocrats, and the Republic had set its seal on their abandoned palace.

The little house next door was left untouched. On the street side a wooden façade was painted to look like marble, and on each side of the door was a window in which shelves held the majolica jars made of clay from Nevers and commonly used by pharmacists. An iron pestle and mortar hung above the door. On a painted wooden arch above this emblem was written the name

'*Michel Fontaine, Apothicaire*'

Marie hesitated. When alone she came and went by the garden entrance, a gate opening on the lane which crossed the Rue St Honoré and led to an open space where twice a week market women sold whatever green stuff and eggs were available. Today she felt a great need to be indoors, safe in the familiar surroundings and away from the horror of the tumbril. She opened the shop door in time to hear her Uncle Prosper say,

13

"Why the devil did you have to make yourself conspicuous?"

He was speaking to a man in a high-backed chair, with his coat off, and his face twisted in a grimace of pain. Prosper Fontaine turned swiftly to face his niece.

"Marie! What are you doing here at this time of day?"

"The supervisor dismissed us all at eleven o'clock. She said we ought to have a last look at the Widow Capet."

"And did you? Yes, I see you did . . . Well, now you're here you can help me with this gentleman."

"Has there been an accident?"

"Merely an incident, mademoiselle, caused by my own stupidity," said the stranger, speaking in correct but heavily accented French. The mere use of the term of respect 'mademoiselle' showed that he was a foreigner. 'Citizeness' was what every Frenchwoman had to be called now.

"This is Monsieur Adam Boone, a visitor from America," said the apothecary. "He had rather a rough welcome to Paris when he ventured too far into the roadway to see the – the Widow Capet."

"I got into trouble with the National Guard," said Boone. "They have their own way of making foreigners get back in line." He was a man of about thirty, powerfully built, with bruised knuckles which showed he had his own way of meeting trouble.

"His shoulder was dislocated in the scuffle," said Fontaine, "but it's back in place again, and fortunately there was no concussion. Heat some spiced wine for him, Marie, and drink some yourself: you look as if you'd caught a chill."

"It's a bitter day," said the American.

Perhaps her hearing had become more acute since she stood on the steps of St Roch's church. Marie wondered if *une journée amère* had a double meaning: a day of bitter cold, or of bitter wrong? She was glad to withdraw to the kitchen behind the shop, where a wood fire was always burning and a kettle of water kept simmering above it on an iron bar with hooks. A second hook supported a crock of potato soup for her uncle's midday meal. Throwing her red cap aside Marie poked the fire to a blaze, fetched wine, sugar and spices from a corner cupboard, and wondered why her uncle had not chosen one of the cordials ready to his hand. Had he sent her to the kitchen to get her out of the way? She could hear a murmur of conversation from the shop. The apothecary seemed to have plenty to say to the victim of patriotic zeal.

The kitchen window was open and Marie heard a sudden resurgence of noise. The tumbril must have turned into the street still called Royale, where no doubt an even larger crowd had gathered to see a royal lady go to her death. Now there was nothing ahead but the Place de la Révolution, where the blood-dabbled dress of Marie Antoinette would be soaked in blood when her head was stricken from her body. Marie shuddered. She poured out a little of the hot wine and drank it gratefully. Then she filled a thick tumbler with the steaming mixture and carried it on a pewter tray to Mr Boone.

He was standing up now and had shrugged his painful shoulder into his coat. It was a grey frock coat worn over a grey waistcoat and trousers, the whole suit stained with the dust and rubbish of the street. Marie had a fleeting impression, as he took the tumbler with a bow and a word of thanks, that he was more accustomed to wear uniform.

Perhaps she only thought so because the shop door opened to admit a tall man who actually was in uniform. Sky blue and scarlet, the first choice of the National Guard, it had to be immaculate to be impressive, and this man's regimentals were creased and shabby. Younger than the American, the newcomer looked slovenly by contrast, thanks to a day's dark stubble on his cheeks and chin. His good looks, which depended on well-cut features, were spoiled by an expression at once sullen and arrogant, as cultivated by most of the leading revolutionaries.

"Sergeant Vautour, citizens," he announced himself,

and looked at the American. "Is this the man who disobeyed the orders of the National Guard?"

"I suppose you could mean me," said Adam Boone, and there was a trace of amusement in his accented voice. "I didn't hear any orders, and I didn't expect to be knocked down and savaged by the Guard."

"Then why did you break through their ranks?"

"To get a closer look at the tumbril."

"Why? Are you a *logographe*?"

"What's a *logographe*?"

"A writer for the newspapers."

"No, but I've friends back there in America who will want to hear my impressions of the queen."

"The *ci-devant* queen," said Sergeant Vautour automatically. "The Widow Capet."

Ci-devant, meaning 'former' or 'formerly', was one of the key words of the French Revolution. Only fifteen at the time of the storming of the Bastille, Marie sometimes felt as if she had no former life before that July day. Her uncle spoke up.

"Citizen Boone is an American visitor to France," he said. "His curiosity was quite natural, and deserves to be excused."

"You're the apothecary? I'll come to you in a minute," said the sergeant, using the egalitarian 'thou' and 'thee'. He turned back to Adam Boone, who drained his glass and set it down on the counter between a small bronze pestle and mortar and a brass balance with weights.

"My men said you claimed to be a citizen of a neutral country," said Vautour. "That doesn't entitle you to defy the laws of France! I want to see your papers – if you can produce them – and ask a few questions about your presence here."

The American, in silence, took some documents from the inner pocket of his frock coat and handed them over.

"This is your passport, is it?" said Vautour. "Name Adam Boone, age thirty-three, born Boston – what's this word? Mass-a-chusetts, occupation wine-shipper. Do they drink much wine in Boston, citizen?"

"We acquired the taste from General de La Fayette."

"H'm! He won't be drinking wine today in his Prussian prison. So! You landed at the port of St Nazaire on the thirty-first of August, obtained a travel warrant for Bordeaux, and went from there to Paris on the first of October. You hold an exit permit to leave the capital on any date between the fifteenth, which was yesterday, and the twentieth of the month."

"That is correct."

"A very brief visit. Your address is given here as the Hôtel Molière – "

"In the Rue de la Loi."

"I know it, near the Théâtre Français. Now, citizen! Is there anyone in Paris who can vouch for you? Who can attest that you are a genuine businessman?"

"The American Minister, Gouverneur Morris."

"Oh! Oh indeed! Citizen Morris is highly respected in Paris . . . You may sit down if you wish."

Boone sat down in the high-backed chair with a breath of relief which betrayed the aching of his body. The apothecary intervened again.

"You can see for yourself, sergeant, that Citizen Boone was treated too roughly by your fellows. Is this long interrogation really necessary?"

"That's for me to decide," said Vautour, handing the papers back to Adam Boone. His movements were well co-ordinated and he knew how to stand while conducting an enquiry, but his pose was theatrical, with his right hand on one of the two pistols he carried in his belt. "Citizen Boone," he said, "I regret the incident. American travellers are welcome in Paris. But you must understand that the barring of the roadway as the Widow Capet's tumbril passed was absolutely necessary. You may not know that when her late husband went to the scaffold a band of royalists planned to seize him near the Barrier of St Denis and take him to a hiding place. They were

17

betrayed and arrested in the very act, for which they paid by death. The National Guard was on duty today to prevent a similar attempt at rescue. Now! One more question. What made you come to Citizen Fontaine for assistance?"

"I saw the sign of the pestle and mortar, and when your men released me I managed to get here."

"All members of the Society of Apothecaries are bound to give first aid to the injured," said Prosper Fontaine, "and now I recommend that Citizen Boone return to his hotel and rest."

"You do, do you?" said Vautour. He turned his dark gaze on the apothecary, who met it squarely. Fontaine was a man of fifty, who in old-fashioned knee breeches and swallow-tail coat of brown kerseymere gave an impression of solid strength. He had given up powdering his grey hair, but still wore it long enough to be tied back with a neat black silk bow. His steel-rimmed spectacles were characteristically pushed up to the top of his head. His smile, which came and went during Vautour's tirade, was small and cool, revealing only large front teeth like a rabbit's. He had been a widower for more than twenty years, but his young wife had liked to tease him about his 'rabbit smile', and called him Monsieur Lapin. When he was genuinely amused his mouth widened, and then his smile was broad and attractive. Prosper Fontaine could be accurately described as a man of two faces.

Before he could answer Vautour a wave of noise broke over the grey street, the sound for which all four people in the pharmacy had subconsciously been listening. It came from as far away as the Place de la Révolution, that shout of blood lust satisfied, of murderous hate gone mad. The *ci-devant* Queen of France had perished by the guillotine, and the executioner was holding up her severed head for acclamation by the people. Marie Fontaine crossed herself and there was silence until Sergeant Vautour exclaimed,

"Justice has been done!"

"If you believe in justice," said Adam Boone. "Am I free to go?"

"Back to your hotel?" said Vautour. "Of course, citizen; you're not being detained against your will. But you understand that we must be very careful in dealing with unaccredited foreigners. France is at war with half Europe, and an allied army of our enemies is only ten days' march from Paris. The fortress of Maubeuge is our last defence, and the Widow Capet had to die because she was conspiring against us with the Emperor of Austria. Is that quite clear?"

"Perfectly," said Boone. He looked for his hat and remembered that he had last seen it being kicked along the gutter. He asked Fontaine what there was to pay.

"For putting a dislocated shoulder back, and a glass of hot wine? Nothing, citizen. It was my duty and my pleasure, and I wish you a safe journey to Bordeaux. Rest that arm!" He moved to open the door, but Boone paused to say, "Thank you, Mademoiselle Fontaine, for your kind attention!" before he went out into the deserted street.

"Fontaine!" exclaimed Vautour. "Are you the apothecary's daughter?"

"My niece," said Prosper Fontaine, putting his arm round Marie's shoulders. "My dead brother's child, Marie."

"And you are Michel Fontaine?"

"You saw the name above the door and jumped to conclusions. Michel was the name of my father and my son. Mine is Prosper." But the National Guardsman was studying Marie.

"I've seen you somewhere before, citizeness," he said.

"Going or coming from my war work, possibly."

"What war work do you do, and where?"

"I work three days a week in a manufactory in the Palais Royal," she said. "Sewing shirts for the army."

"Who supervises the manufactory?"

"Madame – I mean Citizeness Merlot."

The sergeant laughed. "A true patriot," he said, "and

experienced in handling young women. But why only three days a *décade*? You must learn to say a *décade* instead of a week, you know."

"Yes, and the workers must learn to enjoy one day of rest in every ten days instead of every seven," snapped Marie. At the man's bullying tone she moved out of the shelter of her uncle's arm and backed defensively against the counter.

"Why only three days?" Vautour repeated. "Why don't you go to work every day, as other unmarried women do?"

"That was the decision of our Section," said Fontaine. "Would you care to challenge it?" He was on safe ground there. The Paris Commune, which had divided the former districts into forty-eight Sections, was not to be tackled lightly by a member of the National Guard. He went on:

"Our Section knows Marie is my assistant, and reduced her workshop hours accordingly."

"She serves in the shop, do you mean?"

"More than that. Marie has learned how to make certain preparations – "

"This sort of thing?" The sergeant looked quizzically at a shelf which held glass jars of cosmetics, hair oils and creams. These were grouped round an opened fan with the blue, white and red emblem which all shopkeepers found it politic to display.

"I can make rouge and face powder, but – "

"But your fan is faded." He picked it up. Inside the tricolore cockade was a coloured print of General the Marquis de La Fayette as commander of the National Guard. "Faded and out of date," said the Guardsman, and snapped the fan shut.

"Give it to me," said Marie. "It's a souvenir of National Federation Day."

"Three years ago."

"I suppose we should replace it with the latest novelty, honouring Citizen Marat," said Marie, and her uncle frowned.

"I know what my niece was going to say," he asserted. "'Yes, I can make cosmetics, but I'm learning how to measure medicinal powders and liquids and make pills.' If she were a boy she would be my apprentice."

"Apprentice indeed!" said Sergeant Vautour, feigning terror. "May heaven preserve me from a female apothecary! I wouldn't trust a woman to get the measures right. There might be poison in the pills."

"I don't make up poisons for human beings," said Marie. "Only for rats."

"You speak boldly, Marie Fontaine." The man in uniform turned to her uncle. "I wish you joy of your assistant, citizen. Wouldn't your son have been a more suitable choice?"

"My son?" said Fontaine. "Michel was in his second year as a student apprentice at the Botanical Gardens when war was declared. He joined the Army of the Republic. He was killed at the battle of Valmy, just over a year ago."

For the first time the sergeant lost his assurance. "I'm sorry," he said. "My condolences, citizen."

"Michel Fontaine did his duty," Marie said. "When the country was in danger he didn't wait to be conscripted. He didn't think he could serve France by hanging about the streets and harassing civilians. He fell in his first action, *mort pour la France*. My cousin Michel was a brave man!"

2

"What's got into you, Marie?" demanded Prosper Fontaine when he had locked the shop door behind Vautour and followed his niece into the kitchen. "I never heard you speak so wildly in my life. There's no sense in making enemies – and you as good as called that fellow a rat."

"He's more like a rat than a vulture," said Marie. She took a cloth of coarse clean linen and a few spoons from the table drawer. "Sergeant Vautour – The Vulture – what a name! What a horrible man! He tried to bully you, he insulted me. *He's* alive, while boys like Michel go to war and die . . ." Her broken words became a sob, the prelude to a burst of tears.

"Don't cry, my dear," her uncle said. Tender words, like caresses, were seldom exchanged between them, but the pharmacist was visibly moved when he asked her gently if she hadn't been fonder of Michel than she would ever admit.

"Not in the way you wanted – not like that," she said. "Michel was a kind brother to me and nothing more. But that Vautour, bursting in on us just after I saw the queen – "

"You might have been spared that. Damn the Merlot woman! Did she, did the queen, look very ill? Was that what upset you?"

Marie's strength seemed to fail her. She sat down at the table, laid her head on her arms and whispered something which sounded like, "It was her dress – her poor dress!"

Perhaps Fontaine had an inkling of what she meant. He said no more, but poured himself a glass of wine from the bottle opened for Boone, and drank it at a draught. Then he brought dishes from the cupboard, filled a tureen from the pot above the fire, and told Marie to stop crying and drink her soup.

"I don't want anything to eat."

"We both need food, such as it is, so don't be silly."

She was accustomed to obey, and felt guilty at her uncle's making the preparations for their midday meal. Marie accepted the blue bowl of soup which he filled for her. It was one of the staples of their wartime diet – the meat ration had already been reduced to half a kilo every ten days – and Fontaine made a hackneyed joke about what a blessing it was that Auguste Parmentier had promoted the culture of potatoes in France when he was chief pharmacist at the Hôtel des Invalides. Marie achieved a smile and said the potato soup was better than the stale bread and cheese provided at the workshop, and so they got through the soup and the dish of cold stewed apples which followed. Then Fontaine said,

"I ought to do some laboratory work this afternoon. Do you feel equal to taking charge of the shop?"

"Of course I do."

"I don't expect there'll be much trade today."

"But uncle, before I wash the dishes may I ask you something?"

"About our visitors of this morning?"

"Well, about the man Vautour. Could he get you into trouble with the Section because of anything I said?"

Her uncle smiled his rabbit smile. "Certainly not! I stand too high in the Section's favour, like all the members of my profession, for any young popinjay in the National Guard to attack me. Don't worry about the Vulture, Marie. His performance was a bit too theatrical to be convincing. I've a feeling that Sergeant Vautour is a young man who's not all he seems to be."

23

"Have you?" said Marie queerly. "Perhaps he's not the only one."

No more tumbrils came up the Rue St Honoré that afternoon, as if the execution of the *ci-devant* Queen of France deserved to be the one great event of the day. While Prosper Fontaine worked in the laboratory he had installed in the cellar, straining to see by the light of a window grating on the garden, Marie attended to a little crying boy who had been knocked down and bruised in the crowd streaming away from the Place de la Révolution. He was brought in by his mother, whom Marie knew as Citizeness Florette, one of the vegetable sellers in the lane. Normally a quiet woman, she was flushed with wine and the excitement of seeing the Widow Capet's head held up to the crowd in the packed square.

"Why, Jeannot, whatever have you been doing to yourself?" asked Marie. The boy's face was covered in grime and blood.

"We was at the execution, see, and it went off beautiful," said Florette, "but the brat got away from me and started skylarking with some other kids round the scaffold – "

"They pushed me," whined Jeannot. "My head hurts."

"Then the first thing we do is wash your face," said Marie. Her own face was white as she went to the kitchen for a basin of warm water. Skylarking round the scaffold – she tried not to think about it.

Florette offered to "hold on to the little devil", but the boy was docile enough as Marie gently washed his pale face clean and saw that the real damage was on the right temple, from which his own blood was still oozing. She opened the drawer in which bandages were kept in sealed envelopes, and took out a narrow-fold bandage and a pad. On the pad, using a silver spoon, she spread a golden-brown salve from one of the majolica jars.

"What's that stuff?" asked Florette suspiciously.

"It's a salve of white beeswax and sweet oil," said

24

Marie. "Please don't talk, citizeness. This isn't easy to do." It was the first time she had bandaged a real patient, but she had practised on her uncle, and she quickly and neatly kept the pad in place while she unrolled the bandage over it, and round and round again until she secured it in a flat knot above the injury.

"How does that feel, Jeannot?" she asked. "Better now?" At least the child had stopped crying.

"Get him home to bed and give him a hot sweet drink," she advised the mother. "Bring him to see my uncle tomorrow morning. He'll change the dressing and tell you what's to pay."

"You're as good as a doctor yourself, Citizeness Marie!" gushed the woman, and when she was alone Marie felt a new access of courage. She had met a test and met it well enough. Putting away all the traces of first aid she set out an inkstand and a quill pen and prepared to enter all the details of Jeannot's treatment in the day-book.

And sat staring at the blank space where she had expected to see the name of Adam Boone.

After a while she started to dust and polish the fittings of the pharmacy. These were her especial care, for the floor was washed daily by an old woman called Augustine, who lived at the far end of the lane. *La mère Augustine* had been cleaning and washing for the Fontaines for years, but the stairs were too much for her now, and as well as suffering from rheumatism she was almost completely deaf. Her silent presence added one more to the layers of silence which filled the Pharmacie Fontaine.

One wall of the shop was entirely fitted with drawers, each with a glass knob and a porcelain tablet on which the name of the contents was written in Latin. The drawers contained such specifics as rhubarb and senna powders, liquorice and calomel; some, divided to hold bottles, held liquids: paregoric used as an anodyne, tinctures of benzoin and lavender, and aromatic spirits of ammonia. Dangerous drugs were kept in the cellar laboratory, of which Fontaine alone kept the key.

When dusk fell Marie lit a lamp and placed it on the counter before she dusted her uncle's books, neatly arranged on two shelves. I saw that Vulture eyeing them, she thought; I hope they were radical enough for his taste. For while the top shelf held the classics of pharmacology from Gerard's *Herball* in translation to Antoine Baumé's *Dictionary of Chemistry* in six volumes, the bottom held Voltaire's *Candide*, Rousseau's *Social Contract* and several volumes of Diderot's *Encyclopedia*. Fontaine was known in the St Roch *quartier*, long before the storming of the Bastille, as a critic of authority and an anti-cleric.

When all was done Marie turned to the shelf which held the cosmetics and the La Fayette fan which Vautour had despised as out of date. She sat down in the high-backed chair and snapped the faded paper open and shut. Wrenched out of her passive acceptance of the Revolution by the sight of the suffering queen, Marie thought of the early time, when the French Revolution was the inspiration of poets at home and abroad and hailed as the splendid dawn of a new day. Then, in the floods of oratory celebrating the brotherhood of man, the rights of man, the triumph of international man, and so on, the idea of Federation was evolved. One was a Federal, one's duty was 'to federate', and in the humblest villages men and women kissed and danced in the ritual of federation. On the national scale a Federation Day was planned for 14 July 1790, the first anniversary of the storming of the Bastille. The only site in Paris big enough to hold the Federals pouring in from all parts of the country was the Champ de Mars, and in the spirit of federation bourgeois and workers joined in the digging and building required by the spectacular plans. Michel Fontaine, on leave from the Jardin des Plantes, had been one of the labourers, who in his wild enthusiasm had taught his young cousin to sing the new revolutionary song, the '*Ça ira*'. "*Ça ira, Ça ira!*" she sang along with him. "'It will come, it will come!' But Michel, what will come?"

"The greatest day in the history of France!" cried the

young man. "When the king takes the oath to his people, and the people take the oath to their king!"

The great day came, with thunder, lightning and a downpour of rain which destroyed the uniforms and the finery and dampened the spirits of three hundred and fifty thousand citizens who, between the Temple of Concord and the Altar of the Fatherland, heard the General-Marquis de La Fayette, mounted on a white horse, take the constitutional oath to 'the King, the Nation and the Law' in the name of the army and the National Guard. They heard the mass celebrated by Talleyrand, the Bishop of Autun. They did not hear the king take the oath, for Louis XVI, that master of the lost opportunity, was sheltering from the rain on a covered stand. But Queen Marie Antoinette came forward, youthful and beautiful, to present her little son to the multitude as their future king, and the people went wild with joy. The rain stopped about three o'clock, and Marie Fontaine, clutching her souvenir fan as she walked home with her uncle, was justified in asking:

"Is everything going to be all right now?"

"Now we have a constitutional monarchy, my child."

"So that's what Michel's song meant, 'It will come.' They were all singing it today."

"Ça ira? Something will certainly come, but what? When a man pushes a boulder down a steep hill and can't stop it, doesn't want to stop it . . ."

"Then – "

"Then there's a tremendous crash at the bottom."

Marie put the La Fayette fan back in its place. "I've been a fool," she said to herself, "a silly, trusting fool. Why should we live in safety while others go to the guillotine? And how long will our safety last now the Vulture has his eye on us? And that American, who made himself 'conspicuous' – was he meant to be lost in the crowd, and why? I must listen more, think more, try to understand . . ." It was a relief when her uncle came in and said prosaically:

27

"Any customers?"

"Only Florette and her boy." She described Jeannot's accident and her treatment, while Prosper Fontaine smiled approval.

"Good girl! Did you enter it in the day-book?"

"I did. But uncle – "

"What?"

"Did you forget to enter the dislocated shoulder?"

Her uncle was reading the book and did not meet her eyes. "That wasn't necessary," he said. "No material, no medication, and no fee . . . You did the right thing, Marie. You're ready for more advanced work now. Tomorrow I'll show you how to make a many-tailed bandage and put it on. But there's no sense in wasting lamp oil. Light a candle instead, and if any late customer turns up he can use the emergency knocker. Monsieur Guiart may drop in after supper."

Marie followed her uncle and stood in the back door while he completed the locking up process by turning the huge key in the gate on the lane. She drew a few deep breaths. It was not the growing season, but yet the air smelled sweet, as much from their own grass plot and the beds where young Michel had planted salads, pot herbs and simples from the Jardin des Plantes, as from the neglected garden of the Hôtel de Noailles next door. She picked a late lettuce and turned back into the lighted room.

The Fontaines' kitchen, which was also their living room, was more attractive by lamplight than on that grey noon. The family had originally come from Brittany, and possessed some fine pieces of farmhouse furniture, including two rush-bottomed armchairs, well cushioned, drawn invitingly up to the fire. A big rag rug softened the red-tiled floor in front of the hearth, and on the wall the brass pendulum of a clock painted with fruit and flowers ticked the minutes away. Uncle and niece sat down to a supper of boiled potatoes, two almost transparent slices of cold beef and the lettuce dressed with oil and vinegar, with a modest glass of wine apiece. When supper was over Prosper Fontaine asked his niece when she was next expected at the manufactory.

"Tomorrow, uncle. Madame Merlot told all the part-time workers they must put in extra time tomorrow to make up for today's – holiday."

Her uncle grimaced. "Then I advise you to go early to bed, my dear. Get to the Palais Royal before the tumbrils begin to roll. You don't want to run into another scene like this morning's."

"There'll never be another scene like this morning's. And didn't you say Monsieur Guiart was coming in this evening?"

"I expect him, yes."

Louis-Jacques Guiart was Fontaine's closest friend, and the man who insisted that a pharmacist, serving the public and taking no part in politics, had nothing to fear from the extremists who within three years of the joyous *Fête de la Fédération* had subjected France to a Reign of Terror. Monsieur Guiart himself, a master apothecary, continued to work tranquilly in his own laboratory on the Rue St Honoré. As the professor of botany at the Collège de France he had sponsored young Michel's admission to a student apprenticeship at the Botanical Gardens, but his influence had not been strong enough to prevent the same gardens from being partly destroyed by vandals among the revolutionaries. This was after Michel Fontaine was killed in action; Guiart's own son was too young for the conscription which followed.

"Oh, then I must make everything very tidy," said Marie. When the dishes were washed in the tiny scullery and another log put on the fire, she fetched the pewter tray again and set out a bottle of brandy and two crystal glasses before bringing out her mending basket and preparing to establish herself at the table. She had passed many evenings in that way, sitting in the background with a book or her sewing, ready to jump up and replenish the glasses while the two men discussed pharmacology from the lofty altitude of the *Collège de Pharmacie*.

29

This evening, however, her uncle was impatient. "It's nearly nine o'clock," he said. "You ought to go to bed now, Marie."

"Uncle, I feel horribly wakeful. As if I should never sleep again."

"You've had a hard day. I'll bring you up an infusion of lime blossom in a quarter of an hour, and you'll sleep the night away. Things will look better in the morning."

"You're very kind."

Kind, yes; sincere, she doubted it. By the light of a tallow candle Marie climbed the wooden stair. There were three rooms on the upper floor; her uncle's, which faced the Rue St Honoré, and two smaller rooms which faced the garden. One which had been Michel's as a schoolboy was now used for storing pharmaceutical and cosmetic supplies. Marie's was comfortable enough, with a rug on the wooden floor, although the narrow bed was eclipsed by a marble-topped washstand and a Breton *armoire* which held every article of clothing she possessed. She was wearing her long white nightdress with a little white nightcap tied over her fair hair when her uncle came tapping at the door.

"Drink this while it's hot, my dear, and sleep well."

The *tisane* was in a white china cup with a lid, and was too hot to drink. Marie set it on the window-sill, pulled the grey shawl round her shoulders and sat down on the end of the bed to wait. It was a dark night, and nothing was to be seen beyond the high brick wall on the left which hid the Noailles garden. On the right, looking west, there was a glow in the sky of which Marie had long known the sinister meaning. It came from the light of torches so planted round the scaffold in the Place de la Révolution that a squad of men could see to do their nightly work of cleaning the blade of the guillotine, the straps, the plank and the blood-soaked platform, sweeping the red tide into the gutter and making ready for the next batch of victims. By night, too, the death carts took the piled and mixed heads and bodies to the cemetery of Ste Madeleine.

To stop another fit of shivering Marie reached for the posset cup and took a careful sip. It was no longer too hot but too sweet, so sweet as almost to destroy the delicate lime blossom taste. Perhaps the sugar was intended to dominate another taste which Marie had learned to identify; the taste of poppy juice, which her uncle used in soporifics.

Why has he prepared a sleeping draught for me? For my own good or to ensure my silence? Perplexed and fearful, Marie replaced the lid on the china cup, blew out her candle and crept into bed. She kept the shawl round her throat, for the blankets were thin, and closed her eyes.

Instantly a picture formed in the darkness. Again she saw the steps of St Roch, the artist furiously sketching, and the *ci-devant* Queen of France in her bloodstained dress. How long the hideous image would have lasted Marie could not tell. She heard some quiet movements on the floor below. There were footsteps crossing the shop, entering the kitchen, and the subdued hum of talk began. Obviously Monsieur Guiart had arrived.

She was dozing off, lulled by a false sense of security, when her uncle's voice was raised. It was not the tone he ever used to Monsieur Guiart, who contracted out a good deal of his own laboratory work to the Pharmacie Fontaine, thereby adding to a livelihood straitened since the Revolution. It was the acerbity of "Why the devil did you have to make yourself conspicuous?", the challenge she had remembered all day long. Marie slipped out of bed and went on bare feet to the landing. The staircase door was shut, so that she saw only a crack of light from the kitchen, but she could hear the voices of two men. Without shame, though she knew what was said of eavesdroppers, Marie listened intently. The second voice was not the pontifical bass of Monsieur Guiart. It was the very distinctive voice of the American who called himself Adam Boone.

3

The man in the green coat left his modest lodging further up the Rue St Honoré very early next morning, when the concierges of the tall apartment houses were opening their doors for the day. Although the man was wearing no patriotic emblem they knew him well. Some of them had heard him speak in the Convention, rising in his place among the Jacobins on the Left to attack the Girondins on the Right, and they knew his power, although on the Federation Day of 1790 few had ever heard his name. Since that happy, that almost innocent feast day, the new dawn had turned into a bloodstained noon. One year later the royal family had attempted a flight across the eastern border where the armies of Austria and Prussia were mobilising along with Frenchmen who had emigrated to safety. They were discovered and brought back ignominiously to their palace of the Tuileries. Another June, and they had to seek shelter inside the National Assembly when a mob stormed the palace: in August their faithful Swiss guards, nine hundred strong, died to the last man to protect the king and queen, who with their two children were taken to prison in the Temple.

The Commune came to power, the Prussians took Verdun, and for one week in September 1792 the prisons of Paris, full to overflowing, were emptied by the simple process of butchering the prisoners. Now the Committee of Public Safety ruled, and the man who ruled the Committee was the man picking his way as daintily as a cat along the tumbril ruts of the Rue St Honoré. The concierges sweeping out their doorways went inside at the sight of him. In Maximilien Robespierre they saw the Terror walking.

He was a lawyer from Arras, who like so many others saw in the French Revolution an opportunity to lever himself upwards from a mediocre situation in life. The invention of the ingenious Dr Guillotin was exactly suited to his sense of mission. When the guillotine was first used for public executions some spectators complained that it was too quick. There was more pleasure, more private sexual satisfaction, in watching the slow jerking of a hanging body or hearing the screams of a wretch broken on the wheel. But the blade of the guillotine could despatch twenty in a morning, while a ceremonial hanging disposed of only one. Robespierre, pursuing traitors, royalists, non-juring priests and returning émigrés with equal zeal, was just the man to supply the twenty.

In a time when to be slovenly in dress and speech was to be fashionable, when the *sans-culottes*, or breechless ones, went barefoot in their newfangled striped trousers and torn shirts open to the waist, Maximilien Robespierre was a model of bourgeois neatness. On this cold October morning his dark green surtout was worn above a nankeen waistcoat, striped pale green and white, and a red silk cravat. His face was a cat's face, square at the forehead and pointed at the chin, with green cat's eyes looking warily at the world. He was on his way to the Convention, meeting in an all-night session, to demonstrate the guillotine technique of applying a closure. The exhausted debators, on the morning after the Widow Capet's death, would be in the right mood to assent to a purge of his Girondin enemies. He licked his lips at the thought of it, like a cat approaching a saucer of cream.

The National Assembly, which had changed its name to the Convention after the abolition of the monarchy and the proclamation of the Republic One and Indivisible in September 1792, had moved from the *Manège*, or Riding

School of the Tuileries, now called the National Palace, to the upper floor of that home of kings. The Committee of Public Safety met in the Hôtel de Ville. The Place du Palais Royal, where Marie Fontaine sewed shirts for the army, lay between the two, and she walked there rapidly about half an hour after Robespierre had passed, exchanging pleasant greetings with women on their way to the shops. The apothecary's niece was respected in the *quartier*, although few of the remaining inhabitants knew her well enough to see the new firmness in the delicate moulding of her mouth and chin, or to interpret the sad glance she gave at the empty portico of St Roch.

There was as yet no sign saying National Property on the three great doors of the church, but because the priests of St Roch had refused to take the civic oath the doors were locked and services were prohibited. Marie Fontaine had been baptised there, had learned her catechism and made her First Communion at St Roch's altar, for her uncle had never tried to infect her with his own agnosticism. Without the consolations of the Church the girl had lost the habit of prayer; what sustained her in the days of the Terror was the dumb instinct of survival.

The Hôtel de Noailles was not the only mansion to be locked and labelled National Property. In the ancient Rue St Honoré there were other great houses whose owners had either emigrated or died by the guillotine; all of these were National Property now, and some had been looted in the general exuberance. Some had 'Les aristos à la lanterne!' or 'Mort aux aristos!' scrawled on the boarded-up windows, and the shops which catered to their owners' taste in jewels, fans, satin slippers and lace ruffles had gone out of business. In the lanes and alleys of the *quartier* the butcher and the baker sold such food as they had to sell early in the day, and a little man capable of carrying a *stère* of wood in a triangular shaped hod on his back and a dozen bottles of table wine in a hand basket sold wine and firewood to the remaining flat dwellers. The Street of St Honoré had become the Street of the Tumbrils, of death instead of life, and the sluggish tide of commerce had flowed instead into the Place du Palais Royal.

Here too there was an empty palace, for its tenant Philippe, Duc d'Orléans, the king's cousin and rival who had voted for his death, had found that dropping his title and calling himself Philippe Egalité did not redeem him from the taint of aristocracy, and had judged it prudent to leave Paris for Marseille. The gardens and fountains in the square which he had maintained for the public good had fallen into disrepair, and it was nobody's business to sweep the paths and arcades clear of fallen leaves. At night there was a sinister animation about the place, for Egalité's Vaudeville Theatre played to capacity (like all Paris theatres during the Terror) and there was an innovation in the form of 'restaurants' where food was served, opened by men employed as chefs by the defunct *aristos*. In the chilly morning when Citizeness Merlot, like an angry schoolmistress, was herding her sewing women into the bare hall heated only by one small brazier, the Place du Palais Royal was depressing indeed.

Marie understood what Vautour meant when he said the patriotic Citizeness Merlot was experienced in handling women. A week in the workroom, and the ribald conversation of some of the girls taught her that the Merlot woman had kept a well-run brothel before the war, and owed her job as supervisor to the influence of one of her best patrons, now an army contractor. Some of the sempstresses were prostitutes, who paid her a percentage of what they earned by night and went unrebuked for idling and gossiping by day. They were in disgrace for the moment, like every other female in the establishment, for as Citizeness Merlot went among the workers, giving out the cheap material and the needles and thread, she had the same question to put to each.

"Did you witness the execution of the Widow Capet?"

"No, citizeness. Unfortunately – "

There was always some excuse. Caught in the crowd, kept behind the barricade of the National Guard, unable to keep up with younger patriots, thrust away by the knitting women, *les tricoteuses*, whose places were kept for them at the foot of the scaffold – the long and the short of it, said the outraged Merlot, was that none of them deserved the holiday she had so kindly given them. They had profaned the memory of that great man, Citizen Marat.

Citizeness Merlot had a natural turn for invective. She would have been a star of the Jacobin Club, if the Jacobins had admitted women. She was tall and heavy with a florid face, and when she orated her red cap fell forward on her brow, giving her the look of a one-horned animal. She had a cult for the late Citizen Marat, editor of the scurrilous newspaper *L'Ami du Peuple*. Marat had announced that 270,000 traitors should die by the guillotine, which had inspired a young Norman girl called Charlotte Corday to journey to Paris and stab him to death in his own bath tub.

Looking out of the dirty window Marie could see in an arcade across the garden the shop where Charlotte Corday had bought the knife to do the deed. She had been arrested immediately and executed the next day, going to the guillotine smiling in the first tumbril to take the route of the Rue St Honoré to the Place de la Révolution. Then the man she murdered, vile and diseased though he was, became a hero to patriots like the Merlot, who had Marat fans and Marat posters in the dingy workroom, where Charlotte Corday's victim was depicted like a saint, his head surrounded by an aureole of stars.

When the supervisor had said her say there was the silence of fear in the workroom. No one was prepared to comment on the execution of the *ci-devant* queen. No one knew how any remark might be misconstrued, or reported to the Section as royalist propaganda. There were spies everywhere, perhaps among the lively prostitutes, perhaps among the decent older women who helped the beginners with such problems as the setting-in of sleeves.

The Commune, which ruled by intimidation, had done its work well, and fear was everywhere.

Marie Fontaine was learning suspicion. The two visits of Adam Boone to the pharmacy had convinced her that her uncle was involved in some plot, whether for or against the Republic she could not tell. Was he what she had heard Citizeness Merlot call *un mouton*? She thought not, for the 'sheep' grazed in the prisons, where they were pastured to receive and betray the confidences of the prisoners.

She knew that Prosper Fontaine's humorous, cynical and reserved personality had changed since his son fell in battle. Never one to frequent the clubs – Jacobins, Cordeliers or Feuillants – whose windy oratory had done so much to set the French Revolution on the path of violence, he now frequented the Convention. At the night sessions he moved about in the public tribunes, an unobtrusive figure in the vast hall dominated by a giant statue of Liberty. He wandered in the night streets, he told Marie, "to get a breath of fresh air after listening to the Deputies". Did he meet other wanderers in those dark streets? What did he say to them?

When Marie left the workroom the square was lit by lanterns slung on ropes between the pillars of the arcades. Those ropes and others like them had been used for summary executions when the Revolution began, and '*à la lanterne!*' was still a favourite slogan of the mob. By the light of the nearest lamp Marie was disgusted to see, patrolling the path opposite the door, the military figure of Sergeant Vautour.

"Good evening, citizeness!" he said, falling into step beside her.

"What brings you here, sergeant?" said Marie coldly. "Am I under surveillance?"

"The idea!" he exclaimed. "Of course you're not. I wanted to see you again, that's all."

"Don't let me detain you from your urgent military duties."

"I must report at the National Palace in an hour . . . Those cobblestones are slippery: will you take my arm?"

"Certainly not." Marie wrapped her cold hands in the folds of her grey shawl. She walked on, the man keeping pace with her until she said, without looking at him:

"What do you want of me?"

"Two things. First, I want you to forgive me if I said anything to offend you yesterday – I mean about your cousin. You understand, I knew nothing about him, either his existence or his death."

"Forgiving you won't bring Michel back to life."

"Were you in love with him?"

"Good heavens!" cried Marie. "Can't a girl speak up for a man who isn't there to speak for himself? Can't she praise his courage without being asked if she loved him?"

"No," said Vautour. "At least, not the girls I used to know."

"You and my uncle would agree on that, at least."

"Ah!" said Vautour. "That's the second thing I want of you. To tell your uncle something that I think will interest him."

"Tell him yourself."

"It'll come better from you. But we can't talk here," said the man, for the path had become crowded, and they were jostled by the clerks from a nearby ministry, hurrying home with their coat collars turned up. "Why don't you come and drink a glass of wine with me in comfort?"

"I? Sit drinking in a café with a stranger? You must be crazy."

"Was Lieutenant Buonaparte a stranger when you drank wine at the Régence with him?"

"Lieutenant – "

"You heard me. Buonaparte, the little Corsican artillery officer who spent a good deal of time hanging around the *quartier* a year ago, when he was lodging in the Rue du Mail. I remembered last night where I'd seen you before. Of course, you've changed a bit since then. You were all dressed up when you went out with Buonaparte, and you'd done something fancy to your hair. He – "

"Sergeant Vautour," interrupted Marie, "I've been in the Café de la Régence exactly once in my life, and my uncle was there too. He used to play chess with Lieutenant Buonaparte. We were invited to supper with him and another officer, to celebrate his captaincy."

Marie's voice was as steady as ever, but she was glad they were crossing the dark street which led into the Rue St Honoré. Her cheeks were hot, and she knew that she was blushing furiously.

"Citizen Fontaine and Buonaparte, that's a curious couple," said Vautour. "He was a funny fellow, that little Corsican. The Permons used to laugh at him and call him Puss in Boots."

"Who are the Permons?"

"Friends of his from Corsica. He went to their home a lot. Well! Here we are at the Régence. Sure you won't change your mind?"

"Quite sure, thank you." They were in a well-lit place now, for the lamps of the Théâtre Français vied with the lamps of the famous café, and Marie saw that Vautour was closely shaved and far more spruce than on the day before. She told him that if he had any message for her uncle he had better give it to her now, and allow her to walk home alone.

"Very well, if that's what you prefer. I suppose you can guess what the message is about? It concerns your patient of yesterday, the man from America."

"I can guess you lost no time in calling on the American Minister to check the credentials of Mister Boone from Boston."

"Correct. At least, I went to his residence early this morning, only to find that Citizen Gouverneur Morris left the day before yesterday for his country house at Melun. I should have known he would disappear before the execution of the Widow Capet. He's always been squeamish when the people's justice must be done."

"So you're none the wiser," said Marie mockingly.

"Oh yes I am. I went straight to find Citizen Adam Boone at the Hôtel Molière. I was too late by several hours. Boone passed the Gate of the Star at five o'clock this morning, in the first coach of the day to leave Paris."

"Why not? He had an exit permit for Bordeaux, valid for three, or was it four, more days?"

"Quick thinking," approved Vautour. "But the coach he took wasn't bound for Bordeaux, where he said he had business. Boone left for Nantes, which may mean anything. A passage to Boston from St Nazaire, or a disappearance into royalist Brittany. Just tell your uncle that the bird has flown."

4

It was after six o'clock when Marie reached home. The pharmacy was closed, but a note in her uncle's handwriting lay on the kitchen table, announcing that he had gone to the Section office but would be back by seven. Marie was glad of the respite. She heated some milk and sat down in the firelight to drink it and indulge herself in the memory, conjured up by Vautour, of a young lieutenant of artillery called Napoleon Buonaparte.

Marie Fontaine had been completely heart-whole until she was eighteen. The pressures of the times forbade even the mildest sociabilities, and the only young males she ever met were her cousin's fellow-students at the Jardin des Plantes, some of whom came home with Michel on Sundays to talk botany with his father. These earnest youths were scattered now. Two had enlisted along with Michel Fontaine; two more were émigrés in England, where they found employment as Young Gardeners at Kew. Lieutenant Buonaparte, older than the students, was not twenty-three when he came to the pharmacy to consult Prosper Fontaine. He and Marie met in unromantic circumstances, for she was behind the counter while he described in complete detail the digestive upsets which accompanied what he called his bilious condition.

He spoke French with an unusual accent, but there was something so compelling in his way of talking that he appeared to be taller than the apothecary, which he was not. Marie forgot the shabbiness of his uniform and the

41

greasy black hair which hung to his shoulders in the fashion called 'dog's ears' when she saw his brilliant eyes, and when at her uncle's direction she gave him a box of pills he thanked her with a brilliant smile.

"Bilious condition!" said Fontaine when the customer had gone. "Hunger, I call it. Eating the wrong food and precious little of that. Did you notice his sunken cheeks? I've seen him once or twice at the Régence, making one glass of wine last through a long game of chess. It's not a face that's easy to forget."

Presently the apothecary and the young lieutenant were playing chess together, and Fontaine discovered the reason for the young man's penury. He had no right to eat in any army mess, nor even to wear uniform (but he had nothing else to wear) because in February 1792 he had been cashiered from the army. Overstaying his leave in Corsica, his native island, to look after his widowed mother and the brothers and sisters who depended on him, was the reason given. Now he was in Paris to beg for reinstatement, and was cultivating the friendship of Augustin Robespierre, a milder version of his brother, the terrible Maximillien.

Fontaine was impressed by the young man, and invited him more than once to supper at his home. Marie cooked, Marie poured the wine, Marie blushed at the compliments spoken in a Corsican accent, Marie was on the delicious verge of falling in love. His first visit, in the June of 1792, took place two days after the mob invaded the Tuileries, when even the iron shutters of the pharmacy, hastily closed, had not kept out the noise of a rabble in arms. Buonaparte's comments on the episode were severe. The king, instead of going to ground among the Deputies, should have confronted his enemies on horseback. "A whiff of grapeshot," he said, "and the cowards would have turned tail and run."

Those were rash words, and the young man never repeated them. He talked, then and later, and out of his voracious reading, of far-off lands where France could

42

build an empire. With American help France could take Canada back from the British. By the conquest of Egypt and Turkey the road to India, and hence the lost Indian possessions, could be won back. It was heady stuff, and he made his hearers believe in it as he believed in himself. They were not surprised when the Corsican's story had a happy ending. He was reinstated in the army with the rank of captain, and the award of all his back pay since February.

That was when he returned the Fontaines' hospitality by inviting them to a celebration at the Régence, along with his only close friend, an officer called Bourrienne. As the Régence did not serve meals the supper was sent in by a *traiteur*, and consisted of pasta in various forms, not recommended for a bilious condition. Marie, in pale blue muslin, with a rose in the curls into which she had dressed her fair hair, was thrilled by the novelty, the wine and the admiring glances of many men. Most thrilling of all were the eyes of Buonaparte, those astonishing eyes which were neither blue nor grey. She was chilled when the young adventurer announced that instead of rejoining his regiment he was going back to Corsica, escorting his sister Elisa home from boarding-school.

"Too much Corsica," said her Uncle Prosper as they walked back from the café. "Buonaparte might do great things if he could only get Corsica out of his system. He ought to ask for a posting to Paris and let his new friends in high places help him on. Carnot, now, the best military man they've got, might find a job for that young man. Well, I shall miss our games of chess."

And I shall miss you, Napoleon Buonaparte, thought the silent girl by Fontaine's side.

She was so lost in the dream which had no substance that Marie was startled when her uncle came in from the shop carrying a lamp and demanded to know why she was sitting in the dark.

"You've been crying," he said, as the lamplight showed tear stains on her cheeks. "What's the matter, child?"

"It was that horrible man Vautour," she lied. "He was hanging about when I came out of the workroom. He said he had a message for you."

"What message?"

"'Tell him the bird has flown.' That's what he said. He'd found out that Adam Boone left Paris by the first coach this morning."

"I don't blame him, after what happened yesterday."

"The coach was going to Nantes, not to Bordeaux."

"So Vautour wants to make a drama out of that, does he?" said Fontaine tranquilly. "There's nothing to cry about, Marie! I've just been to the Section, where the Vigilance Committee issued certificates of good citizenship to you and me. Look!" he flourished two sheets of paper, "I'm going to lock them in the shop, in the counter drawer. Show them to Vautour if he favours us with another visit."

"But why do we need certificates? Is this something new?"

"It's a precaution against the new Law of Suspects . . . Augustine brought four eggs this morning. You might make an omelette for supper."

He knew already, thought Marie, as she tied on a white apron and began the supper preparations. That's why he took Vautour's message lightly – because the whole thing was planned when Boone came here last night. And I'm too much of a coward to challenge my uncle, to ask him what is the bond between a Paris apothecary and an American stranger who makes himself conspicuous in the street.

They passed a silent evening. Marie read *Les Liaisons Dangereuses*, without fully understanding the subtlety of that study of the sexual corruption of the innocent, while Prosper Fontaine, with his spectacles in their proper place instead of on top of his head, read the war news in the *Moniteur* and understood it only too well. France was encircled by the enemies she had challenged. The English now held the port and city of Toulon, and three of the four fortresses which guarded the eastern approaches to Paris had already fallen to an allied army commanded by the Duke of Coburg. The republican general Custine had been guillotined for his failure to hold Valenciennes, and now only Maubeuge remained, although under siege.

Fontaine sighed, laid down the newspaper and rubbed his eyes. Then he smiled at Marie.

"How often have you read that book, I wonder?"

"Oh, I don't know. I haven't got many books, and you won't let me read *Justine*."

"It's a vile book, and the Marquis de Sade's an odd choice for the leader of the Place Vendôme Section . . . What do you plan to do with the *décadi* tomorrow?"

"Stand in line at the butcher's and baker's, I suppose."

"They'll only be open for a couple of hours on the so-called day of rest. How would you like to take some medicine to the Maréchale de Noailles in the afternoon?"

"At the La Fayette house on the Rue de Bourbon?"

"The ladies have been evicted from that house too. Their kinsman the Duc de Mouchy has lent them his *hôtel* on the Rue de l'Université. You wouldn't be afraid to go to the Left Bank all by yourself, would you?" asked Fontaine persuasively.

"It's no further than the Palais Royal. But uncle, you've always carried the old lady's medicines yourself. It's you they'll want to see, and get your advice – "

"The old Maréchale is senile, she wouldn't know me from Robespierre. And the duchess and Madame Louise will be glad to see you again, after so long."

"Very well," said Marie, shading her face with her hand.

"You don't sound very enthusiastic. I thought you were so fond of the Noailles ladies."

"Madame de La Fayette was the one I really loved. But she's far away at Chavaniac in the Auvergne . . . they're all scattered now!"

45

"Fortunes of war," said the apothecary. It was lightly said, but when her uncle took the heavy key off its hook and went out to lock the gate on the lane Marie could hear that he dropped the seldom used iron bar into place as well, as if a certificate of good citizenship were not sufficient protection against the terror by night.

The terror by day was hard at work next morning, as four tumbrils rolled and creaked their way to the Place de la Révolution, and the Fontaines left by the lane and the Terrasse des Feuillants, which ran alongside the garden of the Tuileries. It was cold enough for Marie to wear a black cloak instead of a shawl, and to relieve the mourning for Michel she had tucked a white pleated frill into the neck of her black dress. The inevitable cockade was attached by a red ribbon to the basket she carried, which held the bottle of medicine.

She was pretty enough to have attracted the admiration of the loungers on the Terrasse des Feuillants on any ordinary day, but it was clear, as soon as they turned the corner, that this was no ordinary day. Men were running out of the cafés and cheering, while the workers turning the Tuileries garden into a potato field pulled off their red caps and shouted too. A crowd of civilian Deputies and uniformed National Guards was pouring out of the main entrance to the National Palace, while children and girls were dancing and singing the *Ça ira*.

"Citizen," called Prosper Fontaine to the nearest shouting man, "What's the cause of rejoicing? Good news from the front?"

"Good news, citizen? The best! Jourdan won a great battle – Maubeuge is saved and the enemy in full retreat!"

It was true. Uncle and niece learned, as they made their slow way through a crowd increased by vagrants and pickpockets from the sordid side streets of the Place du Carrousel, that General Jourdan and his citizen army had won a battle at a village called Wattignies and delivered the key fortress of Maubeuge, driving the enemy back across the Sambre. Despatch riders had just arrived from the Ardennes, bringing the Convention the news that the victory was won on the very day the Widow Capet was guillotined. A happy omen for the Republic!

"There! You'll be all right now, won't you, Marie?" asked Fontaine, dusting his red cap on his sleeve. It had been knocked off more than once during the patriotic embraces they both had to accept, but they were clear of the Carrousel mob now, and near the Seine bridge still called the Pont Royal.

"*I'll* be all right, but what are you going to do?"

"Spend an hour or so at the Convention. When the Deputies sober up after this outburst, there should be some interesting speeches. You're not nervous, are you? Walk quietly, and no one will molest you."

"I'm not nervous of street people. I *am* worried about the ladies."

"Give them my respectful homage,' said Fontaine, as if that made it all right, and Marie nodded as he turned away. She set off across the deserted Pont Royal: the *quais* ahead, running east and west from the newly named Quai Voltaire, had become a gigantic old clothes shop or flea market where the loot from émigré houses was on sale. Sometimes, when there was food to spare, bread and soup were distributed to the homeless who slept on the banks beneath the *quais* of the Seine. Marie stopped in the middle of the bridge. Her life was so circumscribed, so confined to home, manufactory and the streets between, that the mere sight of the Seine was a refreshment. The river flowed on to the sea, with an eddy in midstream, foaming against the pillars of the Pont Royal. On the further bank a poplar tree was dropping its leaves into the water. The poplar was one of the symbols of the Revolution, *le peuplier*, the people's tree, and in the days when federation was all the fashion the villagers danced around it as they would dance to celebrate the victory of Wattignies, which Carnot had organised and Jourdan fought.

Soothed by the sight and sound of the river, Marie was

walking on slowly, her free hand trailing along the stone parapet, when she heard a quick step behind her, and a man's voice saying her name.

"Sergeant Vautour!"

"Did I startle you, citizeness?"

"Nothing you do can startle me. Are you following me?"

"I saw you with your uncle outside the National Palace when I came off duty, and I was curious to know where you were going. Especially when I saw you cross the bridge alone."

"I'm going to visit friends. Is that a crime?"

"It depends on the friends, citizeness. Are you taking them a present in your little basket?"

"It's medicine for a sick woman. Is *that* a crime?"

"Medicine of your own concoction?"

"Don't be afraid – it's not rat poison."

Their speech was so rapid, their antagonism so intense, that Marie was amazed when, a leaf from the poplar tree floating down to the parapet, Vautour picked it up and laid it gently against her hair.

"Just the same colour," he said. "Beautiful. *Couleur de feuille morte.*"

"A dead leaf? A faded leaf? Thank you for the compliment."

"Nothing faded about you," said the man. "You look like the *Petit Chaperon Rouge* with your dainty basket."

"Little Red Riding Hood? My cloak is black, not red."

"But you wear the *bonnet rouge*, like a true patriot."

"So do you intend to play the wolf?"

"Stop hedging and tell me where you're going."

"I'm going to the Rue de l'Université," said Marie.

"To the Hôtel de Mouchy?"

"What makes you think so?"

"Just a guess. I've been learning something about your close relations with your *ci-devant* neighbours, the Noailles and the La Fayettes."

"What have you learned?"

"That the late duke, the old Maréchal, set your grand-father up in business."

"Long before my time, sergeant. And my grandfather was not his private apothecary; the pharmacy has always been at the service of the public."

"Well spoken, citizeness. Shall we walk on?"

She saw there was no getting rid of him, and shrugged. They crossed into the narrow Rue du Bac, the Street of the Ferry used on the Seine for centuries before the Pont Royal was built. It led to the Rue de l'Université, although the university itself had ceased to exist. Where the Schools of Paris had been famous since the twelfth century, the Sorbonne had been put up for auction in 1792. The revolutionaries, condemning the university as elitist, therefore aristocratic, wanted to demolish the building, but when demolition was found to be too dangerous it was divided into sixty small lodgings for working people and called the Museum of the Arts.

The tall man in uniform and the tall girl in a black cloak walked on side by side until Vautour broke the silence.

"Twice in a few minutes you asked me, in your sarcastic way, if I thought it was a crime to visit friends or take them medicine. Do you know the real crime, committed not by you but by your uncle?"

It was such an echo of the thoughts tormenting Marie that she said falteringly,

"I don't know what you mean."

"I mean it's a criminal act to let a child like you go anywhere near those Noailles women. If he hadn't the guts to take them his medicines himself he ought never to have sent you."

"What harm have the Noailles women, as you call them, done to anybody? Three unprotected women and three children, what threat are they to the Republic?"

"They're unprotected, sure enough. The old lady's senile, her daughter the duchess has been deserted by her husband, who's living with his mistress in Switzerland,

49

and her granddaughter the vicomtesse has a husband who's also an émigré, living comfortably in America."

"What a lot you know about the aristocracy!" said Marie with malice. The man reddened angrily.

"That's the right word," he said. "They're *aristos*, and that's enough. That's why they've been put under house arrest, to keep them out of mischief."

"House arrest! I – I didn't know that, and I'm sure my uncle didn't either!"

"So you say. Their relationship with Gilbert Motier hasn't helped them either."

"By Gilbert Motier you mean the *ci-devant* Marquis de La Fayette?"

"Yes – marquis, general, Hero of Two Worlds, what do his fine names matter? I call him a deserter. When he was challenged by the Convention he left an army in the lurch and fled across the border into the Austrian Netherlands, believing the allies would welcome him with open arms."

"Instead of which they put him in prison."

"Did you ever know La Fayette himself?"

Marie remembered the tall man with red hair and a self-satisfied expression, who sometimes came into the Noailles garden when she and his children were playing, and condescended to watch their game. She had been in awe of the general but never of his wife, for Adrienne, Marquise de La Fayette, married at fourteen and a mother at fifteen, was a happy child romping with her girls and boy.

"I never *knew* him," she told Vautour. "I saw him occasionally when I was a little girl."

"How long have you been living in the Rue St Honoré?"

"All my life. My uncle took me home when I was only a few months old. My parents died in the great smallpox epidemic of '74, when the old king died too."

"Giving even smallpox a royal blessing," jeered Vautour. "Don't walk so fast! Can't you understand that I want you to turn round and go back? Why should you run into danger for the sake of a bunch of *aristos*? Is it possible you've never heard of the Law of Suspects?"

"Vaguely."

"Vaguely, vaguely – there'll be nothing vague about it when you're arrested under the new law against consorting with aristocrats."

"Do you intend to denounce me?"

The provoking girl was biting her lips to keep from crying, and still he could not weaken her resolve to carry out her mission. Vautour waited until a group of people had gone by, laughing and cheering the victory of Wattignies, and then he tried another tack.

"No innocent person need fear denunciation," he said. "But how do I know you're not carrying something in that basket which will help the Noailles to cheat the guillotine?"

"Oh, don't be so silly!"

It was a childish retort which somehow made a child of Sergeant Vautour. He muttered something about making sure, and quickened his pace to match her hurried steps as they turned into the Rue de l'Université and approached the closed doors of the Hôtel de Mouchy, guarded by a man armed with a rifle and bayonet. He was a genuine *sans-culotte* in a red cap and the one-piece garment called a *carmagnole*, which took its name from the revolutionary song.

"What's your business, sergeant?" he said aggressively. "My orders are to admit nobody to this house."

"This young woman is on an errand of mercy," said Vautour. "She's bringing medicine for one of your inmates."

"Prisoners, you mean," said the *sans-culotte*.

"I wish to see the Citizeness Louise Noailles, or her mother," said Marie.

"We keep 'em apart," said the jailer. "It's easier that way."

"The woman Louise will do," said Vautour. "Admit us,

citizen, I'll take full responsibility. You're not alone, are you?"

"My mate's in the guardroom."

The guardroom, when they crossed the cobbled courtyard, proved to be a room off the tessellated hall where footmen had waited for their visiting masters. The decent furnishings had been replaced by a littered table and two unmade pallet beds, on one of which sprawled a second *sans-culotte* smoking a short clay pipe. The empty fireplace was obviously used as a spittoon.

"Here, what's this?" said the second man, sitting up.

"Visitors for the Citizeness High and Mighty," said his mate.

"She taking up with National Guardsmen now?"

"I'm not a visitor," said Vautour, "I'm an escort. I want to check the medicine this girl brought from a pharmacy. Citizeness, give me your basket."

"What are you going to do?" Marie protested.

He took out the bottle of medicine, wrapped in white paper, and broke the red wax seal.

"You mustn't do that! You shouldn't break the seal!" cried Marie.

"It is broken. Now, citizeness! Prove to the guards and me that the contents of this bottle are harmless. Drink some yourself."

"Drink my uncle's special bronchial mixture, meant for a sick woman – "

"*Taste it!*"

Marie smiled. "Very well," she said. "Citizen, will you give me a spoon?"

The *sans-culotte* addressed swore, and told her not to play the fine lady. "Drink from the bottle like the rest of us."

"A *clean* spoon, please, if you have such a thing."

The second guard, scowling, produced a spoon from a pile of dirty cutlery on the table. Marie rubbed it with her handkerchief, uncorked the bottle, poured a spoonful and drank it with her blue eyes fixed on Vautour.

"My uncle flavours this mixture with myrrh," she said. "It has an agreeable taste. I'm sorry I can't oblige you by falling dead at your feet – "

"I'm sorry I can't wring your impudent little neck," said Vautour. "Citizen, take this girl to the woman she wants to see, and don't leave them alone together."

"You not coming too?" said the guard.

"I've nothing to say to an *aristo*," growled Vautour.

Louise, Vicomtesse de Noailles, was confined to her bedroom. She was sitting before a very small wood fire, looking dejected and defeated in spite of her luxurious surroundings. The fourposter bed had draperies which matched the satin curtains at the two long windows, the carpet was Aubusson, while above the marble mantel hung one of the twenty portraits of Queen Marie Antoinette painted at Versailles by Madame Vigée Lebrun. The artist, a court favourite, had been one of the first to emigrate after the Revolution. A little knot of black crape had been attached to the picture frame.

The vicomtesse did not turn at the sound of the opening door, and the *sans-culotte* had to speak twice before she heard him.

"Marie Fontaine! Dear little Marie, what good wind brought you here?" Louise de Noailles kissed her visitor for the first time since Marie was a child. She was a woman of thirty-five, whose good looks had been destroyed long ago.

"My uncle sent some medicine for Madame la Maréchale, madame. I'm sorry the seal is broken. I tried to stop the man who did it, but – "

"One of our jailers, I suppose." Louise threw a contemptuous glance at the *sans-culotte*, who in a pretence of tact had turned his back on them and was looking out at the garden. This brought him conveniently close to a window table covered with small bright objects: silver snuff boxes, miniatures in gold frames and Sèvres figurines. Marie saw him slip a couple of the silver boxes into the pocket of his ragged *carmagnole*.

"You were a dear good girl to bring it, and Monsieur Fontaine is always thoughtful."

"My uncle, with his respectful homage, desired me to enquire after the ladies' health."

"What did you say?" asked the older woman, and Marie realised that, like her mother the duchess and her grandmother, Louise de Noailles was going deaf. Raising her voice, she said,

"We're both anxious to know about the ladies, and if you have any news of Madame Adrienne."

"My grandmother no longer knows where she is, so she is spared much, and my mother is allowed to nurse her. The cough is very troublesome, and your medicine will help. Adrienne should have left the country long ago, and would have done, if President Washington had not discouraged Gilbert from returning to America in 1790," said Louise de Noailles. "Poor Gilbert! Such ingratitude, after all he did for the Americans in their time of trouble! It doesn't bear thinking about; even," with a heavy sigh, "even if we could bear to think of anything after the dreadful blow of the queen's death."

"They told you she was – dead?"

"They came in and made jokes about it." She looked at the queen's portrait and crossed herself. Marie Antoinette had been painted in the flush of her youth and beauty, sumptuously dressed, sitting by a table which held a vase of flowers and a crown.

"The queen is at peace, Madame Louise."

"Some day soon, I feel sure, we shall share her fate."

"God forbid, madame!"

"Have you any news of the king, Marie?"

Marie Fontaine hesitated. The king, to her, meant Louis XVI, dead by the guillotine. Then she remembered the child in the Temple prison, brutalised and corrupted since the day he was taken from his mother's care. He was King Louis XVII by the grace of God, but would he ever reign?

"No news, madame," she said. "I believe his sister,

Madame Royale, is well, and at least she has her aunt to care for her."

"That poor Madame Elisabeth! But for how long?"

The girl saw that the vicomtesse was living in the lost world of Versailles. Kings and princesses were more real to her than the fellow by the window, who was now listening to their talk with interest. She changed the subject from the royal family and asked after Madame Louise's children.

"I'm allowed to have them with me every morning for an hour," said their mother. "Some of the guards are kind, and let them play in the garden. Also, a tutor comes three times a week to give them lessons – Monsieur Carrichon."

She spoke the tutor's name with a half smile which Marie understood. Father Carrichon was a priest whom she had often seen about the Hôtel de Noailles and the church of St Roch. He had refused to take the civic oath and now wore a layman's dress with the tricolore cockade. There were many like him who used that simple disguise to visit their surviving penitents. But to masquerade as a tutor – that was masterly!

"And who looks after all of you, madame?"

"Our meals are sent in, I don't know from where," said the vicomtesse. "And we have a cleaning woman called Beauchet who comes in and out when the guards are kind."

Marie nodded. Madame Beauchet had been the personal maid of the Marquise de La Fayette, and since her marriage to a clerk in the Court of Bankruptcy had remained unfailingly loyal to the family she had served. Now, to the girl's surprise, the Vicomtesse de Noailles took her into her arms and began to finger the white frill at her neck.

"How pretty and fresh you look," she said affectionately. "You're growing up, my dear!" Then, dropping her voice, she said quickly, "Don't come back, it isn't safe.

55

Beauchet will come to you. She's in touch with my sister Adrienne."

"Here, no whispering!" said the *sans-culotte*, starting towards them. He was interrupted by his mate, who slammed the door wide open with a cry of "Time's up, citizeness! Sergeant Vautour's got to get back to the National Palace!"

"What does he say?" Louise had to be very deaf not to hear that shout.

"He's saying I must go, madame. The National Guardsman who brought me seems to be getting impatient."

"One of the National Guard? Oh, Marie, I do hope you're being careful!"

"I am, I assure you . . . citizeness. My love and duty to . . . the others." She dropped a curtsey, at which mark of respect one of the men spat on the carpet.

"Well!" said Sergeant Vautour when they were clear of the Hôtel de Mouchy, "how did it go? Was it a happy reunion?"

"Do you expect a prisoner to be happy?"

"As a prison it's an improvement on a cell in the Conciergerie."

Marie ignored his comment. She asked him abruptly what he did at the Tuileries – or the National Palace – or whatever he liked to call it.

"My company is one of those quartered there, to guard the Deputies."

"You must be very proud," said Marie. "You're in the forefront of the battle there. Such arduous duty – guarding the Deputies from the people who elected them – "

He told her to shut up, so quickly that she failed to connect the abrupt *"Ferme ça!"* with what Vautour had seen before she did: a crowd of roughs coming dancing down the Rue du Bac. The celebration of Wattignies had spread to the Left Bank. The men were in motley uniforms, the women wore tattered skirts and shawls which opened on bare breasts, and they were very drunk. They were all singing, and though some were staggering in the gutter they kept time surprisingly well, swinging and setting to partners, joining hands and whirling in a ring. Marie knew the song they sang. She had often heard it hummed in the workroom when Citizeness Merlot was in an amiable mood.

> *Allons, enfants de la patrie*
> *Le jour de gloire est arrivé!*

"It's those damned Federals from Marseille," said Vautour. "Quick, Marie!"

Before she could protest he pushed her into a deep doorway and seized her in his arms. When she struggled he held her closer and stopped her mouth with kisses. The dancers, who had halted for a moment to shout a ribald invitation to the waltz, laughed and continued in their mad career. The sight of a man and a girl, writhing in the apparent approach to climax in the public street, was a commonplace in the Paris of 1793.

"Why – why did you do that?" stammered Marie, when Vautour released her. "It was hateful – cowardly . . ." She had to pretend fury, to cover the shaking emotion his kisses had aroused.

"Did you want to be swept up in that rabble?" said the man. "I was only trying to protect you. Those fellows from the south are the very devil. Bawling the *Marseillaise* till we're all sick of it, and kicking up a row everywhere in the city when they should be at the front – "

"That's where you should be too."

"If my company were ordered to the front that's where I'd be now."

"Did you have to wait for orders at the time of the *levée en masse*? Couldn't you have volunteered, like my cousin Michel? The National Guard's a wonderful excuse for keeping out of danger."

She wanted to goad him, to infuriate him into seizing her into his arms again, to punish her with the violent

57

kisses which fired her whole body with new sensations. But Vautour only flung at her:

"Are you calling me a coward?"

"Yes, I am. A bully and a coward."

"Very well." Vautour looked beyond her at the empty bridge. "You're safe enough now, so I'll rid you of my company. Make your own way home, Marie Fontaine."

5

When Marie returned to her home through the garden, breathless and trying to set right her rumpled frill and disordered hair, she was surprised to hear a woman's merry laugh from the direction of the pharmacy. She had hardly expected her uncle to be back from the Convention, let alone to have opened the pharmacy on a *décadi* unless in the case of an emergency, and the laughter did not sound like an emergency. She laid aside her cloak, cap and basket in the kitchen, took a critical look at herself in a wall mirror, and went to see who the customer might be.

"Ah, there you are, Marie," said her uncle. "Just in time! You waited on the Citizeness Fontenay last summer, she reminds me, and so you must know exactly what her requirements are."

"I hope so," said Marie shyly. The *ci-devant* Comtesse de Fontenay was a young woman of her own age in years, but twice that in sophistication, having been married and divorced, and brought up from her cradle to rank and wealth. She was the daughter of a Spanish nobleman, and had the striking good looks of her race: black eyes, black hair elaborately dressed, and a sensual mouth which had no need of lip rouge. She wore a hat with feathers, and her tricolore cockade was made of feathers too, fastened to the breast of her low-cut dark dress with a cameo brooch. Citizeness Fontenay was seated in the high-backed chair and had flung off her velvet cloak. Marie saw with awe that it was lined with fur. Most impressive of all, a hackney cab, visible through the windows, was waiting outside the door. Horses were being commandeered for the army, but there was a modified cabriolet service at the theatres. Such a thing as a cab in the Street of the Tumbrils had not been seen for many a day.

"Citizen Fontaine has a soul above scent," said the lady roguishly. It was second nature to her to flirt with every man she met, and Fontaine responded with his rabbit smile. "We seem to be out of jasmine scent," he said, "and lavender water and eau de cologne have been pronounced unsuitable – "

"They're far too insipid for me," said Citizeness Fontenay.

"The jasmine perfume from Grasse is in the storeroom," said Marie. "I'll run upstairs and get it at once."

"Oh, thank you! But before you go to all that trouble, let me make sure that I have everything else I need. Six jars of cucumber cream and three vials of hair lotion – yes, that's right. You see, I'm leaving next week for Bordeaux, and heaven only knows the cosmetic situation there. Luckily I remembered the Pharmacie Fontaine . . ."

Marie returned quickly with three glass-stoppered vials of jasmine scent on the pewter tray, and three more which she presented for the customer's approval. "You might like to try this," she said. "It came in what I'm afraid will be the last consignment from Grasse. It's a true carnation, and I think it would suit you."

Citizeness Fontenay bared her wrist, revealing a gold bracelet, rubbed the glass stopper on her pulse, and sniffed. The heavy languorous odour of the true carnation was released in the room.

"It's so exactly right for me!" said the beauty. "You may give me all six bottles – one can never have enough of scent from Grasse."

"Thank you, citizeness," said Marie demurely. "Is there anything more I can show you?"

"Don't tempt me, my dear! One has to travel light these days, and my trunk is nearly full already."

While Marie packed a box very carefully with the scent, the lotion, and the cucumber cream, Prosper Fontaine said politely that the lady had a long journey ahead of her. "I hope you find Bordeaux in a settled state," he said. "You don't propose to travel alone, I trust?"

"Oh no, I'm taking my maid with me. And perhaps my father will join me in Bordeaux, that is if the affairs of the Spanish government permit."

She had a winning way – a politician's way, if Marie had known it – of taking them into her confidence. While retaining the manner of a great lady, she seemed to treat the two shopkeepers as friends. She even shook hands with them when she had paid her bill, and allowed Prosper Fontaine to help her into the cab, giving him a bewitching glimpse of a lacy petticoat and a silk-clad ankle. He returned smiling to the shop.

"Well done, Marie," he said. "You were a bright girl to remember the carnation and make such a splendid sale." The glass shelf now contained nothing but the faded La Fayette fan.

"She has beautiful things, hasn't she?" said Marie enviously. "Who is her father, do you know?"

"The Conde de Cabarrus. She was born Teresa Cabarrus, and I wonder if papa will be glad at having a divorced daughter back on his hands again. Obviously she got a good settlement from Fontenay, and I shouldn't think she'll be long in the marriage market."

He sat down heavily and sighed. Now that the stimulating visitor had gone Marie saw that he was very pale, and looked exhausted.

"Uncle Prosper, what's the matter? Aren't you feeling well?"

"I'm all right," he said with an effort. "Just a bit of a headache from too much oratory."

"I can imagine. But there's nothing wrong, is there? About the relief of Maubeuge, I mean."

"No, Maubeuge is saved. But what comes next? The defeat at Verdun caused the September massacres last year; Jourdan's victory may mean more bloodshed this year. The Committee of Public Safety is riding high – well, never mind all that. Tell me how you got on at the Hôtel de Mouchy."

She gave him a carefully edited version of her afternoon, presenting Vautour as the man who had gained the entrée to the mansion, and omitting the farce of drinking the medicine and the irruption of the Federals from Marseille. She noted how her uncle's hands shook when she mentioned the National Guardsman, and his genuine dismay when she told him the Noailles ladies were under house arrest.

"This Vautour turns up everywhere," he said. "What d'you really make of him, Marie?"

"You said yourself he wasn't what he seemed to be, and I think you were right. He talks like an educated man, he quotes the fables of Perrault, and I think he was afraid to meet the vicomtesse in case she recognised him. I think his bluster is put on to hide the fact that he's an *aristo* himself, who came out for the Republic and maybe regrets it."

Her uncle opened his eyes wide. "You're very observant, Marie," he said. ". . . My God, I wish I could get you to a safer place than Paris."

"Make an émigrée of me, do you mean?"

"If only you could speak English!"

"Why? We're at war with England now, I'm not going there. Besides, who would look after you?"

"Augustine."

"Augustine can't hear a word you say. And you've been telling me for years that the safest place to be is here, right in the eye of the storm."

"No place in Paris will be safe much longer, if Robespierre has his way."

"It's a pity we've no relatives left in the west country to take us in."

"The west?" The man groaned. "The Vendée is in the throes of civil war."

"But that was over months ago. You mean the royalist rising last spring, when the peasants refused to be conscripted?"

"There's been another rebellion, Marie. At least, that was the unconfirmed report at the Convention this afternoon. The Vendéens started a rising that wasn't meant to begin until December."

"A report of actual fighting?"

"Heavy fighting around Nantes."

"How very inconvenient for Mr Boone from Boston."

"What put Mr Boone into your head, Marie?"

"How do you know there was a rising planned for December? Was Boone meant to be a part of it? Were you?"

He looked at her, the girl he had never thought of as a daughter but as an obedient niece. She stood between his chair and the window so that her features were obscured and her body in its black dress seemed taut with menace.

"Listen, Uncle Prosper," she said, "I could have been arrested this afternoon, just for going to see Madame de Noailles. Consorting with aristocrats, it's called. If you're going to be in worse trouble, for consorting with royalists and rebels and American spies, I have a right to know. Because all the certificates of good citizenship in Paris won't save us then."

"What nonsense you talk, Marie! Adam Boone isn't an American spy. He's a man I helped in my professional capacity – "

"Don't lie to me," she said. "He wasn't just your patient, he was your friend – confederate – fellow-plotter, I don't know what. I do know he came back here two nights ago, and talked with you until after midnight."

"You were dreaming. You were in bed and sound asleep."

"I threw the opiate you gave me out of the window."

Fontaine threw up his hands in a gesture of defeat.

"Uncle, tell me the truth. Who is he, and why are you involved with him?"

"I don't know his real name. He's not an American. He's a British naval officer."

"So the passport and the permits were all false?"

"They were forgeries prepared in London."

"An Englishman in Paris. How did he get Gouverneur Morris to vouch for him?"

"He didn't. We knew the American Minister was at Melun, and he took a chance on it when Vautour interfered."

"He interfered because the Englishman made a fool of himself in the street. When you say 'we' do you mean the two of you? Or are there other people involved?"

"Yes, there are others, Marie, all members of the Convention. I won't tell you their names because what you don't know you can't betray."

"The word *betrayal* doesn't come well from you."

Since Marie had revealed that she knew of Boone's night visit, Fontaine had answered mechanically, avoiding her eyes. Now he said in a spurt of rage:

"I've betrayed nobody. I was loyal to the Republic from the capture of the Bastille until the abolition of the monarchy. I only changed when our new masters committed the supreme folly of going to war."

"And Michel was killed."

"Michel and hundreds like him who gave their lives for nothing. Even as recently as at Wattignies two days ago. I believed that if the English joined forces with the royalists in the Vendée and defeated a republican army, the Convention would be forced to sue for an amnesty and declare a general peace. Boone came here to confirm the details of an English invasion and test the support in Paris, but those hotheads in the Vendée have risen too soon and ruined it all."

"I don't believe it."

"It's true, Marie."

"I mean I *can't* believe it. You – Prosper Fontaine,

64

trusted and respected by everybody – you've been planning an English invasion of our country. 'Intelligence with the enemy', that's what it's called, and they guillotined the queen for that."

"It was for the sake of peace, Marie, and the saving of young lives."

"But the English are in Toulon already, and that hasn't saved a single life! Where was the December invasion supposed to take place?"

"I can't tell you that. I've told you too much about a matter where other men's lives are concerned. As for Boone, I don't even know if he's still alive."

A breach was opened between them, and for several days they avoided each other completely. They ate at different times on a corner of the kitchen table, and left written messages on pharmacy business with Augustine, who was too deaf to understand any verbal message correctly. Marie knew that the uncle who had brought her up was afraid of her, afraid that she would report him to the Section, and the knowledge gave her a heady sense of power in the middle of her great dread.

The premature rising in the Vendée was easily put down by republican troops, and after their victory at Cholet there were executions by firing squad and the burning down of many farms and villages. Robespierre declared that Nantes should be the first city to suffer in his new policy of repression in the provinces. But before that, he intended to extend the scope of punishment in Paris.

Robespierre had won his battle with the moderates, and before the end of October twenty-one Girondins had been condemned to death. They were guillotined in a mass execution, singing the *Marseillaise* or shouting *Vive la République* as they ascended the scaffold. After that the tumbrils rolled unceasingly into the Place de la Révolution. Philippe Egalité was brought back from Marseille to be executed in the city where he had voted for his cousin's death. A few weeks later Madame du Barry, mistress of King Louis XV, who had virtually ruled the king and his court for five years and was a thorn in the flesh of Marie Antoinette, was arrested and condemned on a charge of 'wearing mourning for a tyrant'. She went to the guillotine sobbing and screaming, so that all the *aristos* at liberty or in prison sneered at the cowardice of 'the royal whore'. To die bravely was the mark of true breeding and the pride of their class.

Noisy as the shrieks of the du Barry were, the howls of Citizeness Merlot were louder still. Her protector, the army contractor, had been found guilty of embezzlement, and on the principle of guilt by association she was condemned to die with him. She was arrested at the manufactory, and during the uproar Marie Fontaine sat quietly stitching while the frantic woman denounced half a dozen of the sempstresses, on what grounds it was not clear. They were taken to prison along with her, and disappeared for ever from the workroom. New supervisors were appointed: two this time, so that one could spy on the other. Gentle and simple, guilty and innocent followed each other to the guillotine, the knitting women made their patterns of the names and the numbers, and the people who still lived in the Rue St Honoré complained to their Section about the increasing and nauseating smell of blood.

Prosper Fontaine did not join in the official complaint. He and Marie had begun to talk again, on such subjects as the weather and the price of firewood, and he seemed so much more cheerful after the execution of the Girondin leaders that Marie wondered if some of them had been the Deputies favourable to the plan for an English invasion as a way to stop the war. She was sure he spent sleepless nights in the last days of October, for she heard him moving about in his bedroom while she lay awake in hers, both of them waiting for the heavy knock on the door which should announce the patrol with an order for their arrest. But night succeeded night and the dreaded summons never came; gradually Marie began to breathe more easily as the risk of betrayal seemed to recede.

On a bleak day in November the women in the manufactory had been even quieter than usual, exchanging furtive glances when the supervisors' backs were turned because of the unusual fabric issued to each one. The churches had been closed all over Paris, whether the priests had taken the civic oath or not, and plans were being made to set up the Goddess of Reason in place of the Christian God, but the sempstresses had not expected a delivery of surplices, carrying the scent of incense, which they had to cut and adapt as army shirts. It had been a hard day, and Marie was glad to see lamplight in the pharmacy and hear the sound of a familiar voice.

She exchanged kisses with Citizeness Beauchet, once the personal maid of the Marquise de La Fayette and now living with her husband in lodgings above a grocer's shop in the Rue de Courty, on the other side of the river. The Beauchets were a living proof of Fontaine's old theory that the safest place in the Revolution was in the very eye of the storm. They came and went unobtrusively, cheered when it was popular to cheer and hissed when hissing was in order, and of course possessed certificates of good citizenship, while all the time doing their best to serve *aristos* like the Noailles and the La Fayettes.

"How good to see you, Madame Beauchet," said Marie warmly. "Have you come to get more medicine for Madame la Maréchale?"

"Alas, Marie – " The former lady's maid, neatly dressed as ever, pressed her handkerchief to her eyes.

"Madame Beauchet has brought very bad news from the Hôtel de Mouchy," said Fontaine, with something of his old confident manner. "She was just beginning her story when you came in."

"What's happened?"

"You didn't know the Duc and Duchesse de Mouchy had been arrested?" said Madame Beauchet. "Yes – down at their *château* on the Oise, and their daughter the

Duchesse de Duras was arrested too. I don't know what they did with *her*, but the duke and duchess were brought up to Paris and imprisoned in their own house, with extra guards and a regular prison establishment. I was told that my services were no longer needed because the jailers would do all the work."

"How awful for poor Madame Louise!" said Marie. "I mean, it's dreadful for them all . . ."

"While there's life there's hope," said Fontaine sententiously.

"But that isn't the worst of it," said the woman. "My poor Madame Adrienne . . ."

"Don't say she's been arrested too!"

"They've taken her to the local prison at Brioude. She's in a cell with all the rogues and vagabonds of the town."

"How do you know?"

"Her son's tutor, Monsieur Frestel, got the boy away to some hiding place in the hills, and George-Washington wrote to me himself. Do you realise he's fourteen now?"

"I suppose he is. But what happened to the girls?"

"They're still at Chavaniac with the old great-aunt. But this is what George-Washington says his mother wants me to do. You know she has great faith in the American Minister, Monsieur Gouverneur Morris. She thinks that because of all General de La Fayette did for America, the Americans are bound to help her now. She wants me to go and see the gentleman and tell him of her plight."

"Another opportunity for Citizen Morris," said Marie, with a look at her uncle which he understood too well.

"I doubt if even he has the influence to deliver the wife of La Fayette from a state prison," said Fontaine.

"But I must see him!" cried Madame Beauchet. "And this is what I've come to ask. Nicolas, my husband, has friends in several of the foreign ministries. He found out that Gouverneur Morris always attends the Convention on Mondays and Thursdays, I suppose to report to his own government. Thursday, that's tomorrow. I've never been inside the National Palace. I wouldn't know how to get a place in the public tribunes. Monsieur Fontaine, you know all about such things. Could you possibly spare the time to come to the Convention with me tomorrow afternoon?"

Prosper Fontaine appeared to reflect before he shook his head. "I wish I could," he said. "I wish I could be of service to you, and of course to our dear Madame de La Fayette, but – no. I have some important laboratory work on hand which I can't leave on the off-chance that the Minister will be at the Convention and willing to speak to you. Could you not write and ask for an interview at his residence?"

"I don't know where he lives."

"I'm sure your knowledgeable husband can find out."

"Don't worry, dear Madame Beauchet," said Marie. "I'll come with you. We'll find the man and make him talk to us. Two women are better than one for this sort of thing – and they say Monsieur Morris speaks good French."

In the Revolutionary calendar, which had superseded the Gregorian calendar, November was called Brumaire, the foggy month. The weather, as Marie went to meet Madame Beauchet on Thursday afternoon, was not so much foggy as misty and rainy, and cold enough to let her hold up the collar of her cloak so as to cover the lower half of her face. It may have been a subconscious wish to be unrecognisable, in case Sergeant Vautour was somewhere about the premises of the National Palace. She kept telling herself that his disappearance from the neighbourhood was one of the few good things about this wretched autumn, and that she had no wish ever to see him again. In fact she had never forgotten those passionate moments in a doorway of the Rue du Bac.

Madame Beauchet was waiting anxiously at the corner of the Terrasse des Feuillants, and the first thing she told Marie was that she had delivered the bottle of medicine which Prosper Fontaine had given her to the Hôtel de Mouchy.

"And just imagine," she said, "the man on sentry-go was a *sans-culotte* I used to know before. He asked me what had happened to the pretty girl who brought the stuff last time."

"Maybe he'll let the poor old lady have her medicine. If it was a bottle of wine, he wouldn't."

"I see you know him, and he knows you all right. He said tell her Sergeant Vautour, *son cher ami*, had deserted the National Guard."

"Vautour a deserter! I don't believe it," cried Marie.

"He didn't say 'deserted from', he said deserted. Given up, gone away. Your friend left the Guard and joined the army."

"That's exactly what I told him to do," said Marie, and Madame Beauchet looked baffled. But they were caught up in the crowd always roaming about the gates of the palace once called the Tuileries, and Madame Beauchet was distracted by what she thought of as the ordeal ahead.

Marie had heard that two months had been required to remove the furnishings, pictures and possessions of the Bourbons from their ancestral home, and she could believe it when she saw the space of the empty rooms that were left. The whole of the ground floor had been turned into a guardroom, with an area fenced off for beds and bedding, and when she saw the sky blue and red facings of the National Guard uniform Marie thought with satisfaction that she had sent Vautour off to war. Now he'll find out what it's really like! she said to herself. Now he'll know what Michel knew!

All they had to do at street level was to follow the crowd up the grand staircase, now carpetless, to the hall where the Convention met, and which held two thousand people. It seemed to be filled to capacity, for Danton, the most striking orator of the Committee of Public Safety, was said to be attacking Robespierre, his rival and colleague. The two women heard his great voice shouting down the interruptions as they pushed their way into the hall. The president's bell, rung repeatedly for order, was less effective than the voice of Danton himself, and Marie had to raise her own voice as she sought information from an usher.

Yes, citizeness, there were the people's tribunes, where people were eating and drinking as if the Convention were a café, and where they were at liberty to sit or stand if they could find a place. Yonder was the tribune where the foreign diplomats were seated. The American Minister? Fat man in black, seated in the front row. When would he leave? What did she think he was – a fortune-teller? Oh, very well (as Marie slipped a coin into his hand) Citizen Morris was an orderly fellow, usually left about five o'clock. Not that he was likely to leave as long as Citizen Danton was speaking.

A pretty girl and her companion easily found places in the crowded tribune, among spectators who found the Convention nearly as good a show as the Revolutionary Tribunal, though not likely – as yet – to end in bloodshed. "Falling out amongst themselves, they are," said a grimy man, who offered Marie a bite of his equally grimy sausage, "I don't like that." Danton was speaking up for the establishment of a Committee of Clemency, a policy of moderation, and a return to religious festivals instead of the cult of Reason. It was not a popular theme, and only the dynamism of the speaker prevailed against the interruptions; when Robespierre rose to reply it was clear that he carried the Convention with him.

Maximilien Robespierre, as an orator, had started with several disadvantages. He had a weak voice, but he had learned to project it in the Jacobin Club, and he had no physical presence, a defect which he had learned to exploit. The cat's face, the green eyes, the feeble limbs, somehow came together in a synthesis of power. It was as if a snake had been given words to reply to Danton. He was not, he said, a supporter of atheism, but would let the cult of Reason run its course. He was utterly opposed

71

to clemency and moderation in any form. The commissioners whom he was sending out to subdue reaction or rebellion in the provinces had his orders 'to regard all dissidents as criminals' and send them to the guillotine.

Robespierre ended an unusually short speech to a storm of applause, and there was a wave of movement in the crowded chamber. Many of the Deputies left their places, and the diplomatic tribune began to empty. Marie, who had watched and waited for this moment, grasped Madame Beauchet's hand. "Now's the time!" she whispered, and led the way out of the public tribune towards the American Minister, who was exchanging handshakes with several Deputies as he made his way to the main exit.

"*Excellence!*" The formal address, so unexpected in revolutionary France, caused the American Minister to turn round in surprise, increased when he saw that the speaker was a young girl with beautiful fair hair, a heightened colour and a very damp cloak. Her companion, a neat little woman, was actually sketching a curtsey.

"Yes, citizeness!" he replied courteously. "What can I do for you?" He was accustomed to being importuned by Frenchmen who thought of the young American Republic as a mint of riches and unlimited credit, and a man like Prosper Fontaine, for instance, would have been given short shrift by Mr Morris. In his heart of hearts he disliked the French. He was one of the very few Americans to have been in Paris on business at the time of the storming of the Bastille, and he had been a horrified eye-witness of some of the murders which followed. "Great God, what a people!" he had written after seeing the first executions *à la lanterne*, and yet after two years as the United States Commissioner to England he had been willing to return to Paris as the Minister to What-a-People, where the guillotine was queen. He got on with them well enough, although he never achieved the popularity of Benjamin Franklin. To be approached by two women was something new.

"If you please, *monsieur le ministre*," said the girl. "My name is Marie Fontaine, living in the Palais Royal Section, and this is Madame Beauchet, who has brought you a message from – from Citizeness La Fayette."

"From Chavaniac?"

"Alas no, sir," said Madame Beauchet, plucking up her courage, "my former mistress has been arrested and is in prison at Brioude. It must have been one of the new commissioners who did it, sir, because the townsfolk of Brioude all love her; my lady has been very good to them. Her son George-Washington – named for your president, sir – has written to ask if you would use your great influence to obtain her release."

"I didn't know the poor lady had been arrested," said Morris. "News travels slowly from the Auvergne."

He was talking to gain time: what hope could he give these women, what promise of release? Adrienne de La Fayette had been arrested because she was her husband's wife, that husband of whom General Washington, in the war years, had said his great defect was self-satisfaction. Well, La Fayette's self-satisfaction, or self-assurance, had landed him in a Prussian prison, where the foolish faithful Adrienne, in spite of his constant infidelities, had hoped to join him. So now Adrienne was a prisoner too, and her next journey after Brioude could be to a Paris prison and – the guillotine.

He drew the two women into a window embrasure.

"Ladies," he said, "I saw you in one of the tribunes, where youth and beauty are seldom seen." He smiled at Marie. "You heard Citizen Robespierre's speech. Against his absolute determination to punish all dissidents – and General de La Fayette's wife must be considered to be a dissident – nothing I could say on her behalf would make any impression."

"But would not the President of the United States, the friend of General de La Fayette, intervene on behalf of his poor wife?" said Madame Beauchet.

"President Washington has made it known that he

cannot interfere with any foreign government without the commitment of all his cabinet, which he is most unlikely to obtain," said Morris. "But he has already placed over two thousand guilders to General de La Fayette's credit at a bank in Amsterdam. I may add that I myself have augmented that sum by ten thousand guilders since the general was imprisoned."

"Twelve thousand guilders sounds like a lot of money," said Marie, "but money in a Dutch bank isn't much use to a prisoner in Prussia."

What a people! There was the devil's own temper in that girl as well as beauty, Morris thought, and she was singing the same song as all the others. Because La Fayette had drawn his juvenile sword for the American Revolution (though the really effective French general was Rochambeau) the Americans were expected to support him for ever after. Even the great Madame de Staël, safe in Switzerland, had written to the American Minister, saying, 'Pay the debt your country owes to La Fayette!' And talking about debts . . .

"Do you know that I personally lent Madame de La Fayette one hundred thousand *livres* to pay her husband's debts?" he said, addressing Madame Beauchet directly.

"It's because of her gratitude that she ventures to appeal to you," said the diplomatic Madame Beauchet. "But monsieur, with great respect, this is a question of freedom, not of loans or gifts of money. Madame's situation is desperate, cut off from her husband and children – "

"Forgive me for interrupting you," said Morris, "but you said you had a letter from her son. Where is the boy now?"

"A good priest has given shelter to his tutor and himself."

"Can you reach him?"

"I think so."

"I might be able to do something for the boy. I could get him a passage to America, if the French grant him an exit

74

permit. They won't give a permit to George-Washington de La Fayette, but if he uses the French spelling and the family name and calls himself Georges Motier, it might be possible to get him a passage to America. Write your name and address in my pocket book, Madame Beauchet, and I will be in touch with you."

"So one will be saved out of five," said Marie Fontaine.

"I hope they will all be saved," said Morris. "Be sure of one thing, mademoiselle, that if the worst comes to the worst I shall do my best for Madame de La Fayette. But Brioude is a long way from Paris; she has many friends outside her prison walls, and her situation may not be as desperate as you fear."

Brioude is a long way from Paris. Those words of Gouverneur Morris came back to Marie many times in the dreary weeks which followed. No place, not even a small town in Auvergne, was at more than a bullet's distance from the Committee of Public Safety when Robespierre's commissioners, or *représentants en mission*, arrived in the provinces. The commissioners, intimidating figures who wore plumed hats and went armed to the teeth, were accompanied by military bodyguards and travelling guillotines. Sometimes the commissioners lost patience with the speed of the guillotine, as happened at Lyon where three hundred victims were mown down by cannon fire. The commissioners, with very few exceptions, were men of humble birth and mediocre attainments, who delighted in avenging themselves on their superiors in rank or intellect. The lawyer's clerk, the renegade priest, the failed writer and the printer's devil came into their own as they piled up a total of fifteen thousand deaths. One prisoner who escaped the guillotine was Teresa, *ci-devant* Comtesse de Fontenay, who succeeded in charming the viciously cruel commissioner at Bordeaux, a butler's son called Jean Tallien. The true carnation scent from the Pharmacie Fontaine had proved to be a powerful aphrodisiac.

The purge of suspects at Nantes was particularly successful, for there Commissioner Carrier had the original idea of using the Loire to supplement the guillotine. Naked men and women, bound together, were drowned in the river, and *les noyades* or 'Loire Marriages' were highly popular with the spectators. When news of the terrible vengeance in Brittany reached Paris Marie Fontaine was moved to reopen what had been for weeks a banned subject.

"Do you suppose your friend, the British naval officer, was caught in the death trap at Nantes?" she asked her uncle.

"I hope not. I don't know."

"Would he have had time to take a ship bound for any port at St Nazaire?"

"He meant to leave by boat from one of the coastal villages, but he may have reached St Nazaire for all I know."

"Would anyone in Paris know?"

"Not now."

Not after the execution of the Girondins. Marie asked if her uncle had ever received letters from the Englishman, perhaps to announce his arrival in Paris.

"No, never. The only messages were by word of mouth. And if – if by ill chance he fell into the hands of Carrier, a British naval officer would never betray his friends."

She hoped not. But Marie could never be sure that there was not, somewhere, a scrap of handwriting, or a message revealed by a messenger in terror of his own death, which would serve to denounce Prosper Fontaine. She wondered if he realised the utter futility of his peace move when he studied the news from Toulon, where the royalist townsfolk had declared the little boy in the Temple prison to be Louis XVII, their rightful king, and had invited the English admiral, Lord Hood, to occupy their city and harbour. Hood arrived in strength, with Spanish auxiliaries, and he had ordered the captain of HMS *Agamemnon* to bring him reinforcements. Captain

Horatio Nelson obeyed with all the enthusiasm of an officer who had been 'on the beach' for five years. At Naples, where Queen Maria Carolina was a sister of the murdered Marie Antoinette, he obtained six thousand Neapolitan troops, who embarked at once for Toulon. And yet with all this manpower at his disposal Hood had been unable to break out of Toulon, or win the kind of victory which Fontaine and others like him had thought would bring the Convention to sue for peace. It was a deadlock, for first one and then another incompetent republican general, obvious candidates for the guillotine, failed to dislodge Hood from Toulon.

It was all part of the miserable time which, as the year declined towards the winter solstice, was the most wretched Marie Fontaine had ever known. Estranged from her uncle, lonely and afraid, she was without hope of any change in the dreary pattern of her life. She had lost whatever sympathy she might have felt for the principles of the Revolution, and when she saw the new slogan 'Liberty – Equality – Fraternity – OR DEATH' scrawled on walls and fences she knew that *death* was the important word. What could one girl, without the inspiration of a Joan of Arc or the courage of a Charlotte Corday, do to stem the red tide of death?

There was no comfort in the approach of Christmas, for the de-Christianising movement which had spread across France was particularly strong in Paris, where both the cathedral of Notre Dame and the church of St Sulpice had become the scenes of the orgiastic worship of the Goddess of Reason. While Michel Fontaine lived he and his cousin Marie had gone together to the midnight mass at St Roch on Christmas Eve, and while Prosper Fontaine did not accompany them he always provided a good supper for the *réveillon* which followed. For the New Year *réveillon* they had all gone to a merry gathering at the home of Monsieur Guiart. Citizen Guiart was not entertaining this year, but a few days before Christmas he sent the Fontaines a Christmas goose already cooked at the baker's, and a *bûche de Noël*, the traditional Christmas cake.

"Would you mind if I gave half of this to Augustine?" Marie asked her uncle. "We can't possibly eat it all. And she has those two grandchildren to take care of . . ."

"Quite right," approved Fontaine. "But don't starve yourself, Marie. You're taking a long time to shake off that cold."

"Everyone in the *quartier* has a cold this month. We've sold a lot of remedies."

"You're right," agreed Fontaine. "And speaking of sales, I've got another present for you, more portable than a goose."

He put his hand in the back pocket of his tail coat, and drew out a shabby leather purse which Marie recognised as having belonged to Michel.

"Money?" she said, and instinctively recoiled.

"Call it emergency money. Call it your accumulated wages for acting as my assistant. I've never given you anything but an *écu* for your birthday or a trinket – "

"You've fed and sheltered me for nearly twenty years."

"I don't know what shelter you may need before another year is out. There are three hundred *livres* in this purse – "

"One could live for twelve months on three hundred *livres*."

"Thriftily. So I don't want you to accept it now. I mean to put this purse in the counter drawer with our certificates of good citizenship, and I want you to take it as and when you need it."

"Or you need it. I've been saving up my wages from the manufactory."

"That can't be much."

"It's something."

She knew she was being ungracious, knew her uncle was making overtures of friendship, but Marie could not yet return to their old pleasant relationship. It was different next day, when the great news came from Toulon.

Admiral Julien, an alcoholic, and his successor General Carteaux, a former painter, had been replaced in the command of the force attacking the British in Toulon by General Dugommier, aged seventy-five. Dugommier had the sense to listen to the opinions of one of his junior officers, a Captain Buonaparte, who had been sent to take delivery of a consignment of gunpowder at Avignon.

The young captain pointed out that if Lord Hood, who was known to be having trouble with his mixed command of English, French royalists, Spanish and Neapolitans, could be forced to evacuate the tongue of land which divided the bay of Toulon into two harbours, he could be prevented from reaching the open sea, and given the right ordnance the manoeuvre was possible. In six weeks one hundred pieces of ordnance, mostly cannon, were at the disposal of the young man, who was promoted to battalion commander and led the attack. It was a bloody business, executed in a storm of rain, and the young major himself was wounded and might have been killed but for the protection of one of his sergeants. He had his first victory, and Lord Hood told the horrified Toulonnais that he could no longer defend them. He reached the open sea, fighting a rearguard action in which the arsenal was wrecked, nine French warships were burned and sixteen other vessels were carried off: the English admiral also evacuated fifteen thousand citizens and took them to safety at Leghorn. The others were left to the fury of the republican mob whom Hood had held in check, and the British were left with only one base in the Mediterranean, at Gibraltar.

When Marie heard the news from Toulon, her suspicious reserve towards her uncle melted, and almost for the first time since Michel's death they embraced – though this time in rejoicing – to think that their shabby, hungry young friend was the hero of the hour.

"Promoted *général de brigade* at twenty-four!" cried Fontaine.

"I never even knew he was back in France," said Marie.

"Neither did I."

"Oh, but things will be different now he's here!"

She was convinced of that. So completely, that she almost expected him to arrive in Paris to receive the freedom of the city. They would meet again, they would drink wine at the Café de la Régence, and this time he would not go back to Corsica. Leave Corsica to the English and welcome to it! When she went to her room that night Marie rummaged in the *armoire* until she found the blue muslin dress of the memorable supper party, and put it on. The home-made gown, sadly wilted, had never been in fashion, and the fichu made out of yellowing lace which had belonged to her mother was as outmoded as the sash. She ripped out the fichu, pushed her cotton petticoat off her shoulders, and sat before the cracked mirror in the door of the *armoire* to assess the girl who might be seen by the brilliant eyes of General Buonaparte.

Still too pale and thin, but her shoulders and breast were white, and the man Vautour had said her hair was beautiful. So it was, if you admired the colour of the poplar leaves by the Pont Royal, but oh, how straight! Hours of work with curl-papers had gone into the ringlets of the supper at the Régence. The deep blue eyes were serious. They would brighten, Marie knew, at Napoleon's smile.

Part Two

1794
Spring

6

"You've done wonders in the time, citizen commissioner," said General Buonaparte.

He was sitting in the commissioner's office in the Hôtel de Ville in Toulon, the city from which his guns had driven the English two months before. In the hour of victory he had seen French battleship after battleship exploding like a ball of fire, and the buildings round the docks collapsing like houses built of cards. While he was in Marseille the work of reconstruction had gone on apace, largely thanks to the *représentant en mission* sent from Paris as soon as the English withdrew. He was the *ci-devant* Vicomte Paul Barras, a man of nearly forty who had seen some soldiering in the Indies and was now a member of the National Convention. Tall, handsome, florid, a womaniser, Barras was a complete contrast to General Buonaparte.

His dress was an interesting mixture of the regulation and the fashionable. His official hat, bedecked with plumes, lay on a side table, and he wore the obligatory black neckcloth and tricolore sash. But he had not felt it necessary to stick two pistols in the sash, nor wear a sword, and his coat and *sans-culotte* trousers were a subdued shade of olive green. The material was smoothly rich, of a texture seldom seen in France since most textile manufactories had been commandeered for the army.

"I got on faster," he told the recently promoted general, "because there were so few dissidents left to punish. The real criminals of Toulon had been evacuated by their British friends, so masons and carpenters were needed before executioners."

"Hardly the situation I discovered in Marseille."

"So I gathered from your admirable report," said Barras, and smiled. "I shall see that one copy is sent to the Committee of Public Safety without delay, and the other to Citizen General Carnot."

"You will note that I advise doubling the fortifications at the Château d'If."

"It shall be done." He smiled again. The whole report had urged the doubling and redoubling of the existing fortifications, the scrapping of the obsolete, the construction of the new. It was art and part with the personality of the young man who faced him across the desk: the blazing energy, the ceaseless curiosity, the struggle for perfection. He admired the little man.

In two years Buonaparte had changed for the better. He was still thin and gaunt, but his face had filled out enough for the lines of a classical profile to appear, and his black hair, though still hanging in 'dog's ears', was glossy with the application of soap and water, and not with an accumulation of dust and grease. His grey riding coat was creased from hard usage and his riding boots were nearly as high as those of his first regimentals, which had caused the young Permons to call him Puss in Boots, but now he wore about him the aura of success.

"One thing I would like to mention," said Barras, "is that there's been a good deal of talk in Paris about your present posting."

"How so?"

"Some members of the Committee think now you're a *général de brigade* you should be given command of a brigade. Specifically, that Carnot should have given you a brigade in the Army of the Rhine, where a man with your experience of artillery is sorely needed. Instead, you were side-tracked into the unrewarding post of Inspector of Coastal Defences. What's your own view of the matter?"

"With respect, citizen commissioner, I find my employment most rewarding. Nothing can be more important than strengthening the defences of France against France's enemies. When Milord Hood withdrew from Toulon he didn't withdraw from the Mediterranean. His frigates are still there, just out of the range of our shore batteries, keeping station as they call it, and waiting for another chance at invasion."

"Quite so, general, but for your personal satisfaction would you not rather be with troops?"

"That will come."

Not for the first time in his meetings with Buonaparte Paul Barras realised the enormous potential of the man. Command of troops would come – brigade, corps, Army of the Rhine . . . Army, perhaps, of France.

He took up a page of memoranda.

"I see you've minuted for a smaller force to accompany you on the second part of your inspection than the half-company you took to Marseille."

"That half-company!" said Buonaparte. "It was chosen at random while I was recovering from my thigh wound, and not by me. What is needed on a tour of inspection is not a detachment of soldiers, but men with special knowledge of their fields. I would like two experts on bridges and highways, if there's still a Department of *Ponts et Chaussées* in Toulon."

"Most of the departmental experts are now refugees in Leghorn," said Barras drily. "I'll see what can be done. You also want two engineers, two sappers, four troopers – and Sergeant Junot."

"Junot came to my rescue when my horse was shot under me. He's indispensable."

"Twelve men, including yourself. It's a small force, and a big risk."

"Provence is quiet now, citizen commissioner."

"But when you leave Provence, and cross the Var into the county of Nice, you may expect to meet with some hostility."

Allied with the Great Powers at war with the French Republic was a small enemy, the loosely named Kingdom of Sardinia. This included an island in the Mediterranean and the fertile plain of Piedmont, with its capital at Turin. In 1792 the Duchy of Savoy and the city and county of Nice were the first French prizes of the war.

"The Niçois," said Buonaparte, "whether they call themselves Sardinians, Piedmontese or French, can hardly approve of the English presence offshore, or the invasion of Corsica."

"You had your own troubles there, citizen general."

"Yes!" said the Corsican. "Troubles, and a great disillusionment. Pasquale di Paoli was the hero of my boyhood. My late father fought with him when they freed Corsica from Genoese rule. The island became French before my birth. Then Paoli went to England and lived there for twenty years. Result: when I reached Corsica in October '92 I found Paoli back again as a tool of the English, preparing to make war on the French Republic."

"So you, as a soldier of the Republic – " hinted Barras.

"I went to war with my former hero. And what a war! Guerrilla warfare and local vendettas were not on the curriculum of my military schools, either at Brienne or Paris. My own family was in danger. I managed to get my mother and the younger children safely away to Marseille, where we were classified as 'persecuted patriots' and given free soup at the street kitchens."

"Very disagreeable," said Barras. "But that state of affairs didn't last long?"

"Not as far as the street kitchens were concerned. After I rejoined my regiment at Nice I found a suitable house at Antibes for the family, but my little sisters thought Antibes would be too dull. They're growing up too fast! So they're still living in Marseille, of course in a decent lodging, and enjoying all the gaieties of city life."

Buonaparte could have added that he had enjoyed some of these gaieties himself in the intermittent courtship of a pretty girl called Désirée Clary, the daughter of a well-to-do Marseille manufacturer. Désirée was docile and affectionate, but she was unable to compete with the cannon of Toulon in the heart of a man who thought and said that woman was only made to be the warrior's rest.

"Citizeness Buonaparte must have been glad to be in Marseille to welcome her son, the hero of Toulon," said Barras, rising with a smile. "Your thigh wound healed by first intention, the doctors say. Doesn't give you any trouble when riding? Good. Then I wish you luck on your next tour of inspection, citizen general! Especially when you cross the valley of the Var."

Twenty-four hours later the Inspector of Coastal Defences was ready to start on the long road to the Italian border. His first tour to Marseille and back had shown him that a few intelligent men would be more valuable than a cumbersome half-company of republican troops, and only two men on the second expedition had been with him on the first. They were Pierre Dulac, like Buonaparte a King's Cadet of the Ecole Militaire at Paris, and the 'indispensable' Andoche Junot. Dulac had the advantage of being a born Provençal, with a whole network of friends, relatives and informants along the route they had to travel.

The eastward coast road – the only road along the shore – was even worse than the road to Marseille. It was full of potholes, mired from the winter rains, and so narrow that the riders had to proceed two abreast, while their horses' sides were fretted by the thorn bushes of the garrigue. Mid-February had brought an early spring, and round the white farmhouses there were almond trees in pink blossom, adding their sweetness to the scent of violets and broom. If Buonaparte had known it, he was riding through the very landscape of which Captain Nelson's sailors had declared themselves 'heartily sick'. From the blue sea they saw nothing but a sky as blue above red rocks and pines and olive groves. For Frenchmen who had come through the hell of Toulon it was a glimpse of an earthly paradise.

It was also, and had been from the days of antiquity, a vulnerable shore, ravaged by pirates and invaded by the Saracen enemy from Africa. Many of the strong places to be inspected had first been constructed as a protection against the Saracens. Now the enemy was British, not African, and the white sails of a ship of the line, glimpsed far out in the Mediterranean, was a constant reminder of his presence.

For the first hour of their journey Buonaparte rode alone. With his usual lucidity he had decided on the priorities of his inspection: the armament of the existing forts, the construction of furnaces to provide the batteries with red-hot shot, and new plans to protect the coastal trade, on which army supplies depended, from attack by the English. Only his recent talk with Barras had left a faint cloud on his mind. That hint that he should have been given a brigade in the Army of the Rhine – was it an attempt to drive a wedge between Carnot and himself? Barras was very plausible, but since the defection of Paoli to the English Buonaparte had lost confidence in words. It was a relief to know that whatever Barras was plotting behind his back would be counteracted by the presence of Augustin Robespierre, who had arrived at Toulon as an extra commissioner and had praised him to the skies. They must think well of him in Paris now. And nobody, in Paris or anywhere else, knew what part in Buonaparte's destiny he foresaw for the Army of the Rhine.

He turned his mount, and rode back along the straggling line of his followers until he reached Dulac, who was riding rearguard. Before very long the general would have ridden beside every one of the men, getting to know each man, his background and his capacity, wearing down what might be sullen shyness, or nervous impertinence, or even weakness, by his insatiable questions and surprising colloquialisms. But to begin with he had business with Dulac.

Pierre Dulac was a true *méridional*, black-eyed and swarthy, with a heavy torso and short legs. Fifteen years older than his general, he had advanced no further than the rank of captain in the republican army, precisely the same rank as he had attained when Louis XVI was king. Promotion did not come quickly to a former royalist soldier, but Captain Dulac's republican sentiments were impeccable, and whatever Robespierre might say, the military member of the Committee of Public Safety, Carnot, knew quite well that a stiffening of officers of the old army was indispensable to the morale of the ragged levies who were being forged into the armies of France.

Buonaparte and Dulac had both been captains when they first met at Nice, and the discipline of the old army obliged Dulac to address the new brigadier-general in the third person to mark the distance between them. But the Corsican persisted in using the *tutoiement militaire*, and the 'thee' and 'thou' of friendship broke down the other man's reserve. Soon they had dropped a little way behind the others, and were talking confidentially about their mission.

"Citizen Barras seems to think we shall encounter some opposition in Nice," said Buonaparte. "It was quiet enough when we were there last summer. Possibly the Piedmontese were still stunned by their defeat, but they seemed to accept us peaceably enough. What's your opinion, Dulac?"

"The population was peaceable, citizen general, but not the military. They kept their arms and took to the hills. Now they've formed a Piedmontese militia to harass our outposts, and they've mobilised the peasants into a loose band of guerrilla fighters called *les barbets* . . . I don't suppose they'll tackle an armed troop like ours, *mon général*. Robbing hen roosts is about their level."

"*Les barbets*," said Buonaparte thoughtfully. "I wonder why they call themselves 'water-dogs'. No doubt we'll soon find out."

There was no sign of any infiltration by Piedmontese

resistants on the westward side of the River Var. At Hyères, St Raphaël and Antibes the villagers even turned out to cheer the little detachment headed by one of the troopers carrying a tricolore guidon, and the small garrisons of the existing forts were willing providers of food and shelter. Sometimes the shelter was little more than a bivouac with a roof above their heads, and the men were crowded together working on the day's notes by candlelight. Dulac had the task of correlating the notes on roads and bridges (or the lack of bridges) after the evening *soupe* was eaten. He had been one of the *ingénieure-géographes* of the old army, and was still superior in mathematics to every man in the group except Buonaparte himself. The general made his own notes on ordnance in the deteriorating scrawl which few but he could now decipher, and sketched corrections on the sole and inaccurate map of Provence. Sometimes, when the men slept and his was the only candle still burning, Buonaparte studied this map along with another and better map of Italy.

The nearer they came to Nice the more often he thought of Commissioner Barras's good luck wishes when he crossed the Var. Was there a double meaning in the words? Was crossing the Var to be the equivalent of crossing the Rubicon, and was some disastrous decision to be made by him at Nice? General Dumerbion, the commander of the city, he knew to be ageing and indecisive, and the new commissioner of the Republic was an unknown quantity. It might be prudent to put off his arrival in Nice until he and his little troop had reconnoitred the back country and the possible routes to Italy. They would cross the Var – eventually – but first they would ascend the Var river by what was marked on the map as a mountain track.

He had learned last summer at Nice that there was a half-company of troops at Entrevaux, a village high in the mountains which was in the sector commanded from Digne, and therefore not to be considered as part of coastal defence. It had been fortified by Vauban, and defended by the great Turenne, one of Buonaparte's heroes, and must thus have some importance as guarding the mountain passes which led to Italy. With his secret project in view, the general decided to have a look at Entrevaux. If the map was reasonably correct, the place was no more than a day's ride from the coast road.

The map, of course, was wrong. The very nature of the track, winding higher and ever higher by the side of the brawling river, made speed impossible. They rode in single file, for the winter rains had brought down falls of stone, and the riders looked apprehensively at the towering cliffs above their heads. There were several halts while pebbles were removed from horse-shoes, and by midday, when they stopped to eat cold food from their saddle bags, most of the unfortunate mounts were being led. To make matters worse the sun, which had shone on all their journey through Provence, was obscured behind dark clouds, and soon a light rain began to fall. It quickly became a downpour and the trudging men were soaked through. By five in the afternoon it was too dark to see the way, and they had only reached the confluence of the Var and the Tinée, with as far again to go before they reached Entrevaux.

There were some stifled curses but no complaints from seasoned soldiers until Buonaparte called a halt and went forward with Captain Dulac to examine a cavern where some quarrying seemed to have taken place. The size of the rocks strewn about the entrance suggested that the quarrymen had been giants, but in the bowels of the earth there was shelter for man and beast. The horses were rubbed down, fed and watered from one of the many springs which flowed into the Var, now a raging torrent.

"We're the water-dogs now," said the general, as he reluctantly vetoed the lighting of a fire. "We don't want to be caught in a cave if some of the Piedmontese militia come looking for trouble. Bread and wine tonight, soldiers, and a good meal at Entrevaux tomorrow. We move forward at first light."

The exhausted men, wrapped in their sodden great-coats, were soon asleep. The troopers were ordered to stand sentry for three spells of two hours each, but when Captain Dulac awoke in what he supposed to be the middle of the night, he saw that the figure silhouetted against a paler sky was that of General Buonaparte, bareheaded and with his hands clasped behind his back. What was he thinking about, in this wild place beneath the mountains? What did he hope to find at Entrevaux?

The general who had relieved the man on sentry duty was thinking about Turenne. He had always believed Turenne was the greatest of French generals, 'the only one who grew bolder with old age', as he was fond of saying. The hero of the Thirty Years' War was an authentic hero, not a Paoli, and he'd had the good luck to be killed in action at the age of sixty-four. That's how I would like to go, thought the general who was not yet twenty-five. I want to snatch the laurel crown of fortune or die on the field of battle.

What they found at Entrevaux, when they reached that mountain eyrie after a long ride-and-march through the pelting rain, was no Turenne, but a white-haired veteran of the Seven Years' War called Captain Geoffroy, the commander of the little garrison. Warned of the general's approach by a trooper sent on in advance, he had turned out his men in parade order, to be inspected by Buonaparte in one of the quickest reviews of his entire life. For once he was not interested in making an immediate inspection of the forts established by Vauban. There were two: one on the far side of the Var, and one in the form of a citadel beyond the village square. The square itself was the great attraction to the weary men from Toulon. Before they dispersed to stables and barracks they noted two wineshops, a saddler's, a baker's, even a butcher's shop and other evidence of civilisation inside an ancient stone arcade, while on the other side of the square there was actually an inn. The hostess, who announced herself as Madame Catherine, came out to curtsey a welcome to the citizen general, the news of whose gallantry at Toulon had reached as far as Entrevaux, and whose visit to her poor house was an honour indeed.

It was not a poor house, but a very comfortable one, as comfortable as the substantial form and rosy cheeks of Madame Catherine. Her efficiency, and perhaps her youth – for she was not much more than thirty – were a great deal more to the general's taste than the babbling of the elderly commandant, who was torn between apologising for the weather and thanking Buonaparte for an invitation to take wine with him. Madame Catherine whisked him off to a bedroom with a fire in it, where he could change into a dry shirt from his saddlebags and wash in hot water, and then whisked him back to a bright parlour with another blazing fire, in which an iron vessel held a jorum of hot spiced wine. From the kitchen, where his greatcoat and cocked hat were drying, came the appetising smell of roasting chicken.

Although the garrison had had its *soupe* at the usual hour, Captain Geoffroy was delighted to share the general's luncheon. He ventured to suppose that the general must be hungry after the spartan rations of the previous day. So he was; but General Buonaparte was a fast eater, gobbling the good things set on the table by Madame Catherine in person and firing questions at Captain Geoffroy between mouthfuls. The captain was a long-service man, was he not?

"I first stood fire at the battle of Minden, sir."

"Minden? That was thirty-five years ago."

And was the service unbroken, or had he been recalled to duty at the time of the general conscription, called the *levée en masse*? Recalled and posted to Digne, sir. Given command of the garrison at Entrevaux, when? Here the captain was in difficulties. Although a good republican, he found a new calendar confusing, with months called after the seasons and beginning in the middle instead of on the first. He would obviously have preferred to say his tour of duty began in January and ended in June, but he achieved "Began in *Nivôse* and will end in *Prairial*", then, he supposed, back to Digne. Their supplies came by wagon from Digne, and during the month of November – your pardon, sir – of *Brumaire*, there had been two attacks on the wagons by men of the Piedmontese resistance. No, he didn't think they were the so-called 'water-dogs', in Geoffroy's view *les barbets* was merely another name for brigands, who had always flourished in the high country. There had been no direct attacks on the forts at Entrevaux, built to resist an invading army.

"And you are the only officer, citizen captain?"

"I am, sir; but there's one young man I intend to recommend for a commission when we return to Digne. His name? Corporal Vautour."

"Corporal Vautour! There's a *nom de guerre* for you!" Buonaparte's brilliant smile lit up his face, and Geoffroy, an affable man, was relieved to find that the grave young general could smile at all. "Pray what are the Vulture's claims to a commission?"

"He claims nothing, sir, it was an idea of my own. Vautour joined the National Guard as soon as it was formed, and rose to the rank of sergeant in one of the Paris Sections. Last October he applied for a transfer to the army, and joined us at Digne, of course with a loss of rank. He was promoted to corporal when our tour began at Entrevaux. He has initiative, sir, which so many of the men lack. When the mountain patrols go out he makes notes on the terrain and draws maps. Vautour's an educated man, *mon général; he reads books*."

"Where does he get the books?"

"He brought several from Digne in his knapsack."

Buonaparte smiled again at the respectful tone. An omnivorous reader, he preferred tearing the meaning out of a book and throwing it away to carrying it anywhere.

"Point your Vulture out to me, will you, when we visit the forts," he said. "It's time we started, and the rain has stopped."

With a regretful look at an untouched dish of dessert

Captain Geoffroy followed a leader who was constitution-ally in a hurry. The still-damp greatcoat and cockaded hat were reclaimed from the kitchen, the two engineer officers were summoned, and the two from the *Ponts et Chaussées* at Toulon were reported to be already examining the rickety bridge across the Var.

The fort across the river was exactly what Buonaparte had expected, a monument to the seventeenth century. It was built of stone and iron to withstand a siege, but the slits in the walls suggested that the defenders were to use bows and arrows, and Captain Geoffroy went into another fit of apologising for such ordnance as there was: he had seen more modern cannon, he said, at the battle of Minden.

"Can't get modern stuff across these planks, citizen general," said one of the bridge experts. "First thing we'd have to do is build a stone bridge, and is it worth it, for a hole in the hills like Entrevaux?"

"Turenne thought it was," said Buonaparte abstract-edly. They had mounted to the flat roof of the fort, and he was looking at the great peaks to the east. Beyond those mountains lay Italy. What had Turenne seen, more than a hundred years ago? A road into Italy, or out of Italy which he must defend for France? An easier way than the way by Fort Saorgio and the Col di Tenda which Buonaparte had studied on the map? It might be worth discussing the route with the only man in the little garrison who 'made notes on the terrain and drew maps'. He said to Geoffroy,

"Your Vulture isn't here, is he?"

"He's on duty at the citadel, *mon général*."

"Yes, well, that can wait until tomorrow morning. Send Corporal Vautour to me at the inn at five o'clock. I have work to do until then."

Certainly he had work to do, but the general felt a most unusual need to lie back in a comfortable chair and rest the leg in which a bayonet wound had healed by first intention, but which was now aching after the long exhausting climb of yesterday. Madame Catherine came into the parlour with the excuse that the fire needed attention. He suspected that she wanted to have another look at the distinguished guest, for the fire was burning brightly, but she knelt down on the hearth rug with her wood basket and began to add some small sweet-smelling logs to the flame. She wore no fichu, and when she leaned forward he could see the swelling of her breasts. From her coquettish sidelong glance the general knew she was aware of his gaze.

Was she a wife or was she a widow? She wore several rings on her left hand. Whatever she was, Madame Catherine was available, he was sure of that, and suddenly he felt an impulse to possess her. He remembered the big bed in the room where he had changed his shirt, the thick curtains ready to draw around it, and the patchwork counterpane spread above what he was sure was a mattress stuffed with feathers. Taking Madame Catherine to bed would be a double sinking into feathers: that big healthy body was built to be the warrior's rest.

The impulse was not entirely sexual, for sex, in the consideration of Napoleon Buonaparte, ran a poor second to the art of war. His affair with Désirée Clary was conducted on the lines of contemporary romance, and he was even planning a novel about it in which he was called Clisson and she, Eugénie. The great tactician failed to see that the verbalising of his feelings proved their insincerity.

"How old are you, citizeness?" he asked in his abrupt way. She smiled and got to her feet in one supple movement, brushing the wood chips from her skirt.

"Guess!" she said provocatively.

"Twenty-five?"

"Flatterer! Let's call it thirty."

He thought she was more than thirty, but he liked older women, experienced enough to handle his sometimes fumbled attempts at lovemaking. He held out his hand to her and said, "You have beautiful eyes!"

She had just slipped her hand into his when there was

a loud knock on the door and someone, presumably a maid, called, *"Madame Catherine! Venez vite, s'il vous plaît!"*

"A kitchen crisis," she said calmly. "I must go." The parting pressure of her hand said *later*.

The little incident had cured the general of his lassitude. Stimulated and energetic, he picked up the map case and sheets of blank paper he had left when they went to visit the fort, and sat down at the now empty table to put on paper all the details he had committed to memory when they came up to the ramshackle bridge across the Var. Time passed, the afternoon skies darkened with fresh rain, and without his having to ask for it a well-trimmed lamp was carried in by a silent stable boy. By its light the general saw the door opening as the clock on the village church struck five, and a tall figure with its hand raised in a stiff salute.

"Corporal Vautour?"

"A vos ordres, mon général!"

The Vautour of Entrevaux was no longer the Vautour of the Rue St Honoré. Instead of the shabby theatrical sky blue of the National Guard he wore the dark blue uniform of the new army, correct in every detail from the cockaded tricorne hat and the wide skirted coat with the crossed shoulder belt to the tinderbox with the copper handle at his waist. If he had been carrying a rifle with a long bayonet, this Vautour might have stood for the portrait of a model soldier.

"Come in and close the door," said Napoleon Buonaparte. "I daresay you're wondering why I sent for you?"

"Captain Geoffroy said you wanted to see me, citizen general."

"Captain Geoffroy tells me you're something of a scholar. You draw maps and read books. What are you reading now?"

"I have Guibert on *Tactics* in the *chambrée*, sir, and I read the *Campaigns* of Turenne at Digne."

"But not Bourcet's *Treatise on Mountain Warfare*, eh? No, obviously not; there are only a few manuscript copies available. Pity, since you seem to be interested in the subject: now tell me, what set you to map-making?"

"It was something to do after we'd been on patrol."

"You find garrison life at Entrevaux lacks interest?"

"It isn't exactly Paris, sir."

"You regret having left Paris and the military glories of the National Guard?"

"*No!*" It was said so explosively that Vautour apologised. "I beg your pardon, sir. I only meant, when I volunteered for the army, I hoped to be posted to a fighting front. Instead I was sent to Digne, where you never hear a shot fired in anger from one month to another."

"Give it time," said Buonaparte. "You haven't been six months in the army yet. How old are you, Vautour?"

"I'll be twenty-three in July, sir."

"I can't believe that a man of twenty-two takes to map-making, of all skilled occupations, just to relieve the tedium of garrison life. You must have some other motive. What is it?"

The imperative question was a shock tactic which seldom failed. With a heightened colour, and obvious embarrassment, Vautour replied that . . . here in the mountains, sir . . . on the very terrain . . . he got interested in trying to make a plan for the invasion of Italy.

"I share your interest," said Napoleon Buonaparte. "I should like to know what conclusions you've come to. You may take off your hat, corporal, and sit at the table with me. You can't study a small map standing up."

With a sinking heart, and the feeling that he was about to make an abject fool of himself, Vautour obeyed. The general spread out two maps, one, heavily over-corrected, of Provence, the other of Italy.

"Here we are at Entrevaux," said the general, using his pen like a pointer. "Show me how you would proceed."

Vautour took a deep breath and began. "From Entrevaux I would march down to the confluence of the Tinée – "

"Where we spent a wretched night in some sort of a quarry."

"I know that quarry. From there the way leads back up the Tinée till you come to a place called Isola. Then you take to the passes of the Maritime Alps and the river beds till you reach Cuneo, where the plain of Piedmont lies at your feet."

Buonaparte watched the long fingers and the strong wrist as the young man, carried away by his own enthusiasm, traced out his path on the two maps. He was bent over the table with his chin supported on his two fists as he surveyed his goal: the plain of Piedmont and the capital, Turin.

"If you take that route, supposing it to be practicable," said Buonaparte, "you're going to ask a great deal of your men and your horseflesh. Do you realise that before you reach Cuneo you'd have to 'turn the Barricades', as it's called, in the Valle della Stura?"

"I never heard of the Barricades. They're not marked on the map."

"The Valle della Stura is. Never mind! Suppose you do turn the Barricades. Do you expect exhausted men to make a successful attack on Turin?"

"They could be reinforced from the Army of the Alps."

"Executing a pincers movement from the base at Digne?"

"That's what I thought of."

"Not bad strategy, but bad mountaineering. Now think again. Turin is not the ultimate prize, but Turin captured means the Kingdom of Sardinia is effectively out of the war. Where would you strike next?"

"Through Lombardy, sir?" – doubtfully.

"Through Lombardy to Milan. Now that's your real goal, but the Austrian army would arrive in strength to defend it. How would you handle that?"

Vautour was still more doubtful. "Would another pincers movement be possible? Could the Army of the Rhine attack the Austrians in the rear by way of the Tirol?"

The general smiled. "Not bad," he said, "you have the root of the matter in you." He pulled Vautour's ear gently; with him it was a mark of favour. "What you need is training and experience. It's a thousand pities you didn't go to the Ecole Militaire."

"That's where I wanted to go, but my father sent me to the Lycée Louis-le-Grand."

"Did he indeed? Speaking of schools, are you any relation of Edouard de la Tour?"

He saw shock wither the young man's face. "How did you guess?" said Vautour.

"Comte Edouard de la Tour was in my class at military school. I didn't know him well" (he had known none of them really well) "but I've often seen him sitting at his desk with his chin on his hands, working out some problem. You're very like him. Are you his brother?"

"His younger brother."

"Where is he now?"

"Farming in England, I believe."

"An émigré?"

"Like my father and mother."

"When did they leave France?"

From the moment when he knew himself to be recognised, Vautour had answered the hail of questions mechanically. He remembered how often he himself had been the questioner, and for very shame he kept his eyes on the maps before him, without meeting Buonaparte's brilliant gaze. But now he flung round in his chair to face the general, and said,

"Sir, that is their story and not mine. I chose a different way, which I thought was the right way, but I won't criticise them, even to you . . ."

"You may say anything you like to me; it'll go no further than this room. I'm not a commissioner of the republic, waiting to pounce on you and send you to the guillotine for some fancied lack of patriotism or because you were born an aristocrat. I want to help you, corporal. Now tell me your real name."

"I'm the *ci-devant* Vicomte Charles Maurice de la Tour."

"What made you call yourself Vautour? A schoolboy prank?"

"I *was* a schoolboy when the Bastille was stormed in '89. My parents left immediately, like the king's younger brother, the Comte d'Artois, so they were able to take money and jewels with them to England. Edouard had been commissioned into the Flanders Regiment – *you* remember, the regiment whose demonstrations of loyalty to the king and queen started the row that brought the market women of Paris to Versailles. Edouard didn't cheer Their Majesties. He was safely in Wiltshire by that time."

"You were only seventeen then. Didn't your parents try to take you with them?"

"Yes, but they were in a great hurry to leave. I ran away from home . . . Don't ask me to tell you about that time, citizen general, it was the worst time of my life. Then, when La Fayette organised the National Guard, I joined it. You see I believed in La Fayette in those days."

"Had you known him, under the old régime?"

"As a schoolboy knew the Hero of Two Worlds. My mother and his wife were friends; the *ci-devant* marquise and her sisters often came to our house in Versailles. But that didn't affect me; what I admired was what La Fayette stood for. Law and order and a constitutional monarchy. I know he saved the king's life, and the queen's, the night the mob stormed the palace of Versailles. But in the end he betrayed the people and fled the country."

Buonaparte was silent. He had his own and most unflattering opinion of the Hero of Two Worlds.

"What beats me," he said at last, "is that, after four creditable years in the National Guard, and long after the *levée en masse*, you volunteered for the army. Why?"

"I suppose I could make up a story," said Charles de la Tour. "I could invent some noble reason which would turn everything I've told you into a lie. The truth is, I enlisted because a girl called me a coward. She said I should be at the front, so here I am – at Entrevaux."

"Ah!" said Buonaparte, "*cherchez la femme*! Was she pretty?"

"Very. As pretty as she was when you knew her, citizen general."

"*I* knew the girl who called you a coward?"

"I saw you having supper together once, with her uncle and another man, in the Régence café in Paris. Don't you remember Marie Fontaine?"

7

It was odd how the name of Marie Fontaine brought a change in the tenor of their conversation. The general remembered her at once, and called her "a sweet little thing, not the sort of girl to call a man a coward" and he spoke well of her uncle, a fine apothecary and chess player. But he was plainly not interested in the Fontaines, nor Vautour's association with them, and beyond hoping they were well he let the subject drop. He put his own maps back in their case and told the young man to give the maps he had drawn himself ("such as they are") to Captain Dulac. "Ask Captain Geoffroy to come to me," he said as he dismissed Vautour.

Back in the *chambrée* that night, while the other men played cards or made a dash down the arcade to the wineshops through the blinding rain before Lights Out, the *ci-devant* Vicomte de la Tour lay on his palliasse and thought of the girl who had driven him to enlist. On that last day he had tried to protect the little fool, first from the risk she ran in visiting the Noailles and then from the drunken Federals from Marseille, and all she had done was sneer and quarrel, except at the last moment, when he knew quite well she had responded to his kiss. Was he wrong to have left Paris? Ought he to have stayed beside her, coaxed her, begun all over again on a new footing? It had seemed impossible at the time; it *was* impossible. That damned uncle with the rabbit smile would get her into trouble sooner or later, and he, 'the Vulture' (the general had laughed at the name), would not be there to help.

He told himself not to be so sure. This day at Entrevaux might mean the start of a different life for him. If he could get away from the backwater of Digne, and follow Buonaparte, he might find himself sooner or later on the road back to Paris.

He would have been surprised to know that his future was under discussion in the inn parlour, where General Buonaparte had invited Captain Geoffroy and Captain Dulac to dine with him. Dulac confirmed that the young man actually had been on patrol up the valley of the Tinée as far as Isola, and his maps made from observation were very good. Where he was working from the very indifferent Italian maps available at Entrevaux he had relied on imagination, and there his work was bad. "Promising," was the non-committal opinion of the engineer. By this time he had a fair idea of the way the general's mind worked, and foresaw extra duty for himself in the tuition and wet-nursing of a 'promising' new recruit.

Captain Geoffroy, too, was thinking of himself. To his mind, rock-set in the old army mould at the time of the battle of Minden, it was unbelievable that the general should propose the transfer of Corporal Vautour from the Army of the Alps to the Army of Italy, with a change of name thrown in. The paperwork involved would fall on his shoulders, with a probable reprimand from his commanding officer at Digne as well.

"You really think he deserves to be seconded to your tour of inspection, citizen general?" he said with an attempt at dignity.

"Citizen captain, you said yourself he was a valuable man. You talked of getting him a lieutenant's commission."

"Yes, but that was at Digne."

"France isn't ruled from Digne, Captain Geoffroy. Nor is it ruled from Nice, but at Nice I can discuss the matter with General Dumerbion, and if necessary with the commissioners of the Republic. They are the masters – for the time being."

The arrival of a tureen of thick soup and a basket of crusty bread put an end to the discussion, but after the jugged hare and the assortment of cheeses it was resumed in the form of a lecture by Buonaparte, illustrated by references to his own maps and Vautour's. Madame Catherine, coming in to clear the table with a rose in her brown hair, was horrified to see her best linen tablecloth pushed aside and crumpled, as well as stained with wine and sauces carelessly served by a hasty eater.

"Can't you do all this in the morning, citizeness?" said Buonaparte. "We don't want to be disturbed."

"As you please, citizen general. Is there anything else I can do for you?"

"Yes, have me called at five tomorrow. Goodnight, Madame Catherine."

No compliments now on her beautiful eyes! Muttering *"Bonne nuit!"* she left the room in dudgeon, and not long after that the general had pity on his audience – for Geoffroy had drunk enough wine to be in danger of falling asleep – and dismissed them. But Napoleon Buonaparte sat on in the disordered room, over the dying fire, and thought of the invasion of Italy and the capture of Milan. He knew that what had prompted him to consider adding Vautour to his expedition was the young man's suggestion that the Army of the Rhine should attack the Austrians in the rear. No one but himself had thought of that, for Carnot was committed to a defensive policy and Maximilien Robespierre was equally committed to fighting on all fronts. Folly! The Napoleonic way was to attack your enemies one at a time, and Austria was the prime enemy, except for . . .

But England could wait.

Two weeks later Sergeant Charles Latour was riding eastwards out of Nice, the thirteenth man in the group detailed for the inspection of coastal defences, and prepared to believe against all superstition that thirteen was his lucky number.

Inspection of the second fort at Entrevaux had been over by nine o'clock in the morning. At ten o'clock Captain Geoffroy, still protecting himself, had given him written movement orders in the name of Vautour, Corporal Charles, to report for duty to the *Grand Quartier-Général*; these orders were countersigned with a scrawled capital B. By eleven, his few possessions were in his saddlebags, his horse was groomed and the last *soupe* of Entrevaux was eaten. Then the little troop set off down the stony track, in weather so mild that they made good speed on the way to Nice.

As Buonaparte had anticipated there were delays at Nice. General Dumerbion had before him the awful warning of six hundred generals appointed since the Revolution who had been demoted, relieved of their commands or otherwise disposed of, usually by means of the guillotine, and he was anxious to keep his job and his head. The inspector's demands alarmed him; so did the dismissal of that ancient fortress, the Château of Nice, as 'a relic of Saracen times'; so did the man's insistence on proceeding to Mentone, the last village before the Italian border, by the direct route along the coast. The Piedmontese resistance seemed to be petering out, but a band of 'water-dogs' had taken to harassing the picquets and had done damage before they were haled in front of a firing squad. In an accumulation of worries, General Dumerbion saw no reason to object to the transfer of a man with nearly five years' service in the National Guard to his credit. With a very slight alteration in his name and a promotion to sergeant, Charles Latour was duly sworn in to the Army of Italy.

He was in better spirits than he had ever been since the fall of the Bastille and the headlong flight of his parents and brother to England. It didn't seem to matter now that the ancient Tour de Vesle, from which the family took its name, had been destroyed in the advance on Verdun, or that his mother's estate in the Ile de France (she had been a great heiress, and one of Marie Antoinette's ladies) was now forfeit and declared National Property. *Nizza la Superba* was a good place for a young man to be. The guillotine was kept in the background, for the city was too recently annexed and too restless to be stirred up by the mass executions of Paris, and the light-hearted citizens were eager for entertainment. There were theatres, concerts, public balls, and in every café round the harbour, under the umbrella of every flower-seller, telling their beads on the steps of every church, there were girls. Girls who giggled, girls who kissed, girls who spoke Italian but were very willing to be taught French by the soldiers from the north.

For a few days, while the experts conferred on defences, the two NCOs and the four troopers of the inspection detail had many hours off duty. They got on well together, and hunted in couples, Latour and Junot having struck up a friendship at Entrevaux. They enjoyed their freedom and they enjoyed the girls.

There were also newspapers in Nice, and some of the reports they carried, coming in late from Paris, showed that Napoleon Buonaparte was not the only commander who knew how to divide his enemies and tackle them one by one. By now the virtual dictator of the Committee of Public Safety, Robespierre had two rivals at loggerheads with each other. They were Georges Danton, one of the leaders of the Revolution and a magnificent orator, who stood for moderation and clemency, and was now the leader of the *Indulgents*, whom Robespierre regarded as no better than counter-revolutionaries. The other was Jacques Hébert, the editor of a scurrilous newspaper called *Le Père Duchesne*, and the inventor of a horrible story of Queen Marie Antoinette's incestuous relationship with her eight-year-old son.

Robespierre took Hébert first. On the pretext that there were foreign agents among the Hébertists who were planning a demonstration against the government, he had Hébert arrested on 14 March, and guillotined with seventeen of his associates.

This was much discussed at GHQ at Nice, where Augustin Robespierre had arrived from Toulon as a commissioner, along with a Corsican Deputy called Saliceti. The other Corsican present inwardly cursed the delay to his mission: it had been bad enough to argue with Dumerbion, who had some futile reason for wanting the Inspector of Coastal Defences to go the long way round to Mentone, but he had to listen civilly to the commissioners if he was to get their approval to his plan of attack on Italy.

He had not forgotten the 'promising' Latour, but left him up to Captain Dulac. The engineer, sighing, administered a mathematics test to the young sergeant, which he passed with a success reflecting credit on the teaching at the Lycée Louis-le-Grand. His reward was a manuscript copy of Bourcet's *Principes de la Guerre de Montagnes*, which Latour was to read and return to Captain Dulac in forty-eight hours, having made a written digest of the whole work. It was equivalent to being confined to barracks for two days.

"Well done!" said Dulac, when the precious manuscript was returned to him at GHQ. "You may expect an oral exam on Bourcet when the general has time to spare."

"When will that be, citizen captain?"

"When we're on the road again. Word has just come down from on high that we start for Mentone tomorrow – by the coast road."

"The word in barracks was that General Dumerbion wanted us to ride via L'Escarène and Sospello."

"Which would have doubled our journey. Do you know the reason?"

"If we took the long way round by the mountain road we would avoid the Principality of Monaco, where the French are not too popular, because the Princess of

Monaco is in a Paris prison awaiting trial by the Revolutionary Tribunal. But we can't dodge the Principality, sir; Mentone and Roccabruna are part of the territory."

"Well, we won't be climbing up to Roccabruna, to be told it's another relic of Saracen times," said Captain Dulac, thinking Latour was well informed. "I know Mentone, I think the people there are friendly . . . It won't be a long trip, and the general's in a hurry. Tell Junot and the troopers we start at first light."

It was the second of April, and first light came early. By the time they reached Monaco the sun was high in a cloudless sky. Riding down the hill beneath the castle on the rock they heard some muttering about *les bleus* and *notre princesse*, but an innkeeper down by the harbour was perfectly willing to serve the Frenchmen with food and drink, and when he thanked them for their custom he bowed, and said Monaco had always considered itself a protectorate of France. The afternoon was spent in planning a gun emplacement near an ancient look-out called La Vigie, and it was sunset before they reached Mentone. Captain Dulac, who said he knew the innkeeper of the village, rode on ahead with a billeting order.

Buonaparte halted his men at a wooden bridge across a little river which lost itself in trickles of water across the stony beach. A few children gathered to look at the men in uniform, and that was all they saw of the population of Mentone.

"Soldiers!" said Buonaparte, "this stream is the Careï, which is of some importance to the Army of Italy. Up that cart track by the river bed the way leads to Sospello, and from there by the High Valley of the Roya to the Col di Tenda. The road is no worse than the road to Entrevaux, and it is protected by a Piedmontese fort at Saorgio. Once over the Col di Tenda, the way is clear to Cuneo and the plain of Piedmont. It's a much better way than the route by the Valle della Stura." He looked at Latour with a half smile, and added, "Some of you may see the Careï again." He gave the order to ride on.

He meant all that for me, thought Latour, biting his lips as the little troop clattered down the main street of Mentone, where shopkeepers came to their doors to watch. That was his way of reminding me that I made a fool of myself over the damned Barricades. 'Better than the route by the Valle della Stura' – I should think so! I hope I'm one of the ones who get to take the short cut by the Roya! He was not really cast down. The reprimand had not been public, and a reprimand from Buonaparte was worth more than a compliment from . . . say Robespierre.

The next day was a bustle of activity. The men from the *Ponts et Chaussées* were ordered to do a preliminary survey for an entirely new road joining the main street to the Italian frontier, the existing road winding uphill and downhill like the track beside the Var. The engineers and sappers groaned when they saw that the frontier itself was marked by a ravine spanned by a double plank bridge. The deepwater harbour, where the fishermen moored their boats, was an open invitation to any British frigate in the vicinity.

"Coastal Defences!" fumed Buonaparte. "Mentone has *no* defences, none, and the terrain is not defensible unless we mount guns on the Red Rocks with underwater swimmers to fire them! The sooner I get a report away to Paris the better, so let us ride back to Nice as fast as possible."

He scowled as they walked their horses over the shaky Careï bridge, as if he thought it would be some time before they could make Mentone their base for the ascent of the Col di Tenda, and went up the Roman road beyond the village at a gallop. It was the ultimate frustration of the day when the general's horse cast a shoe at the top of the hill, and he swore in fluent Italian as he dismounted.

It was some small comfort to know that they were only a short distance from a smithy, which with a tavern and two or three cottages formed a hamlet on the landward side of the point called Cap Martin. It was not so comforting to find the blacksmith, a burly red-faced man in his thirties, sullen because he was about to sit down to supper, and unwilling to go to work because the smithy fire was out.

"Light it then," said Dulac.

"Let me see the hoof first."

The blacksmith took the shoeless hoof between his knees, shook his head over the 'slovenly ways' of the army smiths, and announced that he must use the hoof clippers. These were found only after a prolonged search in his slovenly smithy.

"This looks like being a long job," said the general. "Dismount, men. Junot, go to the tavern and ask them to bring out some wine." He turned away and strolled off to examine a curious structure, half brick and half ruin, by the side of the road.

"That's an old Roman tomb," said Dulac to the other engineer officer. "I wonder what he's thinking about."

"Nero, perhaps," said the engineer.

"Did you say Nero or hero? Alexander's *his* hero, he told me so himself. Anyway he's not interested in the Roman; look at him."

The general had taken his glass from his tail pocket, extended the single lens, and was studying the promontory.

"Can he be planning a gun emplacement on Cap Martin? He didn't seem interested in the area when we passed through."

He was planning, undoubtedly, for the brain which never rested had dismissed the problems of Mentone and was working on a new idea. All he said when he rejoined the men was, "Is the wine drinkable?"

"It's a good *rosé de Provence*," said Dulac. "Very refreshing."

Buonaparte took a glass from the tray which the potboy from the tavern, a shock-headed youth of about sixteen, was carrying round among the men. "It *is* good," he said.

111

"We have such wine in Corsica . . . Has that fellow got his fire going?"

"At last, sir."

"Take a glass of wine to him, *jeune homme*." The blacksmith came out; surprised but ungrateful, he said *"Merci!"* in a sulky voice.

"How long will the job take you, blacksmith?"

"About an hour. The fire's not drawing well. There's something the matter with the bellows."

Buonaparte took out his watch. "An hour to wait, and a good twenty kilometres to Nice. No chance of *la soupe* for the men tonight . . . You, boy! How are you off for food at the tavern?"

"Oh, we have plenty of everything, sir," said the boy eagerly. "Eggs and cheese, and dry *salame* and *coppa*, if you should please to order supper . . ."

"Go ahead, Jean-Pierre!" said the voice of an angry woman. "Offer to sell all your provisions to *les bleus*, and let the hamlet folk go hungry for a week! Foreign soldiers, taking the bread out of poor folks' mouths – "

"Shut up, Juliette," said the blacksmith. The woman was his wife, young and good-looking in the Ligurian peasant style and dressed in black. As she talked she knitted mechanically, reminding the men from Paris of the women who knitted at the foot of the guillotine.

"Citizeness, your husband gives you very good advice," said Buonaparte.

The woman stared angrily at the little man in the grey coat. She had not the least idea of his rank. From the cottage door which she had left open behind her came the smell of cold burned food.

"And what about my man's supper?" she asked. "Ruined, and you don't care! You come up as bold as brass and say you're on the business of the Republic – "

"Juliette!" shouted the man again. "Hush up!"

"Don't you hush me!" stormed the woman. "I'm a free-born Monégasque, and I've a right to speak my mind!"

"You're a likely-looking fellow," said the general to the

blacksmith. "You could be drafted into the Army of Italy tomorrow. I guarantee our farrier sergeants would teach you to keep your fires burning and your bellows in repair!"

The smith retired precipitately to his anvil and the sound of hammering began.

"Threats now," said the blacksmith's wife, knitting furiously. "Big talk, but you don't scare me. You gentry from Paris are in for some unpleasant surprises, you mark my words. Citizen Danton, your great man, has been arrested by order of Robespierre, and he'll have sneezed into the sack by now."

The innkeeper and his wife, who provided a good supper, confirmed the news of Danton's arrest. The postboy had brought it on his way from Nice; they must have missed the postboy in Mentone. It was news which every man digested in his own way. All realised that Maximilien Robespierre was now a virtual dictator. Buonaparte thought of the effect on his own career if his friend Augustin, the dictator's brother, rose to a position of greater power. Latour, who had seen more of the excesses of the Revolution than any of the others, thought of the great Danton in a tumbril going along the Rue St Honoré and wondered how long Marie Fontaine and her uncle would be safe. 'Sneezing into the sack' – he had heard the vulgar expression often enough, but seldom used it. An insult to death, was how he thought of that description of the last breath leaving the body, and the severed head tumbling into the bloodstained bag.

Supper was eaten in silence, the officers at one table, the sergeants and troopers at another. Jean-Pierre came timidly up to say the citizen general's horse was shod, and the general sent Junot across the road to examine the shoeing and settle with the smith. Then, raising his voice, he told them all that they would bivouac for the night in the woods of Cap Martin, where he had an inspection to make next morning. The innkeeper would provide coffee and bread before they rode back to Nice.

The horses had been fed and watered in the inn stables, and they had only a short distance to go. Back by the road they came, down to the shore, with just enough light in the umbered dusk for horsemen to see their way along a track to an open space where the ruins of an ancient building stood among scented bushes and green grass.

"We've taken to the *maquis*, Dulac," said the general with a laugh. "Thyme and lentisk and rosemary and flowering cistus – it reminds me of the country where my brother Joseph and I played as boys."

"It's certainly a vast improvement on our bivouac by the Var," said Dulac. "The very earth is warm."

"What are those stones, like the foundation of a house?"

"My father told me there was once a chapel here, the Chapel of St Martin. There was even a community of nuns, who harassed the men of Roccabruna by constantly ringing a warning bell when they thought the Saracens were coming."

"Rang bells, did they? Well, bless the good women, we can do better than that," said Buonaparte . . . "You men, see to the horses." He gathered his experts round him, saying there was light enough to talk. "You can take your measurements in the morning," he told the engineers, "and the sappers must decide where to lay the foundations. What I have in mind for Cap Martin," he went on, "is a semaphore . . . Come now, you've all heard of Chappe's invention?"

No one was willing to admit ignorance.

"You could call it a visual telegraph system, if you understand what the word telegraph means. It's a wooden tower with shutters set in frames, which can send messages over a considerable distance: the first messages were passed between Paris and Lille about a year ago. Here it would be possible to send messages across the bay to the harbour at Mentone, or in the other direction to La Vigie at Monaco. Then from La Vigie to the headland of Nice."

"It sounds like a better way than ringing a bell to give warning of an enemy invasion," said one of the sapper officers.

"Exactly," said the general. "Well, let's sleep on it. And don't admit, when we get back to GHQ, that you never heard of Claude Chappe and his semaphore."

Napoleon Buonaparte believed, and often said, that five hours' sleep a night was enough for a man. "Six for a woman and seven for a fool" was his genial allocation, but that night beneath the Aleppo pines of Cap Martin he rather exceeded his own limits. He lay awake longer than usual, profoundly disturbed, though he had avoided discussing it, by the fall of Danton and a new power structure which might threaten his own career. He listened to the heavy breathing of the tired men around him until he was lulled to sleep, and to sleep on, by the evocative scents of the *maquis*.

When he awoke there was a faint light in the eastern sky. The general unwrapped himself from the grey overcoat used as a blanket, pulled on his boots and moved silently over the pine needles away from the bivouac. Even the birds were asleep, and the only sound was the sound of the waves fretting gently against the samphire covered rocks at the point of Cap Martin.

The general walked down to the seashore. There was a certain phenomenon, a vision which was given to the eyes of man at certain seasons of the year. He had never seen it, and April, perhaps, was too late: they said January was the best time to see the vision, and then from high up in the Maritime Alps. But he had to take his chance, so he waited while the last stars paled, and wondered which Star was his.

He heard a stone rattle under the booted foot of someone who moved less quietly than he did. He said, "*Qui vive*?" without turning round.

"Latour, citizen general. I hope I don't disturb you?"

Buonaparte turned with a smile. "You don't," he said. "What's the matter? Couldn't you sleep?"

"Not very well."

"You're not accustomed to sleeping in the open air."

"I like it better than the guardroom at the National Palace. But I'll go back now, sir; I didn't mean to intrude upon your – your thoughts."

"No, stay – stay and watch this splendid sunrise. I was thinking about you, last night."

Latour kept his eyes on the general. In breeches and boots, with his white shirt open at the throat and his lank black hair in disorder, he looked even younger than a man some months short of his twenty-fifth birthday. Amazing creature, to have done so much, so soon!

"When we're back at Nice, I want to arrange for you to do a field reconnaissance for me."

"*A vos ordres, mon général.*"

"You saw for yourself yesterday that the coastal defences of Mentone are a farce. It would cost a fortune to make the place into a base for the Army of Italy. But there's no reason why a man should not use the track we saw that leads by the Careï to Sospello, and then up the Roya to the Col di Tenda. A man who could bring back an accurate map of the area, and a complete description of the route across the peaks and the defences of Fort Saorgio, would be a useful man to me. I think you could do a good job, Latour, and you won't have to worry about turning the Barricades."

I'll never live down the Barricades, thought Charles Latour. He said, "When do I start?"

"As soon as it can be managed. You've read your Bourcet now," said Buonaparte sententiously. "You know his maxim, which I have made my own: never plan a campaign without a reconnaissance in depth of the terrain."

"Am I to go alone, citizen general?"

"You'll have an orderly."

An orderly! That meant a commission! Latour smiled,

and the general, perfectly understanding the smile, gently tweaked his ear.

"That'll be something to write to Marie Fontaine about, won't it? But don't give away any military secrets, mind!"

Marie Fontaine! It was thinking about her, fearing for her safety, that had made Latour awaken. He started to say something about letters and security, when he realised the general was not listening. His eyes were again fixed on the sunrise.

"Look!" he said.

The vision so seldom granted had appeared. On the golden horizon, above the blue Mediterranean, there was now the violet outline of an island, with mountain peaks clearly etched, and cliffs running down to the sea.

"Corsica!" the general whispered.

Without waiting to be dismissed, Latour went away. It was not for him to see the look on his general's face, as Napoleon Buonaparte watched the island of his birth.

At the top of the slope he looked back. The general had not moved, but the violet island was lost to view. Instead, rounding the point of Cap Mortola and out of cannon range, he saw the white sails of a British frigate.

8

Marie's life, as winter gave way to the spring of 1794, followed the same monotonous pattern of keeping house, sewing at the workshop in the Palais Royal, and serving behind the counter in the pharmacy. Trade had picked up there, for a hard winter brought a plague of colds and coughs, low fevers and digestive disorders to the half-starved people of the *quartier*, and Prosper Fontaine's remedies were in demand. There was no sale of cosmetics or perfumes except for eau de cologne. The tradesmen's wives who bought it said a handkerchief soaked in eau de cologne was the best thing to keep the smell of blood from their nostrils. There were more complaints to the Section about the blood-reek rising from the very cobbles of the Place de la Révolution, and there was some talk of removing the guillotine east to the Square of the Throne. But nothing came of it, and the death-carts continued to carry their load of victims, now as many as sixty in a day, along the Rue St Honoré.

One day Madame Beauchet came to show Marie the letter which she had at last received from Gouverneur Morris. Nothing was said about a passage to America for George-Washington de La Fayette, but through Frestel, her son's tutor, Madame de La Fayette had succeeded in getting a message to the Minister, again accusing the American government of ingratitude towards the Hero of Two Worlds.

"Pray tell the unhappy lady, if you can reach her at

Brioude," wrote Morris, "that she does herself no good, and her imprisoned husband no good, by these baseless charges. However, I am prepared if need arises to inform the Committee of Public Safety that the family of General de La Fayette is much beloved in the United States, and that the execution of his wife would impair the friendly relations which exist between our two countries."

"Did you ever hear anything so cold-blooded?" Madame Beauchet interrupted the reading of the letter to say. "He talks about the execution of my dear mistress as something likely to happen! And not a word about the poor boy!"

"If the Minister intervenes with Robespierre and the Committee he might save Madame Adrienne," said Marie. "What else does he say?"

The remainder of the letter referred only to President George Washington's Proclamation of Neutrality in the European War declared by France in February 1793, which made it impossible for his envoy to do anything more in the *affaire* La Fayette.

"Marie, tell me, how am I to answer this?"

"Don't answer it at all. Our best hope now is that Frestel himself will be able to save George-Washington. Poor boy, I hope he's proud of his name . . . And what about Madame Louise de Noailles and her children? What's going to happen to the three poor little prisoners in the Hôtel de Mouchy?"

Madame Beauchet looked wise. "Father Carrichon comes to see me," she said. "He hopes to be allowed to take them to their aunt Rosalie de Grammont in the Franche Comté if . . . if their mother is taken to prison."

Marie privately thought the disguised priest was only echoing the pessimism of Gouverneur Morris: they were both expecting the worst. But she kissed Madame Beauchet and begged her to be careful. Father Carrichon might already be under surveillance under the terrible Law of Suspects which ordered suspected persons 'to be run to earth in their burrows by day and by night'. What if one of his burrows were discovered to be the Beauchets' lodging in the Rue de Courty?

"You be careful too, Marie," said the faithful servant of Adrienne de La Fayette. "I don't mean that you or your uncle would ever come under suspicion, but you really ought to take more care of yourself. The life you lead is no life for a girl."

What Madame Beauchet meant and was too kind to say was that Marie Fontaine was losing her pretty looks. The *armoire* mirror told her the same thing. For a time after his victory at Toulon, Marie expected Napoleon (she never thought of him as General Buonaparte) would return to Paris, would come to see the Fontaines, would invite them again to the Régence, and then, and then . . . life would become a cloud of blue muslin, roses and romance. But Napoleon was still in the south, engaged in some inspection tour or other, and Marie Fontaine was wasting beauty and youth in the shadow of the guillotine.

There were grey wet days in February and March when she felt herself to be as much a prisoner as the caged white mice seen long ago at a street fair, condemned to turn for ever on a wooden treadmill. Days of silence only broken by the rattle of the tumbrils, for there was no longer any real communication between Prosper Fontaine and his niece. He had been deeply disturbed by the death in prison of Condorcet, the philosopher and mathematician whom he had greatly admired, and whose radical writings had done so much to form the intellectual background of the French Revolution. That was in March, and the day was not far distant when Lavoisier, the founder of modern chemistry, was condemned to the guillotine by a tribunal which pronounced that 'the Republic One and Indivisible does not need intellectuals.'

Like everyone still alive in Paris, Fontaine was shaken by the execution of Georges Danton on 2 April, the most sensational victim to pass along the Rue St Honoré since Queen Marie Antoinette six months earlier. The National Guard had no difficulty in keeping the crowds back on that day, for the feeling was that if Danton, that great revolutionary, could be executed, then so could anybody else, and every man who heard his powerful voice bawling, "You will follow me, Robespierre!" had a premonition of whom that somebody else might be. The iron shutters were run down on the Rue St Honoré and the shopkeepers hid behind them; it was a couple of days before Marie could persuade her uncle to go as far as the back garden, where she had been careful to protect Michel's herbs and vegetables from the winter frosts.

It was still very early on a beautiful spring morning when he followed her into the yard, and the birds were practising their songs in the great neglected garden next door. Marie was still wearing her white cooking apron, and in the pharmacy deaf Augustine was washing the floor. She had just told Marie that a man who sold vegetables in the street market at the top of the lane had arrived that morning with a few sacks of potting soil in a push cart.

"I think I'll run up now and ask him to bring a sack of *terreau* down to our yard," said Marie. "The pot herbs could all do with fresh soil." She wanted to run, to feel the spring breeze and the smell of new earth instead of blood.

"Poor Michel set so much store by his herbs and simples," said Michel's father. He had taken to talking more about his dead son, and always in a sentimental vein.

"I'll order some bedding plants if – what's that racket?" exclaimed Marie. There was a sound of heavy steps and voices, a squawk from Augustine, and then four National Guardsmen, led by a man in black, burst through the kitchen door.

"Citizen Fontaine?" said the man in black.

"*C'est moi-même*," said Prosper Fontaine.

"Prosper Louis Joseph Fontaine, and Marie Madeleine Fontaine" (taking the niece for granted) "I arrest you in the name of the Committee of Public Safety, and require you to appear forthwith before the Revolutionary Tribunal, charged with crimes against the Republic."

"Mistaken identity . . . there must be some mistake," stammered Fontaine. "My niece and I are guilty of no crime."

"Save it for the tribunal," said the man in black. "Fall in, the escort."

When the National Guardsmen closed in Marie's first thought was that Vautour had denounced them. Then she realised, when the power of thought came back, that Vautour had joined the army in October, and could hardly be responsible for an arrest in April. She saw her uncle wrench his arms free of the two men who seized them, and heard him ask,

"What is the charge against me?"

"You'll hear it read in court."

"Where I shall produce the certificates of good citizenship issued to my niece and myself by the Palais Royal Section."

"Do you carry them on your person?"

"My niece knows where to find them. Marie!" He produced a small key from his vest pocket. "Bring everything useful from the drawer in the pharmacy."

She knew exactly what he meant, and found voice to say to the man in black, "Have I leave to take off my apron?"

"Get yourself a coat instead, citizeness, you may have a long wait," said the man, not unkindly. Obviously a girl was of no importance: it was Prosper Fontaine who was not to be allowed to move. Marie's shaking limbs carried her into the house. Kitchen and shop were empty. Deaf Augustine had had the good sense to leave by the front door, knowing quite well that when a house arrest took place the servants of the Republic One and Indivisible were in the habit of sweeping into their net anyone who happened to be on the premises at the time.

There was nothing in the counter drawer except the two certificates and the purse of gold which her uncle had given her in case of an emergency. Marie pushed it into the bosom of her dress and hurried upstairs. From the old *armoire* she took a green silk bag on a long ribbon which as a little girl it had been her pride to carry on Sunday excursions with her uncle and Michel. She put the purse into the bag and the ribbon inside her high-necked dress, with a white fichu to hide any possible glimpse of green, and then she slung her black winter cloak round her shoulders. A tricolore cockade was pinned to the breast, but she left the red cap of liberty on her bedside table. How much liberty remained to her she could not tell.

The men were all in the kitchen when she went downstairs, and her uncle had been allowed to put on his brown surtout and carry his beaver hat. One of the guards looked in open admiration at Marie's flowing hair. The man in black took no notice beyond motioning her out through the shop and into a closed vehicle waiting in the street. Thank God, it was not a tumbril. Not yet.

Uncle and niece sat opposite one another, each flanked by a man from the National Guard, while the man in black sat on the box beside the driver. Nobody spoke. Marie herself, after the frantic activity of the last few minutes, lapsed into a kind of apathy from which she only roused when she saw the Café de la Régence. Oh, Napoleon! she said to herself, if he were only here! He would save us, he could save all of France from Robespierre and from the Terror!

She had not prayed before, but she prayed silently now, with unmoving lips and closed eyes. When she opened them again the vehicle had reached a part of Paris she hardly knew, and was crossing one of the bridges of the Seine. Ahead of them lay a high turreted building, with low grated windows almost level with the water.

"Uncle, what is that place?"

"That's the Conciergerie, Marie."

The Conciergerie! The prison from which Queen Marie Antoinette had gone to the guillotine! For thousands of victims the last halt on earth before the Place de la

Révolution! Marie drove her nails into her palms, she would *not* faint under the eyes of her guards. The vehicle rolled on a little further, to the building which housed the Revolutionary Tribunal, and there the Fontaines were herded upstairs into a kind of wooden pen, constructed on the fringes of a mob passionately concentrating on the action in the centre of the hall.

The man in black had been wrong in one detail: there was not likely to be a long wait. Antoine Fouquier-Tinville, the Public Prosecutor, was demanding the death penalty for two terrified girls accused of 'sexual congress with an aristocrat', and this was granted in a matter of minutes by the tribunal. The next persons to be taken out of the pen were a young husband and his weeping wife, denounced by a neighbour for saying Georges Danton was a great man – penalty Death. The last to be tried was an elderly man who made some attempt to defend himself on a charge of speculating in *assignats*, the interest-bearing bonds introduced after the Revolution, which had lost all value in the past three years. For him too the penalty was Death. Then the names of the two Fontaines were shouted out, and the apothecary had just time, as they were moved into another, smaller pen facing the bench of the tribunal, to whisper,

"Did you get it?"

"Yes, but you?"

"I have enough."

"What if they search us?"

Whatever Fontaine might have answered to that question was drowned in the roar of approval from the general public, which always enjoyed the sight of a pretty young girl on the way to the guillotine. The crowd, almost as loyal to the tribunal as it was to the Place de la Révolution, shouted advice to Marie to tie her hair back, dearie, before they cut it off. She shook the bright locks forward to hide her face from the jesters. In fact Marie was too inexperienced to notice the imperceptible signs in their favour. They had *not* been searched, neither had their house or shop; their hands had not been tied, as was the general custom, and they had been brought to the tribunal in a discreet conveyance, free of the stares of passers-by. Even more important, the speech of the Public Prosecutor was less impassioned than was usual.

Antoine Fouquier-Tinville, then forty-eight, was an imposing or as many thought an alarming figure in the red robe of the prosecutor. He was an ugly man with a big pock-marked nose which almost hung over his twisted upper lip. Like a typical revolutionary he had begun life as an impoverished lawyer's clerk, had risen in the world, had gone from poverty to affluence and back to poverty again, and had been glad to accept a seat on the Revolutionary Tribunal. Now he was the Public Prosecutor, a second Robespierre in his vindictive pursuit of all suspects, but he was not quite convincing in his prosecution of the two Fontaines.

The accusation, he told the tribunal, had been initiated by Citizen Jean-Baptiste Carrier, who as commissioner of the Republic at Nantes had carried out a memorable purge of traitors. At a late date in his valued service he had brought before him one Pierre Malouet, a fisherman denounced by patriotic villagers for having given shelter, aid and comfort to a foreign enemy of the Republic.

Under examination, Malouet had declared that the man he sheltered was an American citizen and no enemy. He spoke French with a foreign accent and said his name was Bohun, or it might be Boone. He had been on his way to take ship at St Nazaire when the fighting began in the Vendée, and admitted to being involved in a skirmish with *les bleus* . . . "In other words," interpolated the Public Prosecutor, "this man confessed to bearing arms against the Republic."

He had been wounded and the wound had festered. He was feverish when Malouet found him sheltering in a wooded cove near his village, and took him home. Malouet was a widower, living alone; for humanitarian reasons he tried to nurse the American back to health, but he did not tell the neighbours what he was doing until too late. The *curé* was called in when the man was dying and gave him Christian burial.

Whereupon Commissioner Carrier, scenting a conspiracy, arrested the *curé* as a non-juring priest, and ordered more stringent methods of questioning to be applied to Malouet. Had the so-called American mentioned the names of any others who had helped him, or were in some way involved with him? The man was said to have no identity papers, nothing to go upon, and only a very little money, but the traitor Malouet, before he died under the 'stringent questioning', admitted that the stranger had mentioned one name in delirium, and had asked again and again to be taken to the Pharmacie Fontaine.

The commissioner's deputies, it must be said, had wasted time on the matter – at which some of the feathered heads on the tribunal bench nodded in agreement. They had thought the Pharmacie Fontaine must be in Nantes or St Nazaire, and their investigations had led nowhere. Then enquiries were made in Paris, and the Pharmacie Fontaine had been discovered in the Palais Royal Section.

"Which issued our certificates of good citizenship last October," said Prosper Fontaine. "May I now produce them for the tribunal?"

Fouquier-Tinville shook his head contemptuously. He regarded such certificates as so much waste paper.

"Citizen Fontaine, what do you know of this man Boone?"

"Nothing at all," said Fontaine readily. "I never met an American in my life. Fontaine is a common name. Why didn't the commissioner's men look for the pharmacy in Bordeaux, in Lyon, in Marseille? Why arrest me? Why should I, or my niece, be accused of conspiracy on the word of two, or is it three, dead men?"

"You are accused by the commissioner at Nantes!" thundered Fouquier-Tinville.

"On the strength of circumstantial evidence, given

weeks if not months ago," said Fontaine. "I appeal to the justice of the Republic One and Indivisible, to which my entire loyalty is given."

Marie dared not look at him. This was the uncle she had always known, cool and collected, ready-witted. The president of the tribunal, a red-haired man called René Dumas, believed him, she could see; Citizen Dumas's face grew red too as he kept repeating "Circumstantial evidence!" when the feathered hats leaned together in conference. The Public Prosecutor waited, glaring, and the general public waited, impatiently. The court ushers, who wore silver chains round their necks, clinked and clanked as they moved among the crowd shouting, "Silence!" Cries of "*A la lanterne!*" and "*Mort aux traîtres!*" began to be heard. The crowd wanted quick results and usually got them: it was unlike the Revolutionary Tribunal to waste time on deliberation. At last the president rose and pronounced sentence.

"Remanded in custody pending further investigation."

9

The nine chief prisons of Paris were full to overflowing, and that day's intake from the Revolutionary Tribunal had to wait for nearly an hour after the court rose before it could be decided where they would be imprisoned. Marie and her uncle were separated almost at once. He was among the first to be removed to the Luxembourg, once a palace and the residence of the late king's next brother, the Comte de Provence, and now a jail.

Fontaine's hands were tied, and so there was no farewell embrace. Marie whispered, "You've saved us, uncle!" and the man bent forward to kiss her forehead and say, "Forgive me, Marie." Then the jailers hustled him away, and the girl was left to sit in a locked hall with the others condemned that day, some of whom were taken straight to the Conciergerie.

No food or drink were given them, nor any facilities for the relief of nature, so that the waiting became an endurance test. It was noon before one of the guards came in with a list on which Marie's name appeared and she learned her destination.

"Fontaine, Marie Madeleine! *Aux Carmes!*" the man shouted and she in turn was hustled away. This time it was a tumbril which waited in the courtyard, and in the tumbril, but unbound, the prisoner on remand was taken with the weeping girls, the young couple who admired Danton and the speculator in *assignats* up the long road

128

which led to the prison of Les Carmes in the Rue de Vaugirard.

It was a former Carmelite convent, converted to a prison since the abolition of the nunneries, and there were still some small cells for special prisoners. Men and women were imprisoned there, although in separate quarters both cramped and crowded. When Marie was pushed inside a high, narrow room, one-third as broad as it was long, she saw a surge of women towards her, all staring with what seemed to be the same vindictive intensity as the spectators at the tribunal. The accumulated agonising of the morning overcame her, and the girl who refused to faint in front of the National Guards collapsed in a swoon.

When she recovered her senses Marie first became aware of the familiar scent of eau de cologne, held beneath her nostrils on a delicate handkerchief. She was lying on a pallet bed with her head on the shoulder of a woman with kind eyes, who called her 'poor child!' and asked if she could tell them her name. Then Marie saw two more women kneeling by the pallet, whose drawn faces expressed nothing but concern.

"Marie Fontaine."

"Were you arrested alone?" (glancing at Marie's ringless left hand) "or with your father? Your brother?"

"My uncle. They took him to the Luxembourg."

"Are you 'in secret'?"

"'Remanded pending investigation.'"

"Then you can still hope." The woman smiled. The kind eyes were grey, and there was grey in the brown hair. Her plain dress, too, was of a Quaker grey, worn with a lace fichu.

"Can you sit up now, mademoiselle?" she asked.

"Of course I can. I'm sorry to have been so silly. Please, what am I to call you, madame?"

"My name is Anne de Beaupré. Let me help you up now, the guards will soon be bringing soup and bread. And you must choose your own bed; there are four, today, to choose from. Four ladies left us for the Conciergerie."

In some confusion Marie rose from Madame de Beaupré's pallet and returned the smiles of the watching women. There were a dozen of them in the narrow room, and the atmosphere was stifling, for only one small pane in the barred window was open, the others being closely sealed. Marie chose a bed as near the window as possible. It had been vacated that morning by a girl as young and pretty as herself, who took her first step towards the guillotine with her head held high.

The guards came in, slopping soup out of a pewter urn which had held the breakfast coffee into the tin mugs held out by the prisoners, and distributing hunks of bread. It was not much worse than the bread and stale cheese of the manufactory, but table there was none, and each woman sat on the side of her bed to eat. Somebody brought Marie her cloak, which had been removed. She could feel the green silk bag with the money in a lump beneath the bosom of her dress. While she ate she studied her surroundings. In a corner of the room near the door a screen of sacking hid the buckets which were the only sanitary facilities, and in the opposite corner damp undergarments were pinned to criss-crossed ropes.

"Is that the laundry?" Marie tried to speak lightly to her next-door neighbour, an elderly woman who might have been a tradesman's wife. "Where do we do our washing?"

"At the fountain in the yard. You'll see it next time we go out."

"We're allowed to go out, then?"

"For an hour every morning – officially."

"Is there an 'unofficially'?"

"You'll find out."

After the wretched meal was over, Madame de Beaupré came back to Marie, and presented her to the lady who was, by common consent, the principal personage in this or any other room of the Carmes prison. This was the Duchesse d'Aiguillon, who obviously expected Marie to curtsey, which she did. A woman of forty, like Madame de Beaupré, Madame d'Aiguillon had one thing in common with her: they were both in prison because of an émigré connection. The duchess's husband, like Madame de Beaupré's son, had left France to join the royalist army which, under the Prince de Condé, was a not very useful auxiliary to the Austrians. The *ci-devant* Vicomtesse de Beaupré was the only other aristocrat in the room at that time, but, as a little dressmaker with a taste for fashionable gossip whispered to Marie, the title of de Beaupré was a Canadian title, merely a courtesy since Quebec was lost to France, whereas the d'Aiguillons were descended from Cardinal Richelieu.

Marie Fontaine thought it was an odd title, for *aiguillon* meant a goad or a sting, and there was no doubt that the duchess goaded the other women prisoners and stung them with her remarks on polite behaviour. In some ways she was an aristocratic version of the late Citizeness Merlot, shepherding the sewing women, but her aggressive manner secured the right period of liberty for the others, and sometimes made even the guards quail. Marie realised how important this was on the first morning after her arrival at the Carmes. Groups of prisoners were allowed to go down to what had been the nuns' garden at different times, and then they washed their under-garments in the broad basin beneath a cold water spout. Half the time they were naked under their dresses, for the wet clothes took a long time to dry in the big room. Happily it was a warm April. As for another matter which concerned the younger women, they were not reduced to the straits of Queen Marie Antoinette, for the guards were venal, and for a bribe would furnish lengths of cloth which sometimes looked as if they came from petticoats worn by dead bodies.

'Unofficial', Marie soon discovered, simply meant bribery. Prisoners with money could bribe a guard to let them meet prisoners of the opposite sex, either beyond the brick walls which separated men from women in the garden, or for a night at a time in one of the smaller cells. Prisoners with money got better food, and wine; they also received smuggled letters. In a moment of privacy behind the sacking screen Marie transferred a small sum of money from the green silk bag to the pocket of her dress, and bought letters written a few days apart.

One was from her uncle, determinedly optimistic. Conditions in the Luxembourg were tolerable, he declared, and in less than a month he expected good news from Nantes. Marie must keep her courage up. There was not a word, nor could there be, of the man who had died of wounds and fever in the hut of a Breton fisherman. But Marie said her silent prayers for the soul of 'Adam Boone', that clumsy conspirator who had betrayed them in his delirium, and indirectly had sent Vautour to the army. Once she said a prayer for Vautour too.

The other letter was from the chemist, Monsieur Guiart. Deaf Augustine had not gone home after her unostentatious departure from the pharmacy. She had gone to Monsieur Guiart that morning to tell him what had happened to the Fontaines, and he had courageously gone to the Palais Royal Section to protest the arrest of respected citizens. All he got out of that was a promise to 'investigate' – obviously the key word of the moment – and an opportunity to enter, accompanied by a Section leader, the cellar laboratory of Prosper Fontaine. Guiart wanted to tell Marie, as he had told her uncle, that certain experiments had been dismantled, and that no noxious or dangerous substances remained in the cellar. The 'For Sale' notice was already posted, and he had challenged the Section's right to attach it to the property of a prisoner on remand. He hoped his *chère petite Marie* would soon be back in the Rue St Honoré.

Well done, Monsieur Guiart! thought Marie. It was cheering to know that one friend at least was concerned about their imprisonment. She knew that being 'on remand' was something of a rarity, and had earned her far more consideration from the haughty duchess than her position as a mere apothecary's niece deserved. Marie Fontaine ranked high in the long vaulted room with the barred window which the duchess wanted to turn into a miniature Versailles, with herself playing the part of the queen. She led the general conversation on books and plays in the lengthening evenings, and although not all the women were able to take part they felt the unifying bond of comradeship. The worst had happened: they were without hope, and under the admonitions of the duchess they were able to walk out, on the morning when their names were called for death, without a tear or a shudder, but even with a smile.

On a certain Monday, the twenty-first of April, a prisoner appeared in the women's room who had not gone before the tribunal. While her two children slept, she had been arrested at her lodging in the Rue St Dominique and brought to the Carmes so early in the morning that the prisoners were in various stages of undress and still waiting for their coffee. Marie was at the window, quite frankly looking out at the men sent for early exercise to a part of the neglected garden divided by a low hedge, and the Duchesse d'Aiguillon, sitting by the windowsill, was holding her pocket mirror and applying the treasured stub of a baton of rouge to her lips.

It was Madame de Beaupré, whose pallet was nearest the door, who saw the newcomer first.

She was a pretty woman with a creamy complexion, her graceful slimness muffled in a heavy cloak and her dark head bare. Like so many of the new arrivals she was in tears, and Anne de Beaupré, recognising her, went forward with a word of sympathy.

"Madame de Beauharnais!" she said, "I thought you were at Croissy. How grieved I am to see you here. But not, I hope, 'in secret'?"

A committal 'in secret' was always Madame de Beaupré's fear, for there was no appeal against it; but by that date in 1794 there was no appeal against anything.

"There was nothing secret about my arrest, *chère madame*, except the hour chosen to alarm my household," said Madame de Beauharnais. She had a soft, fluting voice which attracted the attention of all the women around her. "Oh! my poor babies! What will they do when they awake to find me gone!"

"Surely there are people to look after them?"

"Their governess is trustworthy, and so is my personal maid. I've been a fool, Madame de Beaupré. I ought never to have written to the Committee of Public Safety to plead for poor Alexandre . . ."

Here she was unceremoniously jostled aside as the guards brought in an urn filled with the thin coffee drink and prepared to fill the all-purpose tin mugs.

"Who's poor Alexandre?" asked Marie of the duchess, under the noise of the service.

"The Vicomte Alexandre de Beauharnais. They've been divorced for seven years; very generous of her to plead for him," said the duchess drily.

"Is he in prison?"

"Here in the Carmes."

"Heavens! What has he done?"

"Lost a battle."

"And she? Who is she?"

"*C'est une Créole*," said the duchess, as if that explained everything, and Marie perceived that the distinguished lady was one of those who believed that a Creole had native or Negro blood, instead of being a citizen born and naturalised in a colony. She felt faintly indignant on behalf of the pretty fragile creature now seated uncomfortably on Madame de Beaupré's pallet. That narrow bed had been her own first refuge in the Carmes. With her untouched mug of coffee in her hand, Marie made her way down the crowded room to Madame de Beauharnais.

"Please, madame," she said, without waiting for an introduction, "let me give you some fresh coffee. It isn't very nice, but at least it's hot. And mayn't I help you off with your heavy cloak?"

"How kind you are!"

The dark eyes, swimming in tears, looked up at her; the dark hair waving over the woman's temples was not dressed quite close enough to hide the tiny fans of wrinkles beginning to form at the corners of her eyes. When the cloak was removed she was seen to be wearing a high-waisted dress of rose-coloured velvet with a little jacket embroidered with curlicues and galons of gold lace like an officer's uniform.

She made them wait while she dressed in her best to go to prison, thought Marie, remembering her own plea to take off her cooking apron. I'll wager she brought a purse with her too.

A slender hand, with beautifully tended nails, slid into Marie's, and the sweet voice with a suspicion of a drawl in it said, "But this is your own coffee I'm drinking!"

"I wanted you to have it, madame."

"Who is this kind young lady, Anne?"

"I can see you two are going to be friends," said Madame de Beaupré. "Mademoiselle Marie Fontaine, let me present you to Madame la Vicomtesse Marie-Rose de Beauharnais."

"Oh please, darling, *not* Marie-Rose! That name reminds me too much of . . . days gone by."

"You were Marie-Rose when we were neighbours at Croissy-sur-Seine. What is one to call you now?"

"Joséphine."

Alexandre de Beauharnais, the second son of a noble family, was himself a Creole. Like Marie-Rose Joséphine Tascher de la Pagerie, to whom they married him when he was eighteen and she sixteen, he had been born in Martinique, but was taken back to France as a child of five. After a few wretched years and the birth of two children they were divorced, and the young man, still only twenty-eight at the storming of the Bastille, became an impassioned republican. For a time he was President of the National Assembly. Then, having been trained as an officer, he turned to the army, and rose to be the general commanding the Army of the Rhine. In 1793 he was less successful. He failed to relieve the city of Mainz and retired to a little property near Blois. There he was arrested by order of the Committee of Public Safety and now lay in the Carmes prison in Paris under sentence of death. His former wife's ill-advised plea to the Committee had brought her to the same place.

This was the story which, bit by bit, Joséphine told to Marie Fontaine. It was told with tears and sighs, and with so much stress on the youth despoiled and innocence betrayed of the girl from Martinique that Marie's sympathy and admiration increased with every telling. There was only one difficulty: Joséphine was shaky on her dates. Her age at marriage, her age at the birth of her children varied with her mood. At one time it seemed as if she had given birth to her son at the age of ten. Occupied with her infants, neglected by her husband, the young Vicomtesse de Beauharnais had never figured at the court of Versailles. The Duchesse d'Aiguillon, who had, and who possessed an excellent memory for all the alliances of the nobility, declared that *la belle Créole* was over thirty.

Goaded and stinging in repartee, the duchess tried to tyrannise over the gentle clinging creature until the day when Joséphine announced that she had bribed a guard to bring her writing materials. "I mean to write to a friend who's a Deputy," she said. "I know he can help me to go home to my babies".

"Letter writing hasn't done you much good so far," sneered the duchess. "Who is your powerful friend?"

"Jean Tallien, who was commissioner at Bordeaux."

"I wouldn't admit a promoted lawyer's clerk to my confidence."

"Of course not," said Joséphine tranquilly. "Your late father-in-law set you a good example. He was the confidant of Madame du Barry, wasn't he?"

The duchess flushed. Any allusion to the relations between a noble Richelieu and 'the royal whore' touched her on the raw, and the listening women hid their smiles. They were not to know that Joséphine's son Eugène, thirteen years old, had ranged the streets of Paris alone and in vain, looking for Deputy Tallien to come and help his mother.

Very soon the prisoners saw Eugène de Beauharnais. With the help of their governess, who bribed the sentries, he and his sister were allowed to stand for five minutes behind the hedge visible from the window, and Joséphine in tears kissed her hand to the tall manly boy and the beautiful little girl of eleven.

"I congratulate you on your *babies*, madame," said the duchess, and Marie Fontaine muttered to no one in particular, "Why can't she leave that poor girl alone?"

"Not exactly a girl," said Madame de Beaupré. "Marie, listen to me. You've grown very fond of Joséphine, haven't you?"

"I think she's fascinating."

"So she is. But at Croissy-sur-Seine, people thought she wasn't very . . . reliable."

To the devil with village gossip! Marie did not say it aloud, for she was fond of Anne de Beaupré too, though in a different way. Anne, with her unfailing patience and kindness, supplied a motherly element which had been entirely lacking in Marie's life. But Joséphine was the charmer, who beguiled the sultry evenings when the room was filled to its capacity of eighteen women with stories of her girlhood in Martinique and told their fortunes with the tarot cards.

"You predict long life and happiness for every one of us, Madame Joséphine," some weary hopeless girl would say. "Did you never have your own fortune told?"

"Once, by a wise woman on our old plantation, Trois Islets."

"And what did she say?"

"Perhaps I'll tell you when it comes true."

There was one bad moment in every day. It came at six o'clock in the morning when the guards came in and, while the women wrapped themselves in their rags of clothing or sheets, read aloud the names of those 'to be transferred to the Conciergerie'. Some wept when their names were called, others affected a trembling courage; the farewells were soon said. Messages were given to relatives and friends in the faint hope that these might be seen, even at the last moment, in the courtyard of the Conciergerie or at the foot of the scaffold. Goodbye, God bless you, *bon courage*.

After the interlude beside the fountain, the afternoon hours seemed the longest and the hardest to endure. Most of the women lay on their beds. Some slept, and if they slept they dreamed, calling the names of lover or of child, and weeping. It came to be the accepted thing that Joséphine de Beauharnais should monopolise the window for an hour, scrupulously standing back so that some air should reach the sleepers. It was understood that she was hoping for another sight of Eugène and Hortense, but the children never came back, and one day in June Anne de Beaupré asked her if she thought she might one day see General de Beauharnais.

"I only hope he may have seen the children," she replied. "With all his faults, poor Alexandre loved them both." Madame de Beaupré kissed her without speaking. She was surprised when Joséphine said, with more animation: "I've seen a man in the yard who reminds me a little of Alexandre. You know the man I mean. Who could he be, Anne?"

"I think you must mean General Hoche, my dear. Another unlucky general!"

"He commanded the Army of the Moselle, didn't he?"

"And came to grief in Alsace, poor fellow."

It was a simple exchange of words, but it was the first time Joséphine had expressed interest in any stranger. Some of the street girls who shared the long room with the others under sentence pretended to fall in love with this or that good-looking fellow who came in sight of the

138

window, and would whistle or wave to attract his attention; usually the younger men waved back. But that the *ci-devant* Vicomtesse de Beauharnais should single out one man, even a general, was a surprise to Marie. She asked Anne de Beaupré to point out General Hoche to her, and they agreed that he was very young for his rank.

Louis Lazare Hoche was twenty-six. He had been a foot soldier in the royal army, and in the republican had one of the meteoric rises from private to general which were typical of the time, and too often ended at the guillotine. Hoche, like the rest of them in Les Carmes, was under sentence now, and though he had a very young wife weeping at home with their baby he was not the man to deny himself an adventure, presented in such charming form. He also, as a general officer, was imprisoned in one of the small private cells.

How the first contact between Hoche and Joséphine was made remained a mystery. "She fancied him," said one of the street girls, when the *affaire* was obvious, as if Joséphine had made the running, as perhaps she had. Certainly it was with the connivance of the guards, using oiled keys, that she was able to slip out of her bed in the communal cell and into the bed of General Hoche.

The first time she slipped back into the room, in the palest light of a June dawn, two women watched and wondered: Anne de Beaupré, who slept nearest the door, and Marie Fontaine, who raised her head from the pillow by the window to see the graceful figure in the velvet dress lie down fully clad beneath the prison blanket. They did not mention what they had seen to one another. But on the next night, and the next, there were others who watched and giggled: it was a bedroom farce which relieved the tension of waiting for the roll-call for the Conciergerie. 'The General and the Divorcée' – it would have made a good theme for a short story by Crébillon.

Joséphine herself was serenely unconscious of her friends' comments and the duchess's glares. Not that her friends said much about her escapades, except for Marie's remark, "I suppose this is what you meant when you said she wasn't reliable," and Anne's oblique reply, "She likes men younger than herself."

"Oh well, what's the harm?" said Marie. "She's had a rotten life."

And so have I had a rotten life. I want to *live* before I die, I want a man to love me. Marie's romantic appetite for Napoleon Buonaparte was dying of inanition, just as in his heart there was no place for sentiment, or any interest outside the theatre of operations.

Nobody mentioned Buonaparte in the Carmes prison, although Joséphine brought back some scraps of Paris news from her lover's cell. She mentioned them casually, always beginning, "General Hoche was telling me . . ." and the other women learned that Maximilien Robespierre had organised a Festival of the Supreme Being (did he mean himself, by any chance?) followed by Fraternal Suppers, which meant that everyone brought their home cooking to tables spread in the dusty streets. It didn't sound very pleasant, did it? Marie thought it did. Oh to be free and in the open air again, dressed in rags and never mind the dust!

They were all in rags now, except for Joséphine. She had wheedled the guards (and Marie thought that was the right word for her, *la câline*, the wheedler) into delivering a large parcel which her maid brought from the lodgings in the Rue St Dominique with loving messages from her children tucked inside. The parcel contained two thin dresses, silk stockings, and underclothing of silk and fine batiste.

"I would love to give you a dress, Marie dear," she said in her *câline* way, "but you're so much taller than I am, it simply wouldn't fit. I know! You must have a nightdress!"

To a girl who had been sleeping in her petticoat, washed and dried or worn damp for three months in prison, a silk nightdress with lace on the bosom was a gift above rubies. Marie had pleasant dreams when she wore it, dreams of freedom, of a lover's arms about her, and his kisses . . .

and then woke to the everyday terror of the guards' roll-call, and the departure of the victims to the Conciergerie. Day succeeded day, and yet the names of Aiguillon, Beauharnais, Fontaine and Beaupré never appeared on the doomsday list. Joséphine urged her to try again for news of her uncle, and Marie bribed the jailers who for a long time had told her that no letters ever came for Citizeness Fontaine. At last, on a sweltering July day when the room was full of flies, a line came from Madame Beauchet. Unsigned, but Marie knew the handwriting, and it said,

"Madame Adrienne has been brought to Paris and is in the prison of La Force."

It was bad news, but not unexpected: it seemed to be a signpost to worse news to come. Next day the divorced wife of Alexandre de Beauharnais was told by a jeering guard that her 'old man' was in the Conciergerie and would be guillotined next morning.

Joséphine at once went into hysterics. She was always tearful, but this was a bout of screaming, moaning and tearing her hair which terrified the other women, and set off imitative hysteria in some of the more emotionally susceptible. "My children – my husband – my poor Alexandre!" she repeated between her sobs, and Anne de Beaupré's soothing had no effect. It was mid-morning, and the day's supply of drinking water had just been delivered. Marie took a mugful of her own ration, and tried to make Joséphine drink, but clinging to her damp pillow – for she had thrown herself on her pallet – the woman refused with wild shakings of her dishevelled head. Marie poured some water into the palm of her hand and tried to bathe the sweating brow.

Into this scene of total abandonment to grief came the Duchesse d'Aiguillon, carrying another mug of the precious water, who said sternly:

"Calm yourself, Madame de Beauharnais! This is not how an aristocrat accepts the crimes of the Revolution."

."Accept?" cried Joséphine. "Accept the murder of my children's father?"

"Who abandoned you seven years ago," said the duchess. "He left you with a title of nobility; live up to it as you ought to do, whatever may be the custom in Martinique."

The answer to that was a fresh outburst of sobbing.

"Set an example to our fellow-sufferers," the duchess went on relentlessly. "Think of the Queen of France, Marie Antoinette of blessed memory, who saw the king her husband go calmly to his death, and died herself – "

Joséphine's hysterical laughter rang through the vaulted room. "The Queen of France!" she said. "That's what the wise woman predicted, that I should be the queen! When she told my fortune, long ago at Trois Islets, she said *I* would be Queen of France!"

The duchess dashed cold water in her face.

There was no visit to General Hoche that night, and although Joséphine gave way to more than one fit of sobbing she was fairly calm by morning, and only said tearfully and insincerely that she wished her name might be on the death list when the jailers came in to read it aloud. It was very long that day; nearly half the women went to the Conciergerie, and ten more arrived from the tribunal. The number of executions was increasing daily; as many as three hundred and fifty men and women had gone to the guillotine since the Festival of the Supreme Being.

When the time came to take exercise in the yard Joséphine complained of headache, and stayed in the room with the last of Anne de Beaupré's eau de cologne on her dainty handkerchief. Marie stayed with her. From the window, by craning her neck, she could see the Duchesse d'Aiguillon marching up and down like a grenadier and justifying herself to the few remaining inmates of the room. The girl could guess what she was saying, for 'native blood', 'Creole insanity' and 'insult to the monarchy' were phrases she had used in a monologue

142

which lasted until Madame de Beaupré begged her to be silent. Joséphine, after her extraordinary outburst, had said nothing at all.

When she spoke, in the sultry morning, it was not about the duchess.

"Marie dear, what day of the week is it?"

"I've lost count of the days. I'm sorry, I don't know."

"I mean what day of the month is it?"

"When the man read the list this morning he said it was the third of Thermidor."

"So he did. That means it's nearly the end of July, and I've been here for three months. You were here before me."

"Three weeks. Or should it be three *décades*? Oh dear, it's all so confusing. A year that begins in September and months that start in the middle instead of on the first . . ."

Fabre d'Eglantine, the former actor who had drawn up the Revolutionary calendar, had been guillotined in April along with Georges Danton. The charge was political, of course, but some cynics thought the crazy calendar was justification enough.

"I must find out the real date," said Joséphine with her first wistful smile. "My children and I must keep the anniversary of their father's martyrdom."

It was the twenty-fourth of July in the world outside France, and two days later a letter delivered by hand was smuggled to Marie by one of the guards she had bribed. It was written in an unknown hand from an address in the Place Vendôme.

> 'Citizeness!' [the letter ran]
> 'I regret to inform you that my esteemed client, Citizen Prosper Fontaine, is dead. He gave me certain instructions regarding your good self, which I will communicate to you when it is possible to do so.
>
> Fraternally yours,
> Etienne Favart, Attorney-at-Law'

10

More than one revolutionary month before Thermidor came in, the Committee of Public Safety passed the Law of 22 Prairial (10 June) which ensured the death, among a thousand others, of Prosper Fontaine. He and his niece had been lucky in coming before the tribunal in April, when a prison sentence or a remand in custody was still legal, and when a quick-witted citizen could still argue with his judges. After 22 Prairial there was no argument, no evidence nor positive proof of guilt required, and the only sentence which the court pronounced was Death.

Robespierre had ordered every man and woman awaiting trial in the provincial courts to be brought to the capital, and although the farcical 'trials' were carried out in haste there was a backlog of candidates for the guillotine. This was one reason why the apothecary remained in the Luxembourg for the three months spent by Marie in the Carmes before he was again summoned to the tribunal.

The Luxembourg, once a royal palace, was a vile prison. The sexes were separated as in the Carmes, but there was no surreptitious commerce between them, for the guards were more alert and more severe. Nor had Fontaine the means to bribe them, because while he lay sick of the low fever which often afflicted older prisoners his purse was stolen by one of his cellmates, who next day threw it out of the tumbril to his wife before he died.

Fontaine was delirious during this attack of fever, and

when he became sensible again was afraid of what he might have said in his delirium. The guard who gave him some rough nursing care told him he kept calling for 'Marie'. Was she his wife?

"No, not my wife. I'm a widower."

"Ah, so Marie's your *petite amie*, you old dog, you!"

It was not worth the trouble for a sick man to explain to a grinning *sans-culotte* that Marie was not his mistress but his niece. The niece he had undervalued, fed and clothed but never loved, used as a housekeeper, taught some elementary medicine and finally brought to the extreme danger of death. He spent hours of his convalescence in thinking about Marie, and if he had not forgotten how he would have prayed for her.

Sometimes he thought about the English officer he had known as Boone. He had had the worst of luck, and newly recovered from fever himself Fontaine knew that Boone had never intended betrayal when he let slip the name of the pharmacy. Now he pinned his faith to the long delay in finding that pharmacy in Paris. The trail was cold, and they could investigate as much as they pleased in Nantes. He brought himself to believe, there in that over-crowded cell, where vile men forced boys who should have been at school to submit to them, and fights broke out, and the guards came in with whips, that one day he, and Marie too, would receive the order of release.

Instead, on the first of Thermidor, he was taken back to face the Revolutionary Tribunal.

If he had been the Prosper Fontaine of a year ago, even of three months ago, he would have seen a subtle change in the demeanour of the Revolutionary Tribunal. The president, Citizen Dumas, was as intent as ever, the Public Prosecutor as viciously dramatic as ever, but the other members seemed more anxious to mutter among themselves than to follow the proceedings. The spectators were restless too. There was constant movement in the public tribunes, and every time the great doors opened to admit a messenger there was a rustle of anticipation. The

145

apothecary was hardly aware of his surroundings. He sat in a corner of the pen with his eyes on his clasped hands, and when he was brought before Fouquier-Tinville the prosecutor smiled.

He saw a little white-haired old man, blinking nervously – for Fontaine's spectacles had disappeared while he was ill – and looking very unfit to conduct his own defence as he had done in April. In any case the prosecution had a surprise for him. When the charge was read it had nothing to do with the foreigner who had babbled about the Pharmacie Fontaine. The prosecution's case ignored the circumstantial evidence from Nantes. It was a personal charge, based on evidence collected in Paris, against the character of Prosper Fontaine.

Marie's guess had been the right one. Those associated with her uncle in his foolish scheme to stop the war by bringing in the English had indeed been Girondins, and his relief was great at the time when Robespierre had eliminated the Girondin leaders. There was no one left who could bear witness against him. Now here was Fouquier-Tinville declaiming,

"Are you acquainted with Citizen Elie Thibault?"

"I know no one of that name."

"Answer Yes or No!"

"No."

"H'm! Were you acquainted with the late Citizeness Manon Roland?"

"I went to a reception she gave . . . once . . ."

"Answer Yes or No!"

"Yes."

"Citizen Thibault was the waiter hired for the evening by Madame Roland. He testifies that you had a long conversation with her, and appeared to be on the best of terms with a woman whose criticisms of the Republic were notorious, and who was sent to the guillotine in the month of Brumaire last year. Citizens, I demand the same penalty for her intimate friend, Prosper Fontaine."

Fontaine tried to say he had only seen the woman once,

that he didn't like the woman, that their intimate conversation was a monologue by the woman on the writings of Voltaire and Plutarch's *Lives*, for she loved to show off her knowledge . . . but before he said the half of it he was hustled out of the dock and into a waiting room where he sat for an hour before they took him back to the Luxembourg. It was the damnedest piece of luck, because Manon Roland and her husband were two Girondins who had not been privy to his plot, nor aware of the presence in Paris of the man fated to die in Brittany. After his wife's execution Roland had committed suicide. All gone, all silenced, and now Prosper Fontaine had been brought down by a waiter, remembered vaguely as a presence with white gloves (Madame Roland was a terrible snob) offering a salver with food and drink. It was poetic justice of a sort. Death for conspiring with the Girondins, when his real crime was intelligence with the enemy!

"O Liberty, what crimes are committed in thy name!"

Those were Manon Roland's last words, as she looked up from the scaffold at the statue of Liberty which had replaced the statue of old King Louis XV in the square which had borne his name. So like her, the melodramatic apostrophe! Fontaine had been inclined to smile at it. He was not smiling now, he the criminal who put his own concept of Liberty above his country, as they took him back to the Luxembourg and threw him into the crowded cell among the men who had jeered at him and robbed him, but who spoke awkward words of sympathy when they learned his fate.

The least vicious of the guards brought him writing materials, and pocketing the apothecary's last remaining *sous* promised to see that his letters were delivered. In the event his solicitor Maître Favart received a letter, while Marie and Citizen Guiart did not, but the writing of the three took him all afternoon, for his trembling hand took so long to move across the paper. He tried to eat, but his throat closed on the food, and when he lay down he moved his head from side to side uneasily, as if unable to believe that it would soon be stricken from his body.

He tried to recall those who had been dear to him in life. He hardly dared to think of Marie, and he had been a widower for so long that he pictured his wife only as the face in the stiff miniature which hung beside his bed. In the article of death he saw her again as the lively loving girl who had teased him about his rabbit smile and called him Monsieur Lapin. Even so, it was of their son he thought most that night. Would he find Michel again? He knew Christian men and women all believed there would be a reunion of souls in heaven. Prosper Fontaine had given up that belief years ago. But now his fingers moved along the grimy sheet as if he were telling the beads of a rosary.

At last he fell asleep. Only for an hour, but it was a sound sleep, and he awoke calm and composed, to face his last day but one on earth. It was dawn, and soon the muster roll for the Conciergerie was read. But now there appeared to be a hitch in the proceedings. There was a good deal of movement in the corridors, accompanied by the sound of raised voices, and the midday *soupe* was brought in an hour late. A prisoner who asked the guards if there was some disturbance in the city was sworn at. The men in Fontaine's cell were not so fortunate as the women in Marie's, for their window looked out on an inner courtyard from which nothing could be learned: this did not prevent the more optimistic from believing that there *had* been an uprising which would result in their being set free. Nothing of the sort happened; the hot afternoon hours wore away, and at seven in the evening Fontaine and two other men were taken to the prison of the Conciergerie.

The days were long past when the common chamber of the Conciergerie, that waiting-room for death, was a gallant travesty of the court of Versailles. The supply of aristocrats was almost exhausted, and Robespierre's victims now were decent bourgeois, or members of the working class whom the Revolution was intended to benefit. But the women who still possessed some finery were wearing it, and swept elaborate curtseys to the new arrivals, while a gentleman who introduced himself as the Marquis de St Maur was acting, for one night only, as the master of ceremonies.

"My dear Monsieur Fontaine, we have met before," said the marquis, a young man arrested as a returned émigré. "I patronised your admirable pharmacy more than once in the good old days."

"Thank you, monsieur," said Fontaine. "I look forward to seeing it again tomorrow, when we are driven down the Rue St Honoré."

"But have you not heard? The Place de la Révolution is no longer our destination. The Place du Trône is now the scene of the final ceremonies." The marquis took out his snuff-box and with studied detachment helped himself to a pinch of snuff. "Isn't that your understanding, General de Beauharnais?"

Joséphine's divorced husband, tall and fair, was the best-looking man in the room, and, next to the marquis, the coolest. He said indifferently that yes, they were bound for the Square of the Throne. "The Throne Overthrown, the rascals call it," he added. "May I offer you a glass of wine, monsieur?"

Some of the prisoners who still had money had clubbed together to buy the wine. It was an excellent Chambertin, and did them good. Little groups formed, little jokes were cracked and vigorously applauded, little flirtations began which must end in a day. Fontaine, looking about him, saw a sight which dismayed though it could hardly surprise him. The three Noailles ladies, his neighbours of so many years, were sitting against the back wall.

Prosper Fontaine worked his way round the long room until he reached them.

"My ladies!" he said, and bowed low.

The old Maréchale, far gone in senility, looked at him with blank eyes. The duchess nodded mechanically. But

Louise, *ci-devant* Vicomtesse de Noailles, rose with a tearful smile and gave him her hand.

"I wish we had met anywhere but here," she said. "Mamma, don't you know our kind old neighbour, Monsieur Fontaine?"

"*Enchantée, monsieur,*" said the duchess, still mechanically, as if she were greeting some unimportant Versailles acquaintance in the middle of a court reception.

"Mamma has been ill," said Louise anxiously. "We were not well treated in the Luxembourg."

"Neither was I, madame."

"I beg your pardon?" Louise cupped her hand behind her ear.

"I said I too was in the Luxembourg, madame. How long were you and the ladies imprisoned there?"

"Some weeks, I think. One loses count of time. Our relatives the Mouchys were taken first . . . and are gone. But tell me, Monsieur Fontaine – where is dear little Marie?"

"She was arrested with me in April, and taken on remand to the Carmes. I still hope . . ."

"For us the time has come to give up hope, except the hope of a life hereafter."

"Do you believe in that?" the man said urgently.

"With all my heart." She laid her hand confidingly on his. "Sit here by me, Monsieur Fontaine. Do you remember my confessor, Père Carrichon?"

"Very well, madame. He frequently visited my pharmacy."

"He has never deserted us. He must have found out when we left the Luxembourg, for when we reached the Conciergerie he was among the great crowd in the court-yard, and he came close enough to whisper that he would be there tomorrow and give us his blessing at the end. I am so thankful! But very thankful, too, to know *you* will be near us. Will you help me with mamma and grand-mother, when they come to fetch us?"

"I will do everything I can, madame."

Now he was resolute for death. What he could do to help those helpless women Fontaine could hardly tell, but that Louise de Noailles trusted him – he, the untrustworthy – was as comforting as any priestly blessing. He sat on by her side, holding her hand, and watching the marquis, the general, the once-rich, the always-poor, promenading about the room as if they were actors playing their parts in some final scene on the stage of life.

It was easy to join the Noailles women next evening, for they were conspicuous among the forty-five victims of the day. The old Maréchale had emerged from her almost cataleptic silence and was berating the men trying to lift her into the tumbril. "Take your hands off me!" she cried shrilly, while Louise, in a white dress, tried to restrain her. "I shall report you to Her Majesty for gross disrespect!"

"Her Majesty the Queen of France?" jeered one of the men.

"Her Majesty the Queen of Heaven!" – for the old lady had occupied her few lucid intervals in writing letters to the Virgin Mary. Prosper Fontaine intervened.

"Let me handle this," he said authoritatively. "I'm an apothecary. Now, madame!" (to the Maréchale) "you remember me, your old neighbour Fontaine. They're waiting for you at court, and I've come to take you there. Let me help you into the carriage – " With a strength he did not know he still possessed he lifted the old woman clear of the cart wheel and into her daughter's arms. She subsided, mumbling, while the duchess murmured a prayer and Louise climbed up beside them, whispering a "Thank you!" which meant much to Prosper Fontaine.

They were ranged three to a bench, the Noailles ladies on one side and Fontaine with two men on the other, and the guards, standing behind the benches, tied their hands behind their backs. The procession took some time to arrange, but at last the tumbrils crept out of the courtyard of the Conciergerie and took the road across the Pont Neuf. There was the usual outburst of shrieks and jeers from the crowd which had waited for this moment, and Louise de Noailles, so long in close confinement, shrank back from the howls of hatred, but Fontaine, with his hands tied, was at least free to smile at her, and his confident smile was rewarded by her own.

The oppressive heat of the July days had broken, and there was an ominous roll of thunder as the tumbrils turned north and east in the direction of the Place du Trône. The rain began as they reached the road junction, where the crowd was thickest, and Louise shaped the word "Look!" as she gestured with her head. Fontaine saw Père Carrichon, in his workman's dress, making the sign of the Cross in their direction, once, twice, thrice and four times, and knew the words *Ego te absolvo* were meant for him.

The rainstorm was over, but the *faux-bourdon* of the thunder seemed to be continued in the roll of drums which greeted the arrival of the victims. The drummers were drawn up in a square round the scaffold, to which each must climb by a short ladder, and Prosper Fontaine had just time to register that there were no knitting women in the Place du Trône (though plenty of viragoes screeching at the far side of the square) before he was prevented, not ungently, from giving his hand to help the Noailles ladies down from the tumbril.

The executioner, dressed in red, and his assistants had a system which they had perfected. All the tumbrils had to be emptied of their passengers before the killing began: all the victims had to be drawn up in the order of their death with their backs to the terrible Machine which reared up starkly in the middle of the square. Beyond it a large wagon painted red waited to receive the heads and bodies.

Prosper Fontaine reckoned that he would be the twelfth to be executed. He could not see Louise de Noailles, for with her mother and grandmother she was ranged behind him, but the scaffold steps were within his line of vision, and so, further away, was the street leading directly to where the Bastille had stood. After it had been seized by the people, and the governor murdered, the ancient fortress had been demolished, and signs erected saying 'Dancing Here.' He remembered telling Marie, at fifteen half scared and half excited, that the people's will had triumphed, that the fourteenth of July had ushered in a splendid dawn. Now the final symbol of the people's will reared up before him, and over a roll of drums the executioner shouted, 'One!'

In the silence which fell immediately there were just three audible sounds. The elderly man who went up first was seized by the three executioners, the chief taking his left arm, the second his right and the third his legs. Then came the first thud as his body was thrown on the plank. The second thud followed as the neck clamp dropped into place. The chief executioner pressed the switch and the third sound was the whirr of the knife descending. To an accompaniment of shrill cheers and another drum roll the body was detached from the plank and thrown, with the head, into the wagon.

Prosper Fontaine had hoped to be brave, and he had been brave ever since his meeting with Louise de Noailles. Now an abject terror seized him, and with the fear of death came the fear that he would lose control of his bodily functions. He was more concerned with his bladder and bowels than with his hope of heaven. The man next to him, who had drawn the unlucky number Thirteen, had obviously lost control, for the front of his trousers was dripping, and not with rain. He was muttering, "*Mon Dieu mon Dieu mon Dieu!*" in a desperate monotone.

The old Maréchale was Three, and somehow achieved dignity; the drums rolled on. General de Beauharnais's contemptuous smile survived the humiliating tumble on the plank; the Marquis de St Maur took snuff before he mounted the scaffold. Ten was the duchess, praying. Eleven was Louise de Noailles, who turned to smile at Fontaine from the foot of the ladder. He thought she looked like a girl in her white dress, and a moment later her voice was a girl's voice as the executioner tore her bonnet off her head and a pin caught in her knotted hair.

"Oh, you're hurting me!"

Thud. Thud. Whirr. Sound of a toppled body.

Twelve.

He had not lost control and he was on the scaffold. He had just time to see the monstrous wagon, swimming in blood, before his left arm was grasped and he was thrown forward.

Michel – Marie – peace on earth –

Then it was peace.

11

A few days later, peace of another sort came to France in the downfall of Robespierre.

The prisoners who had sensed unrest in the Revolutionary Tribunal, even in the disorganisation of the prison system, had shown more flair than many members of the Convention. Robespierre was the president of the Convention, the president of the Jacobin Club, and with his two staunch allies, Couthon and Saint-Just, virtually the dictator of the Committee of Public Safety. In April he appeared to be unassailable. But in a convulsive upheaval of opinion (Gouverneur Morris would have exclaimed "What a People!") by July the people's Deputies, who had condemned the king to death, were shouting for the death of Robespierre.

When the rot set in was difficult to say. Those who claimed to have seen it coming said it began with Danton's great cry on his way to the guillotine, "You will follow me, Robespierre!" Others thought the Festival of the Supreme Being on Whit Sunday touched off the Convention's dissatisfaction with the man who organised it. More potent was Robespierre's recall of the commissioners who had carried his message of death to the provinces, for these men, hardened and brutalised as they were, had no hesitation in criticising their master. Most important of all, the people were sick of slaughter. In the eight weeks preceding the execution of Fontaine, St Maur, de Beauharnais and the Noailles ladies, fifteen hundred lives had been lopped off by the guillotine.

Among the returning commissioners was the dictator's brother Augustin, bubbling over with praise of Napoleon Buonaparte, and Paul Barras, who had been with him in Toulon, knew that Augustin would stick to his brother through thick and thin. He said as much to Jean Tallien, as they took wine together in the Café Procope on the Left Bank, far enough from the National Palace to be reasonably secure from Robespierre's spies.

"I agree," said Tallien, who had practised the most vicious cruelties in Bordeaux while at the same time falling in love, "but we can dispense with Augustin. You and I, Barras, and Carnot certainly, should command enough support to challenge Robespierre. And the sooner the better. I have a special reason for despatch."

"What's your reason?"

"I want to get married."

"A civil marriage can be performed at any time. You don't need Robespierre's permission for that."

"No, but there's a difficulty. The lady is my prisoner."

"For God's sake, man! Sign an order of release."

"I know; I should have done it before we left Bordeaux. But I brought her here under guard, and now it's she who imposes conditions on her freedom."

"Unusual!" said Barras drily. "Who is she, this strong-minded citeness?"

"The *ci-devant* Comtesse de Fontenay."

Barras whistled. "The daughter of the Conde de Cabarrus! Can't he arrange a prison break?"

"Can't . . . shan't . . . won't, I don't know. But anyway there's no time to lose."

"For the usual reason?"

"Yes."

Barras set no store by the sanctity of marriage. He had left his own wife in Provence, a meek little creature who was probably as glad to be rid of him as he was to be rid of her. He said, "In such cases it's usually the woman who's impatient for marriage – without conditions. What conditions does the Citeness Fontenay impose?"

156

"She wants me to set the prisoners free."

"No one man can do that."

"A group of men could."

The conversation was abruptly broken off, for the next two arrivals at the Procope were members of the Revolutionary Tribunal, and there was much handshaking and exchange of fraternal greetings. Paul Barras was left wondering how Tallien, that rampant revolutionary, had become so enslaved to a woman as even to listen to her plea to set the prisoners free. He remembered Teresa de Cabarrus when she first came to Paris, a lovely creature whose whim was law to her adorers. But – a prisoner and pregnant, and still dictating terms to her lover? The situation amused him, and when they left the café and came out into the Rue de l'Ancienne-Comédie, he took Tallien's arm and said,

"Listen, Jean. Suppose I go and see Robespierre in private – not at the Committee, where Couthon and Saint-Just never leave him alone – and urge him to follow a policy of clemency? If he agrees, you could tell your lady we'd made a beginning . . ."

"Danton tried the clemency line, and look where that got him."

"To the guillotine, yes; but Robespierre has discovered God since then. Else what's the Festival of the Supreme Being all about?"

"I suppose it's worth a try." And Tallien, the terror of Bordeaux, heaved the sigh of a lovesick youth. Barras hid a smile in the summer darkness. He thought the butler's son was still susceptible to the charm of a title, and found love all the sweeter because his lover was a *ci-devant* comtesse.

He was not smiling next morning, when he left Robespierre's lodging in the house of a carpenter, and made his way down a long entry to the Rue St Honoré, doing his best to avoid the planks and lumber which were the carpenter's stock in trade. Robespierre had flatly refused to listen to him. He was in his dressing gown, having just returned from the hairdresser, and his green cat's eyes flashed as he shook hair powder over Barras, and spat on the floor at his feet as he brushed his teeth. He made his contempt for Barras obvious, and the former commissioner at Toulon, as he strode off down the Rue St Honoré, vowed eternal enmity to the man who thought himself the master of France.

More enemies were made at the Festival of the Supreme Being, when Robespierre kept the Deputies waiting for an hour in front of the National Palace until he appeared, to inaugurate a pageant in which the effigy of Atheism was to be destroyed by fire and replaced by the effigy of Wisdom, which rose from the ashes black with soot. Ridicule, always a powerful element in French politics, took the place of respect for the strutting little man who believed himself to be the apotheosis of Virtue and divinely appointed to purge the sins of France by blood.

In six summer weeks Barras and Tallien so undermined Robespierre's position, abetted by all the Deputies who expected to be his next victims, that when on 8 Thermidor he made a two-hour speech denouncing most of the leaders of the Convention he was met with a furious counter-attack. That day it was by words only, but on the next, after his creature Saint-Just had prepared a list of Deputies to be guillotined, Tallien threatened him with a dagger and screamed that he would kill the tyrant if the Convention failed to arrest him.

What-a-People was in great form that day. The *journées* of the first Fourteenth of July, the Terror, the September Massacres, the executions of the king and queen became insignificant in comparison with the Ninth of Thermidor. Robespierre and his friends were arrested, but no prison would take him in, and he was rushed from one place to another while the Commune ordered out the National Guard to fight the Convention, and the Robespierrists took refuge in the Hôtel de Ville. Barras, the former soldier, led a column against that place. A National Guardsman with the significant name of Merde or Merda, who appeared to have changed allegiance, shot Robespierre in the jaw. His brother Augustin jumped out of a window and broke his leg. Lame Couthon fell downstairs and cut his head open. These scenes of farce ended only when Robespierre, his jaw roughly bandaged by a surgeon, and his confederates were taken before the Revolutionary Tribunal and condemned to death. Meantime What-a-People danced the summer night away, and huge crowds gathered along the route of death to see the last progress of the tyrant.

The knitting-women were early in their usual seats, because for such an occasion it had been decreed that the Place du Trône was not suitable. The guillotine was hastily brought back to the Place de la Révolution, where the King and Queen of France had lost their heads. Now it was the turn of Robespierre. Far less dignified than they had been, he lay on the ground with his eyes shut until his turn came.

"Monster! Vermin! Death to the tyrant!"

He was carried up to the scaffold, and the executioner tore away the bandage that had bound his jaw. A great gush of blood spurted from his mouth, and the man who had ruled by Terror died in terror, in a veritable river of blood.

That was about half past seven in the evening. Next day Joséphine de Beauharnais, looking listlessly out of the window in the Carmes prison, motioned Marie Fontaine to her side.

"Look at that old woman, Marie. What in the world is she doing there?"

"What's any old woman doing there?"

Behind the hedge, where Joséphine's children had once been seen, and where the male prisoners waved to the women at the window, a stranger had appeared. She was not waving. Once she was sure that she had caught their attention she went through a series of actions, three in number and repeated again and again. She lifted her skirt and held it in front of her so that it formed a bag. She dropped what seemed to be a stone into the bag. Then, with a hideous grimace, she drew the flat of her hand across her throat.

"What's she *doing*?" said the puzzled Joséphine. Marie, quenched and silent since she had news of her uncle's death, solved the riddle when the stone dropped for the third time.

"It's a message!" she cried, more excitedly than she had spoken for weeks. "Come, Anne, come, all of you, and watch this! See what she's telling us! A dress – *une robe*, a stone – *une pierre*: Robespierre! And then the hand across the throat – *la guillotine*!"

"Robespierre is dead!" screamed the prisoners.

"Robespierre is dead!" came the echo from the men's cells. The woman behind the hedge heard the cheering and slunk away.

From a hundred despairing throats came one long sigh: "Now we shall be free."

Part Three

1794
Autumn

12

Freedom seemed so close that every day of imprisonment was a fresh offence against humanity. In some jails there were riots in the men's cells. Guards were injured and went armed, and the names of the rioters went automatically to the foot of the lists of liberation. In Marie's cell in the Carmes the women showed more patience, and what they heard of the violence in Paris after Robespierre went to the guillotine and the Commune was overthrown suggested that they were safer in prison than on the streets.

It was still Thermidor by the revolutionary calendar, but 4 August in the outside world when Marie Fontaine was released from the Carmes. On the record as 'remanded in custody' she was one of the first to go, and the ten women remaining in her cell overwhelmed her with kisses, good wishes, and more messages than she could ever hope to deliver. Even the Duchesse d'Aiguillon condescended to shake hands, and tell her she was a very good girl. Marie's influence, unobtrusive at first, had developed during the anxious months, and by the end was powerful. She was a model of patience and confidence, and women much older than herself relied on the girl to stand up for their rights with the guards.

It was known that she was homeless, and two homes were at once offered to her. Anne de Beaupré and Joséphine de Beauharnais were due to be released on 6

August, and Anne begged her to go straight to Croissy and wait for her at the riverside villa.

"Dear Anne, it sounds wonderful, and I'd love to come to Croissy some day, but not yet. I must stay in Paris until I find out more about my poor uncle's death, and have a talk with his man of business. I want to know what's happened to our house, and the pharmacy . . ."

"But you can't stay there!"

"No, I can't, it's National Property," said Marie. "Joséphine has asked me to stay with her."

"I have a villa at Croissy too," said Joséphine de Beauharnais jealously, "but I'm counting on Marie to be with my darlings in the Rue St Dominique until I get home. My poor babies must have their father's last letter as soon as possible."

"Of course they must," said Marie gently. "You can rely on me."

"Dear Marie, you're such a comfort. I want Eugène and Hortense to understand that their father died a hero's death, and remember him that way. Only that way!"

Marie nodded. Joséphine's real distress at the execution of her children's father had evaporated when it came to light that he had employed his last days in the Carmes in a violent sex affair with a prisoner named Delphine Custen, who had survived him, and was boasting about his virility. Marie was as unlikely to tell the children about their father and Delphine as about their mother and General Hoche.

"I don't think I'll come down to the yard this morning," said Joséphine. "I want to write to Mademoiselle de Lannoy about you, as well as writing to the children."

"Please do," said Marie. "They might let me go quite early tomorrow, and I'd like to be ready. No more calls for the Conciergerie!"

She linked her arm through Anne de Beaupré's as the guards flung open the doors for exercise, and said lightly, "Please heaven this is my last cold-water laundry!"

But Madame de Beaupré was not ready to speak lightly.

When they took their turn at the big stone basin where the spout of water played she said to Marie, "Perhaps I was selfish to ask you to come to Croissy to keep an old woman company – "

"You're not an old woman!"

"But I wish you weren't going to the Rue St Dominique. You don't know whom you might meet there."

"After four months in the Carmes I can't be too particular, can I?" asked Marie flippantly.

"It's no joke, Marie. Joséphine de Beauharnais isn't the right friend for you. She behaved very badly last summer down at Croissy, when she rented Madame Campan's furnished villa – gave wild parties which kept her neighbours awake, and had some most unsuitable guests. She left owing money to every tradesman in the place – "

"Good heavens, Anne! She isn't going to present me at the court of Versailles, you know! She's giving me shelter for a few days until I find my feet in the new Paris."

"Which is what you really want," said Anne de Beaupré shrewdly. "The new Paris. We none of us know if it'll be better or worse than the old."

"I know I've got five years of living to make up," said Marie.

She began to live next day: not in the morning as she had hoped, but in the late afternoon, after the endless forms of bureaucracy had been filled in and the prison gates were opened. She was quite lost in the Rue de Vaugirard, and one of the *sans-culotte* sentries had to tell her gruffly to turn to her left if she wanted to reach the Rue St Dominique. Before she started down the long grey street she walked on just far enough for a backward view of the prison she had left. She saw a belfry and a dome with a cross above the rows of windows and remembered that the place had been a Carmelite convent, which young women of her own age had entered to follow the strictest of all religious Rules and spend the rest of their lives in silence and in prayer. And she had complained about the privations of four lost months! Marie started to walk quickly in the direction of her friend's home.

Some of the older prisoners, on being released, found difficulty in walking, as if their terribly cramped quarters had also cramped their legs. They had to rest in archways or against gateposts if they had far to go. With every step she took as a free woman Marie felt energised. She walked faster and faster, feeling instinctively that there was freedom in the air. Whatever the future might hold for France the heavy pall of suspicion had lifted, and the people she passed – some of them even smiling – had animation in their faces. She entered the aristocratic quarter, the Faubourg St Germain; there indeed it was depressing to see all the signs of 'National Property – For Sale', but there were no mobs, no drunken dancers like the *fédérés* from Marseille from whom Vautour had shielded her, and no *sans-culottes* guarding the innocent prisoners in their homes. It was very quiet in the Rue St Dominique. She found the tall grey house where Madame de Beauharnais rented an apartment. It was on the ground floor, so there was no concierge to face, and when Marie let the heavy knocker fall the door was opened by a little maid in a clean apron, who bobbed a curtsey to the tall young lady in a black cloak too heavy for the August heat.

"*Vous désirez, madame?*"

"I have a letter from the Citizeness Beauharnais to the Citizeness Lannoy."

"A letter from *madame la vicomtesse!*" The little maid looked delighted; decidedly this was a household of the old régime. The door was opened wide. "Please to wait in the little salon, madame, and I'll fetch Mademoiselle de Lannoy."

The little salon was modestly furnished, but it contained a long mirror in which Marie saw her reflection for the first time since she entered the Carmes. There she had sometimes seen her face in someone's pocket mirror, or on a still day in the waters of the fountain. Now she saw herself as a shabby figure in black, with fair hair tumbling out of the knot in which Anne de Beaupré had fastened it, and a face pale with the prison pallor and the perspiration of the day. She could see the unbecoming bulge under her bodice made by the purse of money which as far as she knew was all that stood between herself and starvation. She pinned her hair, she set her jaw, and waited for Mademoiselle de Lannoy.

The governess came in quickly, with Joséphine's open letter in her hand. She was a gentle little woman in a grey dress, with a black crape fichu, and she was followed by another woman in black with a white lace apron, whom she introduced as "Agathe Rible, madame's personal maid." Her welcome to Marie was perfect.

"Any friend of the Vicomtesse de Beauharnais would be welcome – but her companion in captivity . . . her affectionate helper, she says here! Mademoiselle Fontaine, you are to make our home your home . . . and is it true our dear lady will be free in two more days?"

"I believe so, mademoiselle," Marie interrupted the broken phrases with her reassuring smile.

"And you have letters for the children. May they have them now? Do you feel equal to meeting Hortense and dear Eugène? Agathe, take mademoiselle's coat . . . Such a hot evening for a winter cloak, but I suppose in prison . . ."

Marie said, "Mademoiselle de Lannoy, I reek of prison. I've lived in the clothes you see for the past four months and they're only fit to be burned. Mayn't I at least wash my face and hands first?"

Agathe intervened. "We have hot water in the kitchen, mademoiselle, and I'll prepare a bath for you as soon as I can. But the trouble is, the children know you're here and have letters for them, and they're very impatient. Hortense is crying, and the boy is trying not to cry. I think it would be better if you saw them now."

"Very well." And get it over with, said Marie to herself. She was not accustomed to children, and to these bereaved children she dreaded saying the wrong thing.

He died a hero's death, remember that. She remembered, too, that the letters were in the pocket of her cloak, which Agathe had laid across a chair, and rescued them while the governess, in her fussy way, was whispering her condolences on "your own dear uncle. Madame says he died on the same day as the general . . . don't use the word 'guillotine' to the children!"

"But surely they know – "

"Oh yes, they know, but they hate the word . . ." She said no more, for the children were in the room, the little girl holding fast to her brother's hand.

"Hortense, Eugène, this is Mademoiselle Fontaine."

They were beautiful children, Marie saw as they bowed and curtsied. They favoured their father in looks, being very fair, and the boy looked her straight in the eye.

"Mademoiselle Fontaine," he said, "you've been with mother in – that place?"

"I left your mother there this afternoon. She was well and longing to see you both. She'll be home the day after tomorrow."

"Oh, Eugène!" exclaimed the girl. Her brother hushed her.

"Did you know my papa in – that place, mademoiselle?"

"I saw him in the yard from time to time. He died a hero's death," said Marie Fontaine, remembering her lesson, "and I have a letter from him here. One from him and one from your mother, for you both."

She held out the letters, and Eugène de Beauharnais stepped forward to take them with a bow.

"Do you know when papa wrote to us, mademoiselle?"

"I think it was just before he – went to the Conciergerie."

"Went to the scaffold," said the boy who for the rest of his life would never use the word guillotine. "Did he write to my mother too?"

"Yes he did." Marie had been shown the stilted note in which her former husband sent Joséphine his fraternal greetings.

"That's all right then." The boy smiled for the first time, and Marie understood that for the child of divorce, driven from pillar to post during most of his short life, the idea of any sort of rapprochement between his parents was a kind of stability.

"Well, but aren't you going to open your letters, Eugène?" said the governess reprovingly.

"I think Hortense and I would rather read them when we're quite alone. May we go back to the schoolroom now?"

"Of course you may," the older woman said. "Thank mademoiselle and wish her good night, because she's very tired. She'll talk to you again tomorrow."

"And tell us more about mother," said Hortense, holding up her face confidingly.

Marie kissed her. "Mother will soon be here to tell you about herself," she said. "Good night, my – my dears."

Agathe, who had been waiting by the door, shepherded the brother and sister from the room and came back to tell the guest that her bath was ready. Only then Marie realised that the excitement which had sent her headlong from the prison to the Rue St Dominique, and sustained her through the awkward little interview, had completely ebbed away. She let the woman lead her through a corridor of what was obviously a large apartment to a room which held a dressing table with a ewer and basin full of hot water, and the little maid was pouring more hot water into a chair-shaped bath with a high back. Here Mademoiselle de Lannoy left them, and Agathe took charge of Marie with the skill of an experienced lady's maid. It was delightful to be babied: to be given a scented shampoo while being told that her hair was "such a wonderful colour, and so thick!" and then to lie back in the tub soaping herself while the little room slowly filled with perfumed steam. Four months of the prison fountain and now this luxury! Marie was half asleep when Agathe helped her out of the bath and into a silk nightdress too short for her long legs, and across the corridor into a little guest room where a sunburst clock marked a quarter to eight.

"Is that really the time, Agathe?"

"Certainly, mademoiselle."

"It's very early to be going to bed!"

"Not for you. Now try to stay awake until I bring you supper. Would you like a bowl of bread and milk, like the children?"

"That would be wonderful."

The little maid must have had it ready and waiting. The bread and milk were fresh and hot, pleasantly sugared and with a touch of nutmeg, and Agathe waited to take the bowl away, while the hair that was the colour of poplar leaves in autumn fluffed out and dried on Marie's bare shoulders.

"Shall I draw the curtains, mademoiselle?"

"Please don't, Agathe. I want to look out tomorrow morning and know I'm free."

She knew it as soon as she was left alone. Free to sink into the embrace of a feather bed instead of the strips of rotting leather which made the prison pallets, to rest her cheek on fine linen and feel the silk nightdress sliding under the fresh white sheets – free, above all, of the closeness, the moans and the smells of her fellow-prisoners. In freedom, Marie slept.

When she awoke the sunburst clock still said eight o'clock, and she had to look out at the early sunshine and hear the cheeping of late summer birds before she realised that it was morning now, and that her dreamless sleep had lasted for twelve hours. She got up and went to the window. As in her old home it looked out on a garden, this one a formal affair of gravel walks and low boxwood hedges which gave out their special scent. Someone had been in the bedroom, for over the single chair lay a chemise of fine white batiste and a pair of black silk stockings. Her own shoes, highly polished, were set beneath a table with a wooden wedge under one leg.

Apart from the comfortable bed, the room was not luxurious; in Marie's eyes it was a palace.

A tap at the door announced the arrival of Agathe, with something black and soft across her arm.

"Awake already?" said Agathe. "I hoped mademoiselle would sleep longer."

"Longer than twelve hours?" Marie laughed. "I've had the most wonderful sleep of my whole life."

"So far," said Agathe with a sideways smile. "There will be better nights to come. There!" seeing the girl's blush, "no need to take offence. One can easily tell that mademoiselle is – inexperienced."

This was a different Agathe from the nursemaid of the night before. Now she was a soubrette from a Palais Royal farce, verging on the impertinent, and Marie changed the tone by asking, "Did you bring me these pretty things?" indicating the garments on the chair.

"I did; and see what else I brought you." Agathe shook out the dress she was carrying. It was made of plain black chiffon, with long sleeves and a ragged rose of the same material at the neck, and it had a deep frill at the hem.

"I made this dress last summer for madame to wear in the mornings," the maid explained, "but I knew it would be too short for mademoiselle. I had some of the chiffon by me, so I sat up late after supper to add the frill. Had you no hat?"

"I left the cap of liberty behind when I was arrested."

"The red cap's out of fashion now. I'll find you something. And by the way you left your purse behind, after you had your bath. It's quite safe in the table drawer. Now get back into bed; don't catch cold at the open window, and I'll bring you some coffee."

Marie caught impulsively at the woman's hand. "Agathe, you're spoiling me!" she said.

"Make the most of it," said Agathe pertly. "When madame comes home she'll demand all my attention."

"She'll deserve it, too." Marie felt a wave of gratitude to Joséphine. The hospitality, the absolute repose – how could she repay them? Please God there's no hitch at the prison, she thought. Those children will break their hearts if she doesn't come home tomorrow.

The breakfast tray arrived, with a fresh cloth and pretty china, a pot of coffee and a jug of hot milk, two slices of new bread and a little jar of quince jelly. Marie enjoyed it slowly. No guards to come bursting in, no list of victims for the Conciergerie, no wringing out of her intimate possessions beneath the chilly waters of the fountain! She dressed slowly too, washing in the room with the bath, and then drawing on the black silk stockings, which had rose satin garters attached. The chemise was very short, but the chiffon dress was a good fit, and Marie took it off again to do her hair with the brush and comb and the hairpins she found on the table. She was still brushing and pulling the bright locks across her face to smell the freshness, when Agathe returned.

"You're getting dressed – that's right," she said abruptly. "Mademoiselle de Lannoy would like you to come downstairs. There's a very early visitor, a woman, and she says she knows you – "

"Is it Madame de Beaupré?"

"No, that's not the name. She says she comes from Citizen Tallien, whom poor little Eugène tried so hard to see . . . and these days one never knows . . ."

The woman's fear reached out to Marie. She threw down the brush and started to her feet.

"Oh, my God, I hope nothing's gone wrong at the prison!"

"That's what we're afraid of."

"But doesn't this woman give a name?"

"The *ci-devant* Comtesse de Fontenay."

172

13

Mademoiselle de Lannoy was obviously terrified by the latest visitor. Marie Fontaine, shabby and shy, was to be pitied, but Teresa, *ci-devant* – and divorced – Comtesse de Fontenay, was to be feared. Not that she was fearsome in appearance. She was handsome, smiling, elegant in a hat with bronze feathers and a new dress of yellow silk arrogantly chosen to show by its cut that she was expecting a child. It was her rapid speech, her surprise that Madame de Beauharnais was not at home and her frequent references to Citizen Tallien, one of the new powers in the land, which had flustered the governess. Wringing her mittened hands, she turned with relief at the entrance of Marie, who was enthusiastically greeted by the newcomer.

"It is – it really is – Marie Fontaine from the Rue St Honoré! I could hardly believe my ears when this good lady told me you were here! I must apologise to you both for this most untimely visit. I seem to have upset the people of the house, but I was *most* anxious to make the acquaintance of Madame de Beauharnais, and I was told positively that she was released yesterday . . ." She stopped with a pretty gesture of pretended embarrassment.

"It was I who was released yesterday," said Marie. "Madame de Beauharnais is expected tomorrow. I think her – her staff thought you'd come to tell them there

173

would be a delay. Citizeness Fontenay, I'm glad you're free and well. We heard you were in prison in Bordeaux."

"Oh, I was, I was!" Teresa laughed. "I'm quite an expert on prisons. Citizen Tallien took me out of La Force ten days ago. Let me give you a piece of advice, my dear. If you're ever arrested again – the jailer is the man to know."

Mademoiselle de Lannoy gasped, and Marie joined in the infectious laughter. Teresa's boldness was a welcome contrast to the crushed despair of the women of Les Carmes. It was typical of her tact that she asked no questions about Marie's imprisonment or her uncle's fate, but turned charmingly to the governess and asked if she might meet Monsieur Eugène de Beauharnais.

"Citizen Tallien has been telling me about him," she said. "He must be a remarkable boy."

When Eugène came in with a little pug dog at his heels, for which he apologised, Teresa kissed his forehead and said he was very brave to go through Paris day after day looking for Citizen Tallien, to ask him to set his mother free.

"I never did get to see him, madame. I went to the Convention and the Commune, and even to the Committee of Public Safety, but they always told me to go away."

"Citizen Tallien was very busy at that time," said Teresa gravely. "You know why, don't you?"

"Because of Citizen Robespierre," the boy whispered.

"Yes, because of Robespierre, who has paid for his crimes, but there were people who told Citizen Tallien how you looked for him everywhere, and that made him examine your mother's case, and after he had freed me, he freed her. So you see, when your *maman* comes home tomorrow, it'll be because of *you*." Teresa saw that the boy was too much moved to speak, and went on, "Citizen Tallien and I are going to be married very soon. When we have a house of our own, will you come to see us, Eugène, and meet him properly?"

The boy looked at her adoringly. "I'd like that," he said. Teresa had charmed him as she charmed everybody, and

Marie, watching, thought, Why couldn't I be like her, last night? So stiff, it was an effort to say 'my dears' to a young boy and a little girl!

Eugène de Beauharnais, very conscious that he was the surrogate master of the house, was offering refreshments. Would madame like a cup of chocolate? A cool drink? Might he present his sister Hortense? Was Fortuné (the pug dog, nibbling her skirt) being a nuisance? Down, Fortuné!

Teresa laughed and kissed him again. "I must go now, dear Eugène," she said. "I have to look at a house Citizen Tallien may want to buy. But I'll come back very soon, and quite likely you'll see a lot of me. Marie, are you going out too?" for Marie was wearing gloves and a straw bonnet provided by Agathe, and carrying what looked like a reticule of faded green silk.

"I have to see my uncle's solicitor," Marie explained. "I thought I might as well get it over with today, and be quite free tomorrow when Joséphine comes back."

Mademoiselle de Lannoy, who raised her eyebrows at the Christian name, said disapprovingly that she had hoped mademoiselle would spend the morning in bed and get a thorough rest.

"Far better to be up and doing," said Teresa. "Where is this solicitor's office?"

"In the Place Vendôme."

"Perfect; then I can drop you on my way. I have a cabriolet at the gate."

A cab in waiting, just as she had on the day she bought the carnation scent! Typically Teresa; and assuring Mademoiselle de Lannoy that she wouldn't be overtired and would be back in time for the midday meal, Marie followed the yellow dress into the Rue St Dominique and took her place in an unexpectedly smart turn-out.

"This is Jean's own cab," explained Teresa. "He lends it to me when I go house-hunting. So we don't have to worry about the driver, he's a safe man."

"Jean being Citizen Tallien?"

"Yes."

"And we still have to worry about safe men?"

"We can't wipe out the tragedy of five years in five weeks." Teresa laid her gloved hand gently on Marie's. "Forgive me, dear. I didn't want to say anything painful in front of that old lady and the boy, but – your uncle's dead, isn't he?"

"Yes, he's dead," said Marie steadily. "He was executed not long before Robespierre. On the same day as General de Beauharnais."

"And the Noailles ladies, and forty more. Oh, what slaughter! I keep telling Jean it's got to stop."

"*Which* Noailles ladies?" said Marie, horrified.

"The old Maréchale, and the duchess, and the Vicomtesse Louise."

"Oh my God! But not Madame Adrienne – Madame de La Fayette?"

"Adrienne de La Fayette was in La Force with me, and then they moved her to Plessis. Her husband's been moved too – to Olmütz in Austria."

"Can't your – Citizen Tallien set Madame Adrienne free?"

"Not yet. Poor woman, she's in prison because she's the wife of La Fayette, and he's hated in France because he's a deserter."

Marie was silent, thinking of Madame Beauchet's grief. I must go to her as soon as I can, she thought. Those poor ladies, dying together, and for what?

"But you, Marie!" said Teresa urgently. "What are you going to do?"

"That's what I may find out from Uncle Prosper's solicitor."

"Perhaps your uncle's left you all his money."

"He can't have had much to leave. It was all tied up in the house and the pharmacy, and they're National Property now."

"We'll save them for you," said Teresa confidently.

"Jean and Paul are planning to bring in an Order of Restitution for most of the confiscated property."

"Who's Paul?"

"The *ci-devant* Vicomte Paul de Barras, who was a *représentant en mission* at Toulon."

"And the National Property is going to be given back to the real owners?"

"Not the church properties, they're rated as *biens nationaux.*"

"Well!" said Marie, "I see there are going to be big changes, but there's one thing that hasn't changed. They haven't dismantled the guillotine."

The cab had driven through the quiet streets of the deserted faubourg, and emerged upon the bridge originally called, like the great square it approached, by the name of the old king, Louis XV. The guillotine reared up in the middle of the Place de la Révolution, empty of victims and spectators, a mute reminder that while dictators might come and go, the Republic One and Indivisible still kept the right to chastise. Marie Fontaine covered her face with her hands.

"Don't, dear!" Teresa's arm was round her shoulders. "Don't give way! I know it's hard to lose someone you loved, but we have to think of ourselves, haven't we? We've escaped from the Terror, and we've the right to enjoy life now. Just give me a couple of months until the wedding's over and the baby's here, and I'm going to give balls and dinners that'll put Paris on the map again – a different sort of map from Robespierre's!"

The cab horse reared between the shafts, and the driver called down to know where the citizeness wanted to go first.

"To the Place Vendôme, and then up the Champs Elysées, please."

"I'll go by the Rue St Honoré, then. I won't come back this way," the man shouted. "The horse hates the smell of blood."

It was true that the blood-smell clung to the cobbles of

the Place de la Révolution. Some old women were still knitting on their stools at the foot of the scaffold. Force of habit, or the expectation of a new batch of victims?

"Would you like me to come with you to the solicitor's?" Teresa asked.

"You're very kind," said Marie, "but I think this is something I ought to do alone. And you've given me a lot of your time already, besides going out of your way."

"Not very far," said Teresa, "and between ourselves, I'm not enthusiastic about this house Jean wants me to see. The Champs Elysées is too far out in the country for my taste, I want to be in the centre of things. However, if the rooms are big enough for entertaining, it may do."

The horse had steadied down since they entered the Rue Royale, and took the street at a trot.

"Tell me one thing," said Teresa de Fontenay, "shall I like Joséphine de Beauharnais when I meet her? Is she as beautiful as all the men say she is?"

"Joséphine is very lovable," said Marie seriously, "and very charming. She makes you believe she's beautiful, though with her it's the gentleness – the grace . . . I really can't explain. She's fascinating."

"I can't wait to meet her." And Marie, aware of the slight stiffening of the arm still laid protectively round her shoulders, wondered if Teresa sensed a rival in the new Paris which she so obviously meant to conquer.

"Here we are," she said, as the cab stopped at the number she had given in the Place Vendôme, and she got out. "Thank you so much, Madame de Fontenay. When shall I tell Joséphine to expect you?"

"Oh – at the end of the week, probably. Listen, Marie!" (leaning out of the cab window) "if you can get any money out of your lawyer man, buy yourself a new dress, and one that fits."

"I thought this one fitted very well when Agathe arranged it for me."

"It's far too narrow across the shoulders. You'll feel

twice the woman in a new dress, and not a black one either."

"I'm in mourning. I feel as if I've been in mourning for half my life."

"I know, dear. Try white, or even lilac. There's a shop at the top of the Rue du Bac where you can buy a frock for twenty *livres*, or there's a new place just opened in the Palais Royal, Madame Germaine. Good luck to you!"

The advice of a worldly-wise woman had lasted long enough for a small group of idlers to drift across the square, attracted by the sight of the beautiful Teresa in a horse-drawn carriage. Someone recognised her, for there were murmurs of "*La voilà! La voilà!*" and then a louder cry:

"*Vive Notre Dame de Thermidor!*"

Teresa, smiling and bowing to the onlookers, waved to Marie as she was driven away to the sound of cheering, and Marie, seeing the crowd's attention now turning to herself, hurried inside the *porte-cochère* of the house forming part of the exquisitely proportioned square. A good deal of rubbish and débris had been removed since the days when the Marquis de Sade was head of the Vendôme Section.

The concierge directed her to Maître Favart's office, which was at the back of the building, looking out on a sunless courtyard. An elderly clerk announced her, and the lawyer came out of an inner room at once, expressing his surprise and delight at her arrival.

Etienne Favart was a man in his thirties, squarely built and square of jaw, with his brown hair tied back with a ribbon in the old-fashioned way. In the new fashion he wore a black coat with a very high collar and an elaborately knotted white cravat: the empty right sleeve of the coat was pinned to the breast.

"Sit down, Mademoiselle Fontaine," he said, pushing forward a chair. "Fortunately I don't have to ask you for proof of identity, for I've often seen you going about the *quartier*. I'm glad to see you got my letter, though deeply sorry for what I had to tell you. Monsieur Fontaine was an old and valued client of our firm, going back to the days of my father."

"He never discussed his business affairs with me," said Marie.

"No, of course not. Did you get a letter he wrote you to Les Carmes?"

"No, monsieur."

"Neither did Citizen Guiart. Fortunately the one to me arrived."

"The jailer must have pocketed the bribe and destroyed the others," said Marie.

"Probably. Where did you go when you were released?"

"I'm the guest of Madame de Beauharnais in the Rue St Dominique."

"Then you had a long walk on a very hot day."

"Madame de Fontenay brought me here in her cabriolet." Marie leaned forward: the ice was broken, and she liked this straightforward, simple young man, so different from the double-dealing *notaire* of the fiction she had read.

"The people in the square cheered Madame de Fontenay and called her Our Lady of Thermidor," she said. "Do you know why?"

Favart smiled. "I don't know the lady personally," he said, "but I do know that in less than two weeks she's become a heroine to the Parisians who welcomed the end of Robespierre. They're convinced that it was her influence on Citizen Tallien which led to the great events of Thermidor."

"Maybe so," said Marie, "but she seems to think our troubles aren't over yet. I believed, and so did the other women in the Carmes, that all the prison gates would open and everybody would go free."

"Not yet, alas," said the lawyer. "When Robespierre and his men went to the guillotine the royalist element – which does exist – thought the time was ripe for the restoration of the monarchy, meaning the poor little fellow

180

in the Temple prison. There's been another rising in La Vendée which is disturbing the Convention."

"A rising backed by the English?"

Favart looked surprised. "No indeed, it's entirely local, and so far very successful. Citizen Carnot is about to appoint a general to put it down."

"General Buonaparte?"

"Who's General Buonaparte?"

"You've never heard of Napoleon Buonaparte? Who drove the British out of Toulon last December?"

"Last December I was in hospital in Maubeuge, recovering from – this." He touched the empty sleeve. "My souvenir of Wattignies."

"You were wounded in action! Oh, Maître Favart!"

"We delivered Maubeuge," Favart said laconically. "My general, Jourdan, would be the man for La Vendée. He won a battle at Fleurus some weeks ago which gave us Belgium, but he's in Occupied Brussels now, and not available."

"I'm so sorry about your arm, Maître Favart."

"Thank you," he said. "I'm learning to write with my left hand . . . Why did you ask if the English were backing the Vendéens?"

The question came more sharply than he had spoken yet, but Marie was prepared for it.

"I expect you know," she said, "that when my uncle and I were arrested we were accused on some trumped-up charge of intelligence with the enemy – of knowing, or helping, an Englishman who was mixed up in an invasion plot. The tribunal couldn't prove it, though Fouquier-Tinville did his best, and we were remanded in custody. I was let alone in prison but my uncle was executed. What I came here to ask you, as quickly as I could, was simply this: when he went to the guillotine, *was it still on the same charge?*"

"It was not. No indeed, it was on quite another charge. Fouquier-Tinville found him guilty of consorting with the Girondins, specifically with the late Madame Roland."

Marie drew a long breath. Consorting with the Girondins! She had thought so all along. Caught out at the end, only days before the great event of Thermidor, because of some slip as silly as Adam Boone's in the Rue St Honoré! She said as calmly as she could:

"I know that he and General de Beauharnais and – the others – were executed in the Place du Trône. What did they do with the bodies?"

"They were buried in the Picpus cemetery."

"Picpus. I'll remember that. Thank you, Maître Favart."

"You may like to know that Citizen Fouquier-Tinville has been relieved of his position as Public Prosecutor."

"I hope he goes to the guillotine himself."

Etienne Favart, an exceptionally well-balanced man, thought how strong was the French desire for vengeance, even in the heart of this gentle and lonely girl. He said, "You came here to find out more about Citizen Fontaine's death. Don't you want to know about the terms of his Will?"

"I didn't know he made one. I told you, he didn't discuss such things with me."

'Then you had better read it."

The whole back wall of the lawyer's room was occupied, almost to the ceiling, by iron strong-boxes. Taking a bunch of keys from his pocket he opened one of these, and then stood nonplussed by the difficulty of lifting out a smaller, but heavy, iron box with one hand. Marie hurried up to help him and set it on the table. "May I open it for you?" she asked.

The box contained a leather bag, which clinked; a shabby leather jewel case, and a folded parchment which Favart handed to her in silence.

It was Prosper's Will, dated in February of that year, and it left the whole of his estate, the house, the pharmacy and their contents, with a parure of seed pearls which had belonged to his mother, and a sum in cash of three thousand *livres*, outright and without condition, to his beloved niece, Marie Madeleine Fontaine.

Marie sat stunned. The lawyer opened the jewel case and showed her a fringed necklace of seed pearls, with dangling earrings in the style of an earlier day. "They need cleaning, I'm afraid," he said.

"Everything for me . . . outright?" Marie managed to say.

"I will admit," said Favart, "that I tried to persuade your uncle to appoint a trustee. Either Citizen Guiart, whom of course you know, or myself, or both of us together, but he wouldn't hear of it. 'My niece is a girl of strong common sense,' he said more than once, 'she won't throw the money about. And in these times I want to be sure that she's provided for.'

These times! Marie looked at the Will again. Beside her uncle's copperplate signature, and the witnesses', appeared a date in February 1794. Just when he thought there were to be no reprisals for his ill-starred attempt to bring about peace on earth! "How kind he was," she said with brimming eyes. "How I wish I'd been nicer to him – he was always good to me."

"I think you must have been very nice to him. He was obviously very fond of you. Now you must understand that as far as the house and pharmacy are concerned, nothing can be done as long as they are National Property. Monsieur Guiart succeeded in getting the Section to stop the order for an immediate sale."

"I knew he was trying to do that," said Marie.

"It was a generous act, because I have a strong impression that Monsieur Guiart wants to buy the property himself."

"But what if the Order of Restitution is passed?" said Marie.

Favart raised his eyebrows. "You've heard about that already, have you? Well, if the Order goes through the Convention, the property reverts to you, and you can sell it to whom you please."

"Oh, Maître Favart, if I could only keep it for myself!"

"What, the pharmacy? Put in a manager, d'you mean?"

"No, no, I mean – to run it myself. If only my uncle had taught me a little more! He began, you know, after Michel was killed, and I could make simple medicines and pills. I loved the work, and it made me feel useful. But I never did any laboratory work or studied the *materia medica* in uncle's books, so I could never join the Society of Apothecaries, could I?"

"I never heard of a lady apothecary," said the lawyer.

"Why not?" Marie's fingers tightened on the jewel case. "Women are allowed to be shopkeepers and dressmakers and actresses, aren't they? Why shouldn't they be doctors and apothecaries too?"

14

Eugène de Beauharnais was not present at the simple midday meal in the Rue St Dominique, and the governess told Marie between sighs that as the son of an *aristo* he had to do a given number of hours of manual labour every week. The boy was apprenticed to a carpenter on the Left Bank. "He goes off with a lunch of bread and cheese tied up in a red handkerchief, like a common working man," said the governess, "and do you know, he actually seems to enjoy it!"

"It doesn't seem to be doing him any harm," said Marie. "He's so tall and strong for his age."

"Yes, but have you seen his poor hands? Don't make too much of it to his mother, it'll only distress her."

"But surely she knows about it?"

"Oh yes, he started work on his thirteenth birthday. She knew there was no alternative: many boys of thirteen have gone to the scaffold because of their father's name. But if she comes safely home tomorrow there may be a change."

"Thanks to Our Lady of Thermidor," said Marie, and explained the nickname to the disapproving Mademoiselle de Lannoy.

Eugène came back very late, having worked overtime to secure a holiday for his mother's return, and he came back jubilant. One of the stall-holders on the Quai Voltaire had started selling flowers as well as old clothes, and had promised to keep fresh roses for the boy if he came early the next day. Flowers for *maman*! She loved roses, and there was nothing in the garden of their lodgings but boxwood! He was off to the Quai Voltaire long before breakfast next morning, and came back with his bouquet before seven o'clock. The Provence roses, yellow and pink, had the sweetest scent of all, and the boy himself arranged them in his mother's bedroom and the salon.

Marie, hurrying from room to room like the other members of the household, placing newly washed crystal and newly polished silver where they would show to most effect, now realised that the furnished apartment contained only gimcrack furniture and mended carpets. She hugged to herself the thought of the fine old Breton farmhouse pieces in the Rue St Honoré, hers by the right of inheritance. She wanted to discuss her visit to Maître Favart with Joséphine, as worldly-wise in her own way as Our Lady of Thermidor, but not immediately: the children's welcome must come first. Eugène was in the garden, playing a gentle game of bat-and-ball with his little sister, who had been arrayed in a white muslin dress with a blue sash since before midday: Marie hoped they would not have to wait until early evening before they could greet *maman*.

Joséphine came home at four o'clock. When the sound of a horse and carriage was heard in the quiet street they all rushed to the windows, expecting to see the arrival of Our Lady of Thermidor, but it was Madame de Beauharnais herself who stepped out, wrapped as Marie had been in her prison cloak. Then there was a stampede to open the door, headed by Eugène, and such a kissing and crying, a hugging and petting as only a hysterical woman could begin. Even Agathe and the little maid of all work were kissed, while Mademoiselle de Lannoy wept and blessed the day. But Marie, when she had given her friend the three kisses of ceremony, looked beyond her to the pavement where, quietly telling the driver to wait – 'not more than ten minutes!' – stood Joséphine's prison lover, General Lazare Hoche.

"The citizen general is here," she said warningly, and Joséphine, disentangling herself from the children's arms, held out her hand to the man. "Come and meet my little ones," she said, and they all went into the house together.

Joséphine, freed of her cloak, sank gratefully into a deep *bergère* in the salon, and breathed, 'What lovely roses! Your gift, my darling boy?" before she said to the soldier, "General Hoche, let me introduce you to my dear companion of the Carmes, Mademoiselle Marie Fontaine," and he bowed low.

"You were in the Carmes too, mademoiselle? For how long?" he said.

"Far, far longer than you, citizen general," Marie smiled. "I remember when we first saw you – from the window."

"Ah, the famous window!" The young general smiled too. "I was only imprisoned for twenty days. Twenty memorable days!" He and Joséphine exchanged a sidelong glance of complicity. She had taken Hortense on her lap, while Eugène, as close to her knee as he could get, was gazing in fascination at the general.

Lazare Hoche was six years younger than his prison mistress. He was handsome, with dark hair worn long and an olive skin slightly flushed with what might have been excitement, but to Marie Fontaine looked suspiciously like the early hectic on the cheeks of customers who came to her uncle for a lung remedy. He had been arrested in a uniform not much damaged by twenty days' imprisonment, and the jailers had given him back his sword, so that he was a figure to arouse the envy of the youngster who spent his days with carpenters. Hoche had embarked on a long and unnecessary story about how he had bribed one of the guards to fetch a carriage from as far away as the Louvre in order to bring Madame de Beauharnais home in comfort.

". . . And now I must take leave of you, madame," he interrupted himself to say. "I told the man to wait. I must go straight to the Convention and see if I can find Citizen

Carnot. I want to hear about my next posting before I go – anywhere else."

The man had remembered that he had a wife. Joséphine smiled languidly and said he must come back soon and tell them about his plans. "I shall be impatient to hear your news," she said, and on the strength of that promise Hoche kissed her outstretched hand before beginning his formal adieux. *Au revoir, ma petite fille; au revoir, jeune homme; au revoir, Mademoiselle Fontaine –*

"Citizen general," said Marie desperately, "have you any news of General Buonaparte?"

"General Who?" said Joséphine.

"General Buonaparte, madame, is the Corsican officer who did so well at the siege of Toulon," said Hoche. "I don't know him, mademoiselle, for we never served in the same theatre of war. I believe he was seconded to the Army of Italy, but he hasn't been much heard of lately."

After General Hoche left, Joséphine said very little to Marie beyond "Anne de Beaupré sent you her love, she was released yesterday," before she was swept off by Agathe for the same shampoo and bath treatment as had refreshed Marie. She came downstairs later, in a trailing négligé of pale blue silk, but it was to preside alone at the children's supper, and tell them in a hushed voice about their heroic papa. She followed them when they went upstairs to bed and heard their prayers; then, declaring herself "broken with fatigue", she went with Agathe's help to bed herself. It was eleven next morning before she sent a message to Marie.

"Come in, darling," she said, when Marie tapped at her door. "I've neglected you shamefully. But all I was able to do was sleep . . . and sleep . . ."

"I know," said Marie, drawing up a chair to the bedside. "I slept for twelve hours myself, the first night."

"And they looked after you nicely?"

"Perfectly. Joséphine, I can't thank you enough for

letting me come here, and making me more comfortable than I've ever been in my life!"

"You'd rather be here than with Sainte Anne de Beaupré at Croissy?"

"Poor Anne," said Marie. "You have a house at Croissy too."

"We'll go there very soon. But we must plan our future seriously. Did you go to see that man in the Place Vendôme?"

It was difficult to take Joséphine seriously when she lay in bed. It was the perfect setting for her, propped up on lace pillows so that her nightdress revealed the shape of her beautiful breasts, and the faint signs of ageing were hidden by the bed curtains of silk muslin hanging from a circle of gold laurel leaves. She was an odalisque, a houri, a woman made for love, but with the sharp look of a calculating brain in her dark eyes. She listened attentively while Marie described Our Lady of Thermidor and the possibility of an Order of Restitution, murmured "Bravo!" when Marie spoke of her inheritance, and was horrified when the girl said she had brought away the pearl parure and two hundred *livres*, and left the rest in the lawyer's hands.

"You mean you let him *keep* it?"

"Not keep it. Hold it for me, and let me have it as I need it."

"But can you trust him?"

"My uncle trusted him," said Marie. "Maître Favart insisted on signing a document with his clerk and the concierge as witnesses, saying he held three thousand *livres* on my behalf and I had drawn the first two hundred yesterday. Then I signed too. Joséphine, what else could I do? The money is safer in his strong box than carried through the streets of Paris in the new reticule I bought afterwards in the Place Vendôme! I have all I need at present – I had money in the prison, you know that."

"We all knew that," said Joséphine with a giggle. "It

189

showed. But you won't need any money while you're living with me."

"Oh yes, I will."

Then Marie spoke with the firmness she had learned in the hard school of Les Carmes. She would gladly spend a month – two months – three months – with Madame de Beauharnais, on condition that she paid her way. Her share of the rent, her share of the household expenses, her independence.

"But why do you make a month-by-month condition?" said the bewildered Joséphine. "At home, at Trois Islets, our friends came and stayed as long as they liked, and no one ever dreamed of *paying*!"

"Dear Joséphine, we're not in Martinique, and you're not a rich woman. I want to pay my way by the month, because if I get the house and the pharmacy back I may make other plans."

"Such as?"

"I might sell the shop, or I might let the house, I don't know yet."

"Darling, you have such a head for business," sighed Joséphine. "I was hoping you'd stay and be my *dame de compagnie*. We set each other off so well! And I'm sure I could find you a good husband . . .'

"Are you?"

Joséphine winced at the mocking tone. "Have you never been in love, Marie?"

"I don't know. Have you?"

"No."

"General Hoche thinks you're in love with him."

"Oh, General Hoche! He's very amusing." When Joséphine said *Il est drôle* her Créole accent turned it into *Il est drolle*, and Marie laughed.

"Don't let's talk about love and marriage," she said. "Let's talk about the Order of Restitution instead."

'I'd rather go back to sleep.'

"So you ought."

"Agathe's going to bring me a bowl of soup, and then I think I will have a nap. What are the children doing?"

"Eugène is at his carpentering, and Hortense is playing with her dolls in the garden. I'll take her out for a walk this afternoon."

"You're sweet," said the sweet voice, and Marie drew the curtains round the bed, creating the half-light of her friend's childhood in the long siestas of Martinique. She ran downstairs to look for Hortense. The little girl was a good excuse for not doing what her conscience told her should be done. After the midday meal she ought to go to the Rue de Courty, such a short distance away, and listen to Madame Beauchet's tale of woe. "I can't face it," she thought. "Not yet. I'll go next week. I don't want to talk about the poor Noailles and my poor uncle and poor everybody. Maybe I'm a selfish beast, but *I'm alive!*"

She took the delighted Hortense to the Rue du Bac in the afternoon, and bought a dress of pearl-grey silk with the new high waist for fifteen *livres*.

She modelled the dress before supper, for an audience of Joséphine, Agathe and little Hortense, who excitedly confirmed that the shop lady insisted that high waists were in and wide flowing skirts were out.

"I'll have to throw half my wardrobe away if that's true." Joséphine got out of bed and sent Agathe for a striped Roman scarf, which she knotted over her night-dress immediately below her breasts. "It'll seem strange not to wear a corset," she said, "but that's passable, isn't it, Agathe?"

"Passable indeed!" cried the sycophantic maid, "with a beautiful bosom like madame's the effect will be sensational! I'm sure I can arrange something for madame to wear until she can go to the shops and see the new styles for herself. As for mademoiselle, she had better wear her hair in curls for the present."

It was true that the prim chignon into which Anne de Beaupré had taught Marie to dress her hair looked all wrong with the new dress, and the girl resigned herself to a painful course of rags and curl papers. She wasn't complaining; it was so pleasant to be talking fashion in Joséphine's bedroom, warmed by the long sunny hours and scented by the powders and perfumes on the dressing table. It was a kind of relaxation she had never known before.

Joséphine, fresh and rested, came down to breakfast next day, and was feeding extravagant morsels of sugar to the pug Fortuné when a messenger was announced. It was an orderly in a more correct uniform than was usually seen in Paris, who saluted the company smartly and presented Madame de Beauharnais with a bouquet of red roses and a letter. "From General Hoche, citizeness," he said, and Joséphine told the little maid to take him to the kitchen for a glass of wine.

"Lovely roses, *maman*," said Eugène.

"Yours are just as beautiful, my darling," said his mother tenderly. She was turning Hoche's letter in her fingers, and half whispered to Marie, "I do hope he isn't going to be importunate!"

"He did promise to tell you his plans," said Marie.

"Yes, well, let's see if he got what he wanted."

"What does he want?"

"A command, of course; what else?" Joséphine cut away the seal of the letter and read the brief contents with a smile and a frown. Written in the third person, the message said that General Hoche would do himself the honour of calling on Madame de Beauharnais at five o'clock that afternoon. Meantime he thanked her for her interest in his future posting . . .

"Wretched boy, he doesn't mention what the posting is," said Joséphine. "Now I can't go to the dentist this morning – I can't run the risk of having a swollen face this afternoon . . . and it was the first thing I meant to do – "

"Do your teeth hurt badly, mother?" asked little Hortense, coming to lay her cheek against Joséphine's. "Eugène and I have toothache too, sometimes."

"Only when you eat too many sweets," said Mademoiselle de Lannoy, putting the empty cups together. Marie had noticed, almost as soon as Joséphine arrived at Les Carmes, that the one blemish of her beauty was in her mouth. Her front teeth were beginning to decay, and to disguise it she cultivated a tight-lipped smile which altered the expression of her face in certain lights. It made her look older, and General Hoche was young.

The Marie of the Rue St Honoré would have been shocked at the idea of a liaison between a married man and a divorced woman. She had been sufficiently infected by the moral standards of the prison to regard the affair as right in itself: a grasp, perhaps the last grasp, at the sweets of life. Back in the conventional atmosphere of the Rue St Dominique she was still prudish enough to wish that all knowledge of the affair could be kept from the children and their credulous old governess. That Agathe would have to know about it if General Hoche remained in Paris she had no doubt. Marie Fontaine had already summed up Agathe as the soubrette who knows all the secrets of her mistress, and may even use them for blackmail.

"Eugène, come up to my room, I want to talk to you," said Joséphine, rising from the table.

"Please, mother, it's my workshop day."

"Then you'll have to be late for once, this is important. Marie, could you amuse Hortense for half an hour? Then we can all go for a walk as far as the Rue du Bac. I want to see the new fashions for myself – and by the way, wear your new dress this afternoon."

Although General Hoche had announced himself for five o'clock, they were both dressed and in the salon by four, and Marie realised what Joséphine meant when she said they set each other off so well. The sophistication of Joséphine in a dark blue dress, the heightened waist indicated by a girdle of plaited red velvet to match the roses which filled the room, was complemented by the ingénue in pearl-grey silk, with golden ringlets which owed much to the skilled hands of Agathe. They were posed, as in the days of the old régime, with trifling pieces of embroidery in their hands.

The clock had hardly struck half past four when three unexpected guests arrived in a burst of noise and laughter which seemed to come from the one woman who led the party. The two men at her back contented themselves with bowing low. Marie said quickly, having picked up the formula, "Madame de Beauharnais, may I introduce Madame de Fontenay?"

"Madame Tallien!" said her bridegroom.

"Paul Barras," said the other man. "Forgive this invasion, citizeness, but Madame Tallien insisted on it. She has been so eager to meet you – "

"As I have been longing to meet her, and to thank Citizen Tallien for securing my release from Les Carmes," said Joséphine prettily, and the two women kissed. Madame Tallien was bare-headed, with a fillet of golden flowers, like the prize of the Queen of Beauty at a medieval tournament, securing the curls of her black hair. She wore a dress of shot silk, silver and gold. She turned to kiss Marie – she was lavish with her kisses – and said, "You look wonderful! Rue du Bac or Palais Royal?"

"Rue du Bac," and Marie curtsied to the gentlemen, to whom Joséphine now named her, and helped to push forward chairs.

"I know my maid has put champagne to cool," said Joséphine. "We must drink the health of the bride and groom. Marie dear, would you ring the bell?"

For all her social grace, Madame de Beauharnais was a little surprised by her visitors. Not by the woman, who was her equal, and whom she was mentally circling like a duellist looking for his opponent's weakness, but by the two men, Barras and Tallien, who had overthrown Robespierre, and for the time being represented the highest power in France. Paul Barras, the *ci-devant* vicomte, was a man of her own world, extremely attractive to women, but Jean Tallien, the former lawyer's clerk, had a hangdog look which belied his masterful conduct of the Thermidor revolt. He avoided all eyes except his bride's, and sat worrying a hangnail on his right thumb while he nodded assent to Joséphine's repeated thanks for "all he had done for her".

The arrival of the little maid with champagne and glasses seemed to revive him, and he spoke a whole sentence of thanks when the health of Monsieur and Madame Tallien was drunk by the three others present.

Marie kept the guests' glasses filled and passed a silver basket filled with *petits fours*. Moving behind Tallien she saw that his red hair spread in bristles down the back of his neck and round his jaw, and thought he was repulsive. Nor was she impressed by Barras's flashy good looks. If the two men had been paladins of medieval chivalry, stainless knights come to redress the wrongs of a suffering people, she would have been ready to adore them. But they were men who had served Robespierre before they overthrew Robespierre, who had sent thousands to the guillotine in Toulon and Bordeaux: would they in turn create a White Terror instead of a Red?

She began to talk to Teresa about the house in the new Avenue des Champs Elysées. No, it had been quite unsuitable, at the end of a muddy lane, with small rooms and poor stabling; Paul had a marvellous idea, which she wasn't allowed to talk about, for a far more *suitable* residence for them all. Marie saw 'Paul' glance at her once or twice, as if doubting her discretion, but he was absorbed by Joséphine, who was sounding him on the possibilities of an Order of Restitution. Tallien joined monosyllabically in both conversations, and the rising hum of a successful party filled the room when Agathe announced Citizen General Hoche.

He came forward with great aplomb and kissed Joséphine's hand. He was freshly groomed and wearing new regimentals: his cocked hat, which he placed on the floor beside his chair, bore a bright new tricolore cockade. He looked supremely confident, but his natural flush deepened when he said to Barras:

"Citizen Barras, I didn't expect to meet you again so soon."

"I didn't know you had the honour of Madame de Beauharnais's acquaintance."

"We were in prison together." Teresa gave her infectious giggle. Hoche and Joséphine, with her airs and graces – now who would have thought of that?

"Agathe, champagne for the general," ordered Joséphine. ". . . General, we want to know about your posting."

"You haven't told them?" Hoche appealed to Barras.

"It didn't occur to me," said Barras drily.

"I've been given command of the Army of the West."

"Against the Vendéens – oh! Surely that's a post of honour?" said Joséphine.

"I like to think so, madame."

"And when do you leave?"

"We thought next Monday, didn't we, Citizen Barras?" said the young commander. "I'll lose no time in getting my staff together."

"We must all drink your health," decreed Joséphine, and Agathe, who had lingered in the room in order to miss nothing, opened another bottle of champagne. She filled Marie's glass again. It was the first time the girl had tasted champagne since the days when Uncle Prosper opened a Sunday bottle for Michel and his botanical friends and she was allowed a sip, not that there was any comparison between that champagne and this marvellous vintage. Marie saw that the health-drinking was intended to cover Joséphine's embarrassment. Madame de Beauharnais knew as well as Marie Fontaine that General Hoche had left them to report to Carnot, the military expert of the Committee of Public Safety. Now it seemed that he owed his appointment to the Army of the West to Paul Barras. Had Carnot been removed from the Committee? Had he even been guillotined? Clearly there were pitfalls ahead for those who had spent four vital months in prison. They must learn as fast as possible who was in power and who was out.

Carnot's name was not mentioned, but Hoche himself mentioned Napoleon Buonaparte. He did so very quietly, when the hum of conversation was renewed and he leaned towards Marie.

"You asked me about General Buonaparte, mademoiselle," he said. "I'm afraid the news isn't good. An order for his arrest was sent to Nice last week."

15

General Buonaparte's plan of campaign, the prelude to his master project for the invasion of Italy, had been carried out by the end of May, with three French divisions established along the crest of the Alps and Apennines. His credit was very high, and Augustin Robespierre, leaving for Paris, intended to tell his brother and the Committee of Public Safety about what he called 'General Buonaparte's transcendent merit'.

Then came the crushing news. By order of Citizen Carnot the attack on Piedmont was halted, and there was a stalemate along the whole Italian front. It was no consolation to the general to be sent on a secret mission to the neutral Doge of Genoa. The need to get food for the men in the mountains, either through the port of Genoa or through the Mediterranean harbours controlled by Genoa, was great, and Buonaparte was not pleased to find that the British had been beforehand with him. They needed facilities for revictualling their Mediterranean squadron, and had sent Captain Horatio Nelson to arrange matters with the Genoa government.

Although the audience he gave the envoy from France was not productive, the Doge received Buonaparte with all honour, in robes of state and in an ancient council chamber which gave a man who had never seen a palace some idea of what it would be like to live surrounded by great wealth and the adulation of courtiers. He returned thoughtfully to Nice, where he was greeted by the news of Thermidor.

Napoleon Buonaparte was arrested in his billet in the Rue de Villefranche on 6 August, the same day as Joséphine de Beauharnais was released from Les Carmes.

The charge against him, to which he listened with cold dignity – only asking leave to put some books, writing materials and a change of linen together before he was led off to fortress arrest – was based on his friendship with Augustin Robespierre, guillotined along with Maximilien. He realised that Barras, so affable after Toulon, had done nothing to save him from imprisonment. He had never had many friends, being described as 'dissocial' on his army record; but now another step was taken in the making of Napoleon: in prison he learned to trust nobody.

Fortunately, the men at GHQ who hoped for the downfall of the ambitious Corsican tried to make capital out of his visit to the Doge of Genoa, representing it as a covert act of intelligence with the enemy. This wild exaggeration ended his imprisonment, for Saliceti, the Corsican Deputy who had been one of Robespierre's commissioners but had not been ordered back to Paris, was able to produce documents which proved that Buonaparte's mission to Genoa, while undertaken in secret, had been planned by the *représentants en mission* themselves. Saliceti clinched the argument for setting him free by saying in a massive understatement, "We need him in the army!", and fourteen days after the arrest Buonaparte was dining with his liberator in a little restaurant at Nice harbour.

"Jean, I'm eternally grateful to you," he said between gulps of food and wine, "but for God's sake give me something to do now. The men in the mountains are longing for action, and I'm rusting here at Nice. Rotting here, I could say: I could have rotted in prison for months before Barras lifted a hand to free me."

"My friend, we have to face it: Barras is in the saddle now, but he's following Carnot's line exactly in refusing to give battle without good reason. I've no authority to command an action – "

"Oh yes, you have, if you get General Dumerbion and that local fellow, what d'you call him – Masséna, on your side. And have we no good reason to attack the Austrians, the first of all our enemies? Carnot and Barras are ready enough to give battle in the north, I notice, and what about sending off Hoche to kill Frenchmen in the Vendée? What about giving us a chance to show what we can do in the south?"

"South of Lyon the country is more unsettled than ever, and Lyon is in the throes of another royalist revolt. The Army of Italy is needed here for police action: we can't send it into Piedmont yet."

Eventually Buonaparte was successful, and the men who had stormed the mountains were brought back to the littoral. The attack they mounted on a town called Dego, on the coast between Genoa and Nice, was a classic Napoleonic manoeuvre with the general interposing his forces between the Piedmontese and the Austrians, who beat a retreat which the French were forbidden to follow up. It was a short, sharp encounter, and Charles Latour, serving with the 4th Artillery, caught a glimpse of the general wreathed in cannon smoke and thought it was his native element. He looked for the general when the battle was over, and was rewarded with a tweak of the ear and a "Ha! Latour, things haven't turned out quite as we expected when you were exploring the High Valley of the Roya! Come and see me at my billet – you know the place – and we can talk. I'm needed at Army Forward now."

Three nights later they met in the Rue de Villefranche. Latour thought Buonaparte changed: he seemed to have lost the confidence he had shown at Entrevaux and Cap Martin, and to be brooding on his own misfortunes. He looked haggard and ill, and the parlour of his billet was a comfortless place on a September night of thunder and rain.

"So we won the battle of Dego," he said sarcastically,

pouring a glass of wine for Latour. "What a victory! What a triumph! Another revictualling post secured for the Army of Italy, which should be marching on Milan!"

"Supposing we'd lost instead of winning?" Latour suggested.

"We couldn't lose, I tell you! I was with Saliceti all afternoon, trying to make him see that the army would soon be demoralised if we confined it to piddling little actions like Dego. All he could suggest was that a large part of the forces – he never gives an exact figure – should be amalgamated with the Army of the Alps at Digne. You know yourself what Digne is. Do you want to go back to that outpost as a lieutenant in the 4th Artillery?"

"With yourself in command of the forces?"

"Oh no. Impossible. They have other views for me. I am to stay here in the south and rejoice in the victories of other men. Jourdan, the hero of Fleurus. Hoche, putting down rebellion with an iron hand, as the saying goes. And Pichegru, massing his troops on the north-eastern frontier for another attack on the Austrian Netherlands. That's where the new Committee wants to fight Austria. In Holland. The Prince of Orange is expected to flee at the mere approach of General Pichegru. I never thought much of him as a tactician."

That was where the shoe pinched, thought Latour. A man aware of his own genius was jealous of the chances being given to lesser men. He asked what views the Convention now had for Buonaparte.

"It's a funny thing," said Buonaparte moodily, "funny, the way history repeats itself. Exactly a year ago today I was at Ollioules, bringing back a convoy from Avignon, when I was halted by a vedette with an urgent message: I was to take command of the artillery at Toulon. Three months later I had risen from captain to brigadier general, with a stunning victory over the English to my credit. Today I'm a man who's been in prison, a suspect like so many more, with the fact on my army record for ever, and now I'm ordered *back* to Toulon, to work – so the briefing runs . . . in close co-operation with the Navy."

"With the Navy, *mon général?*"

"The Navy is smarting under their defeat by the English Channel Fleet last June. The Glorious First of June, they're calling it in Britain, so the papers say: our fellows, of course, are blaming it on the Americans."

"But why? They're on our side."

"They ought to be. The king's government lent them huge sums of money during their Revolution, and don't forget, we sent them La Fayette, for what that was worth."

The American government had repaid its debt to France by instalments, and sometimes in kind. In the spring of 1794 they made their payment in grain, very necessary to hungry France, and a convoy of grain ships set out from the United States. A French flotilla from the Brest squadron went to protect the convoy as it approached the shores of France, and the English Channel Fleet, forever lurking round the Channel Islands, duly attacked the enemy. The American convoy got through safely and with its cargo intact, but Admiral Lord Howe cut the Brest flotilla to pieces with the loss of several capital ships. That was the Glorious First of June which the French were now planning to avenge.

"I suppose they mean to tackle the British in the Mediterranean?" said Latour. "At Gibraltar, maybe?"

"Gibraltar is impregnable. No, they mean to recapture Corsica from the British. Paoli has been disappointed in his plan to rule the island. A man from Scotland, one of their barbaric possessions in the north, has been sent out as viceroy. Sir Elliott, they call him, and he's made Bastia his seat of government. Not Ajaccio."

Ajaccio was Buonaparte's birthplace. Latour, remembering the young general in the dawn at Cap Martin, gazing at the violet vision which by some trick of the early light appeared and disappeared in minutes, ventured to say that it would mean a great deal to the general if his birthplace became French again.

Buonaparte shrugged. "It would mean a great deal to my mother if she could go home. Marseille is no place for her, or for my sisters. But I don't welcome the job they've given me. Cannon is my weapon, but fighting a ship larboard and starboard was never part of my training, and I doubt if the Navy at Toulon will be willing to teach me – they're too set in their ways."

He got up, and took a few restless steps through the room.

"Those fellows in Paris have no imagination, Latour! No vision! They've all come round to Danton's way of thinking, that if France regains her natural frontiers all will be well! We ought to be looking far beyond our natural frontiers, if those are the Rhine and the seas. We should conquer Italy, Austria, Prussia, Spain, and then complete our empire by the conquest of England before we return to the east . . . When I was under fortress arrest I improved the time by studying the campaigns of Alexander. He was the greatest soldier in the world, but even he had not the scientific knowledge we possess. Do you know what I would do if I had the power? I would lead a French army into Egypt, and when I had beaten the Mamelukes I would construct two canals – one from the Red Sea to the Nile at Cairo, and one from Cairo to the Mediterranean. That would shorten the way to India, and the Indian colonies we lost to perfidious England would be ours again!"

He had raised his voice, there was colour in his gaunt face, and the blue-grey eyes were full of a strange light. To Latour he looked like a man possessed. Then as swiftly as the mood began it ended, and Buonaparte said in his ordinary voice:

"Now, tell me about yourself, Charles. Do you ever hear from your family in England?"

The abrupt question was almost as shocking to Charles Latour as the visionary outburst which preceded it. If a man had an émigré family he never mentioned it, and those of his friends who knew it never questioned him:

the subject was too dangerous. Buonaparte knew this as well as Latour did and was quick to reassure him.

"Anything you tell me will be in confidence, of course. But talking about my own mother made me think of yours. Do you hear from her?"

"Not directly, no. But the family solicitor, who stayed in Paris, wrote to me a couple of weeks ago to tell me that she and my brother were very anxious to come back to France. They seemed to think, after Thermidor, that there would be a general amnesty and all the émigrés would be made welcome. Not my father, he's got too much common sense, and I fancy he enjoys being the Marquis de la Tour in England. I wrote to Maître Vial to say my mother and Edouard must be warned that the Republic has no place for émigrés, least of all those who might be expected to work actively for a Bourbon restoration."

"Quite right, it's much too dangerous. But have another glass of wine and tell me something. How did this Maître Vial know where to find you? Have you kept in touch with *him*, all these years?"

"No, I haven't. But once I was based at Nice and had an army address, I wrote to him and asked him to find out something for me. I wanted to know what had become of Marie Fontaine."

"Marie – oh, the apothecary's pretty niece. And what did you find out?"

"She's dead, *mon général*. She and her uncle are both dead, and their house is National Property."

"Dead for the usual reason?"

"I don't know about the usual reason, but by the usual means." He slammed his fist on the table. "Damn that old fool of an uncle. I knew he was a traitor, he reeked of treachery. And he dragged her into it – that poor Marie . . ."

Buonaparte respected his emotion. It was not an occasion for ear-tweaking, but he patted the younger man's shoulder sympathetically. Cold-hearted as he was, he had just enough tact not to tell Latour that the world was full of pretty girls.

16

Marie Fontaine, alive and well, did not find time hanging heavy on her hands as the month of Thermidor became the month of Fructidor. Two surprising decisions made by Joséphine in the earliest days after their release from prison kept both women busy, to say nothing of Mademoiselle de Lannoy and Agathe Rible. Joséphine announced tranquilly, two days after General Hoche's command of the Army of the West was made public, that her son Eugène would accompany him to the front.

"To the firing line? You can't mean it, Joséphine!" said the incredulous Marie.

"He'll be kept in the rear to begin with. He'll be a sort of junior ADC."

"A boy of thirteen! Does he *want* to go?"

"He wants to be a soldier like his father, and his father held a commission in the royal army when he was much about the same age; most sons of the nobility did. Your friend General de La Fayette for one."

"But Eugène loves you so much! How can you bear to send him away from you, so soon?"

"Eugène may look like a schoolboy, but he's already a man, Marie. He doesn't want to stay tied to his mother's apron strings for ever. We had a long talk in my room the day the Talliens and Hoche came to call, and he jumped at the idea. He may go to school later, or have a tutor at home, but he's too old for a governess now, and active service with General Hoche is the perfect answer."

Marie said no more. She realised that, for Joséphine, the 'answer' was killing two birds with one stone. His command in the West brought the affair with Hoche to a timely conclusion and relieved her of all the expenses of an adolescent boy. Hoche himself advanced the money for Eugène's uniform, and the boy was wild with excitement when a military tailor came to the house to measure him. The garments were to follow, for Eugène was to go to the front in the personal charge of General Hoche, and there was not a moment to lose in getting his clothes and possessions ready. In a whirlwind of embraces and good luck he left Paris early on Tuesday morning.

"The house seems so strange without that dear boy!" lamented Mademoiselle de Lannoy, and she and little Hortense went about sniffing for the rest of the day. Joséphine shed a few token tears. Her face was swollen with toothache, and in the afternoon Marie went with her to a dentist who gave her oil of laudanum for the pain but could do little for the decaying front teeth. "They must have been neglected in your childhood, citizeness," he said, and Joséphine acknowledged that in Martinique dentistry was even more backward than in France. With a scarf wrapped over her mouth they set out for home, and in the Rue du Bac were alarmed to hear the heavy tramp of men. It was not far from the place where 'Vautour' had protected Marie from the *fédérés* from Marseille.

The men approaching were not republican fanatics. They were obviously of the bourgeois class, but dressed alike in paramilitary uniforms with low boots and very high cravats. Their hair was worn long and plaited at the back, and they were armed with short sticks, obviously weighted, and postboys' whips. Twenty in number, they were marching four abreast, and the leading rank courteously saluted Joséphine and Marie as they went past.

"Who on earth can they be?"

"They're not *sans-culottes*, at any rate."

"They're all of military age," said Marie. "Why weren't they conscripted?"

"They may be auxiliaries of the National Guard. Citizen Tallien will know."

How she depended on a man's opinion, and a woman's sympathy! When Marie gave Joséphine into Agathe's care, and left her to drowse away the effects of the oil of laudanum in her comfortable bed, she slipped out of the house without telling anybody where she was going. It was high time she went to see Madame Beauchet, and in the rooms above the grocer's in the Rue de Courty she wept again in the arms of that old friend.

"Oh my dear, your uncle, your poor uncle!" Marie-Josèphe de Beauchet wept too. "He was so brave, Father Carrichon told me. The good father was there, you know, and saw your uncle die with my poor ladies in the Place du Trône."

"And Madame de La Fayette?"

"Still in Plessis prison. At least she's allowed visitors there. I go to see her every second day. Father Carrichon goes, dressed as a carpenter, and the new American Minister, Monsieur James Monroe. It was he who told her that General de La Fayette was in prison at Olmütz in Austria, farther away than ever."

"Oh, has Gouverneur Morris gone? He never did a thing for her."

"He did write one letter to the Committee, which Monsieur Monroe says saved her from death. But he never did anything for poor George-Washington, and his mother has no idea where he is."

Gouverneur Morris had indeed left What-a-People to their fate, and returned to the more congenial occupation of organising the decimal currency of the United States. Before he left Paris he made one oracular remark, often quoted: "I have long predicted a single despotism in France!" Some thought he meant Robespierre, but Robespierre was already dead, and none of his successors had the quality of a despotic ruler. Not Barras, and certainly not Tallien: was there then Someone, Somewhere, who would make the American's prediction come true?

The two women discussed many other topics. Marie's experiences in the Carmes prison, and her refuge with Madame de Beauharnais; her inheritance and the prospect of getting back the house on the Rue St Honoré.

"You couldn't live there alone, Marie!"

"I could if I took old Augustine to live with me."

"But Augustine's dead, my dear, didn't you know?"

"How could I know? Oh, poor old creature, don't tell me *she* died by the guillotine!"

"No, no, it was natural causes, a heart attack. She was seventy-five, they said."

"I knew her all my life," said Marie piteously. "Oh, Marie-Josèphe, is everybody dead or dying?"

"Of course they're not," said her friend robustly. "You're very much alive, and prison hasn't done you any harm. You're prettier than ever!"

She changed the subject adroitly to her husband, Nicolas, who in his inconspicuous post at the Finance Ministry saw a great deal of what was going on at the temporary Bourse installed in a wing of the Louvre. The New Men, as he called them, the men of Thermidor, were speculating in *assignats*, in commodities, in futures, and were growing rich while the rest of France was starving, and there was hardly enough money to pay the Sections for the workers to attend their meetings, or for the upkeep of the National Guard. The *jeunesse dorée*, of course, paid their own expenses.

"What's the *jeunesse dorée*?" asked Marie, and Madame Beauchet described exactly such a body of men as she had seen marching in cadence on the Rue du Bac.

"They attack anybody wearing the red cap of liberty, and they fight the *sans-culottes* with their clubs. A free fight can break out at any minute. Marie, I don't think you should go about the streets alone."

"*You* do, when you go to Plessis, and I did it all through the Terror when I went to the workshop in the Palais Royal. Do you think I should volunteer to sew shirts again?"

208

"It's all done in the textile shops now. And the Palais Royal's much too far from the Rue St Dominique."

Next morning Marie learned that she was to be living even further from her old *quartier* when Joséphine informed her household of her second great decision, to remove to another lodging, in the Rue de l'Université. Seeming no worse for her ordeal at the dentist's, she had used lip rouge and a fine brush to draw a new outline of her mouth, making the lips fuller to hide the effect of her tight-lipped smile. But when she announced her decision her reddened lips closed more firmly than ever, and the determined woman showed beneath the assumed pathos.

"We've been very comfortable here, madame," ventured Mademoiselle de Lannoy.

"But *I* have not been happy," breathed Joséphine in her best tragic style, with the tears she could summon at will in her eyes. "How do you expect me to feel at ease in an apartment where so many horrid things have happened? The disputes with poor Alexandre's lawyers . . . and then that terrible night when I was torn from my sleeping babies and thrown in prison . . . no, no my dears, I have too many bitter memories of the Rue St Dominique." She dabbed at her mouth cautiously with her table napkin. "Besides, it's much too expensive."

"Is that the real reason – money?" demanded Marie, when she and Joséphine were alone that afternoon in the salon of the apartment in the Rue de l'Université. It was not far from the Rue St Dominique, but quite far, in the long Rue de l'Université, from the Hôtel de Mouchy-Noailles, where nearly a year ago she had gone at the request of a dead man to carry medicine to the women who had gone to the guillotine along with him. It was not as attractive as the apartment Joséphine meant to leave: the rooms were smaller and got very little sun, and there was no garden. "Joséphine!" (as she got no answer) "will you save much money by moving here?"

"Enough, Marie. Enough to let me pay the rent of the

house at Croissy. I don't want to give that up until I must, and there's room for us all there if we're sensible. Agathe and the kitchen maid must share a room, and Hortense must sleep with Mademoiselle de Lannoy and do her lessons in their room until she goes to school. The little guest-room will be yours, of course, and we don't need a schoolroom any more – "

"Do you mean to send Hortense to boarding-school?"

"My landlady at Croissy, Madame Campan, has opened a school for girls at St Germain. I'd like to send Hortense there when the new term begins in October."

"Then," said Marie, "why don't you consider cutting down on staff? I could teach Hortense quite well for the next few weeks, and that would save a governess's wages. She isn't learning much from Mademoiselle de Lannoy."

"Marie, how can you be so heartless? I could never let poor old de Lannoy go. She protected the children while I was in prison, and besides – besides, I owe her a good deal of money."

Bit by bit the story came out. The Tascher de la Pageries, Joséphine's Creole family, had not been rich, and her unlucky marriage was intended to mend their fortunes. After the divorce Alexandre de Beauharnais had been delinquent in the payment of her settlement, and even in paying for child support, and Joséphine was now largely dependent on her income from her mother's estate, paid regularly by a banker in Dunkirk. There had been letters from him at the Rue St Dominique, but the money orders enclosed were smaller than she had hoped. There had been a revolution in Martinique too, and some of Madame Tascher's sugar plantations had been destroyed. "It isn't enough to live on," said Joséphine. "I'm pinning my hopes to the Order of Restitution."

"Which hasn't passed into law yet."

"Citizen Barras is pushing it through the Convention."

As a result of this conversation Marie sent a message to Maître Favart which brought the lawyer to the Rue St Dominique within twenty-four hours. He looked very well in a dark blue frock coat and a new beaver hat, and when after a private talk with Marie he was presented to Madame de Beauharnais he at once won her tearful sympathy for his empty sleeve.

What he had to tell her was that his client, Mademoiselle Fontaine, wished to pay for her board and lodging for three months in advance, dating from 4 August, with payment to be made through Maître Favart's office.

"Is that really what you want, mademoiselle?" the lawyer had asked. "I thought you meant to pay on a monthly basis."

"I did: but I know she's desperately short of money, and I want to give it her."

"Very generous, but don't let your generosity run away with you. I've made enquiries about Madame de Beauharnais, and before she was imprisoned she was known to be heavily in debt."

"She'll be all right once the Restitution Order goes through. Have you any information about that?"

The lawyer had not, but Teresa Tallien had it at the source, and ran in and out to report on the prolonged debate in the Convention during the week preceding the removal to the Rue de l'Université. In the quiet faubourg, where so many houses were standing empty, it was not easy to organise a removal, even though they were going from one furnished flat to another, and only three pieces of mahogany furniture, Joséphine's escritoire, dressing table and cheval glass, had to be moved in a cart which looked alarmingly like a tumbril with the seats taken out. The surly man who owned it came back for the big Beauharnais trunks, and they carried the rest. Teresa Tallien carried nothing, giving her condition as the reason, but she kept them all in good spirits, and when the new apartment was opened she insisted that they crack a bottle of champagne, one of a case sent in by Citizen Barras, and drink success to the new home.

"Drink up, Marie!" she urged. "Drink up, Joséphine! I've got wonderful news for you. I didn't want to tell you until we were safe indoors, or you might have dropped your valuables in the street, but it's this: the Restitution Act became law last night."

"Oh, thank God!" breathed Joséphine, and Marie, clapping her hands, cried, "I wonder if Maître Favart knows?"

"Sure to, by this time. You're both beneficiaries under the Act. They finally worked it out that restitution of property, goods and gear or the equivalent, should be made to the legal heirs of all those 'judicially executed' (I like that, don't you?) after the tenth of March 1793."

"Now my poor children will get their patrimony," sobbed Joséphine. "Oh Teresa dear, how grateful I am to Paul and Jean!"

"Tell them so," said Teresa Tallien. "Let's celebrate! Joséphine, you must give a housewarming party, and Marie can send an invitation to her Favart."

"A housewarming party? When?"

"The day after tomorrow."

"Darling, the place won't be in order then. And a dinner party costs a lot of money," said Joséphine.

"Who's talking about dinner parties? They're out of style. It's much more fun to eat informally, and we'll see that you've got plenty."

"Couldn't we put it off till next week?"

"Next week I'm having a baby, so the doctors say. And then Jean and I have *our* removal – no, I'm not going to tell you where! – so the next housewarming party will be mine."

Eventually a date three days later was fixed, and the maids worked hard to get the new abode in order. The trunks were opened and Marie counted table napkins and dried the crystal glasses and china as these were washed. She sent a written invitation to Maître Favart, but she made time to hurry to the Rue de Courty and invite Monsieur and Madame Beauchet.

The invitation was refused. "We don't belong with your new friends, Marie," said her old friend. "A lady's maid and a *petit fonctionnaire* like Nicolas wouldn't mix well with the aristocracy."

"I want to have somebody of my own there. I may be back in the Rue St Honoré sooner than you think."

"I'll come to you when you really need me, you know that, but don't insist on the party."

The new salon was not as roomy as the old, but it had six glass girandoles on the walls, and when these were washed and filled with new wax candles the lighting was soft and flattering. There were candles on the little tables too, set in wreaths of flowers sent by Paul Barras along with a quantity of choice fruit and another case of champagne. Joséphine accepted these gifts complacently, and going into the kitchen herself prepared some savoury dishes which she said were Creole favourites. The maids cooked them next day while the ladies dressed.

The party numbered ten in all. The Talliens and Barras arrived in a carriage, followed by a Deputy called Fréron who had joined them in the attack on Robespierre, and another sympathiser called Reubell. Maître Favart arrived on foot in a black dress coat, and last, in a cab, came *ci-devant aristos* called Monnier who had been in the prison of La Force with Teresa.

Marie, as she moved about the room pouring champagne, had no idea how many admiring glances were given to her fresh young beauty. She wanted the evening to be a success for Joséphine, and it looked at first as if all the attention would be monopolised by Our Lady of Thermidor. Teresa, effulgent in her approaching maternity, lost no time in announcing:

"Now it can be told! Now you must all hear where our new home is going to be! Paul has arranged it, and we three are going to live in the Palace of the Luxembourg!"

"The Luxembourg!" The surprise and congratulations were everything Teresa wished. Joséphine's were slow in coming, because the Luxembourg made the Rue de l'Université look very shabby. She said, "I thought it was still a prison," and Marie reflected that only weeks before her uncle had gone from that prison to his death.

"The Luxembourg prison is empty now, madame," said Barras, with his special smile for her. "So is Les Carmes. But it'll take a month to make the place habitable."

"I'm glad you're going to live there, Teresa," said Marie. "You'll help to lay the ghosts." Jean Tallien smiled one of his rare smiles. "Your own property will soon be habitable, Citizeness Fontaine," he said. "I've had a word with your solicitor about it."

"Thank you very much, Citizen Tallien."

Perhaps Our Lady of Thermidor had made her sensational announcement too soon. There was a limit, after all, to what could be said about the glory of living in a former royal palace, and the service of supper, dividing the company into three small groups, meant the start of three different conversations. All agreed that it was delightfully original to eat at small tables instead of the banqueting boards of the old régime, and no one mentioned that at least five members of the company had recently been accustomed to eat sitting on their prison pallets, dipping stale bread into a watery soup.

When the tables were cleared the *ci-devant* Vicomtesse de Monnier, a pretty young woman, asked her hostess for some music, looking at the harp which stood in a corner of the room.

"Alas!" said Joséphine, "the harp is part of the furniture, and I can't play it. I want my little girl to learn, but not on that instrument: the strings are broken."

"Didn't you learn when you were young?" said Teresa bluntly.

"There were no teachers of harp in Martinique when I was a girl. My sisters and I used to play and sing to the guitar."

"Then do sing for us," insisted Madame Monnier.

"I haven't touched my guitar for months."

But she rose and took the neglected guitar from a

drawer in the bookcase, pronounced the strings in tune, sat down and began to play.

In the old days the harp, rather than the pianoforte, had been the favoured instrument of young ladies who wished to show off a pretty arm. Joséphine's arms were bare to the shoulder, as white and slim as they had been at twenty, and her drooping head, on which she wore a coronal of roses sent by Barras, was the expression of delicate submission. Her voice, while not powerful, was husky and sweet, and she had the wit to sing the folk songs of Martinique. It was no time to revive the melodies of Versailles, nor sing the patriotic ballads of the day. Joséphine's songs in the Creole dialect took her hearers into another and simpler world. Marie saw that she had regained her ascendancy. She was *la câline*, the wheedler, and her music suited the mood of the September night, the scent of fruit and flowers, the harvest time of life. Marie wondered if, when she sang of her island home, Joséphine remembered the wise woman who predicted that she would be Queen of France.

Two mornings later, while Joséphine was composing one of the innumerable begging letters she was to write to the diminished Committee of Public Safety on behalf of her two children, a cab called at her new home and the driver presented a letter for Mademoiselle Fontaine. It was from Maître Favart asking her, if she were free, to drive at once to his office in the Place Vendôme. The Palais Royal Section had surrendered the keys to the pharmacy and dwelling in the Rue St Honoré.

Pausing only to seize bonnet, gloves and reticule, and tell the abstracted Joséphine where she was going, Marie hurried out to the cab. The driver whipped up his horse, they were across the bridge and the Place de la Révolution, and both her hands were in the warm hands of her lawyer.

"Congratulations, mademoiselle!" he cried. "What a thing it is to have friends – well, we can't quite say at

215

court, can we? But friends in high places, certainly! Monsieur Guiart wanted to be here to greet you, but I thought you'd rather enter your home alone. Was I right?"

"Of course," said Marie. "But I thought the Palais Royal Section was disbanded."

"It is, but they keep a small office open to deal with cases like your own. Here are your keys; now, shall we go?"

He saw that she was agitated, and on the very short drive to the Rue St Honoré talked of nothing but the most agreeable *soirée* given by Madame de Beauharnais, and the charm of her playing and singing. Marie acknowledged the compliments by a few mechanical words. She was back in the Street of the Tumbrils. Here she had seen the Queen of France going to the guillotine; here she and her uncle had been driven away as prisoners, and he had not come back. The notice saying National Property had been removed from the sign of '*Michel Fontaine, Apothicaire*', and the iron shutters were run down. A couple of *sans-culottes*, smoking and idling outside the Noailles mansion, came up to stare as the one-armed man struggled with the key to the iron shutter over the door. They did not offer help, and it was Marie herself who pushed the shutter up when the rusty lock was free.

"Can you see, mademoiselle?"

"When the kitchen door is opened it will be light enough. There!"

In the half-light Marie saw that the pharmacy was almost exactly as they left it on the April morning of their arrest. There was a thick film of dust on the counter and shelves, but the balance and the pestle and mortar were in place, and so were the volumes of Diderot, Rousseau and Voltaire by which Prosper Fontaine had set such store. Only one object was missing from the glass shelf, and Marie's quick eyes found it on the floor.

"Some of the men did it, I suppose," she said, as if to herself, and Favart saw that she was looking at a fan torn

216

in half and crumpled, on which he could just distinguish the faded portrait of a man in uniform.

When the wooden shutters of the kitchen window were flung open, and the back door as well, the sunlight showed dust and mouse-droppings on the floor, but a breeze from the garden brought fresh air into the fusty atmosphere of the room. Marie lit a tallow candle and inspected the cellar laboratory, where everything was in order. The garden appeared to have suffered most, for the pot-herbs and simples had withered in the dog-days of August, and the plot of spring vegetables had produced a fine crop of weeds.

Maître Favart was appraising the good old Breton furniture. "You've been very fortunate," he said. "No looting, no vicious damage . . . are the contents all intact?"

Marie closed the doors of the *armoire*. "As far as I can see," she said. "It'll take time to go through the drawers, of course. Maître Favart, won't you please sit down? I want to go upstairs by myself."

"I quite understand." The man sat down in one of the comfortable chairs near the grate full of wood ashes, where the blackened pots swung on their rod. He remembered the Marie Fontaine of two nights ago, pouring champagne, smiling and engaging in her white dress, and compared her with this stern composed creature confronting her violated home. He listened to her footsteps climbing the steep stair.

Michel's room, used for storage and chemical supplies, was the same as ever, and the only difference in her uncle's bedroom was that his writing desk had been completely gutted, the empty drawers upended on the floor. There had been a search for incriminating evidence, something to back up the story relayed from Nantes; something, no doubt, which had led to the new charge of dealings with the Girondins. A little group of miniatures, of Prosper Fontaine's wife, his parents and Michel as a child, which hung on the wall beside his bed, had also disappeared, probably for the value of their gold frames set with pearls, and probably by the man or men who had rifled the writing desk. There was nothing in Marie's own room to tempt a thief. She stood looking out of the window, now rimmed with cobwebs in which dead flies were caught, and vowed that she would not be sentimental. She had slept for years in that little white bed, and what years they had been! Years of the Terror, of violence and the smell of blood! Months, at the end, of personal fear of the trap her uncle had unwarily laid for both of them!

She emptied out a carton which held a few bottles of scent in the store room – perhaps, for it had a Grasse label, the same carton as had held the carnation scent used to such aphrodisiac effort by Teresa de Fontenay. Into the carton Marie placed all she possessed by way of clean underlinen, her one pair of silk stockings and a cameo brooch which had been her mother's. The well-worn dresses were not worth carrying away. As for the blue muslin, that souvenir of the one romantic evening of her life and the dinner with Captain Buonaparte, it would only make Joséphine laugh. She rolled it into a ball and thrust it to the back of the *armoire*. Then she went back to Maître Favart.

"Everything all right upstairs?" he asked, rising to his feet.

"My uncle's desk has been ransacked and all his papers are gone."

"*Acte de naissance, certificat de mariage* – all that?"

"I suppose so."

"Then it's a blessing he lodged his Will, and your own papers, with me. It'll simplify matters when you come to sell the house."

"I'm not going to sell it."

"But – "

"This house and shop are on one of the choicest sites in Paris. Don't you think I'd be foolish to sell them to the first buyer – say Monsieur Guiart – when I could get more money by holding on?"

"With half of Paris up for sale?"

"That won't last for ever. People are coming back since the Ninth of Thermidor, and new people like the Talliens are coming in. Soon there'll be a big demand for house property. I'm going to wait until then."

"Leaving an empty house to deteriorate? Do you see that patch of damp on the kitchen ceiling?"

"I'll let it furnished, to Monsieur Guiart or another, and let the new tenant look after the damp. By the way, is Monsieur Guiart your client too?"

"Certainly not!" Favart reddened with annoyance. "He and my father were friends . . . and of course he takes a sympathetic interest in you."

"I'm sure he does," said Marie. "Does he want this place for himself or for his son?"

"For a former student, a research chemist invalided out of the army medical service. That's all I know. That, I think, is why Monsieur Guiart wanted to meet you today."

"Thank you," said Marie. "Would you be kind enough to tell him where I live? I shall be glad to see him in the Rue de l'Université – along with yourself, if you can spare the time."

"I'll make the time," said Etienne Favart. He looked at his watch. "If you've seen all you want to, mademoiselle, let me fetch you a cab from the new rank in the Place Vendôme."

"You're very kind, but I intend to walk home. I have a headache, the fresh air will do me good."

"Then at least let me escort you."

"I couldn't think of it. I'll take the short cut by the Tuileries garden, unless it's still laid down in potatoes."

"No, the potato experiment was a failure. Monsieur Robespierre, deceased, had the garden returfed for the Feast of the Supreme Being. Won't that cardboard box be too heavy for you?"

"No, it's very light. Just a few personal things: I'll send over for the books later."

The heavy bar on the back gate was checked, the back door locked and the heavy shutters run down on the front. Favart held the iron keys.

"Do you want me to keep these for you?"

"I'll take them." Marie dropped them into her reticule. "Thank you for all your kindness, Maître Favart. I hope to see you before long."

He stood with his hat in his hand while she turned away and went off down the alley leading to the Terrasse des Feuillants. He felt rebuffed and irritated. There had been no time for sentiment in his life since the Revolution, but he had begun to be sentimental about Marie Fontaine – so pretty, and so plucky as she seemed to be, and today so damnably independent. She'd as good as hinted that he was in some sort of conspiracy with old Guiart to get her property dirt cheap. He was her lawyer, *avocat au barreau de Paris*, and she wouldn't even trust him with her keys!

Marie crossed the Terrasse des Feuillants, thinking not of the present but of the past. Here she had walked with her uncle on the day the news came of victory at Wattignies, where that poor man had lost his arm, the day when Vautour had followed her across the Pont Royal. The terrace looked much less cheerful than on that day, in spite of Thermidor; the café loungers more tense and threatening, the beggars more importunate. Inside the National Palace the Convention was in session, for the Tricolore floated on the roof, but there was now no barrier to the great garden, once the preserve of monarchy. People were moving about on the gravel pathways, newly hedged with boxwood, and the turf was growing green where Robespierre's fireworks had burned it brown.

Marie sat down on one of the new benches and surveyed the scene. Her headache, no fiction, was better already. She drew a deep breath. For the rest of her life, she thought, she would remember the smell of boxwood as the scent of freedom.

17

Two days later Teresa Tallien gave birth to a baby girl, and Joséphine took Marie to congratulate the new parents at their hotel. Teresa, in a bed draped with exotic shawls, was radiant, while Tallien, presiding in the salon, was still worrying his fingernails and unable to look any of his visitors straight in the eye. He was heard to mutter that they had "wanted a boy". The baby, in the arms of a fat nurse arrayed in lace and a goffered bonnet, had a head of red hair and a miserable expression.

The salon was crowded with people come to congratulate: elegant women and well-dressed men whom "nobody" said Joséphine, "had ever seen before." Where had they come from? Where, for that matter, had the *jeunesse dorée* come from? They were Paul Barras's force of law and order, but they were behaving more like shock troops of the counter-revolution, and their nightly brawls with the *sans-culottes* were alarming people emerging from the crowded theatres. At the time of the Tallien baby's birth they were hunting out all the busts of Marat they could find and using their clubs and whips on the owners. The cult of Marat had been destroyed immediately after Thermidor, when his body, interred in the glorious Pantheon, had been flung into the Montmartre cesspool. His bust in the Convention had been destroyed, as General de La Fayette's had been destroyed in 1792, but there were literally thousands of replicas of the bust in the city:

finding and smashing these was the latest sport of the *jeunesse dorée*.

This was much discussed by the guests, of whom only a few were allowed to see Teresa, who had already quarrelled with her doctor about her right to see her friends. Joséphine and Marie were the exceptions, for Tallien, coming back from the bedroom, was heard grunting, "She wants to see you again. Wants you to be the kid's godmother."

"But Jean, you know we can't have a religious ceremony . . ." Joséphine began as they were ushered into the bedroom, and Teresa, who heard, retorted, "Never mind, we'll have a party when Jean registers the birth. If that fool of a doctor thinks he can keep me shut up in a hotel room for a month – 'the usual time for a *lady*' he had the impudence to say – I'll teach him different! There's too much going on, too much I can't miss, and I can't wait to get into the Luxembourg! But you will be her godmother, won't you, darling? She's going to need someone beautiful to take an interest in her, poor ugly little devil."

"Of course I will, dearest." Enthusiastic kisses followed, and Marie, who had only kissed the baby's hand, the smallest hand she had ever seen, was surprised to hear Joséphine say, after they left the hotel, "What a wretched-looking child! That won't last, you know."

"It's perfectly healthy, isn't it?" said Marie in dismay.

"I didn't mean the baby, silly, I meant the marriage. Oh yes, I know we owe Tallien a great deal, but he really *is* such a clod! Once Teresa's in the Luxembourg he'll have to take a back seat, and when the parties begin someone more exciting will come along, and she'll have another *affaire* – you'll see."

"Why did she have an *affaire* with Tallien then, if he's so awful?"

"If you had to choose between the guillotine and the risk of having a bastard child, which would you choose?"

"The child, of course."

"Well, then."

*

At the end of the week Monsieur Guiart, the distinguished chemist, appeared in the Rue de l'Université. He was accompanied by Etienne Favart, who had recovered from his spurt of ill-temper, and had come, he said, "to hold a watching brief on behalf of his client". Marie received both men with a grace which surprised the master apothecary, who was sufficiently lacking in imagination to believe that he was going to meet the girl whom he had known for years as the child in the background of Fontaine's house, curtseying to him, pulling up a chair for him, pouring wine, and then perching on a stool with her book or her sewing while he and her uncle talked of matters beyond her comprehension.

Instead he encountered a young lady quite at home in a salon of the Faubourg St Germain, chaperoned by the Vicomtesse de Beauharnais, and prepared to listen to, but not to accept, his proposal to rid her of what must surely be a burdensome property.

At first he thought all would be well. Madame de Beauharnais, her head gracefully bent over her embroidery, took no part in the conversation, and the new fashionable Marie had tears in her eyes when he spoke sympathetically of her uncle, and the tragedy of his execution so few days before the Ninth of Thermidor.

"I went to see the place where he is buried, yesterday," said Marie. "The Picpus cemetery, so-called, is nothing but a common pit where those who died in the Place du Trône were tumbled headlong, with nothing to mark their names . . ." It occurred to her, unhappily, that she might have said 'tumbled headless', and the lawyer, who had thought the same thing, spoke very gently.

"That will surely be looked after, Mademoiselle Fontaine."

"I hope so," said Marie.

"But now we must look to the future," the chemist said.

"Yes, tell me about the young man who wants to buy my house and pharmacy."

Monsieur Louis Rocroi, it appeared, was a young pharmacist of great promise who had worked for a time in Monsieur Guiart's own laboratory before he was conscripted into the *Service de Santé*, where his constitution had been seriously undermined. Restored to health, he had married two months ago and recommenced his research into the alkaloid known as morphine, into which Prosper Fontaine had begun some investigations. Had Marie ever heard of this? Marie had.

"How old is he?" asked Marie.

"Twenty-five, and his bride is twenty. She is perfectly prepared to serve in the shop, though she has never done anything of the kind before."

"Good of her," said Marie. "Tell me, how can a young couple, the husband at the very start of his career, afford to buy property in the Rue St Honoré?"

"His father-in-law is a man of means – an army contractor, I believe," said Guiart delicately. "He is prepared to lend some money, and so am I. Those premises are absolutely ideal for young Rocroi's purpose, and we believe he has a great future as a research chemist. Such a purchaser would perpetuate your uncle's memory, and even, if you wish, retain the name of Fontaine for the pharmacy."

"Including the invisible asset which is called goodwill," said Marie. "I'm sorry, Monsieur Guiart, but I'm not prepared to sell."

"My dear young lady – "

"I'm not prepared to sell to anybody at today's prices, and see my property sold again five years hence at its real value, when the new owner makes the profit that should be mine. I'll tell you what I *will* do, monsieur. Of course I should have to meet the Rocrois first and decide if they will be suitable tenants. Because I want to rent the house furnished, except for my uncle's books and some of our good glass and china, which Madame de Beauharnais will let me store here. The equipment of the pharmacy and the laboratory would be included, with all the supplies in the store room. I would grant a lease of three years from the first of October, the rent to be paid quarterly in advance to Maître Favart's office: does that sound suitable?"

Clever girl to include the furniture, thought the lawyer appreciatively. If she wants to put them out at the end of three years, they can't claim that they're 'in their woods', as the usual plea runs. He saw that Monsieur Guiart was speechless, and asked Marie what rent she had in mind.

She named a sum so large that Joséphine lifted her head sharply and the chemist cried out in protest.

"That's exorbitant, Marie – Mademoiselle Fontaine!"

"I don't think so. It's what my uncle would want me to require, I'm sure."

"Monsieur Rocroi's father-in-law would never agree."

"He only has to be a little bit cleverer with the army contracts. As for yourself . . ." Marie paused to choose her words. "There's one condition on which I might reduce the rent."

"What is that?"

"That you take me into your own laboratory and teach me advanced pharmacology."

"You know that's quite impossible."

"Why?"

"I've no time to teach young women, and my research assistants would never share the laboratory with a girl."

"You know I helped my uncle with his preparations after Michel died."

"Making carminative pills and herbal salves, that was all! My dear child, I do beg you to put this foolish idea out of your head. There may be women apothecaries in the next century, but not now. When you are married, which I hope will be soon, and have a home and a husband to look after, and some – "

"Spare me the rest," said Marie, rising. "I'm sorry you can't accept my offer, *cher monsieur*. In that case, the rental stands."

Favart noted that Monsieur Guiart, indignant and red-faced, did not withdraw immediately from the aborted negotiations. Muttering words like 'consultation' and 'preposterous' he took his leave of the two women, while Favart, with his eyes on Marie, was equally incoherent but silent in his appraisal. Beautiful, wrong-headed, strong-minded, aggressive – but what a wife for an ambitious man!

When Agathe showed the visitors out and they heard the front door close, Joséphine turned to Marie. "How well you spoke, darling!" she said. "I never heard any woman speak so clearly. But whatever put the idea of being an apothecary into your head? That old man was right – it isn't work for a woman."

"So you're on their side," said Marie wearily. "I *like* pharmacology. I *want* to do something more useful than sewing shirts for soldiers! But now we know: the Republic One and Indivisible is run by and for men. Women can get drunk and dance in the streets, or they can bear bastards to save themselves from the guillotine, but that's all. *Vogue la galère*: let's take a leaf out of Teresa's book. Let's go dancing!"

Marie Fontaine danced, for the first time in her life, in what had been successively a royal palace, a prison, and the home of some of the New Men who had saved the Republic by executing Robespierre. The occasion was the housewarming party of the Talliens, shortly after the October day when Louis Rocroi and Marie, in Maître Favart's office, signed the documents which gave the young man a three years' lease of the Fontaine premises. His father-in-law and Monsieur Guiart were his guarantors, and the first quarter's rental, paid on the spot, met the price named by Marie.

So the girl had a light heart as she dressed for her first ball in a thin gown of lilac which the dressmaker assured her rated as half-mourning. A narrow silver ribbon was tied beneath her breasts, and another was the fillet holding her bright hair low upon her brow. "Too *much* hair," said Agathe, struggling with the ringlets, "it's a shame to cut it, but long hair is out, and it would suit you cropped."

"Madame de Beauharnais still wears hers in a chignon."

"Madame is much older than you. Ask the hairdresser's advice next time he comes."

The dance was held in the grand salon of the suite occupied by the Talliens, and Teresa, greeting her guests, was obviously in her element. She had risen from childbed refreshed and slender, long before the conventional month in seclusion was up, and the intrusive baby had been handed over to a wet-nurse, the wife of a market gardener at Courbevoie. "Quite near," said the 'god-mother', presenting the infant with a coral and bells. "You'll be able to go and see her often." But Teresa was too busy to go much to Courbevoie. She had a new home to organise and furnish.

The furniture, carpets, pictures and curtains had come from the government warehouses where the loot from pillaged houses was stored, and Teresa, having an early choice, had done wonders in assorting colours and fabrics. She pouted that Barras, who had chosen an even bigger apartment, had selected some of the best furniture and she was sure his rooms would look like a jumble sale. The guests reassured her: her taste was perfect. Assembled for the Grand March to the sound of music these guests, 'whom nobody has ever seen before' represented the new Paris society which Teresa aspired to lead, and in that crowd of strangers Marie despaired of finding a partner until Citizen Reubell, one of the guests at Joséphine's *soirée*, invited her to join the Grand March and dance the first dance with him.

Dancing, at the end of 1794, was a pleasure renewed, but it was an art in limbo between two moods. The minuet, so much in favour under the old régime, was out never to return, while the waltz had not yet begun its mad career across Europe. This resulted in a go-as-you-please style of dancing, body touching body and breaking away to whirl and pirouette, change partners and swing, while the beat of the music held more than a hint of the *carmagnole*.

Citizen Reubell was a good dancer. He piloted Marie skilfully through the crowd, and she, after the first stumbling steps, discovered that she had a sense of rhythm. Others were aware of it too, and after the first dance was over she was besieged by half a dozen strangers who had no time for formal introductions but begged for the favour of a dance with the pretty girl who danced so well. After that the evening was a whirl of strong hands and nimble feet, of glasses of champagne between dances, of young men in fancy waistcoats and astonishing cravats who called her *chérie* instead of mademoiselle, and music which never seemed to stop.

"You were a great success, Marie," said Joséphine when they were in the hired cab on the way home. "You danced every dance."

"Did I? I suppose I did," said Marie from a champagne haze. "It was lovely! And didn't Teresa look superb? Those barbaric colours suit her so well."

"I thought she looked like a Circassian slave girl," said Joséphine, tired and peevish.

"Whatever they look like," giggled Marie.

"The de Monniers have invited us to a party at Frascati's on Thursday night."

"Wonderful!"

Frascati's was the top place for the New People. Opened since Thermidor on the Rue de la Loi near the Opéra, it boasted that great novelty, an ice cream terrace, and opera-goers soon formed the habit of dropping in for ice cream after the theatre closed. It was at the corner of one of the boulevards laid out along the line of the old fortifications which marked the urban limits of Paris until the time of Louis XIV, and on the boulevards too new places of entertainment had sprung up. Garchi was the great rival of Frascati, offering firework shows outside his café and terrace, and the restaurants of the Palais Royal, opened by former chefs of the *aristos*, took on a new lease of life. Serious gourmets went to Méot's for suppers *à l'orientale*, but everywhere it became the custom to dine or sup in public. Why not, since there was so little to buy in the shops?

For the young there was always dancing, and from ten o'clock until far into the night they danced. Girls like Marie Fontaine grew accustomed to dancing every night, dancing with strangers, dodging or accepting a kiss on the neck or the cheek, dodging or accepting the whispered plea for *"un tout petit moment* – just half an hour alone with you!" Most of the new dance halls had private rooms where the dancers could proceed to further intimacies if they wished. It was debauched, it was lively, it was the absolutely natural reaction to the Terror and the fear of death.

Marie liked to sleep until ten in the morning and spend the rest of the time until luncheon with the dressmakers, the hairdressers and the manicurists who flocked to the residence of Madame de Beauharnais. In the afternoon she always helped Joséphine to compose her begging letters, sometimes even writing them in the copperplate hand which was one thing Prosper Fontaine had taught his niece thoroughly. In the name of her orphan children there was nothing Joséphine would not ask, and yet she obviously was no longer short of money. Her debt to Mademoiselle de Lannoy was paid in full, and the tearful governess assisted to join a sister at Asnières when Hortense was sent to boarding-school. Eugène was thriving with General Hoche, and only complained that 'they' wouldn't let him go too near the front. The front in La Vendée was fluid, for the Vendéens were fighting for God and their little king in the Temple prison, and Hoche had to burn and kill his way through mobs of peasants armed with scythes and reaping hooks.

Marie helped as much as she could, but the real helper was Citizen Paul Barras. It was remarkable that a man with such a load of responsibility could leave the Convention every afternoon to call on Madame de Beauharnais.

He never stayed very long nor went further than the salon, but there was an unexpressed intimacy in the hum of conversation and Joséphine's low laughter, and Marie went quietly to her own room at five o'clock and stayed there until she heard the carriage drive away. It was her time for reading her uncle's books, sent over from the Rue St Honoré. She found them heavy going, for she had never been taught to read systematically, but she absorbed the ideas of Voltaire, Diderot and Rousseau in a general way. These were the intellectual foundations of the Revolution, the liberal and pacifist opinions which had motivated Prosper Fontaine's fantasy of world peace, and Marie sometimes reflected that the liberal thinkers had died quietly in their beds while the next generation died by the guillotine.

The readings did not last long, and always ended when Marie heard Joséphine going softly to her bedroom. She went to her dressing table after Barras's visits, perhaps to brush disordered hair or redden her lips before she joined Marie. Then they sat gossiping by candlelight, while Joséphine described some new helpful suggestion made by 'Paul', until it was time to dress for the gaieties of the evening.

The wonder was that half the society women of Paris were not dead of pneumonia by the beginning of what turned out to be a very bitter winter, as bad as the winter of 1788 which preceded the Revolution. The fashionable dress was neo-Grecian, skimpy and clinging so as to stop just short of nudity, and the footwear was thin sandals tied with ribbon at the ankles, which were sometimes embellished with gilt anklets. Teresa Tallien, who wore no underclothes except the tight fleshings of the circus, rouged her nipples and wore a jewelled brooch suggestively placed between her thighs. The young women who followed her example, although few went so far, became known as *les merveilleuses* and their escorts as *les incroyables*, effete young men with an affected lisp and elaborate coiffures who, like the *jeunesse dorée* but far less aggressive, seemed to have appeared from nowhere.

Marie Fontaine was a *merveilleuse*. Her height and her really beautiful complexion earned her the title, and though her dresses were not so *outré* as some she was conspicuous for the variety of arrangements of artificial flowers and feathers she wore in her cropped hair. Agathe had been right, the style suited her, and could be dressed with far less trouble by the use of curling irons. The bright tendrils, waving round the Grecian fillet, were the envy of women whose mousy locks had not responded well to dyeing.

She had no *incroyable* as her escort – indeed she seemed to look down on the limp-wristed fraternity – but danced happily with many partners, and the man most regularly seen in her company was a one-armed lawyer who appeared at Frascati's twice a week. He did not dance, but seemed delighted to take a few turns through the overheated rooms with Marie and later to escort her home with Joséphine. One day he invited them to luncheon in his bachelor apartment in the Rue Royale, round the corner from his *étude* in the Place Vendôme. The luncheon, sent in by a *traiteur* and served by his manservant in white gloves, was excellent; the company, regrettably, was dull.

The other guests were two men who had been in law school with Favart, and their monosyllabic wives, with a lieutenant of Hussars who had served with him in Jourdan's army. Lieutenant Lacombe and Joséphine saved the day, for he was an agreeable rattle with a talent for mimicry, and she played up to him with her grace and wit, so that 'this poor Favart' should not think his entertainment was a failure. She had a shrewd idea that it had been got up to show Marie Fontaine the comfort and solidity of his background. Etienne Favart was an orphan, whose parents had bought the apartment when they married in 1758, and all the furniture was pure Louis XV, the pictures by Boucher and Fragonard. It was hard to tell if Marie had been impressed or not.

The most striking example of Barras's helpfulness arrived about this time. When General Alexandre de Beauharnais was dismissed from the Army of the Rhine he left Strasbourg so suddenly that he left behind him his carriage and horses. He also left without Eugène, of whom he then had custody, but that self-reliant little boy made his way to other relatives and eventually to his mother. It was the carriage and horses of which Madame de Beauharnais now asked restitution. Citizen Barras took the matter up, and one day a magnificent equipage with painted panels, drawn by two black horses, arrived in front of 371 Rue de l'Université.

"But what on earth are you going to do about stabling?" asked Marie when the first excitement was over.

"Oh, Paul has arranged all that," said Joséphine. "You know the Hôtel de Mouchy, further down the street? It's still National Property and standing empty, so there's room for several carriages in the stables, and beds for the coachmen too. Joseph – that's this man's name – will come for his orders every morning at ten and take me wherever I want to go. Won't it be fun, Marie? No more walking in the mud, or waiting for a draughty cab outside the theatre! Get your coat and let's go driving now!"

So the Hôtel de Mouchy, which had given shelter to the unhappy Noailles ladies, now sheltered the horseflesh of the New People! Marie did not dwell on the thought. It was too exhilarating to be sitting beside her friend in a well-swung carriage, open although the day was cold, with the blacks responding to the slightest touch of Joseph's whip, and people on the street staring as they went by. They drove along the Left Bank of the Seine as far as the Tournelle bridge, crossed it and came back by the Right Bank to the Pont Royal, where there were still a few leaves left on the great poplar tree.

The sight of the river must have given Joséphine a new idea, for she began to talk about the house for which she was still paying rent at Croissy-sur-Seine. "I know I ought to go and look at it," she said, "but I simply couldn't face the coach when the coach service began again. With my own carriage it'll be easy. Paul wants to see the place, and he'll tell me what to do; why don't we make up a party, and organise a daytime picnic at Croissy-sur-Seine?"

"In a *closed* carriage, please," said Marie, and Joséphine laughed. There came a few days of St Martin's summer when a trip to the country was not impossible, and after Joséphine had driven alone to St Germain to see her little girl at school the picnic was arranged. Madame Campan, who owned the school and was also Joséphine's landlady at Croissy, reassured her by saying she had visited the villa recently and found it had suffered no damage from wind or weather during the nine months since Joséphine went back to Paris.

"Does Madame Campan know Anne de Beaupré?" asked Marie.

"Yes, of course, she saw her when she was at Croissy. Poor Anne! She's worried to death about her son."

"I hope we can see her when we go down there."

"Certainly! I'll ask her to lunch."

Joséphine was right to dread the lumbering coach service which had recently been reinstated along the Seine valley, but she had no fear of it for Agathe, who was despatched on the day before the 'picnic' to light fires in the little house and clean the neglected rooms. The picnickers made quite an imposing procession as they swept through the Gate of the Star with Barras in the lead, to whom the guards took off their hats, driving the Talliens. Teresa, for a day in the country, was dressed *à la sauvage*, the savagery being expressed by a wool dress instead of chiffon but split up both sides to the thigh, and by the absence of paint on her toe-nails. In her own carriage Joséphine took Marie and Etienne Favart, in return for his hospitality, and the rear was brought up by the de Monniers, invited at the last moment. They were driving an English tilbury, the last word in fashion.

233

It was a day of chilly sunlight and leafless trees. The land was lying empty and idle, and the few peasants they passed looked as hungry as in the days of the famine which helped to bring down the monarchy. In one or two hamlets there was a withered poplar tree in the middle of the square, and the windows of the churches were boarded up. Croissy-sur-Seine looked prosperous by contrast. There was smoke coming from the chimneys of all the little villas, and the sign 'National Property' was nowhere to be seen. There was one shop, and even a post house where the Tricolore was flying, and where, said Joséphine as she alighted, she had been issued with a certificate of good citizenship.

"Much good it did me in the Carmes," she said lightly. "Come in, all of you, and be the welcome guests."

The view across the Seine was charming, but the best thing about the villa was the roaring fire which Agathe had lit in the living room, and the sight of the set table. Not set enough to please the hostess, for when Agathe had gone out to carry in the provender Barras had brought in his carriage, and Etienne was bringing in the bottles, Joséphine drew Marie aside as she took off her hat, and whispered, "I didn't allow for the de Monniers, and there aren't enough plates and things to go round. Run to Anne de Beaupré's, it's the villa next door, and ask her to lunch, then ask her to lend you what I need. I'll send Agathe after you with a basket. Oh, and give Anne my love."

"Of course." Their old friend of the Carmes prison was quietly happy to see Marie. There was no fire in her parlour and she was wearing a heavy shawl; Marie thought she looked pale and ill and aged since the prison days. She smiled when Marie gave Joséphine's love and invitation to lunch, and positively laughed when she heard the rest.

"I knew when I saw the vehicles draw up that I'd be asked to lend something," she said. "It used to happen all the time. No, dear Marie, I won't come to lunch. I'm not good company for anyone just now."

"You're worried about your son, aren't you?"

"When I got out of prison there was a letter here, but it was written as far back as June. He was in Verona then with the late king's brother, the Comte de Provence, but who knows where he is now?"

"But there's no fighting in Italy, Anne. He's perfectly safe in Verona."

"If he went to Ghent, to the Army of the Princes, then my Raimond is in mortal danger. I pray for him day and night, but I don't believe I shall ever see my boy again."

Marie kissed her friend and tried to comfort her, but it was almost a relief when Agathe appeared, and with the air of one who had done this many times before loaded two place settings of glass and china into a raffia basket and hurried off.

"You know, Marie," said Madame de Beaupré, "you were right to choose Joséphine instead of me, because this is no place for a bright young girl. Luxury suits you, and do you know how lovely you've become? When I think of you in the Carmes prison . . ."

She looked at the tall girl affectionately. Marie had bought a winter coat of fine dark green cloth, cut like a man's riding coat with three little shoulder capes, above which her curled head rose like a bright flower. Madame de Beaupré kissed her and blessed her, and told her to hurry back to where her friends were waiting.

Another sad heart, another grief! Marie flung herself into the preparations for the impromptu lunch, cutting bread, setting out a kilo of butter from Normandy, and helping Agathe to start the coffee in the tiny kitchen. They were all ready for the good things Barras had brought: a jellied tongue, a couple of roast chickens, a salad, a circle of Brie cheese, and the reversed apple pie called a *tarte tatin*. "Simple country fare, my friends," he said as the shouts of appreciation arose. "You shall have something more *raffiné* when I move into the Luxembourg."

Although much was said about the virtue of fresh air

and the beauty of the countryside, no one wanted to experience them directly, and after lunch six of the company, all inveterate gamblers, proposed a game of cards. Etienne Favart, having received an encouraging nod from Madame de Beauharnais, said to Marie, "I know you're not afraid of a chilly day, mademoiselle. Will you come for a stroll with me beside the river? We mustn't spend all the time indoors."

"I'd like to." He helped her into the green coat, and they started off down the garden where no flowers grew, across a pasture to the Seine. It was narrow here, and calm, with a few dead leaves floating on the surface; they paced along the towing path and watched the water.

"I can't believe this is the Seine that flows through Paris," said Marie. "It's like a little village river here."

"Same old Seine."

"Yes."

She knew what was coming, and stood still, passive, while Etienne kissed her hand, and in set phrases surely culled from some *Letter Book for Lovers* asked her to become his wife.

She felt she should reply in words equally grandiose, like "Sir, I am highly sensible of the honour you have done me . . ." but what she did say was, "I thank you, Etienne, very much. But it wouldn't do. I'm sorry, but it wouldn't."

"Marie, why? We could have such a good life together – "

"Etienne, you are a good man, and you'll make some girl very happy. But it won't – it can't be me."

He touched his empty sleeve with his left hand. "Does this disgust you?"

"Oh," she said in swift distress, "how can you say such a thing? It doesn't disgust me, and it honours you. But I don't want to be married . . . at least, not yet."

He seized on this. "I spoke too soon," he said. "Give me leave to hope, and wait, and try again. You're not

236

much more than a child still, for all your ordeal; I don't believe you know what you really want."

Marie stared at the darkening river. Oh yes, I do, she thought. I've known for a long time what I want. But I don't know if I'm ever going to get it.

18

As the claw of winter tightened its grip on France a murmur of protest began to arise from the people. The death of Robespierre and the collapse of the Commune had not filled their stomachs, and the poor were still huddled in garrets and cellars while the mansions of dead *aristos* stood empty. The protests got no further than Section level, for the Sections were now dominated by the Right, but they were there, a hidden groundswell under the euphoria of Thermidor.

A new wave of punishment was a welcome distraction from hunger and cold. The guillotine in the Place de la Révolution was brought back into service, and some of the commissioners who had taken the Terror to the provinces were among the first to die. The most popular death, to judge by the howls of execration and insult which filled the square, was that of Carrier, who had supplemented the guillotine by the drownings of the Loire. He was executed on 16 November, and Marie Fontaine, reading the account in next day's *Moniteur*, remembered how Carrier had tortured the poor man who sheltered Adam Boone, and extorted the name of the Pharmacie Fontaine before his victim died. It was no thanks to Carrier that she was alive today!

One by one the former commissioners mounted the scaffold. Collot d'Herbois, the cannoneer of Lyon, got off with the sentence of transportation to the penal colony of Guiana, but Le Bon, a renegade priest who had terrorised the populations of Arras and the north, died like Carrier, screaming. The irony of the fact that these sentences were approved by Barras and Tallien, the commissioners responsible for hundreds of deaths in Toulon and Bordeaux, seemed to escape popular attention.

In the Convention these two men were being hard pressed by the Girondins who had escaped Robespierre's purge by hiding, and who now returned as Deputies seeking vengeance on their old enemies of the Mountain. A number of Montagnards were sent to the guillotine, and the knitting women, back in their usual places, told each other, as the heads fell, that it was quite like old times. So the National Circus played to a crowded house in the Place de la Révolution, but the Bread supposed to accompany Circuses was in short supply.

For three days after the picnic at Croissy Barras was too busy in the Committee to pay his afternoon visits to Madame de Beauharnais, but when he reappeared he was categorical in his advice: the villa by the Seine should be given up at once. The November rent had been paid? Good. Now Joséphine must write to Madame Campan and give up the lease. The villa was all very fine while the children lived at home; they had freedom and fresh air in the country, but things were different now, and their mother's place was in Paris.

"But what am I going to do?" wailed Joséphine when the man had gone. "I've got clothes at the villa – and the children's things – and some books of Alexandre's which Eugène will want to keep. Really, men are thoughtless! If Paul had spoken out while we were at Croissy, I could have brought everything back in the carriage!"

"He didn't want to spoil the picnic," suggested Marie. "Is there a lot of stuff?"

"As much as would fill a trunk."

"Then if that's all, why don't I go down and pack it up for you, and arrange with the people at the post house to send the trunk to Paris?"

239

"But then you'd have to stay for at least one night, and I can't let you have the carriage. There's no decent stabling at Croissy."

"Not even at the post house? Never mind. Agathe said the coach wasn't too bad, so I'll take the coach there and back."

"But you can't do it all in a day, and you can't sleep at the villa, the beds are damp."

"I'll write and propose myself to Anne de Beaupré, and stay with her."

"You'd like that, wouldn't you?"

"Yes, I should. I feel guilty about Anne – "

"Why?"

"Because I don't think we were very nice to her that day. We borrowed her things, but we never went back to talk to her, and she was so sad and lonely . . . I certainly meant to go, but the horses couldn't be kept waiting, and so much else was going on . . ."

"You may well say so," snapped Joséphine. The two women had had their first quarrel when they came back from Croissy. The drive home with Favart and Marie in her own carriage had been one long embarrassment for Joséphine. The stilted conversation of the couple, the many silences, and their avoidance of each other's eyes were so marked that only a fool would have failed to know that there had been a crisis of some sort between the pair. Joséphine was far from being a fool. She had given Favart a chance to propose to Marie; had he taken it? And she had said No? Then *she* was a little fool, where did she think a girl like herself, out of an apothecary's shop, would get a better husband? A man of substance, with a good home and an assured career? Joséphine was bitterly disappointed in Marie Fontaine.

Marie stood proudly silent during this tirade. When Joséphine ran out of breath she said only that her marriage was her own business and none of Joséphine's, and went to bed. The subject of Favart was not renewed next day, but it was in the air between them, and was the reason why Marie's offer to go back to Croissy was agreeable to them both. They needed a little time away from one another.

The stage coach was lumbering and uncomfortable, but not crowded, for few people had business in the Seine valley on a freezing November day. None of her fellow-passengers said more than *bonjour* to a girl travelling alone, and the coach set her down in Croissy as it was beginning to grow dark. Anne's welcome was prompt and satisfying.

"Come in, come in, Marie dear! What a nice surprise to get your letter, and have you all to myself with time for good long talks! Take your coat off and come sit by the fire – you're frozen!"

"*Café au lait* and cake – how lovely, Anne!"

The steaming bowl of coffee, which Madame de Beaupré had already prepared, was exactly what Marie needed. For a moment she felt like a child again, warming herself at the kitchen fire and drinking a hot drink made by her Uncle Prosper. She smiled tremulously as her hostess spoke of Joséphine ("So she's giving up the villa? Very sensible. She never fitted in at Croissy") and asked what was the latest news from Paris.

"There was a big riot yesterday, but luckily it didn't spread. The *jeunesse dorée*, or the *muscadins* as their opponents call them, smashed up the Jacobin Club and closed it down – for good, they say, but I don't know."

"I wish some of these young hooligans would smash up the Temple, and deliver Madame Royale to her friends," said Anne.

"I'm afraid there's little chance of that."

Marie had not heard anyone speak of Marie-Thérèse de Bourbon, called Madame Royale, since she was in the Carmes prison. Then there had been great lamentation when her aunt Madame Elisabeth, the sister of King Louis XVI, was sent to the guillotine, and the girl of sixteen was all alone in the Temple prison. Her little brother, whom the royalists called their king, was kept apart from her, and said to be in a decline. The New People never talked about the fallen monarchy.

Madame de Beaupré did, and at length. Royalist prospects, royalist plots, brave royalist peasants and fisherfolk fighting in the Vendée, were the subject of her 'good talk', which led inevitably to her own son. No, she had no news of him, but she kept on hoping, and she was saving every *sou* against his return.

"You mustn't deprive yourself, Anne. You'll make yourself ill if you do."

Deprivation was written large in the little villa. The fire was replenished with one log at a time, the evening meal was scanty, and Anne admitted she had no maid – a woman from one of the farms came in to clean once a week. She had sold her jewels long ago – before the prison time, and she was wearing out her old clothes.

"If only your husband were alive to look after you," said Marie.

"He would be with the Army of the Princes too, like Raimond. Oh, how I regret his decision to leave Canada! I was just a girl then, newly married and eager to see France; I didn't object. But even if we couldn't keep Beaupré, we might have bought a little *seigneurie* somewhere in Quebec, and Raimond would be the *seigneur* now – happy and busy and out of danger's way."

Anne roused herself from a contemplation of the past, and spoke briskly of what must be done tomorrow.

"I'll lend you a big shawl," she said. "Or else you'll get your death in that cold house, and you can't pack in an overcoat. Come back for lunch at twelve, and then try to finish before the Paris coach comes in, so that you'll have plenty of time at the post house. They can be very difficult, Marie; I wish I could help you there, but I might do more harm than good."

"I never expected you to come with me," said Marie. "But why harm?"

"Because I served a prison sentence, and I'm still an

émigré mother. An object of suspicion to the country folk."

"I thought that was all changed since Thermidor."

"Thermidor doesn't mean much down here. But I'll tell you what I can do, Marie: if you leave the keys with me and the permit from the post office, I'll see that the trunk is picked up and sent to Paris. And if Madame Campan has received notice about the lease, you may believe she'll be here as fast as she can travel from St Germain, to be sure that all's well with her property."

"Thank you so much, Anne. Joséphine will be very grateful to you."

Anne de Beaupré made no comment on that, but suggested they recite the evening prayer.

The Campan villa was bitterly cold next day, and Marie had her work cut out to find and fill the leather trunk in the bedroom, on which a vicomte's coronet had been obliterated with a red hot poker, with all the objects on Joséphine's long list before it was time to walk to the post office. There she found three men still wearing the red cap of liberty and the tricolore cockade, with a shotgun laid suggestively on the desk behind which they sat, and Marie stood, during half an hour's interrogation on her right to despatch Joséphine's effects to Paris. She had to produce her own certificate of good citizenship, a copy of which Favart had procured for her, a letter of authorisation from Madame de Beauharnais, and a sum of money for her own return trip by coach and the expedition of the trunk before, with much grumbling, she was given an inkstained document heavily stamped on behalf of the Republic One and Indivisible by the postmaster and his two deputies. They proceeded forthwith to a stableboy's duties of leading out fresh horses for the coach from Paris, arriving in the next ten minutes.

She and Anne laughed at the local authorities' passion for *la paperasserie*, the paperwork, common to all French petty bureaucrats, and enjoyed a better supper than the night before. One of the farm boys, an accomplished poacher, had sold Anne a rabbit at the back door, and they had rabbit stew with mashed potatoes, with hot chocolate to follow. They retired early, for the coach to Paris left at seven in the morning, and not until the evening prayer was said did Anne send her regards to Joséphine.

"I suppose the Hoche affair is over," she said casually.

"It ended at the prison gates, I think," said Marie. "General Hoche took Eugène on his staff, but Joséphine refused to see him when he came on leave to Paris."

"Poor General Hoche! And has he had no successor?"

"Not so far as I know."

"So much the better. But Marie dear, be careful in that woman's house."

It was pleasant to come out of a foggy November afternoon into the warm and scented atmosphere of 'that woman's house', and pleasanter still to know by Joséphine's kisses and words of thanks that the little cloud between them had disappeared.

"Your face is so cold," murmured Joséphine. "Was it awful, at Croissy? You weren't tempted to stay down there with Sainte Anne de Beaupré?"

Marie drew back. "Of course not," she said. "But please don't make fun of Anne, Joséphine. She's not well, and she's very sad and lonely."

"She ought to come and live in Paris then, and hobnob with her royalist friends."

"She couldn't afford to live in Paris. And she did help me, about sending on your trunk."

"When will it be here?"

"In two or three days, the man said."

"You've done wonders, Marie. And now I've a reward for you, an invitation to a very grand dinner . . ."

"Oh, whose?"

"Paul Barras has finally moved into the Luxembourg. He's going to give a big dinner party there on Thursday night. He's asked me to be his hostess, and of course you're invited too."

"You the hostess at the Luxembourg! Lovely for you, but Teresa Tallien won't be pleased."

"Teresa doesn't own the Luxembourg."

Who did? As the de Beauharnais carriage swept up the Rue de Tournon on Thursday evening Marie thought the palace, until 1789 the residence of the king's brother, the Comte de Provence, still looked like a prison. There were too many sightless windows from which the bars had not been removed, for not all the apartments had been remodelled and fewer were tenanted. The Barras apartment, which included the royal reception rooms, was on two levels, and Joséphine stood beside the host at the top of the grand staircase, setting everyone at ease with her indescribable charm of manner. The dining table was spread in the old style, in a room with a vaulted roof longer than the women's cell in the Carmes and three times as broad. Thick tapestry curtains were drawn across the windows, and Barras had commandeered enough Gobelins friezes to cover the rest of the walls. He had also commandeered, or 'acquired', or 'liberated', enough gold plate for a company of twenty-six, with three-tiered épergnes in silver gilt, loaded with fruit and flowers, set between silver gilt game cocks, crouched low and ready for the fray.

When dinner was announced Barras and Joséphine took their places in the centre of the table, opposite each other, with six guests in their best clothes and on their best behaviour seated on either side. The younger people sat at the further ends, and Marie, being on the same side as Barras, had a good view of Joséphine. She was seated in a gilt armchair with a high back like a throne, wearing a new dress of violet velvet and a new headband of brilliants – or could they possibly be diamonds? Marie remembered the wise woman's crazy prediction to the child in Martinique that she would be Queen of France some day.

Whatever the future held for Joséphine, she was the Queen of Paris for a night.

"So you're Marie Fontaine," said her dinner partner. "I've heard a lot about you."

He was a hulking young man in his early twenties, who had been introduced to her briefly as Monsieur Pierre Langlade. He was wearing a conventional black dress coat, of a style coming into fashion, but the cut of his hair gave him away: the plaits at the back were the mark of the *jeunesse dorée*. For further identification he was sporting a fine black eye.

"Have you been fighting, monsieur?" enquired Marie sweetly. The question unloosed a torrent of words. Yes, Monsieur Langlade had been in a fight, a memorable fight, earlier in the week, when he and his comrades had beaten up the Jacobins, and reduced their infamous club room to rubble. Every bit as good as Thermidor! The narrative kept Monsieur Langlade happy for the length of two courses, until he rounded it off by saying unexpectedly: "You're the prettiest girl in the room, do you know that?"

"Flattery will get you nowhere," said Marie flirtatiously. She knew that she was looking her best in an evening gown of clinging white chiffon and her grandmother's seed pearl parure, cleaned by a jeweller. Her hair was restrained by a bronze fillet which matched her curls, and a ribbon of the same colour outlined her breasts.

"It's true, you know," said the hulking youth. "Who's there to touch you? Marie-la-Merveilleuse, the toast of Frascati's! Look at La Tallien – once you've seen all she's got there's no fun in looking twice; look at little de Monnier, ready to sit up and beg like a dog; look at the Beauharnais – now she's got the style, I grant you, but she's an old woman, though my cousin doesn't think so."

"Your cousin?"

"Paul Barras is my mother's cousin, that's why I'm here."

"Really," said Marie. "I thought it might be because of your prowess at the Jacobin Club."

"Smart girl, aren't you?" growled Langlade, and Marie turned to talk to her neighbour on the other side, until presently he recalled himself to her attention by muttering that this dinner party was devilish slow.

"You can't say that of the waiters, at least," said Marie. The waiters, hired through the same chefs as had prepared the stupefyingly elaborate and expensive dinner, were flying up and down the room in an excess of zeal, spilling sauce on bare shoulders and filling glasses over the brim. Marie had been drinking champagne steadily during Langlade's discourse on fighting the Jacobins, and the service having reached the burgundy stage, each guest had a ring of red on the damask cloth beneath his goblet, like spots of blood.

"I still say it's devilish dull," insisted Langlade. "I say, Marie! As soon as they've finished playing at Versailles, let's go to Liliane's and dance."

"I don't know Liliane's."

"New place – just opened in the Palais Royal. You'll like it. Let's get up a party and go!"

Why not? What did it matter? The party *was* dull, even if the chatter was growing louder as the imitation grandeur was stripped away. Her neighbour on the other side was trying to pinch her thigh. One could say this for Langlade, he was very correct, he kept his hands to himself. Teresa Tallien was sulking. She had chosen a pastel-coloured dress which was drained of colour in the candlelight, and she was scowling at the vision in violet velvet in the armchair like a throne. Marie's head was whirling, and the burgundy on top of champagne made her ears buzz. Why not go dancing? The string orchestra Barras had hired was playing classical music, not the dance tunes she loved. When the guests finally rose from table and began strolling about the salons, admiring their decoration, Langlade lost no time in collecting four more young people from the other end of the table, all of whom were eager to go on to Liliane's.

"Madame de Beauharnais, may I present Monsieur Langlade? He wants me to go dancing with his friends."

"Off to the boulevard, you naughty girl?" said Joséphine. "Wrap up well in your *sortie de bal* and don't catch cold. Bring her safely home, monsieur."

"I will, madame. *Mes hommages.*"

Marie's *sortie de bal* was an evening cloak of red velvet, with a *capuchon* which, as she disarranged her hair by slipping it on, made her think of Red Riding Hood. Who called her Red Riding Hood, centuries ago? She found herself laughing aloud as she remembered Sergeant Vautour. She was in a cab with straw on the floor, and Langlade's powerful arms were round her, ready to help her down at the door of Liliane's. The dance hall was exactly opposite the place where Citizeness Merlot had terrorised the sempstresses until the day of her arrest.

Liliane's was – what was the word – *louche*, and not very clean, but the band was magnificent and Langlade a splendid dancer. He nearly swept her off her feet twice, and then he laughed and said, "Steady now!" as if it was all her fault. She danced with other men, she drank some brandy and choked on it, she was dancing with Langlade again and he was nuzzling her ear.

"Let's be alone, Marie. Let's be tremendously alone!"

"Alone, where?"

"Here." He pulled her into a doorway that seemed to open of itself, and gave on to a little room painted a sickly shade of blue. There was a couch with a stained blue spread on it, a couple of chairs, and the usual furnishing of a *cabinet particulier* – a table set with a roast chicken and a bottle of champagne.

"You can't want to eat more after that huge dinner," Marie heard herself say. Langlade seized her in his arms. "No, I don't want to eat," he said thickly. "I want to make love to you." He kissd her passionately. His mouth tasted of brandy; so did hers.

248

Je voudrais faire l'amour avec toi, je voudrais te baiser. The sense of what he was saying came through Marie's whirling brain, and she pushed him away so violently that he almost fell.

"Get away from me," she stammered. "You're horrible . . . I want to go home."

He lunged out to take her in his arms again, and Marie struck him in the face.

"*Garce!*" he said with his hand to his cheek. "*Allumeuse!* You led me on!"

"You lie."

"Don't try to play the little *Sainte-N'y-Touche* with me, *espèce de grue!* Everybody in Paris knows what you are – "

He was forcing her back against the supper table, his heavy shoulders pressing her down to the couch. Marie reached out and seized the carving knife lying on the table.

"If you don't let me go I'll kill you," she said clearly.

The hero of the Jacobin upheaval should have been able to wrest the knife from a girl's hand. The bully moved back, intimidated by the Fury he had aroused.

"Go, then," he said, "I can buy a whore anywhere."

"Is that what you think I am?" Marie was icily sober now, and the knife was steady in her hand.

"You're the girl who covers up for Madame Joséphine. The little lamb who whitewashes her – as if all Paris didn't know she's Barras's mistress!"

The dancing was so wild at Liliane's that no one paid any attention to the opening door of a *cabinet particulier*, nor the girl who sent a knife spinning across the floor before she ran to claim her coat and throw herself into one of the cabs waiting for custom. The driver was an old man and his horse an old horse; during the slow jolting ride in the night air Marie's head cleared of the fumes of wine. She was able to speak quite naturally to Agathe when the maid opened the door.

"Please pay the man, Agathe. He brought me from the Palais Royal."

"Alone, mademoiselle? Madame hasn't come home yet."

"Say goodnight for me when she does. I'm tired, I'm going straight to bed."

"Shall I help you to undress, mademoiselle?"

"No thank you, that isn't necessary."

She caught Agathe's smile of complicity, and was thankful when she was alone that she had not even allowed the woman to remove her cloak, for the marks of heavy fingers could be seen on her bare right arm and her girdle was undone. She made the briefest possible preparations for bed. As soon as she blew the candle out, the pretty flowered *toile de Jouy* became the sickly blue-painted walls of Liliane's, and the sharp knife was back in Marie's hand.

Would I really have done it? If he had thrust himself upon me again would I have tried to kill him, stabbing true and straight until he lay writhing on the floor? Now Marie Fontaine for the first time understood the Revolution, the anger of a people, the lust for vengeance on a despotic power. She hid her face in the pillow, too distraught for tears.

What a hypocrite I am! Only a few nights ago reciting the evening prayer with Anne de Beaupré, in that humble room with the Crucifix on the wall, and last night dancing at Liliane's, drunk on champagne and inviting humiliation! *Garce, allumeuse, grue* were not words she had ever expected to be flung at herself.

'Everybody in Paris knew' – it was a lie, of course. How could everybody think of Marie Fontaine as the screen for the loves of Joséphine de Beauharnais, whom Barras himself had showed off to the leaders of his world, and made his gracious Creole the Queen of Paris.

Part Four

1795

19

The restored coach service from Toulon was well up to time on its forty-mile trip to Marseille on a certain day in January (or Nivôse) 1795, and when the clumsy vehicle reached the post house in the Vieux Port the first passenger to descend was a small man in a grey military overcoat. Four women waiting on the cobbles at once enveloped him in a collective embrace, a tangle of shawls and slender arms, and called him by the Corsican name of his childhood, "Nabulione! Nabulione!"

Napoleon Buonaparte kissed his three sisters, kissed his mother's cheek and kissed her hand with the deference he always paid her. Madame Letizia Buonaparte was the only woman he never dismissed as *le repos du guerrier*, the warrior's rest, for she had been a warrior herself, a guerrilla fighter with Paoli in the maquis of Corsica when she was pregnant with her second son, Nabulione. She was taller than he was, with broad shoulders and a harsh, handsome face, and in her middle forties there was not one grey hair in her black head. "My son, my dear son!" she kept repeating. "How glad I am to see you!"

It was not very far to the decent lodging he had found for them, and the three girls chattered all the way, while Madame Letizia clung to her son's arm. Napoleon told the girls that they had grown – "grown prettier, too," he added genially, noting that the youngest, Pauline, had turned into an authentic beauty who exchanged languishing glances with every handsome fisher boy who passed. The rented apartment had been tidied up for his visit, but it was full of the overspill of family living, like any place inhabited by three lively girls and visited by three young brothers. After eighteen months in barracks and billets, Napoleon found the family atmosphere immensely satisfying.

"And what do you girls think of your new sister-in-law, Madame Julie?" he asked when he had wolfed down the meal prepared for him and they were all seated at the round table.

"She's a nice little thing . . ."

"I always liked Julie Clary . . ."

"Joseph's quite foolish about her . . ."

"Are they living with her people now?" asked Buonaparte.

"They're on a visit to her aunt in the country, but they'll be back in a day or two."

"That's good. I should be sorry to miss Joseph."

"How long can you stay with us?" said the mother anxiously.

"I must be back in Toulon a week from today. I was made to feel it was a special favour to get seven days' leave."

"Are they so busy in the dockyard?"

"They will be when I get back. There's two months' hard work ahead for everybody, that's why I was determined to come and see you now."

"You're a dear, sweet brother!" cried Pauline insincerely, jumping up to kiss him again.

"Sit down, Paolina, and behave yourself. You won't think me so sweet when I tell you what I've come for – to take you all with me when I go back to Toulon, and to put you under safe conduct when you journey on to Antibes."

"Antibes!"

"Yes, to the house waiting for you there. You girls must make up your mind to it, Marseille is no place for your mother or you either, and I want to be sure that you're in

254

a clean decent town, as far away from the Vieux Port as you can get."

He paid no attention to the storm of protest, but when his eldest sister asked, "What about my wedding?" he answered her,

"Elisa, if you and Bacchiocci want to marry, you can be married as easily at Antibes as here. Think of your mother for a change, and don't be selfish."

"I'm not selfish!"

Buonaparte got up: he was in no mood for quarrelling and tears. "Listen," he said, "you'd better start planning the removal. Write an appreciation on one sheet of paper and let me see it when I come back. I'm going out for an hour or so before it gets dark."

"Where are you going, my son?" asked Madame Letizia.

"I think Joseph would like me to drop in at the Clarys, as a courtesy."

This sent his temperamental sisters off into more giggles, and to whispers of "Joseph, indeed," and "Désirée!" the little general took up his cocked hat and left the house.

It was several hours before he returned, and as he had hoped his mother was alone. Not sewing, or knitting, but sitting with folded hands in front of the little stove, and waiting for him.

"I'm late," he said. "Were you getting worried? Did you think some wharf rat had pushed me into the harbour?"

"I'd be sorry for any rat who tried. I was beginning to wonder what was keeping you at the Clarys."

"Madame Clary insisted that I stay for dinner."

"Very civil."

"More civil than Monsieur Clary. He made it clear that *two* Corsican sons-in-law was more than any Marseille bourgeois could be expected to stand."

"Did you propose to become his son-in-law?"

"No."

"And Mademoiselle Désirée?"

"She seemed pleased to see me."

Napoleon's stern face was set, and his mother knew

she would get no more out of him on the subject of Désirée Clary. She said, "The girls have gone to bed exhausted. Your military order about an appreciation on one sheet of paper was too much for them . . . Don't be too strict with your sisters, Nabulione. They're good girls at heart, and they really are willing – now – to go to Antibes."

"I worry about them. And about the boys. Lucien's a clever fellow, he'll get on in Paris, but the other two – " He raised his hand and let it fall in an expressive gesture.

"You're a good brother to them all. It's strange, Joseph has been the head of the family since your father died, but you're the one who really cares for us."

"I only wish I were able to do more for you. But mother – things haven't turned out as I thought they would, a year ago."

Madame Letizia looked at him sadly. "You're disappointed about Toulon, aren't you?"

"It's a very, very difficult position. I've had one row with the Port Admiral already, and I'm sure there'll be more. The Navy men resent me, and my God! why shouldn't they? A land officer put in charge of naval artillery is an upstart to them, and they mean to make me feel it. Meantime Kellermann is given the command of the Army of Italy, which is inactive, and Pichegru, with seventy thousand men, liberates Holland and is revelling tonight in Amsterdam . . ."

His mother held out her arms to him. "There'll be revels in Toulon when thanks to you the British are driven out of Corsica," she said. "You'll win greater victories than Pichegru or Kellermann. Kiss me, Nabulione. Remember, your mother is proud of you."

Ten days later, when he saw their hired carriage leave for Antibes in an army supply convoy, Napoleon knew that he would miss his mother and sisters more than he had ever done before. That week of simple domesticity in the crowded, happy-go-lucky Marseille apartment had for the first time kindled in him the desire for a home of his own, shared with a woman who loved him and with their children. He knew now that the woman would not be Désirée Clary, and that the romance of Clisson and Eugénie would never be finished. She was too young and unformed, too *bourgeoise*, and where once her coquetry had tantalised him, the general now found it merely embarrassing. He saw her twice more during his seven days' leave, and when she realised that he was cooling off she became pathetically anxious to please. It was an unhappy business. Perhaps his brother Joseph could arrange for her to meet some man who would be a good match for a pretty little girl with a rich father.

After the family apartment where his sisters were always laughing, quarrelling, cooking or singing as loudly as their canaries in the window cages, Buonaparte's quarters in Toulon were quiet and dull. As a general officer he was allotted two rooms in an hotel near the dockyard, one of the few made habitable after the destruction of the year before. They were wind- and water-tight, but no more; a little brazier took the chill off each room, and the furniture was an assortment of tawdry pieces. He spent a good deal of time there when the day's work was done, gobbling the unpalatable food brought to him on a tin tray, and then reading such books on naval strategy and tactics as were made available to him. He was not often invited to dine at the Port Admiral's table nor in the flag officers' mess.

Buonaparte was made to feel that the directive from the Committee of Public Safety appointing him artillery adviser to the Mediterranean Squadron was resented by the Navy, proud of its own officers and its former victories. At first, facilities for visiting the ships of the line in harbour were denied him, for a variety of reasons trumped up by their jealous captains. His complaints brought about the icy intervention of the admiral, who was thirty years older than the young general, and one by one the wooden vessels were towed beyond the tongue of land Major Buonaparte had known so well and out to the open sea. The Mediterranean resounded to the firing of blanks.

The general, trained in target practice and actual combat on land, had some difficulty in adapting himself to the confines of a warship, and to dealing with gunners who opposed a dumb obstructiveness to his innovations. One was the use of red-hot shot, for which he had ordered furnaces to be built during his coastal inspection, and which the British were to condemn as 'devilish unsporting'. The other, in which he was more than a generation ahead of his time, was the practice of simultaneous loading, meaning that the cartridge, wad and shot should be rammed home together for the quicker delivery of the broadside. He cursed the powdermen for being too slow in the race to the magazine, and the magazinemen for 'idling' in the delivery of the ammunition. Their officers protested that they were handicapped by the darkness of a magazine lit only by a horn lantern and covered by curtains of woollen frieze. Buonaparte ignored the protests and weeded out the slower men relentlessly until the race for ammunition became a matter of pride to the fleet of foot and sure of hand.

One of his suggestions which was received with contempt from almost every officer from the admiral down was that the warships of the French Navy were firing at the wrong targets. They concentrated their fire on the enemy's sails and rigging so as to prevent him from manoeuvring, whereas the English fire was concentrated on the hulls and gunports for a greater loss of life. Almost the only officer who agreed with Buonaparte was a gunnery lieutenant in the *Ça Ira*, whose opinion was not asked by his superiors. Lieutenant Plougastel came from Brest, and was still smarting under the defeat of the First of June.

"I know you're right, citizen general," he said. "The British fire into the hulls and gunports was what did for the Brest squadron when they tackled the Channel Fleet. That was clear from the condition of the ships able to limp into port after the action. But you'll never get that old stick-in-the-mud to see it."

They were alone in a wineshop near the dockyard hotel when Plougastel ventured to criticise his commander. He was the only naval officer with whom Buonaparte struck up any sort of friendship, being nearly as lonely as when he was sent at nine years old to learn French and the art of war at Brienne, where his schoolmates either tormented or despised him. An occasional glass of wine with Plougastel was his only recreation, for Toulon was still on a war footing, and sensible men aware of the danger of syphilis avoided the wretched drabs who offered the only female companionship of the dock area. It was better to stay at his desk and write his bi-weekly reports to the Committee of Public Safety, a necessary precaution to forestall the reports sure to be written about himself.

Time passed less tediously at sea, when the general put the gun crews through quick and horizontal firing, first at wooden butts and condemned sloops, wreckage from the year before, and then firing by distance, beginning at a hundred metres and working up to five hundred metres, the exercises punctuated by damning the gun crews for their slovenly use of worm and spike in cleaning the great guns. In the last week of February the admiral, who could never remember if it was Pluviôse or Ventôse, announced his intention of making a complete inspection of each unit of the fleet which was to invade Corsica. Accompanied by the captain of the fleet he went in his barge to every one of the fifteen ships of the line 'worked up' by General Buonaparte. It was a lengthy business, accomplished in two days of vile weather, as the beat of drums followed by one ruffle called each gun crew to exercise. When it was over and they were back on shore he asked the crucial question:

"In your opinion, citizen general, is the battle fleet now ready to attack the enemy?"

"As ready as it will ever be, *Monsieur l'Amiral*."

The ambiguity of the answer was lost on the admiral.

He ordered the fleet to sea on 5 March, the very day on which Carnot, who had held the Army of Italy in reserve for so long, left the Committee of Public Safety. That news would have been cheering to Buonaparte, who stood alone on the harbour wall when the *Marseillaise* was played and the battle flags broken as the imposing fleet put out to sea. He had no feelings about the suffering presumed to be in store for the island of his birth; his chief desire was that the usurper, the viceroy, 'Sir Elliott', otherwise Sir Gilbert Elliott of Minto, would either be taken prisoner or forced to flee to his barbaric Scottish home. Then he went back to his books, to the campaigns of Alexander and the contemplation of his own eastern dream. When he had conquered Egypt he would penetrate as far as Darfur and recruit the blacks of the Sudan to the cause of a new French Empire . . . or failing that, there was always Turkey . . .

The British Mediterranean Squadron, lying off Leghorn, was numerically equal to the French. It consisted of fifteen ships of the line, fourteen being English and one, the *Tancredi*, being Neapolitan. When the patrolling frigates brought the news that the French were out of Toulon the English sailed from Leghorn on 10 March and came up with the enemy a day later. Then the French were fortunate indeed that the English commander was a sailor of the calibre of Admiral Hotham, whose motto in another day and age might have been 'Safety First', an attitude not much to the liking of his most daring captain, Horatio Nelson.

What followed was one of the most inconclusive sea encounters ever to take place between the British and the French. The latter, in spite of their preparedness and their panache, declined to give battle when they saw the force arrayed against them, and Admiral Hotham, when he saw the French in full retreat, decided to risk his ships in a stern chase. 'A stern chase is a long chase,' the naval adage ran, and the two fleets were in contact for three days until the French returned to Toulon on 14 March.

There was only one action in that time, when HMS *Agamemnon*, Captain Horatio Nelson, engaged the *Ça Ira* for two hours, firing broadside after broadside into the hull and gunports of the Frenchman. The *Censeur*, trying to come to the aid of her sister ship, also experienced what was beginning to be called 'the Nelson touch', and Hotham could legitimately claim a victory. Nelson himself wrote to his wife, "England yet remains Mistress of the Seas!"

Lieutenant Plougastel was one of those killed in action in the *Ça Ira*, where the French casualties numbered seven hundred and fifty to *Agamemnon*'s thirteen. Buonaparte heard of his death without emotion, beyond thinking it was bad luck that the one man who understood his theory of direction firing should have died when it was proved right. While Toulon was shattered by the fleet's ignominious return and before the storm of recrimination broke over the whole naval establishment, he had despatched a letter to Paris. He regarded his two months in Toulon as little better than his two weeks of fortress arrest, but now that Carnot, that obstacle to his career, was out of the way he hoped for better things. He wrote to the Committee of Public Safety, asking them to give him a command in the field.

20

After the drama of the Barras banquet and its aftermath, the situation at 371 Rue de l'Université deteriorated rapidly into farce. Overnight, Joséphine was attacked by that enemy of romance, a severe toothache accompanied by nausea and retching, requiring the administration of oil of laudanum by Agathe and the application by Marie of eau de cologne compresses to the agitated head. The sufferer, drifting into a drugged sleep, looked very unlike the vision in violet of the night before. Impossible not to feel pity for her! Towards the middle of the afternoon Joséphine roused herself sufficiently to ask for a hand mirror, and looked long at her damaged mouth.

"Does it show very badly, Marie?"

"It hardly shows at all. Is it still hurting?"

"Not as much as it did last night."

"Last *night*? You mean at the Luxembourg?"

"Yes, but I don't think anybody noticed . . ."

"You looked wonderful."

"I didn't want to let Paul down. Now, Marie darling, will you write one of your nice little notes to Angèle de Monnier, and tell her we can't go to her card party tonight. You don't mind missing it, do you?"

"Of course not."

So the first day passed, and by the afternoon of the second Joséphine was able to lie on the sofa and discuss all the details of the banquet. It was only then that she touched lightly on the subject in both their minds.

"Monsieur Langlade undertook to bring you safely home, Marie. Agathe tells me you came back alone."

"I didn't stay long at Liliane's. It's not a nice place."

"Oh dear. But who were the other young people there?"

"I don't remember any of their names, if I ever heard them." Marie added with a touch of malice, "Of course I knew all Citizen Barras's guests would be very nice people."

"I'm sure they were. But Marie dear, if I'm not with you, I think you should have some married lady as your chaperone – "

"Teresa, for example?"

"Angèle de Monnier would be delighted to look after you."

That was all that was ever to be said about the night at Liliane's. Marie, as her nerves steadied, realised that Pierre Langlade, the terror of the Jacobins, was not likely to make a story out of his defeat at the hands of a woman, while Barras, if he heard of his kinsman's offence, would lose no time in packing him off to fight the royalist rebels in the Vendée.

The dentist came, and repeated his visits: Joséphine refused to appear in public with a badly swollen mouth. Her indisposition put a check on their ceaseless round of gaieties, and soon they had a happy distraction in the arrival of Eugène de Beauharnais on ten days' leave. Hortense was brought from school to see him, and the quiet house echoed with laughter and noisy games, played as if they were still children thinking of nothing but amusement. But they were growing up; Eugène was taller than his mother now, and while he still adored her the old tender deference had become the indulgence of a man towards feminine foibles. The deference was transferred to General Hoche, who could do no wrong.

They tried to get out of him some details of his life in camp, for Hoche was fighting a guerrilla war and had no fixed headquarters. The boy spoke highly of the sergeant who was instructing him in musketry. Certainly he was allowed to carry firearms – didn't *maman* know that papa had taught him how to handle a pistol when they were at Strasbourg? No (reluctantly), he had never yet fired a shot in anger, but that would come next, when General Hoche pursued the traitor Cadoudal into the Quiberon peninsula to the north-west. In the south La Vendée was almost pacified, and Eugène's jaw dropped when his mother told him that as soon as peace was declared he would be sent as a boarder to the Collège Irlandais at St Germain. What! Be a schoolboy again after the great adventure of hunting down *les Chouans*? The rebels took their name from *le chat huant*, the screech-owl, whose wild cry they used to rally their forces, and the brother and sister imitated the screech-owl up and down the apartment with such spirit that their mother sighed even while she called Marie to witness that they were 'only babies still'.

Hortense, at twelve, was not a baby, but a tall girl well on the way to becoming a woman. She had learned to imitate sophistication at Madame Campan's school, and felt qualified to criticise her mother's friends. She snubbed Citizen Barras when he tried to kiss her, and thought the Talliens were the worst kind of *nouveaux riches*. "How *can* you know such people, *maman*?" she asked scornfully, after they had all been at a party in the Talliens' apartment in the Luxembourg which exceeded in vulgar display even the famous Barras banquet. Her mother was angry enough to promise her a whipping if she dared to say such a thing again.

She relented next day, for Joséphine's anger never lasted long, and told Hortense she might be the hostess at a New Year's Eve party for young people if she could demonstrate what good behaviour really was. The result was a gathering of girls from Madame Campan's and adolescent boys sick with envy of Eugène's uniform and army rank who all behaved with such correctness as to recall the days of the old régime. The Beauharnais children, delighted with their success, went their separate ways on 2 January, and on the afternoon of that day another model of correctness, Maître Etienne Favart, called to offer his New Year wishes and bring Marie the next quarter's rent paid by her tenant, Louis Rocroi.

"You have business to discuss, and I ought to leave you," smiled Joséphine. "I ordered the carriage for five o'clock, and I mean to call at the Luxembourg. Dear Teresa is full of a scheme for what she calls 'prison balls'. I can't think what she means, but I'm sure it'll be amusing."

"Do you go to balls every night?" enquired Etienne bluntly when the door closed behind Joséphine. "You must be exhausted if you do."

"Not every night," said Marie. "We had a really wild time here on New Year's Eve. Twelve young people under sixteen played charades and guessing games until half past eight, and Madame de Beauharnais told all their fortunes with the tarot cards. It's too bad you weren't here."

"You enjoy teasing me, Marie."

"Perhaps I do."

He was very good-looking in his earnest square-jawed way, and very well-dressed, with his silk hat and his gold-topped cane laid on the carpet at his feet. He was arrayed for a formal courtship, but he said, "Let's talk about your business," and took a small bundle of papers from his pocket.

"The Rocrois have made a very good beginning," he said. "Prompt payment of the second quarter's rent, and only some minor claims for dilapidations. The damp course in the kitchen you know about, and I'm afraid you're liable (I have the receipts here) for a new gutter in the roof and the repair of the fireplace. On the other hand your tenants have spent money on new wallpaper and paint in the upstairs rooms, and I understand they have great plans for a herb garden. Of course they can do nothing in the yard while this frost holds, but Madame Rocroi is very enthusiastic. I think her husband spends more time in the laboratory than in the shop, but that was understood, wasn't it? And she runs the shop very well. I'm sure you'd be impressed if you cared to call on them."

"They'd probably think I was spying. I'm glad they're doing well, but I don't want to see the Pharmacie Fontaine again until – "

"Until when?"

"Until their lease expires in 1797."

The lawyer said nothing, but laid the receipts and the rent money on a table by Marie's side.

"Thank you, Etienne," she said. 'I'm fortunate in having you to look after my small affairs."

"There is one other affair I'd like to know about. In November, before that day at Croissy, you instructed me to pay a second term of rent to Madame de Beauharnais. The third term is due on 4 February. Am I to pay it? Do you want to go on living here?"

"Oh yes, I think so. Where else could I go?"

It was exactly the opening he had been waiting for. Etienne Favart said, "You could marry me."

He rose to his feet as he said it, and Marie, unsure of herself and him, rose too. He resisted the temptation to draw her close to him. He had rushed his fences at Croissy, it was the time for caution now.

"Marie," said Etienne Favart, and he laid his left hand on her shoulder as he spoke, "you refused me, that day in November, but somehow you gave me leave to hope. I stayed away for six weeks. I've kept away from the places where I used to see you, so lovely, so admired, in the hope that you would miss me a little. Did you?"

With the searing memory of the night at Liliane's upon her, Marie whispered, "Yes."

His hand slipped down from her shoulder, his arm went round her waist. "Darling," he said. "Look up, and tell me one thing. Why are you living your life on such short terms? Three years for your tenants, three months at a time for yourself . . . why can't you take a longer view?"

"You forget," she said, "there was another short term in my life. Four months in the Carmes prison."

"And that's what makes you afraid to commit yourself to the future? It's all over, Marie, *ma pauvre chérie, ma pauvre petite Marie*! Put it all behind you, and be my wife."

He drew her close to him and kissed her. It was not a kiss of passion, but it was an honest kiss, just as his words were honest words, very different from the copy-book phrases of his speeches beside the Seine. Marie shook her head, but she let her cheek rest against his own.

"Is there anyone else?" he asked her roughly.

She could not wound him by saying, "I always dreamed of marrying a soldier." This man had been a soldier too, had lost a limb in the service of his country, and he was a good man, constant in what he felt for her. She answered "No one."

Etienne lost his head a little at that, and began kissing her again, whispering that he would always take care of her, that he was sure bad times were coming again for France but in his home she would be safe from harm. It was possible that if he had continued to caress her, to accustom her to his endearments, Marie Fontaine would have yielded and promised to be his wife. It was true that she would be safe with him, but safe from what? He had used the wrong argument when he said bad times were coming again for France. She drew away from him and asked what he meant by bad times coming.

"The people are starving, dear. This bitter winter has brought unemployment and high prices, just like '88. And this time there's no Bastille to storm, no king and queen to be the scapegoats. The *sans-culottes* will look elsewhere for revenge."

"Oh, revenge!" she said. "Is there never to be an end of it?"

"Not while they see the New People riding in their carriages, gambling all day and dancing all night."

"How moral that sounds. I suppose you mean people like the Talliens and the whole Luxembourg set?"

"And Madame de Beauharnais."

"I don't like your tone, Etienne. Joséphine has been very nice to you." She did not add, "She even advised me to marry you."

"She's a charming woman, I admit. But it's a dangerous charm."

"Now you're being silly."

He tried to recover the lost ground. "Darling, I do understand. You're fond of the lady because she gave you shelter after the Carmes, and your uncle's – death. But now I'm offering you a real home where you would be my honoured wife, not just the *dame de compagnie* of a selfish woman – "

"Lady companions get paid, and I pay my way."

"I think she uses you, Marie. You've been her protection in the eyes of the world."

"Protection from *what*?"

"From the scandal she couldn't hide for ever. All Paris knows that Barras is her lover."

There it came, from the lips of a sober, sensible man, the charge of 'All Paris knows' which she had first heard from a lout called Pierre Langlade. *'Le tout Paris'* – what did an attorney know of *le tout Paris*? She had held a knife on Pierre Langlade. Could she stab Etienne to the heart by calling him a smug, self-righteous hypocrite?

She said, "If that's true, it's their own business, and neither yours nor mine."

"Marie! You mean you condone it? But that's one of the reasons I want you to marry me. To get you out of this house, this atmosphere of corruption – "

"To shut me up for life in the Rue Royale? No, Etienne. You've said enough. We're too different, we should never be happy together. I don't want to marry you. Is that quite clear?"

"Perfectly clear," he said with a bow. "I never meant to force myself upon you. I shall be happy to continue our business relationship, if it's not too distasteful to you." He picked up his hat and stick. "Goodbye, Marie. I can't help admiring your loyalty to your friend. I hope she'll prove equally loyal to you."

The prisoners' balls, or prison balls, were inaugurated, and proved to be a great success. They were held in those of the several Paris jails which had been completely cleared of prisoners since Thermidor: the perverse charm being that while the dancers were dressed in the height of fashion, no attempt had been made to decorate the large cells in which the balls were held, except for the addition of an orchestra. The *merveilleuses* and their *incroyables*, always in search of sensation, found a new stimulus in the bare walls, sometimes covered with the last messages of prisoners condemned to the guillotine, and the barred windows; for others there was a claustrophobic feeling in the mere sight of the doors which had been locked against them.

"I was sure we'd be locked in again," confessed Madame de Beauharnais, after she and Marie had accompanied the Talliens to the prison ball at La Force.

"You could always bribe the jailers," suggested Teresa spitefully. She and Joséphine were having a little tiff because the latter had given a thousand francs to a man called La Bussière, who claimed to have eaten her dossier in the files of the Committee of Public Safety. Teresa said the man was a fraud who had tried his eating-the-dossier story on too many people. He was trying to invent one of the legends of the French Revolution, like that other legend of the mysterious Englishman who spirited victims out of prison and left a small red flower as his irritating signature. The Tallien marriage was heading for the rocks, but Teresa remained faithful to that other legend of Jean Tallien, inspired by herself, engineering the fall of Robespierre and the success of Thermidor.

"I didn't enjoy the ball at La Force, and I refuse to dance at Les Carmes," said Joséphine, and Marie agreed. "I couldn't go back to that horrible room," the girl confessed.

"I think I'd keep seeing the faces of the women who were with us, and died."

"Paul agrees with me that these balls are in bad taste," said Joséphine. "He's looking forward to giving another of his splendid banquets soon."

Citizen Barras's good taste might have been questioned, since he had chosen the date of 21 January, the second anniversary of the execution of King Louis XVI. Most of the regicides had followed their king to the guillotine since that day, but there were at least three men at the sumptuous table who had voted for his death, and who toasted each other with hilarity. Marie's dinner partner was Citizen Reubell, who always entertained her, and who would certainly not invite her to dance at Liliane's. Pierre Langlade was nowhere to be seen.

For this banquet Joséphine had a new gown of gold lamé. Either he gave it her or she's running into debt again, was Marie's thought when the splendid dress arrived from Madame Celeste's new dressmaking establishment, but she forgot the cost in admiration of her friend's appearance when Joséphine stood to receive with Barras at the head of the grand staircase. It was a sight to see the *ci-devant* Duchesse d'Aiguillon, the scourge of the Carmes, entering the Luxembourg and making a grand court curtsey to the pair of them. Madame d'Aiguillon was *ci-devant* in more senses than one, for on being released from prison she had divorced the émigré husband who was the cause of her imprisonment. Now she was all smiles. Her sarcasms at the expense of the Creole lady were forgotten, and like *le tout Paris* she bowed to the rising sun.

There was one prison where no ball was held, because it was still in use as a jail, and that was the prison of Plessis. There were only a few prisoners in Plessis, and one of them was a woman who had suffered as long a term of imprisonment as any innocent victim of the Revolution. Her name was Adrienne de Noailles, *ci-devant* Marquise de La Fayette, and she had been under house arrest in her *château* of Chavaniac, then in the common prison of Brioude, where she had been the lady of the land, and then in Paris, where every day she had expected to hear her name called among the twenty selected for the guillotine. American influence had saved her life, but failed to give her liberty: the fatal name of La Fayette kept her in Plessis long after Thermidor until she was released on the second anniversary of the king's execution, which Barras celebrated in the Luxembourg.

One friend, and one alone, waited for Adrienne at the gates of Plessis. The faithful Marie-Josèphe Beauchet, who had stuck to her former mistress through thick and thin, was there with a cab to take her to the house of one of her few remaining relatives, and with her hand clasped in Madame Beauchet's Adrienne looked out on the streets of Paris which she had never expected to see again. Madame Beauchet described that ride to Marie Fontaine when four days later she visited 371 Rue de l'Université for the first time.

"I would have come sooner," she said (Joséphine listening sympathetically) "but it was impossible to leave her. She is very weak, very much changed, and needs constant care which Monsieur de Liancourt, being a widower, has no idea how to provide. She's stronger today, and asked after you, so could you come and let her talk about the poor ladies who died with your good uncle, and ease her troubled heart?"

"Of course I'll come."

"Yes, go, go, Marie," said Joséphine. "Stay as long as you like. I'm giving a luncheon party," she explained to Madame Beauchet, "and of course I should have liked Mademoiselle Fontaine to be there, but if she can help Madame de La Fayette in any way . . ."

"Did you know my poor mistress, madame?"

"No, I never met her, but my – General de Beauharnais was a great admirer of General de La Fayette."

Monsieur de Liancourt, a distant cousin of the Noailles, was a withered little gentleman of seventy who had never done anything to offend the revolutionaries. His house in the Rue de Bourbon had never been declared National Property, and one old manservant had remained with him when all the others ran away to dance the *carmagnole*; he counted himself as one of the few lucky *aristos* in Paris. He was prepared to give poor Adrienne shelter as long as she pleased if only she would continue as the invalid gentlewoman she appeared to be on her arrival, but now she was stronger she had begun to pester him with awkward ideas, and make him open his doors to ill-assorted strangers. One of them, the Comte de Ségur, had arrived while Madame Beauchet was absent, and was exciting Adrienne and himself by proposals which made Monsieur de Liancourt shudder.

Now here came the good Beauchet with a *merveilleuse*, a tall young beauty from another world than his, and here was Adrienne in tears again, limping across the salon to kiss the girl, Mademoiselle Fontaine, as if she was one of her own daughters.

"Marie! Dear Marie, grown so tall! How glad I am to see someone from the old days, when we were all so happy! And your poor uncle – they've been telling me; but you've found friends – how wonderful for you . . ."

The broken sentences came from lips twisted by suffering, the hair was grey, the hands trembling with a nervous tic, but Marie saw at once that Madame Beauchet was wrong when she thought Adrienne wanted to talk about the dead. There was life in the blinking eyes which looked only to the future, and an indomitable purpose, which the prisoner of Plessis at once explained.

"Monsieur de Ségur has brought me splendid news, Marie. My son is on his way to me, along with Monsieur Frestel, his faithful tutor and friend."

"That *is* good news, madame."

"You'll like to see George-Washington, you and he were little playmates once. And when he comes, Monsieur de Ségur hopes to arrange an exit permit and passage on an American ship to take my son to President Washington in Philadelphia."

"The American Minister will help in that, won't he?"

"Yes, but my own countrymen are doing more. Next, my daughters will come here from Chavaniac as soon as they hear of my release."

"It's a long journey from Auvergne, madame."

"They're not afraid of the distance. And when they arrive, we shall all go together on a longer journey" – she took a deep breath, and a smile lit up her ruined beauty – "we shall go to join my dear husband in his Austrian prison."

Monsieur de Liancourt groaned.

That was the theme of Adrienne de La Fayette's days. Her son to the United States, her daughters by her side, and then Gilbert! Gilbert! the husband she had adored through all his infidelities and mock heroics: she would cross half Europe to share a prison cell with him.

Nobody could shake Adrienne from those fixed ideas. Marie Fontaine persuaded Tallien to have the National Property order lifted from a small house the La Fayettes had occupied in the Rue de Bourbon, not far from Monsieur de Liancourt's, who thankfully contributed some furniture to the empty rooms, and Adrienne moved in there to await the arrival of her children. George-Washington appeared, a tall handsome youth of sixteen made vigorous and self-reliant by months of hiding in the Auvergne countryside. His sisters came next, fine young women who unquestioningly accepted the quixotic and foolhardy destiny their mother was preparing for them. For a few days the joy of their reunion kept them calm and happy, but Adrienne's impatience flared up again; she wanted to be off to Austria immediately, and raged at the long delay in procuring exit permits. The new American Minister, Mr James Monroe, while unfailingly civil, grew as tired of her importunities as Gouverneur Morris. His advice was to wait in Paris with her daughters until her husband was free to join them. Mr Monroe was in correspondence with

England: he assured her that La Fayette had friends in high places there, and that Charles James Fox, the statesman, had personally appealed to the Emperor of Austria to let the prisoner of Olmütz go.

Nothing he, or any of her friends, could say shook Adrienne's purpose. Madame Beauchet told Marie, with comical despair, that as soon as her 'dear lady' was able for an outing she had gone to call on Madame de Simiane, who had been her husband's mistress for many years, to ask if she wished to join the expedition to Austria. "You should have seen the Simiane's face," said Madame Beauchet. "She's had her own troubles, I suppose, and now she's comfortably settled in the Hôtel de Beauvau; *she* isn't going off on any wild goose chase to Austria, trust her! Oh, my poor dear lady! I wonder if Père Carrichon could persuade her to stay in Paris?"

Adrienne said nothing about her abortive visit to Madame de Simiane, and very little about her journey across the Seine to the Place Beauvau. To Marie alone she confessed that she had been unnerved by the sight of the guillotine, still in use in the Place de la Révolution, and for the first time wept bitterly over the execution of her grandmother, her mother and her sister Louise. "My father could have saved them," she said between sobs. "He could have insisted that they join him in Switzerland, if he hadn't been so besotted with his mistress!" The infatuation of the Duc de Noailles was a very sore point with his daughter.

"Would *you* consider going to Switzerland, madame?" asked Marie, and when Adrienne raised her eyebrows she added lamely, "It really would be healthier for the girls."

"Virginie and Anastasie are as anxious to join their father as I am." Adrienne limped out of the room, and Marie went to take the advice of Père Carrichon. The good priest, who had assumed so many disguises for the sake of the Noailles family, now appeared in the Rue de Bourbon dressed as a mason, with a hod on his shoulder.

"Father, couldn't you persuade her to give up this mad

scheme of joining the general? She's not well, she could hardly walk today. Those varicose ulcers in her legs, which began in prison, keep growing worse however many hot fomentations Madame Beauchet applies. How can she survive another spell in prison, even by her husband's side?"

"My child, I cannot use my spiritual authority to forbid it, because it is a wife's duty to cleave to her husband. God sees her sacrifice: God will give her strength to fulfil her purpose."

Marie was silent. It was a long time since she had listened to pious words.

"Dear Marie," said the priest, "I may call you so because I remember you when you really were a child, making your First Communion at St Roch's church – this is the first time I have seen you alone since Madame de La Fayette came to the Rue de Bourbon. I have never yet been able to tell you that I saw your uncle die – and he died a brave man."

"You were *there*? Does Madame Adrienne know?"

"I told her all she could bear to hear. I put myself in the path of the tumbrils as the Noailles ladies went to the guillotine, and when I saw your uncle supporting them by his example of steadfastness, I gave him my blessing as well as them. He went to the scaffold with an unfaltering step. Do not weep, my child. He died a Christian."

"Thank you for telling me that," said Marie with a sob. "I wish – oh, how I've wished – that he had lived a few days longer. He might have been released after Thermidor like so many others. We could have gone back to the pharmacy together, and he would have taught me more and more ways to prepare medicines, and help him . . ."

"Had you done that before?"

"I did simple preparations, yes." And Marie found herself telling a sympathetic listener about her desire to study pharmacology and become a qualified apothecary – stopping only when the inevitable smile appeared on Father Carrichon's gaunt face.

"My child, you know that would have been impossible. No woman could undergo the rigorous course of study required by the Society of Apothecaries – her brain wouldn't stand it. What has kept your mind on this bent for so long?"

"Because there must be a better way to make sick people well than by chopping their heads off. And because this is such a bitter winter and so many are suffering and starving."

"'The poor ye have always with you,'" said the priest. He looked curiously at the fashionable young lady in her prune-coloured silk dress with the matching satin slippers. "Are you serious, Marie? Do you really want to feed the hungry?"

"Yes, but how can I?"

"Some of my brethren," said Father Carrichon, "priests like me who refused to take the civic oath, are trying to do the Church's work in other ways. A friend of mine, who calls himself Citizen Vincent now, has organised a soup kitchen under the arches of the Quai Voltaire. Would you like to try helping him to serve the midday meals?"

"Oh, I *would*!"

"So if I say meet me tomorrow at eleven o'clock at the corner of the Pont Royal, will you be there?"

"I'll be there."

"Then I'll take you to meet Père – Citizen Vincent."

Joséphine, as might have been expected, poured cold water on the idea. Already plaintive about Marie's daily visits to Madame de La Fayette, the idea of her going among a crowd of beggars and cripples was appalling. She was growing more and more nervous about the unrest in the city, although it was hardly felt in the Faubourg St Germain. Teresa Tallien, whom nobody cheered as *Notre Dame de Thermidor* any more, had had an unpleasant experience when some ruffians threw stones at her carriage, and actually scratched the paintwork. Joséphine's own pampered pug, Fortuné, who never went out alone, had disappeared for a whole day and was found on the doorstep with a chewed-up ear. Undoubtedly the work of *sans-culottes*! Worst of all, poor Agathe returning from market had opened her purse to give a *sou* to a beggar, and the wretch had snatched the purse and made off howling with laughter! If Marie insisted on going to that dreadful place tomorrow she must be sure not to carry money.

"Father Carrichon told me to wear my oldest clothes," said Marie. "The trouble is, nearly all my things are new."

She was at the Pont Royal at a quarter to eleven next morning, wearing her oldest black dress, a black straw bonnet from which a wreath of flowers had been cut, and a brown shawl borrowed from the little maid of all work. Marie walked up and down the bridge to keep warm, smiling at the thought of Joséphine's last dismal predictions – she expected Marie to bring home the infection of every disease from scrofula to smallpox, thanks to the kind of vagrant who stood in line for free soup.

The Seine was said to be frozen from bank to bank in some places, but not here. The little eddy flowed freely against the arches of the bridge, and a few leaves of the poplar tree floated on the water. She wondered if Sergeant Vautour were alive or dead. Then she saw Père Carrichon approaching, with his mason's hod on his shoulder, and his face clearing at the sight of her. He wasn't sure of me, she exulted. He didn't think I'd come!

Marie Fontaine hurried to meet him, gave him her cold hand, and let him lead her down the icy staircase to the underworld.

21

After the bitter winter the unrest in Paris continued to grow. The coming of spring made no difference to the malcontents, for the food rations were constantly being cut, and the cost of living was thirty times higher than five years before. In the Faubourg St Antoine, where the Bastille had stood and the first great passionate rush of the Revolution began, the *sans-culottes* met in the wine-shops and alleys as their brothers had done in 1789, and cursed the new tyrants, to them no better than the old. The extravagance of the Bourbon court had been described and magnified a thousand times, but Versailles was a long way from Paris, and the fabled luxury had not actually been seen. Now the thirty theatres, the innumerable dance halls and gambling hells were filled every night by the rich, while the poor stood in the gutter with hatred in their jealous hearts and watched the parade go by.

But the *sans-culottes* lacked leadership. A demonstration planned for 1 April was easily put down. Instead of invading the Convention with the simple call of "Bread!" the demonstrators, with the French passion for dates, yelled for "Bread and the Constitution of 1793!" and were driven from the National Palace by a contingent of the *jeunesse dorée* armed with their loaded clubs and whips. There was an easing of the tension during May, by which time news had been received of the signing of peace treaties with Prussia and Holland, and the connoisseurs

278

of the Place de la Révolution had been treated to a super-guillotining. Fouquier-Tinville, once the Public Prosecutor, at last met his just fate among the execrations of an enormous crowd. No man was ever more hated in those dreadful times: he had sent thousands to the Machine which now took his life, and when his head was held up to the crowd there was a huge sigh of the sexual satisfaction and release of the early days.

Even this circus did not stifle the cry for bread, and another demonstration was planned for 20 May. The excitement was whipped up on the preceding day, so that a massive body of men and women, accompanied this time by three battalions of sympathisers from the National Guard, marched on the embattled Convention. Three times the mob forced its way through locked doors in an increasing pandemonium, shouting for "Bread!" Mass arrests and murder followed, while Tallien shouted above the din that the rioters were trying to wreck the Republic. After a lull during the night hours a second attempt was made, with demands for the Constitution of 1793 and the disbanding of the *jeunesse dorée* as well as for bread, but by this time the Convention had assembled a sufficient military force to disperse the rioters. Then the punishments began. By 23 May 3000 'suspects' had been arrested and thirty-six condemned to die by the guillotine. Government by intimidation had returned, and the city lay in a paralysis of fear.

Next day Napoleon Buonaparte came back to Paris.

Three months had passed since the ignominious retreat of the French squadron to Toulon, and it had taken all that while to get any sort of reply to his request for a command of troops. He wrote a second time after he left the dockyard for the landward side of Toulon and made work for himself by inspecting the armaments installed since he drove the British from the port. "We must make sure our cannon are efficient," he said sarcastically to the garrison commander, "else we shall have Captain Nelson sailing in to capture the city as Milord Hood did in '93."

Eventually a letter came from the Committee of Public Safety, signed La Revellière, a name new to Buonaparte. It stated that the Committee had a command in view for him, and ordered him to Paris to discuss it with Citizen Barras. It was not precise enough for a man of his habit of mind, but at least it was action, and since as a *général de brigade* he was entitled to an ADC he wrote to Charles Latour in Nice, asking him to set out for Toulon at once, "and bring Junot with you if you can."

Latour was prompt to obey. Junot held a commission now, but General Kellermann was willing to release him, and when the two young men, his old comrades in arms, rode into the courtyard of his hotel Buonaparte was only prevented by military discipline from embracing them both. Their smiles and jokes over dinner were a welcome change from the glum faces of the naval officers to whom the general said *au revoir* next day before they started on their long and tedious journey to the north.

They travelled by stage coach when coaches were available, or on hacks hired from post houses, and at first their talk was all of the Army of Italy, still inactive, and of the command waiting for Buonaparte.

"It can't be the Army of Italy," he said, "because if they meant me to supersede Kellermann I'd have been ordered straight to Nice. It can't be the Army of the West, because Hoche announced a victory in La Vendée as far back as February. Prussia left the war by the Treaty of Basle: Holland followed suit, and Spain is ready to sue for peace. So what command does the Committee have in mind?"

"The Army of the Interior," suggested Latour.

"Which is in bad shape under General Menou. Yes, they might offer me that."

"Or the Military Governorship of Paris," said Junot.

"I haven't been in Paris for three years," said Buonaparte.

"You'll see some changes, *mon général*," said Junot.

"Just before I left for Corsica I saw the mob attack the Tuileries and massacre the Swiss Guards who died to the last man in defence of the king. The royal family fled to the National Assembly – it was in the Riding School then – and from there they were taken to the Temple prison. My God! It seems like a hundred years ago."

At the last post house they heard of the three days of riot in Paris, and were amazed to find, when they reached the coach station and hired a cab to take them across the city, that the theatres and restaurants were as brightly lit and crowded, in the May twilight, as if no riot had ever taken place. And then the women! then their dresses! the transparent gauze and the rose-coloured fleshings! The three young men tried to look in all directions at once, and at supper Latour and Junot could talk of nothing else. But the general left them to find a porter and send him with a note to Citizen Barras, saying he would wait upon him at ten o'clock tomorrow morning.

The Convention was sitting in what Napoleon called the Tuileries and they called the National Palace. That was one of the big changes, and the place itself was not only shabby but bore the marks of the recent riots. He gave his name to an usher and was taken upstairs to a small ante-room, where he was kept waiting for an hour and ten minutes before a civilian clerk came in with a file in his hand on which Buonaparte's keen eyes read his own name.

"Citizen Barras will see you now, citizen general," said the clerk, and opened the door of an inner sanctum where Barras was seated behind a handsome mahogany desk. He rose at once and gave Buonaparte his hand in welcome.

Such a manicured, well-kept hand, and how different from the general's, who never committed the extravagance of buying gloves! Such a well-kept man, with his florid face and sensual mouth and his exquisite tailoring! In one graceful movement he motioned Buonaparte to a seat, took his file from the clerk, and directed the man towards the door.

"My dear fellow, I'm very glad to see you again," he

began. "We met last at Toulon, didn't we? How long has it been – one year? Two years?"

"One year and five months," said Buonaparte.

"Quite so. And you've been back in Toulon since then, of course. An unfortunate affair at sea, that retreat in the face of the English."

"For which I was not responsible," said the general quickly.

"Nobody dreamed of saying so . . . Unluckily it was the sort of episode which doesn't look well on a man's record." He began to turn the pages of the file. "Ah, here are your two letters requesting a command in the field. We were rather disturbed by their tone."

"In what way?"

"You sounded aggrieved. As if you had been assigned a duty inappropriate to your talents."

"Citizen Barras, when you and I talked at Toulon you implied that I should have been given command of a brigade instead of the Inspectorate of Coastal Defences. I didn't agree. I thought that posting most important."

"Yes, you did well there. But my dear general, you must admit you haven't been lucky since those days."

"I was very lucky in my plan of attack for the Army of Italy until Citizen Carnot called off the advance."

"Then there was another affair that doesn't read too well – fourteen days of fortress arrest."

"That was the price I paid for my friendship with Augustin Robespierre," said Buonaparte. "You and he were as thick as thieves when you were commissioners at Toulon."

Barras caught the flash in the blue-grey eyes and decided not to irritate the dangerous little man any further. He said, "Well, we must let bygones be bygones and look to the future. Citizen general, we have decided to give you the command of the Army of the West."

Buonaparte sat back in his chair, astounded. "Of the *West*," he said. "But I thought General Hoche . . . he claimed a victory in La Vendée!"

"In La Vendée, yes, but the Chouans are still in revolt in Quiberon. And we have other plans for General Hoche."

"What sort of plans?"

"Plans classified as Most Secret, and not for the knowledge of the general public." Now the little Corsican's offended again; too bad. He doesn't need to know that when Hoche is well he's going to lead an assault force by way of Ireland, where the Irish will be delighted to help us descend in strength on the west coast of England.

"The plans are in abeyance for the moment," he said. "General Hoche suffers from a weak chest, and he had a bad attack of pneumonia in April. That's why we want you to take his place."

"You're asking me to fight a guerrilla civil war, Republican Frenchmen fighting royalist Frenchmen?"

"It amounts to that, I suppose."

"I can't do it."

"What!"

"I will never order Frenchmen to fire on other Frenchmen. I decline the command of the Army of the West, and beg to apply for sick leave."

Barras riffled the pages in his file and smiled unpleasantly. "Sick leave?" he said. "That's been a favourite move of yours. You were cashiered and reinstated with difficulty in 1792 for taking too many 'sick leaves', mostly spent in Corsica. I suggest you reconsider your rejection of the command I offer."

"I *must* reject it, Citizen Barras."

"Very well. You were a mere lieutenant in 1792, now you're a general with one great success to his credit, and one only. You may have two months' leave, beginning today. Report to me here in July – I mean in Messidor, and be prepared to accept the next posting you are offered."

"Which will be?"

"I daresay I can find a little niche for you in Plans."

"What's the alternative to Plans, if any?"

"You will be placed on the inactive list – indefinitely."

Buonaparte got up. "Thanks for your consideration, Citizen Barras," he said. "On leave I have no right to an ADC. Lieutenant Charles Latour is with me in that capacity. Can you find a little niche in Plans for him?"

"That could be managed, I suppose."

"And Lieutenant Junot – you remember him."

"Ah yes, he saved your life, didn't he? I'll keep him in mind."

The formal goodbyes were soon said, and the general found himself in a vast outer hall. From behind closed doors he heard a confused shouting, and presumed the Deputies were debating some motion before the House. He ran down the crowded staircase, past the door of the guardroom of which Latour had told him, acknowledged the salutes of the slovenly sentries and stood in the open air. The bastard, he was saying to himself, the sneering, supercilious bastard! Talking to me about sick leave as if I were a second lieutenant! Offering me a guerrilla command in a French province – I, who should command the Army of Italy!

He turned at the gate of the Tuileries and looked at the great building with the bustle of shabby people and the dirty windows. This place was once a palace, he thought. It could be a palace again, if only –

If only I'm a lucky general.

Since the February day when she first went to help at the soup kitchen Marie Fontaine's life had taken on a new dimension, and she was happier than she had been for many months. At first she was frightened by the dark cavern Father Vincent – Citizen Vincent – had fitted up with charcoal braziers to keep the food hot and the water boiling to wash the dishes and a long trestle table to dispense the food. She was disgusted by the smell of river water fouled by rubbish, of unwashed bodies and human excrement. Too often the *soupe* they served was just that: a thin broth made from vegetables thrown away on the cobbles under the market stalls, served with a hunk of stale bread begged from bakers who had any to spare. Citizen Vincent's other helpers did the begging. They were women considerably older than Marie, silent and smiling; she was fairly sure they were dispossessed nuns.

Their example helped her to greet the people who came for food cheerfully, though their looks terrified her at first. Prosper Fontaine had had many poor customers from the alleys and byways of his *quartier*, but none so steeped in poverty and ignorance as those for whom the Revolution was supposed to bring better times. She dreaded their brutish, vulpine faces, their claw-like hands snatching at the bread. Although she hid her dresses with enveloping aprons and her curls with a mob cap, she felt they hated her for being clean and pretty: to them she was an *aristo*. Then, literally by accident, she became their friend.

An old woman coming for *la soupe* slipped on the icy stair and fell several steps to the bottom. Putting out one hand to save herself she was taken up with the hand oddly twisted, and Citizen Vincent diagnosed a fractured wrist.

"How I'm to treat it I don't know," he said. "We didn't make any provision for accidents."

"I can bandage a simple fracture," said Marie calmly. "My uncle taught me how."

"But what with?"

"This!" and Marie ripped up her apron to put on a bandage and improvise a sling for the poor woman before taking her home to bed in a cellar behind the Rue du Bac. The crowd who watched the proceedings murmured their approval.

"Prosper Fontaine must have been a remarkable man," said the *ci-devant* Father Vincent to Father Carrichon when they next met. Carrichon asked him why.

"Because his niece is a remarkable girl. The day after we had the broken wrist she came armed with a supply of bandages and medicines she'd begged from an apothecary called Guiart, and announced that her uncle taught her

285

simple anatomy as well as pharmacology. She had four patients waiting for her and the next day there were twice as many, with every ailment from lupus to running sores. She does her best for all of them, and when there's a case beyond her skill she says so, and advises them to go to the Hôtel Dieu."

"Are they grateful?"

"They've accepted her now as one of themselves. The nuns are most impressed, and Sister Clare – you know her emotional way – told the girl she was doing God's work among the poor."

Father Carrichon crossed himself. "God chooses his own agents," he said. "Even a *merveilleuse*. How did Mademoiselle Fontaine react?"

"She seemed embarrassed. I think what she likes best is that our people have stopped calling her 'Citizeness'."

"What do they call her?"

"Just Marie."

Marie herself was happy. She spent an extra hour each day at the soup kitchen, which was possible because she was no longer needed in the Rue de Bourbon. Madame de La Fayette and her children had gone to pay a long visit to a friend living in seclusion at Fontainebleau, from which retreat she was continuing by letter her campaign on behalf of her husband and her son. It was Joséphine who was the invalid now, requiring petting and attention in the afternoons, for Joséphine had caught cold on a treacherously warm spring day, driving in the open carriage to see her son. Poor Eugène, having lived as a man among men in the forests of La Vendée, was making a very bad adjustment to life as a schoolboy at St Germain, and after an interview with his headmaster Joséphine returned to Paris in tears. Disappointment did not prevent her from going to a ball that night, wearing gauze and tulle and very little else, so that the cold became bronchitis, and a doctor had to be called in. Joséphine's old doctor had died of a heart complaint, and his successor was a true product of the Revolution. "Little better than a *sans-*

culotte," she indignantly said. He prescribed efficiently, but he was 'disrespectful'; he forced her to admit that she was thirty-two, and then said it was folly for 'a middle-aged woman' to go capering around to banquets and balls. "Leave dancing to the young folks and wear some sensible clothes," was his advice, and Joséphine wailed to Marie that he talked as if she was a woman of fifty!

Her convalescence lasted for a long time, and she refused to receive Barras, who sent flowers and fruit with devoted regularity, until she was back in her salon, elegantly dressed and subtly made up. She had not missed much in the way of gaiety, he assured her. The craze for prison balls was over, and the wilder crowd, the *jeunesse dorée* and their women, had taken to dancing in churches and copulating in the confessionals, which he thought was going too far. As soon as Joséphine was really well they would give some parties at the Luxembourg . . . and Joséphine smiled, hiding her teeth. But the May riots put a stop to that.

In June the fashion was for *bals des victimes*, which were a great success. The guests were those whose family or friends had perished by the guillotine, and they wore knots of black crape on their garments and thin red ribbons round their necks to simulate the gash of the knife. Men turned their collars back and women piled their hair high to be ready for the executioner. It was great fun. It was also the ultimate expression of the contempt for death, the lust for life which had driven Paris dancing-mad since the Terror ended.

"Darling Marie, Paul wants us to go to the *bal des victimes* in that new dance place on the Right Bank tomorrow night," said Joséphine on a June evening when she was restored to health and beauty. "Some of our friends are going, and we shall have a nice little group. Paul thinks he should put in an appearance at one of those affairs."

"That's understandable," said Marie, reflecting that Citizen Barras, while he was Robespierre's commissioner at Toulon, had contributed a fair quota of victims to the total. "But I've nothing new to wear."

"That's because you've been neglecting yourself since you started going to that horrible soup kitchen – and nursing me," said Joséphine. "Poor Marie! You haven't had much fun since you sent your lawyer friend away." The Rocrois' April rent, promptly paid, had been brought to Marie by Maître Favart's clerk.

"*He* wasn't much fun either," retorted Marie. "All right, let's go to the ball. After all, we both qualify! Shall I wear my green dress?"

"Yes, do. It suits you. I'm going to wear an old dress too."

"Quite right," said Marie. 'A *bal des victimes* could end up as a terrible romp."

"Don't criticise it, Marie, at least not in front of Paul. I want you to be specially nice to him tomorrow night," said Joséphine in her wheedling way.

"Aren't I always?"

"He thinks you're rather cool and distant. He's being so childish just now! He wants me to give a party for him here, where there simply isn't room for that sort of entertaining."

"Hasn't he got room enough at the Luxembourg?"

"This is to be an absolutely private party, with the American Minister as the guest of honour. Well, I made it clear to the Vicomte de Barras," said Joséphine self-righteously, "that if he wants that sort of help from me he ought to see that I have a suitable house."

22

About half past ten on a fine June evening General Buonaparte left his hotel, Le Cadran Bleu on the Left Bank of the Seine. He was expected at a reception given by an old friend who lived in the Quai de Conti, but as he had no desire to be the first guest and involved in a tête-à-tête with the lady, he walked northward across the Pont Neuf and paused to watch the water.

It was too hot for a cloak, and Buonaparte was wearing the gold-laced uniform of a general officer, put on to please Madame Permon and impress her guests, which attracted some attention from the passers-by. He ignored their stares and leaned on the parapet, gazing upriver at the place which had been the landing-stage when he arrived by barge from Burgundy, a boy of fifteen come to Paris to take up a King's Cadetship at the Ecole Militaire. That was in 1784, five years before the Revolution, and the schoolboy's boundless ambition had not yet been fulfilled.

It was the eighteenth of June, a date of no special significance for the general except that it was ten days since an event took place which might have some effect on his own future. On 8 June the pathetic little prisoner whom the royalists called King Louis XVII died of tuberculosis of the bone, and it could not be long before his uncle claimed the succession to the throne. Then, if the prince made a move from Austria, might not the Army of Italy be reactivated, and the man who had done so much for it be spared that little niche in Plans? The general bitterly regretted now that he had allowed himself to be baited by Barras into applying for a 'sick leave' which still had five weeks to run. He was out of everything just as the Revolution entered a new phase, dependent on what he could learn from his few old friends and on the news brought back by Latour and Junot from the Rue des Capucines. They had been given very minor jobs in Plans.

One thing was clear: there was no effective commander of the City of Paris. The delay in subduing the May riots was a sure proof of that. If he had arrived a week earlier he might have made his mark on the Convention by forceful and immediate action. But he had missed out on that, and he supposed he ought to be thankful that Barras had not put him on half pay. By economising, and lodging in the Rue de la Huchette, he was still able to send money to his mother and sisters – those helpless ones who depended on him.

Once across the bridge he struck away into the Rue de l'Arbre Sec. It was a very old street, and the 'dry tree' had been the hangman's tree in the days before the guillotine; now to his surprise it was brilliantly lighted by a row of lamps outside a dance hall where a *'Bal des Victimes'* was advertised. A victims' ball! what in the world might that be? It was just as he had said so often since coming back to Paris, the French were giving themselves up to pleasure. Dancing, the theatre, and women seemed to have become the great business of life. On an impulse, and to delay his arrival at Madame Permon's, he decided to investigate the victims and their ball.

Either one had an invitation card or one paid the price of admission at the door, but the doorman, impressed by the gold-laced uniform, assumed that Buonaparte was going to join someone of importance, and said, '*Passez, mon général*' without hesitation.

The ballroom was decorated with all-too-realistic drawings of the guillotine in action, of coffins, of tumbrils, of the skull and crossbones. All round the room people were drinking at little tables, seemingly in high good humour, and a dance was in progress. The dancing at Paris balls had steadied down since the first wild exuberance, but the mazurka they were dancing seemed wild enough to Buonaparte. He was staring at the women in those dresses which revealed nearly everything, when the music stopped and one of the women, coming face to face with him, gave a gasp, blushed deeply and dropped a curtsey.

"General Buonaparte!"

She was a tall girl in sea-green chiffon, with the obligatory red ribbon round her neck and a black crape sash under her breasts. Her bright curls were piled on top of her head and knotted in readiness for the action of the knife. He had never seen her before.

Buonaparte bowed. "I regret, madame . . . I must appear to be remiss . . ."

"It's not madame, it's mademoiselle. You mean you don't recognise me? Don't remember Marie, from the Pharmacie Fontaine?"

The memories of three years back awoke in Napoleon Buonaparte. He remembered the older man he had played chess with, and the pretty blushing girl who poured their wine. He said, "Marie Fontaine – and grown so lovely! I can't believe it. They told us you were dead."

"My uncle is dead. That's why I'm here at a *bal des victimes*."

They were both stammering, blurting out questions and answers, bridging the three years since the dinner at the Régence, and Marie's partner in the mazurka had discreetly disappeared. The orchestra began to play.

"I ought to ask you for the honour of a dance, mademoiselle, but I will spare you the ordeal." The brilliant smile she remembered lit up his face. He was not much changed, except for the stern lines about his mouth and a slight thickening of jaw and neck. The gold-laced uniform was new, the lank black hair hanging over the collar was the same.

Half dizzy with delight, Marie tried to make sense out

of what he was saying to her. It sounded like "Marie, do you trust me?" and she answered, "Oh yes, I trust you, of course I do."

"Then will you come away with me?"

"Away – " Was this the dream come true, the fantasy turned into fact, all in so short a time?

"Only for an hour. I would like to take you to the house of a friend of mine, not ten minutes' drive away. She is giving a *soirée* tonight and would be delighted . . . but perhaps you would rather not leave the ball?"

As if the ball mattered, when she could be with him! She tried to speak like a woman of the world. "Who is this friend? I may know her already."

"I don't think so. Madame Permon is a widow with a grown-up family. She's a Corsican like myself, and they live on the Quai de Conti. Please come."

"I will," said Marie, "but I must tell the lady I live with where I'm going. Come and meet her."

Joséphine's idea of an old dress was the violet velvet, which she had certainly worn on many occasions since last January. Nothing became her like the imperial colour, and Barras, alone with her at a big table, was looking at her with admiration and toying with one of her long diamond earrings with the complacent air of the man in possession. At the same time he was shaking his head slowly, and Marie guessed that she was talking about the purchase of a new house.

"Madame de Beauharnais, may I present General Buonaparte?"

"*Enchantée, mon général.*"

Barras, who had risen to his feet, murmured, "The hero of Toulon, my love," and bowed to Buonaparte. "Good evening, general," he said. "I didn't know you were a dancing man."

"I could walk a minuet," said Buonaparte, "but I believe I was the worst performer in our dancing class at the Ecole Militaire."

"Then sit down and have a glass of wine with us."

"Thank you, but I am engaged to attend a *soirée* at Madame Permon's. And since Mademoiselle Fontaine and I are old friends, meeting here by a happy accident, I have asked her to accompany me to the Quai de Conti for an hour or so – "

"Old friends?" said Joséphine. "Madame Permon? You know so many people, darling. Who is this lady?"

"A charming and respected Corsican lady who has lived in Paris for years," said Barras. "I was acquainted with her late husband."

"Then do run along, dear," said Joséphine to Marie, "but don't stay long. We're having supper here at half past twelve, and you mustn't break up the group."

"I'll be punctual." The formal adieux were said, Barras adding that he was glad the general was enjoying his sick leave.

When a cab came up, the driver shouting, "*Citoyen et citoyenne*! Places for two!" and Buonaparte told him to go to 13 Quai de Conti, Marie said, "What did Citizen Barras mean by sick leave? You haven't been ill, have you?"

"Only politically. Barras is fond of his joke . . . Madame de Beauharnais is a beautiful woman. Is she the widow of General de Beauharnais?"

"He was her *victime* tonight. He was executed on the same day as my poor uncle."

"How did you happen to meet her?"

"We spent four months in the Carmes prison together."

"Poor child. So you had to bear that too." The general laid his hand on hers. It was not an intense pressure but the sympathetic touch of a friend. "Where are you living now?" he asked.

"Madame de Beauharnais has an apartment at 371 Rue de l'Université."

"May I call on you there? We mustn't lose sight of one another."

"I'm always at home after two o'clock." She wondered if, by the lights on the Pont Neuf, Napoleon could see her blushes.

"What do you do before two?" he said teasingly.

"I help in a soup kitchen."

"Brave girl. I had some experience of soup kitchens when my family and I were refugees in Marseille."

"There's so much I want you to tell me," she murmured. 'Isn't this an adventure?"

"An adventure with a surprise for you at the end of it."

He laughed at her excited questions and refused to answer. Very soon they were at the Quai de Conti and climbing the stairs of a tall old building to Madame Permon's apartment. A maid took Marie's cloak and ushered them into a large salon, comfortably but not richly furnished, where about a score of people, mostly middle-aged, were enjoying sweet cakes and wine. Madame Permon, who came hospitably forward, was a woman in her forties with a grown son and a pert young daughter whose name was Laure. They all made Marie Fontaine welcome, but when Napoleon left her side to move among the guests Marie felt unsure of herself among strangers who seemed to look at her with doubtful eyes. They were not *aristos*, but their manners were those of the old régime, and she felt self-conscious in her red ribbon and crape sash, for Madame Permon's friends were not the sort to attend a *bal des victimes*. Then Napoleon was by her side again, holding by the arm a tall young officer who was looking at her with – could it be disbelief?

"This is the surprise I promised you. Do you like it?" said Napoleon.

"Sergeant Vautour!"

Napoleon laughed uproariously, as she had never ever heard him laugh before. "Come, come, my child," he said, "haven't you learned to distinguish between uniforms yet? This is the *ci-devant* Sergeant Vautour of the National Guard, true, but now in his own name and new rank he's Lieutenant Latour of the Department of Plans."

It was doubtful if Latour heard him. He was staring at Marie with an expression which made her colour rise, and all he could say was, "I don't believe it. I don't believe it! I thought you were dead."

"What made you think that?"

"I was told by our – by an *avocat* I know, that the pharmacy was National Property and you and your uncle had been – had been – "

"Executed," said Marie. "My uncle was, but I was spared – this." She touched the thin red ribbon round her neck. "The pharmacy isn't National Property any longer. It belongs to me."

"Are you a real lady apothecary now?"

"It's rented to a real apothecary – male of course."

It was so like their old sarcastic exchanges that Napoleon intervened. "Now, you two," he said, "don't start fighting the moment you meet again! Charles, get mademoiselle a glass of wine – Marie, he's been really worried about you."

Latour came back with the wine as Napoleon moved away to answer a summons from Madame Permon, and said, "We've got to talk."

"I know," said Marie. "Where do we begin?"

Where indeed? It was nearly two years since they met, and for each of them the world had changed. She was not prepared for his answer: "In the Rue du Bac. Let's sit down on this sofa and go on from there."

"Nobody else is sitting down. I think we're supposed to move about."

"Madame Permon likes to keep her guests moving. Confound it! Here comes Junot." Another young lieutenant was approaching, hand in hand with Laure Permon. Introductions and small talk followed, and then Madame Permon herself appeared to take Marie on a tour of the room. "Napoleon tells me he's got to take you back to a ball," she said. "You must meet everybody before you go. And come again soon, this is much too short a visit . . ."

Charles Latour captured her after twenty minutes. "This is hopeless," he said. "Last time we met you called me a coward and sent me off to war – "

"Which doesn't seem to have done you any harm – "

"Now you're ignoring me. Where do you live? When can I see you alone?"

The ormolu clock on the mantelpiece struck twelve, and Marie said, "I must go. There's the general, looking for me – "

"Are you playing *Cendrillon* now? You used to be the *Petit Chaperon Rouge*."

"You're forgetting your Perrault," said Marie. "Cinderella had to leave the ball, I'm going back to one."

"Marie, *please*!"

She relented, told him where she lived, and – remembering Joséphine was going to St Germain next day – asked him to come at six o'clock. She thought Napoleon heard, for he was at her elbow, but only to tell her the Permon boy had gone to get them a cab. "I must keep my promise to Madame de Beauharnais," he said, "to take you back in time for supper."

"I must get my cloak," said Marie. Laure Permon, who had been hovering on the outskirts of their little group, said instantly, "I'll show you where it is."

It was unusual, but the servants seemed to have disappeared, and Marie followed the young girl to a bedroom where the ladies' wraps had been arranged. While she was looking for her own wrap she heard young Laure say,

"How long have you known Napoleon?"

Marie turned to face the chit, and said coldly that they first met three years ago.

"Oh, we've known him much longer than that. Ever since he was a cadet."

"I imagine you were the sharp little girl who used to call him Puss in Boots."

Laure giggled. "Yes I was," she confessed. "He was so conceited when he got his commission, and so proud of his blue and silver uniform, I couldn't help teasing him. And the boots were ridiculous, they really were."

"You wouldn't dare call General Buonaparte Puss in Boots now."

"I'm lucky I don't have to call him Papa."

"What do you mean?"

"When he came back to Paris Napoleon asked my mother to marry him."

Biting back the words, "She's old enough to be *his* mother!" Marie said coldly, "What did Madame Permon say?"

"She laughed at him and told him not to be a silly boy."

"You were there, were you?"

"We were all together in a box at the theatre."

"And acting out the comedy, I suppose. When you're grown up you won't take joking quite so seriously. Good night, citizeness."

23

It was nearer three o'clock than two when Marie came home next day, and Joséphine's carriage was waiting at the door with the coachman on the box. She spoke to Agathe in the hall, and when Joséphine heard their voices she called to Marie to come and talk to her in her room. She was trying on a new bonnet and coquetting with her reflection in the mirror when the girl leaned wearily against the door jamb.

"I don't want to come too near you," she said flatly. "It was rather a messy day today, and Agathe's preparing me a bath."

"Oh, horrors!" said Joséphine, taking up a perfume spray and waving it in the air, "I do wish you'd stop going to that foul place! I just wanted to tell you, I'm having dinner with Madame Campan at St Germain, so I won't be back till late."

"All right. Give Eugène and Hortense my love, won't you?"

"I will. Oh, and Marie, what do you think? Your old friend General Buonaparte paid a morning call on me!"

"He did?" Marie came a step further into the room. Joséphine did not turn round, but Marie saw her face in the mirror, and saw – or perhaps imagined – a sparkle of malice in the dark eyes.

"Why – what time – didn't he ask for me?" she achieved.

"Of course he did. He said he was sorry to miss you.

But he really came to see me and apologise for taking you away from your friends last night. He only stayed for about twenty minutes."

"I don't think any apology was necessary."

"Nor do I, but he went on making those funny little pompous speeches, like he did when you introduced him to us . . . I think he likes to hear himself talk."

"You think he's funny, do you?"

"*Oh, qu'il est 'drolle'!*" said the soft Creole voice. "Darling, I must hurry. Try to get a rest this afternoon – you look so tired."

Marie lay in the tub while the water turned from hot to warm to tepid, trying to get her thoughts in order. He came in the morning, when I told him I was never there. He came to see Joséphine, not to see me. And she liked it; even if Barras is her lover, she's greedy for admiration from any man. If I'd ever told her I cared for Napoleon, it would amuse her to take him away from me. Was that why I asked Vautour – Latour – to come at a time when I knew *she* wouldn't be here? Because I was afraid if she saw him, young and – yes, he is handsome – she would make a dead set at him . . .

"She likes younger men." Who said that? Anne de Beaupré, probably, in the Carmes. And if Napoleon proposed to Madame Permon, he likes older women. But I don't believe he did, I think that mischievous little brat was only teasing me, just because he brought me to their house.

I don't suppose he gave me a thought in all those years. I remembered Napoleon because I had nobody else to remember, no one like him, a figure of romance. But he seemed so glad to see me, yesterday night . . . when he remembered who I was.

Long before Latour was expected, Marie had passed from incoherence to a fatalistic calm. When he came, he found her in a dark dress, with her curls brushed down and held with a gilt clasp, the opposite of her 'victim' style. He apologised for being a little late, and said he had been kept at the office. It was all conventional and very polite. Agathe brought him a glass of madeira wine.

"What exactly do you do at Plans?" asked Marie.

"Nothing much. Plans is not very important, but when General Buonaparte gets there it'll be a different story."

'Oh, he's going to Plans too, is he?"

"Yes. It's ridiculous, because he ought to be on a battle front. But Paris is a hotbed of jealousy – "

"Did he ask Madame Permon to marry him?"

She hadn't meant to ask that question, but it had been on the tip of her tongue since the night before. Latour did not reply at once. When it came, his answer was cutting.

"Does it matter?"

"No – oh no, of course not. It surprised me when I heard it, that was all."

"Who told you? I wager it was Laure Permon. She told Junot the same rigmarole, and he told me. Junot's rather sweet on Laure, you may have noticed. Personally I would take everything she says with a grain of salt – the little cat! There may have been some *tendresses* between the general and Madame Permon, I don't know. Perhaps he went to her for comfort, they're old friends, and he's been out of spirits since his *affaire* with Désirée Clary came to nothing."

"Who's Désirée Clary?"

"A girl he was courting in Marseille, before I met him."

"Tell me how you came to meet him."

Latour began his story at Entrevaux, omitting his enlistment after her taunt and the months at Digne which followed. He described the 'wonderful time' which came next, the general's interest, the bivouac at Cap Martin and the bright vision of Corsica, fading too soon, and then his own reconnaissance of Fort Saorgio. As he relived that time his excitement communicated itself to Marie; he went to war, and she was with him on those mountain peaks above Italy; she heard the firing and saw the cannon smoke of Dego. This was no longer the slouching sergeant of the National Guard, this was a soldier, trained and disciplined by Napoleon's example. By the light of a clear June evening, even more than by the candlelight of Madame Permon's sombre rooms, he was also very handsome.

"You admire the general very much, don't you?" she said when he paused.

"I'd follow him across the world," he said. "And besides . . . it's to him I owe this meeting you again." He leaned forward from the sofa where he was sitting, and took her hand. "Marie!"

Not drawing her hand away, she murmured, "Why did you call yourself Vautour, two years ago?"

"Oh – I'd had a row with my family, and didn't want to join the National Guard under their name."

"Is your family in Paris now?"

"No. And you? Tell me about your uncle – and the pharmacy – tell me everything."

"Poor uncle!"

"What were you charged with, Marie? Was it under the Law of Suspects? Anything to do with the Noailles?"

"No, it was the Girondins. Uncle Prosper went to the guillotine because of his acquaintance with Madame Roland."

"Good God! And you were sent to prison – for how long?"

"Four months."

"Poor darling."

The tenderness in that *'pauvre chérie'* touched Marie. His warm hand tightened its clasp on her own.

"I was with a lot of other women," she said. "We weren't molested, or beaten, or flung into dungeons. We saw the light of day. But we were locked up, Charles," she said his name for the first time, "and we waited every morning for the roll call of death."

"My God," he said again. "And you were released after Thermidor?"

She told him about watching with Joséphine from the window when an unknown old woman showed them, in

301

sign language, the fate of Robespierre. She explained how she came to share a home with Joséphine, and it seemed important to tell Charles Latour that thanks to her uncle's provision for her, she was able to pay her own expenses.

"Sounds like a good arrangement," said Latour. Like all the officers in Plans, he knew that Paul Barras was the lover of Madame de Beauharnais, but unlike Etienne Favart he had no intention of saying so. Again unlike Favart, he did not believe that Marie's reputation would suffer from her association with Joséphine. He had some previous experience of Marie's strength of character.

"What do you do when you're not dancing at victims' balls?" he asked. "You were sewing army shirts when I knew you first."

"Now I work at a soup kitchen on the Quai Voltaire, from ten to two every day of the week."

"Do you indeed! I thought the booksellers along the *quais* were selling old clothes now. The whole capital's one vast rubbish heap, it seems to me."

"Our place is *underneath* the Quai Voltaire – under the second archway next to the steps leading down from the Pont Royal."

"And you dish out the soup?"

"Not now. I run a small dispensary and do first aid. There's so much distress among the underground people, they're willing to accept pills from a female apothecary . . . One day I even put a dislocated shoulder back in place."

At that reminder of their first meeting he kissed the hand he held and let it go. "Forgive me, Marie," he said humbly. "I was a brute and a bully in those days. Now I admire you, truly I do. It can't be easy work."

"It's volunteer work, at any rate. Everyone who works with Citizen Vincent – that's the *patron* – is a volunteer. The Convention has no time for organised charity, and that may bring down the Convention, one of these days."

"Are you predicting another Revolution?"

The talk went on, as impersonal as any talk between

two French citizens could be in 1795, and yet suffused by their intense awareness of each other. Marie hardly realised that almost two hours had passed until Charles Latour suddenly took out his watch and said it was eight o'clock. "I must go," he said. "I'm dining with some men at the Café Procope. Can I see you again tomorrow?"

Marie rose with a gesture of protest, and the man got up too. 'Oh, not tomorrow!' she said, and then, making a quick decision, "Come the day after tomorrow. Madame de Beauharnais is giving a small *soirée* then, starting about ten o'clock. I know she will be glad to see you."

Latour bowed. "I shall be honoured," he said. "I too shall be happy to meet Madame de Beauharnais." He took both her hands in his own. "We've learned more about each other this evening, haven't we? Real names, real feelings, everything?"

Not quite everything. Latour had said nothing about his émigré parents; Marie had concealed the original charge against her uncle. So far, each hoped to conceal the truth for ever.

"This is our real beginning, isn't it, Marie?"

"All beginnings have their endings, Charles."

He grinned. "I'm looking forward to the ending!" He dropped a light kiss on her cheek, and left.

Napoleon Buonaparte was one of the men at dinner in the Café Procope and dominated the conversation.

"Seen your inamorata? Make any headway?" he asked Latour without waiting for an answer. His table talk was not on the second-class subject of women – not on Mademoiselle Fontaine, nor on Madame Permon and her mischievous daughter, though he had thought more than once of a graceful dark-eyed woman with a seductive Creole voice. He held forth on politics, having spent several hours in the public galleries of a Convention in travail.

What the Convention was debating was a new Constitution for France. The rioters of April and May had been bawling for the Constitution of 1793, which of course was still in force after being eroded by the events of Thermidor. Determined to anticipate new riots, the Deputies were being asked to consider giving the People what they wanted, but in a different form, for a fashion set during the Revolution and continued for nearly two hundred years was 'when in doubt, change the Constitution.'

"I tell you, the Revolution is working itself out," insisted Napoleon. "The Convention has lost the power to govern and must delegate its authority to a new system . . ."

"I heard it predicted today that the Convention would be brought down by its failure to organise charity," said Latour, and Napoleon shot him a quick glance.

"By its failure to organise anything," he said. "What is lacking in France is a *central* authority."

"General Buonaparte thinks the Revolution is working itself out," announced Lieutenant Latour at Joséphine's *soirée*. He did not add that Buonaparte thought France needed a central authority, or dictator, nor would he have said as much as he did if Barras had been present. But Barras was conspicuous by his absence, and from Joséphine's complaint that 'Paul was being very tiresome' Marie guessed that her lover was resisting her blandishments about the purchase of a house. The Talliens were also absent, and the *soirée* was not one of Joséphine's more raffish parties. The guests fell with appetite on the thesis that the Revolution was working itself out, and since people were no longer afraid of speaking their minds in public there was one of the discussions at which the French excelled: piquant, expressed with clarity, with reasoning for or against the revolutionary principle.

"What an evening! Really one might as well have been at a Section meeting," complained Joséphine, who hated politics, when the guests were gone.

"I enjoyed it," said Marie. It was true, but she had enjoyed even more the attentions of Charles Latour who, once he had set the discussion going, had eyes for no one but her. She had taken the risk of inviting him to meet

Joséphine, who made every man her slave, and he was obviously not impressed by Joséphine nor she by him.

"What a very opinionated young man your Lieutenant Latour is," she said crossly. "Are you going to see him again, if I may ask?"

"If I'm at Frascati's on Friday night, I shall."

"Rather you than me."

The rendezvous at Frascati's, for which Charles had begged, proved only that they danced together in perfect physical harmony, and a day or two of afternoon walks and talks in the Tuileries garden indicated that there was indeed 'nothing much' doing in the Department of Plans. Then a series of events took place which sent all the staff officers in Paris back to their desks, and added fire to the debates on the new Constitution.

The first event had been expected. Stanislas Xavier, Comte de Provence, the brother of the late king, announced that since the death of his nephew he was King of France, and would reign as Louis XVIII. When he returned to France he would restore the social system exactly as it was before the Revolution, revive the power of the Church and punish the regicides.

This programme was not alarming, since the Comte de Provence was far away in Verona; where the danger lay was in an attack from the east led by the Prince de Condé. The Army of the Princes, as it was called, had been fighting with the Austrians, but was now preparing to advance independently in support of the man who had proclaimed himself king. The Republic was equipped to deal with the Army of the Princes. What was unexpected was the outbreak of a new rebellion in the west.

At first the cry was "The English have invaded!" A huge body of men wearing English uniforms had landed from English ships lying off Quiberon Bay, and joined forces with Cadoudal, the royalist leader in Brittany. General Hoche was recalled and attacked the rebels with the same vigour as before. He discovered, when the first prisoners were taken, that they were not English, but

Frenchmen wearing English uniforms, émigrés from England for the most part, paid, clothed and set ashore to try their luck in one last desperate throw against the Republic.

The old sad story began again, of farms destroyed and villages set afire, for Hoche, although he knew the terrain so well and had arms and man power on his side, could not immediately subdue an enemy with nothing to lose but his life, and the cry of the screech owl, the *chat huant*, was heard again as the Chouans rallied behind Cadoudal.

"Have you *no* news from the front?" Marie asked Charles Latour when the fighting had lasted for over a week. She had been strangely excited by the invasion of Quiberon Bay. It revived painful memories of her uncle's belief that an English defeat of the French in La Vendée would cause the Republic to sue for a general peace.

"They've taken some English prisoners, genuine Englishmen acting as officers, and sent them to the rear. Frenchmen in English uniforms are being shot out of hand. They deserve it too," said Charles moodily. "Why did they have to dress up as what they're not, those damned émigrés? Invade if you must, and take the consequences, but don't behave like a crowd of play-actors into the bargain!"

"They needed English ships to cross the Channel," said Marie.

"And it only ends in Frenchmen fighting Frenchmen. The very reason General Buonaparte refused the command of the Army of the West!"

"Is that why he's on 'sick leave'?" asked Marie, suddenly enlightened.

"That's why, and he doesn't regret it. He hates the idea of civil war."

"Which does him credit, but does he say so in public?"

"No, only to Junot or me. He was being unusually sociable at the Talliens' dinner the other night, murmuring sweet nothings to Madame de Beauharnais. I was rather sorry for the girl sitting between them, they talked across her most of the time. By the way, Teresa Tallien has a new admirer, a banker fellow called Ouvrard. What's the matter?" for Marie had given a heavy sigh.

"Nothing. Except that I'm rather tired of the Luxembourg merry-go-round – all those women and their lovers, changing partners as we used to in a square dance, without a notion of truth or fidelity."

"I thought you enjoyed being one of the New People."

"I enjoyed my escape from the guillotine, and all the freedom and fun we had at first. I liked being with Joséphine, and pretending to myself that I was part of a family. Now I think I'd like to live somewhere else. Only – where?"

He seized her in his arms – they were alone in Joséphine's salon – and said, "I'll tell you where! Marry me, and let us have our own home and our own family. Marie! I fell in love with you that day we went to the Hôtel de Mouchy, and I forced you, brute that I was, to drink your uncle's medicine in front of those two *sans-culottes*. You were so brave and so determined – and then, when I hid you in my arms to protect you from those drunken *fédérés*, so very sweet. I love you, darling. Can you say 'I love you' too?"

With her face once again hidden on his shoulder, Marie whispered, "I don't know."

"You'd know fast enough if you would let me possess your body, as you possess my mind."

With that he kissed her, not the light caress on cheek or hand of his skilful wooing, but with the passion which in spite of herself she had never forgotten, and in that long kiss Marie felt her body melting, telling her that he was right, he was the one who could thrill her and teach her a love she had never known. It was with a great effort that she begged him to give her time. "Only a little time, Charles, just a few weeks longer. We need to know more about each other."

In just over three weeks General Hoche defeated the Chouans and the émigré invaders and the dreadful tale of reprisals began again. The British ships lying off the Breton coast sailed for home while Hoche ordered the execution of seven hundred émigrés in addition to those who fell in battle. Not to be outdone Charrette, one of the rebel leaders, executed one thousand Republican prisoners of war. It was a death toll which disgusted a nation inured to mass executions, and made the Convention more determined than ever to bring in a new form of government.

About ten days after the victory Marie Fontaine was at work as usual in her amateur clinic beside the Seine, when she saw a man walking along the cobbles from the direction of the Pont Neuf. Any stranger was an object of suspicion to the vagrants and cripples who frequented the soup kitchen, and Marie felt a prick of alarm as she realised that the newcomer, whose face was not yet instantly recognisable in Paris, was Napoleon Buonaparte. Bare-headed, wearing a black coat and a cravat which had once been white, he was somehow less impressive than in his well-worn uniform. He came straight up to her, but not so close as to hamper her in what she was doing – putting a very efficient bandage round the forehead of a ragged man who had been set on by the gendarmes for loitering with intent.

"*Bonjour, citoyenne,*" he greeted her, and Citizen Vincent came up to inspect this stranger on his territory.

"*Citoyen,*" said Marie, "this is a medical man of my acquaintance, Dr Guidici, come to see the work we're doing here. Dr Guidici – Citizen Vincent."

"You're welcome, doctor," said Father Vincent, looking relieved, and the two men stood chatting while Marie dispensed a calamine lotion to a child with impetigo, and compassionately told a young woman, hugely pregnant, that the right place for her was the Maternité.

'Dr Guidici' was invited to taste the soup, and did so, talking to the women turned out of their convent, then he waited while Marie locked her bandages and medicines into an iron safe brought down to river level with great difficulty, and offered her his escort on the way home. They had climbed the Pont Royal staircase and were on their way west, well out of earshot, before Marie said, "Why did you come? It was very dangerous."

"It might have been dangerous if I'd been in uniform. That's why I borrowed this coat and cravat from one of the servants in my hotel."

"Out of uniform you could be taken for a police spy. Those underground men are dangerous, they might have set on you, and do you think old Citizen Vincent and half a dozen women could have saved you from being flung into the Seine?"

"As bad as that?"

"Every bit as bad."

"So that's why you passed me off as a doctor. Quick thinking, Marie! But why did you give me an Italian name?"

Marie looked abashed. "It was the first one to come into my head," she said. "I used to know a Dr Guidici who bought his medical supplies from the Pharmacie Fontaine."

"Do I look like him?"

"Not a bit." But in the black coat and cravat borrowed from a servant Marie knew whom the general did look like: one of the Italian waiters at Frascati's.

Buonaparte had been thinking, lately, that his own name was too Italian and should be changed. He had even taken to scribbling it on scraps of writing paper: *Napoleon Bonaparte*. He thought it looked well.

"What made you visit the soup kitchen?" asked Marie, and Buonaparte began to enumerate in military style the reasons for his walk along the *berges de la Seine*.

"One. This is the last day I shall be free in the morning; I start work in Plans tomorrow. Two. I wanted to see what you were doing, and I saw you doing it very well. Three. I want to be able to reassure Madame de Beauharnais, who's very worried about your – occupation. Only last night she was talking about it – "

"Where did you see her last night?"

"Er – I looked in at Garchi's for an hour or so. Now Four, and it's the most important. I want to say a word for my former ADC, Lieutenant Latour."

"Does he discuss me with you?"

"He told me he asked you to marry him, that's all. And since he told me that, he has had some very bad news about his family, and is tormenting himself about what you'll think of it. No, I can't tell you more, it's Latour's own story. Be kind to him if he tells you the whole thing tonight."

"I'm not seeing him tonight. I'm having dinner with a friend who's got an exit permit to leave France." Marie was talking to General Buonaparte boldly and bluntly, as she never dreamed of talking on the night of their exciting meeting at the *bal des victimes*, and as Joséphine never spoke to any man in her life.

"Then whenever you meet next, I do beg you, Marie, be kind to him. Charles Latour deserves a woman's love."

Marie was taller than the little man in the shabby black coat. She looked down at him with a bitter smile. "What am I to understand by that, citizen general? That you positively advise me to marry Charles?"

"There used to be a saying that a woman needs six months in Paris to know what is her due and her empire. You were Parisienne born, Marie; do you know what is your empire yet?"

"I'm trying to find out, *mon général*."

310

24

Marie and Joséphine had tea together, with the pug dog sitting between them, begging for cake. An artist could have painted a charming conversation piece of the two pretty women in their summer dresses, with a silver tea service and a bowl of roses on the lace-covered table. No painter could have interpreted the silences beneath the smiles.

Marie said nothing about Buonaparte's visit to the soup kitchen; Joséphine said nothing about having met him at Garchi's. His name was seldom mentioned between them now.

Joséphine, however, had plenty to say. That morning Barras had driven her to see a charming villa on the Right Bank, on which he had at last decided to take a lease in her name. It was a two-storey stone house set in its own grounds, with a whole suite of reception rooms, one with a bay window on the garden, which made it ideal for entertaining.

"I know what you're going to say, dear," said Joséphine. "It isn't as good a residential district as the Faubourg St Germain, but the house is special, so secluded, hidden away down its own lane. I fell in love with it at first sight."

"Is anyone living there now?"

"Did you never meet Julie Carreau, the wife of Talma the actor? They've split up, and she's moving out in a few weeks."

"It was a sensational split, as I remember someone saying."

Joséphine giggled. "*Everyone* saying! Poor Julie, she really was outrageous. Just imagine, the ceiling of her bedroom is covered with mirror glass!"

"Shall you have it taken down?" asked Marie drily.

"That might be too expensive. But I mean to have the bedroom walls covered in the new straw-coloured china silk. Won't that be fresh and pretty?"

"Very. But Joséphine, a whole suite of reception rooms! What are you going to do about furniture?"

"Dear Paul is giving me some lovely new things. A mahogany suite with brass inlay for the dining room, and a horsehair sofa and chairs, the very latest fashion, for the big salon . . . and a harp for Hortense too."

"You're a lucky woman, Joséphine. Citizen Barras is very generous."

"Tell him so," said Joséphine swiftly. "He's coming here this evening, and he loves a compliment from you."

"I'll pay him compliments to his heart's content, but not this evening. Don't you remember I'm going to dinner with Adrienne de La Fayette?"

"I'm so sorry," said Joséphine. "I declare the house on the Rue Chantereine has put everything else out of my head. Poor Madame de La Fayette, how is she now? You did tell me she'd got an exit permit and was planning to leave France?"

"Yes, but her plans have changed."

"How?"

"She means to go from Hamburg to Vienna, seek an audience of the emperor, and implore him to set her husband free."

"She expects to be received by Francis II while we're at war with Austria? The woman's mad!"

"It's a noble madness, Joséphine. For if her mission fails, then she'll go to Olmütz to share her husband's prison."

*

When Joséphine slipped away to make herself beautiful for Barras, Marie left the house earlier than she need have done to reach the Rue de Bourbon. She wanted time, walking through the quiet summer streets, to think about the changes the day had brought. She was in two minds about the new home in the Rue Chantereine. Either it was what it appeared to be, the gift of a rich man to his mistress, the public acknowledgement of their liaison – and Marie remembered that the abode of the notorious Madame Talma had been nicknamed 'The Temple of Love' – or else it was a goodbye present, marking the end of a chapter. She had thought now and again that Barras, who had a roving eye, was tiring of an affair which had lasted for nearly a year. In that case, who would be his successor? Who would watch his reflection entwined with Joséphine's on the mirrored ceiling? Would it be Buonaparte?

Their talk that morning had destroyed Marie's last illusion that Napoleon took anything more than a kindly interest in herself. He had walked along the river not for her sake but for Joséphine's, to soothe the anxieties which were more connected with her own fear of infection than with fear for Marie's safety. Marie was a realist; she admitted that her romantic feeling for Napoleon had been the fantasy of a lonely, frightened girl of eighteen. Now she was a woman of twenty-one, who had come through the Carmes prison and the corruption of the Luxembourg set, and was not going to throw away the substance for the shadow of a dream. Could she be sure that Charles Latour was the substance? Etienne Favart, an excellent man with an assured position in life, had asked her to marry him, and she had sent him away. Who was Vautour/Latour, and where was the family of whom he had bad news?

These questions might be answered tomorrow night. In the meantime Marie was glad to forget her own hesitations in the constancy of Adrienne de La Fayette.

Adrienne's stay in the country had done her good. She still suffered from oedema, but lying on a *chaise longue* in a secluded garden she had recovered slowly from her long imprisonment. The delay in getting any practical help from the French or the American authorities had only increased her determination to go to Austria. She had no news of her husband except the assurance of John Parish, the American consul at Hamburg, that he was still alive in Olmütz. Mr Parish added gallantly that he was prepared to pay the expenses of the journey to Vienna. His colleague Mr Coffyn, the consul at Dunkirk, had offered to lend Madame de La Fayette enough money, on her note of hand alone, to bring herself and her daughters from Paris to Dunkirk.

It was for the daughters Marie asked as soon as she found Adrienne alone in the bare little salon. "Where's Anastasie? Where's Virginie?" she said. "I was hoping to see them too."

"They'll be back quite soon," said Adrienne with a kiss. "George has taken them to see the fountain display at the Jardin de Marboeuf, to celebrate."

"To celebrate your exit permit, dear madame?"

"*George's* exit permit!" cried Madame de La Fayette, clapping her hands and laughing like a girl. "Isn't it wonderful? He got it yesterday, when we'd almost given up hope, and who do you think arranged it? The President of the Convention himself."

"Citizen Boissy d'Anglas?"

"The same. My kinsman Ségur laid the case before him, and Monsieur Boissy d'Anglas came to see me yesterday with the document. He said that as a Protestant he had always admired the stand my husband took on religious toleration and the abolition of slavery, and was glad to be of service to his son. It was so good to hear a man in his position talk admiringly of my poor Gilbert."

"Yes, that must have made you happy," said Marie. "And when does George go?"

"At the end of next week. A gentleman from Boston, a Mr Russell, will take him to Le Havre and on to New York. Our good Frestel hopes to go with them, and be with George until he reaches President Washington in Philadelphia."

"But you and the girls aren't leaving as soon as that?"

"Our passages are taken in *The Little Cherub*, an American ship sailing from Dunkirk to Hamburg at an early date."

"I'm sorry the family will be broken up," said Marie.

"We're not a family while our head's in prison. And George will find his own place in America, where his father's name is still revered. Marie, you've a good mind. I'd like your opinion of the letter I'm going to send with George to President Washington. It's only in draft form at present."

Adrienne got up and began hunting for her spectacles. Her eyesight had failed in prison, and Marie watched with pity as she limped to her *escritoire* and fumbled through the drawers. So frail and so foolhardy, and prepared to sacrifice everything for the man she loved! She made Joséphine, wheedling for new furniture, look very small.

"Here it is," said Adrienne. She cleared her throat and began to read. Marie had listened to some of her letters before. The wife of La Fayette was not a good letter writer. The letters were too long, too chilly or too condescending, and sometimes defeated their own purpose. The letter to President Washington was no exception.

"Monsieur, I send you my son," [the letter began].
"Though – because your views and mine were
not in agreement – I have not had the consolation of getting your ear and obtaining
from you the kind of help I thought
necessary to free my husband from the hands
of our enemies, my confidence in you has been
in no way diminished. I now place my dear
son under the protection of the United
States . . ."

"Why are you shaking your head, Marie?"

"I think you should take out the part about not getting help from him," said Marie. "I'm sure the President of the United States doesn't like to be scolded."

Like most writers inviting criticism, Adrienne only wanted applause. She said sharply:

"It isn't scolding to write the truth. President Washington should know I think he hasn't done enough to help the man he taught to call him 'father'; who shed his blood for him in the American War – "

It was true that La Fayette had sustained a flesh wound at the American defeat of Brandywine Creek.

"Look at this very room, Marie!" Adrienne continued passionately. "Poor and shabby as it is now, when we were rich it was the place above all others where Americans in Paris were made welcome. Nothing was too good for Gilbert's American friends. Who comes near me now? It's the ingratitude that makes me weep, the forgetfulness of all my husband did for them – "

"Dear madame," said Marie pitifully, "it was nearly twenty years ago."

"Does time matter? Do you think you'll have forgotten, twenty years from now, what it was to live through the Terror and be a prisoner in Les Carmes?"

"That depends on what the next twenty years may bring."

The romantic impulse might be dead but the admiration remained, and Marie Fontaine believed that the next two decades would be the years of Buonaparte. But she was wise enough to be silent, and the bitter little scene was ended by the return of George-Washington and his sisters and their merry conversation over dinner. How right Marie's warning had been was proved weeks later, when a letter from Adrienne at Hamburg, dark with tear blots and exclamation marks, told how her son had been welcomed in the United States. He was coldly received by President Washington and informed that his presence was not desirable in Philadelphia, the seat of government.

He was sent back to New York and placed under the care of his father's old ADC, Mr La Colombe. President Washington, in short, was too busy earning the title of Father of his Country to have any time left for the Hero of Two Worlds.

That disappointment lay in the future when Charles Latour was driven along the Rue de l'Université on the following evening. He could hear at some distance from her apartment that Madame de Beauharnais was giving a party. Teresa Tallien's loud laugh rose above the conversation audible through the open window. He was prepared, when Agathe answered his knock, to ask that Mademoiselle Fontaine might join him in the hall.

She came at once, very pretty in blue and ready with a remonstrance.

"Charles! Why are you standing there? Do come in, Joséphine's entertaining friends – "

"I want you to come for a drive," he said. "I brought an open barouche, the fresh air will do you good. Better get a wrap."

He was so grave that Marie merely nodded, and without making an excuse to the company fetched her pelisse of blue and green shot silk and joined him at the door.

"A barouche, how stylish!" she said as they drove away. "Where are we going, Charles?"

"Downriver first. There's something I want you to see."

The driver had been instructed, for they came out on the bank of the Seine and headed for the Pont de la Révolution. What Latour had hoped to show her was a square where the guillotine had been dismantled, the stools of the knitting women had been removed, and, where death and ghoulish appetite had ruled, nothing but an empty space. Instead, the terrible Machine was there as usual, and the few people obliged to cross the square were giving it as wide a berth as possible.

"I was told they dismantled it today. Too good to be true," said Charles grimly. "Coachman, don't cross the bridge. I think there's going to be a storm."

A peal of thunder sounded in the distance.

"Where to, then, citizen lieutenant?" asked the man. "You said up the Champs Elysées and into the country."

"Not in a thunderstorm. We'll go straight to the Quai Voltaire."

"Back to the soup kitchen?" said Marie. "It's closed at night."

"No, to an apartment I'd like you to see."

"General Buonaparte visited the soup kitchen yesterday."

"I know, he told me. He was very impressed by what he saw."

"And he started in Plans today?"

"He did indeed. He turned the whole place upside down in half an hour."

The man's tone was so sullen, his replies so abrupt, that Marie said no more. What *can* have happened, she thought, to turn poor Charles back into Sergeant Vautour?

The barouche set them down at 17 Quai Voltaire, a tall grey house with a huge wooden door banded and studded with iron. When Charles pulled the handle of an iron chain a bell clashed in the interior, and a section of the door swung open, wide enough to admit one person at a time. The first heavy drops of rain were beginning to fall as Charles helped Marie to step over the wooden framework.

"Ah, it's you, citizen lieutenant," said a surly voice. "I thought it might be. You want your key?"

In the semi-darkness of the long covered entry Marie saw a man who might have been the archetypal concierge of a Variétés farce: middle-aged, ill-tempered, and who while he addressed Latour was raking Marie with his eyes.

"This is Citizen Bélard, the concierge," said Latour, and Marie's civil "*Bonsoir, monsieur*," was acknowledged with a grunt.

"Is there a light on the staircase?" asked Latour, and was told No, and not in the apartment either. "I can sell

318

you a candle," said the concierge, "else you won't be able to see a thing."

They waited under the archway, protected from the rain, while Bélard ran across a cobbled yard to his *loge* in another wing of the ancient building, and came back with a tallow candle in a tin holder and a huge iron key. When he was given the price of the candle he stood juggling the *sous* in his hand, making no effort to open a second door with two glass panels which led to an inner staircase.

"Be careful, Marie, the carpet's frayed," said Charles. "Take my arm. Just two flights of stairs to climb, and then we're there."

"It's a strange old place, isn't it?" Marie's voice was strange in her own ears. She was not fanciful, nor given to introspection, but she had the feeling that hands were stretching out towards her from the doors they passed, that inhabitants dead one hundred and fifty years ago were telling her that this house on the Quai Voltaire was going to be more important to her than any other dwelling she had ever known.

"Here we are," said Charles, and ushered her through a little hall into a large salon with a bare parquet floor. Its noble proportions were betrayed by the shabby furnishings. There was a superb marble mantel with no grate beneath it, and darned wall hangings in imitation of the Bayeux tapestry. The nondescript furniture included a day bed with a faded velvet cover, a scarred mahogany table and some mismatched chairs. Marie went to the tall window and looked out through the rain at the Seine and the Pont Royal, and beyond the bridge to the south wing of the Louvre, the Tuileries and the trees in the garden.

"How extraordinary!" she said. "We must be almost on top of the place where the soup kitchen is, under the arches."

"And not much further from the place where I slept rough under those same arches, when I was a boy."

"Charles!"

"Come away from the window," he said automatically,

319

for a jagged flash of lightning pierced the clouds, followed by a closer roll of thunder. Marie retreated to the daybed, while Charles took one of the chairs beside the table and set the candle between them.

"You don't know much about me, Marie," he said. "I'd like to tell you a little more, tonight . . . By the way, this is not a planned seduction; when the rain goes off I'll give you supper at that new place on the corner of the Rue des Saints Pères. That's if you still want to, after you hear what I have to tell you."

"Tell me first," said Marie, "who owns this flat? Who lives here?"

"The owner is an émigré, living in Switzerland. As for the present tenant, I suppose I am. At least, I paid a deposit yesterday on the rent for the next three months. Marie, listen. When I asked you to marry me, a month ago, you asked for time, and I've given you time. I want to show you now that I can give you a home, a roof over your head, as well as a man to love you. Oh, I know this isn't much of a place," he went on, as Marie was silent in sheer amazement, "this room and the bedroom are all right; the kitchen isn't good, while the sanitation is medieval, but it could be a home, a place for you and me alone – "

"For three months," said Marie.

"Renewable," said the man with the ghost of a smile. "Three months is as far as anyone can look ahead these days."

"Unless he follows Buonaparte. And surely the general's not your problem."

He waited for another lightning flash, another thunder peal, before he said, "My problem is my family, Marie. I have to tell you that my father, my mother and my brother Edouard were all émigrés from the very beginning of the Revolution. I ran away from home rather than go with them."

"Where did they go, Charles?"

"To England. They had money, they bought an estate

320

in Wiltshire, and took no part in émigré conspiracies – until this summer . . . And now – I've just been told that Edouard joined the expedition to Quiberon Bay. And died."

The fatal name of Quiberon silenced Marie, and Charles went on, articulating painfully, with his face turned away. "Edouard was three years older than me. When he was commissioned into the Flanders Regiment we were all so proud, and I wanted to be a soldier, just like him. And now he's been shot by a French firing squad, wearing an English uniform – a returned émigré and a traitor to his country."

She would have gone to him then, kissed him and comforted him, but the mute male misery frightened Marie Fontaine. All she could say was, "How do you know?"

"An eyewitness to the – the execution escaped, got away on an English ship, and told my father. Father wrote to me through our attorney in Paris – his first letter for six years."

"Charles, who *is* your father?"

"The Marquis de la Tour de Vesle."

So she had been right at the very beginning: Sergeant Vautour was an *aristo* by birth who had chosen the Revolution, slept rough beside the Seine while his family fled to England, and then – as he was reminding her now – joined the National Guard. "*You* know what that meant," he said. "Strutting and cursing in the streets, bullying innocent citizens – "

"Not always, Charles."

He had made his confession to her; now it was Marie's turn to tell the truth.

"My uncle wasn't innocent," she said. "Nor was the man who called himself Adam Boone."

He saw again the rabbit smile, the bluff and treacherous exterior of Prosper Fontaine. "Who was Boone?" he asked.

"Adam Boone was an English spy who died in the

Vendée fighting, not very long after you first suspected him."

Marie told him the whole story then, of the real charge in which she herself had been involved, and the false charge by which Fouquier-Tinville sent her uncle to the guillotine. "Don't you see?" she said. "Quiberon was the invasion they were plotting in '93, only the Vendéens rose too soon and were defeated. As for my uncle's belief that an English invasion would bring us peace on earth, I can only think he was demented, and forgive him."

"Forgive him?" said Charles Latour. "When he might have caused your death too?"

"As you must forgive your brother for the English uniform at Quiberon Bay."

"You're very understanding," said Latour, getting up and in spite of his warning to Marie going close to the window where the streaks of lightning played. "It *is* the uniform I can't forgive. If Edouard had gone to Ghent to join the Army of the Princes, and fallen in action against Pichegru's men when they took Belgium, that I would have understood. He'd have been fighting against Frenchmen, but still wearing . . . the uniform he was trained to wear . . . the king's . . ."

"Darling!"

He had kept his face averted in case she saw the tears in his eyes. But at that gentle appeal he turned, and saw she was holding out her hands to him. With a cry he took her in his arms and laid her down on the old velvet daybed, kissing her neck, her cheeks and at last her lips. The thin silk dress slipped easily from Marie's shoulders, the chemise and the silk stockings followed, and she lay like a statue of living alabaster beneath Latour's adoring eyes.

"You're lovely, my darling, lovely . . . I love you . . . *Je t'aime* . . ." The incoherent words of love came to both their lips. His uniform was an encumbrance, but it was shed, and Marie closed her eyes against the revelation of his bare body. Charles lay with her and began to make

322

love to her, gently at first and then with a passion which broke the barrier of flesh and spilled over into a fountain of desire. Marie gripped him with her quivering arms and knew the joy of certainty at last.

In the abandon of physical love Marie shed the last vestiges of the reserve with which Joséphine had sometimes reproached her. There was no more need for secrecy or pretence: she loved, and her lover was insisting on an early marriage. His gratitude to her verged on adoration, for Marie had learned compassion in the prison of the Carmes, and knew how to help Latour over the shock of his brother's death. She reminded him that Edouard had chosen to fight in France wearing an English uniform, as Charles had chosen first the National Guard and then the service of Buonaparte; she reminded him that his parents still had one son left to them.

"The black sheep of the family, Marie."

"You won't be their black sheep for ever, not when you meet again. Barras talks of an amnesty. Some day your father and mother will come back to France."

"They had better stay in England. The old Tower is in ruins, my mother's estate was sold to speculators, and our house at Versailles was vandalised."

"But you and I will be here to welcome them."

Gently, Marie drew the poison from his mind as she led him on to talk about his childhood, the schooldays when he studied the same radical writers as her uncle, and the happy times he shared with her now. Their friends wished them joy, and would have entertained them every evening, but what Charles and Marie liked best was to be alone in the shabby flat on the Quai Voltaire. On closer inspection it had some decided drawbacks. The dismal kitchen, for instance, was down two deep stone steps, and had one erratic cold water spout.

"Can you manage to cook on that wretched stove, Marie?"

"I used to cook on an open fire. Oh, darling!"

All their conversations ended in 'Oh darling!' until they had to decide on the witnesses at their civil wedding, the only form of marriage now legal in France. The bridegroom's easy "Why don't we ask Napoleon and Joséphine?" made Marie shake her head, not because of the familiarity, but because of the ring of inevitability in the two names. Napoleon and Joséphine – no! "I'd rather have someone I've known longer," she said, and chose Madame Beauchet. Lieutenant Junot was to be the witness for his brother officer.

If Madame de Beauharnais felt hurt at not being invited to take part in the civil ceremony, she never showed it. Her reaction to their news was entirely practical. "Well done, Marie!" she said. "When his father dies you'll be the Marquise de la Tour de Vesle."

"In republican France?" smiled Marie.

"France won't be a Republic much longer, Buonaparte says."

It was one of Joséphine's possessive tricks to quote the opinions of her men. Hoche says, Barras says, and now it was 'Buonaparte says', without the style of 'General'. Perhaps he's her lover already, thought Marie coldly. If he wants a woman six years older than himself, with a mouthful of rotten teeth, there she is.

But Marie was too happy to be spiteful for more than a moment. Joséphine was being sweet and sympathetic, a striking contrast to Maître Favart who on being informed of Marie's betrothal wrote her a sharp letter to say he could not congratulate her on her marriage to the *ci-devant* Vicomte de la Tour, a man who had nothing to bring into settlement but his cloak and his sword. He added that he was more than ever certain that Monsieur Prosper Fontaine should have left his modest fortune in the hands of trustees.

Joséphine was in high good humour, for her removal to the Rue Chantereine was to take place at the beginning of October, and her plans included the hiring of a larger staff. More maids, a chef, a coachman-gardener, and the return of Mademoiselle de Lannoy as lady housekeeper and companion were part of a scheme which showed that Joséphine was facing the future with confidence. Marie's own removal consisted in borrowing the carriage to take her uncle's books and his fine glass and china to the Quai Voltaire, where they were unpacked with the help of the concierge. Citizen Bélard was a good deal less surly when he found that the lieutenant and Citizeness Fontaine were actually going to be married; he had an old-fashioned concern for the respectability of the house. His wife, Camille, was a pleasant woman, willing to clean the flat and bring firewood from the cellar when Marie was at the soup kitchen.

Citizen Vincent and the former nuns rejoiced in the coming marriage as soon as they knew Marie would not desert them. "I wouldn't dream of it," she said. "Think how convenient! I'll only have to cross the *quai* now!"

"You really want to go on with your first-aid job?" asked Charles when this was reported to him.

"Of course! What else should I do with myself when you're away all day at Plans?"

"I tell you we earn our pay at Plans since the general took over." The days of long leisurely lunches for the Plans officers were over. General Buonaparte, content to gobble a morsel of bread and cheese at his desk, expected them to do the same, and more was accomplished in two weeks than in the previous two months. Buonaparte knew the composition and location of every regiment in Paris and the Ile de France, and the location of every piece of ordnance as well as the reliability of every contingent of the National Guard. He had an interview with General Menou, the commander of the Army of the Interior, which left that indecisive officer shattered, and he showed scepticism about the most important Plan, which was the invasion of England by way of Ireland. Since Hoche had been delayed by a whole month in the action begun at Quiberon Bay, Buonaparte said it was too late in the year to contemplate an invasion, and furthermore he had no faith in the Irish as allies. He cited the campaigns of Montrose in Scotland, of which nobody in Plans had ever heard.

Charles Latour was made to put in a full day's work on the fifteenth of August, which had been fixed for his wedding, and he arrived breathless at the registry of the St Germain Section only moments before his bride. Marie wore the white which became her best, with two rosebuds in her hair, and carried the white roses Charles had sent. The witnesses were waiting with smiles and congratulations, but somehow the roses seemed out of place in that office, where the only decoration was a Tricolore flag stretched across the wall behind the desk, surmounted by the familiar legend "Liberty – Equality – Fraternity – OR DEATH!"

Madame Beauchet had expected to weep all through the ceremony, but it was so short that she had hardly time to produce her handkerchief. The registrar merely said, "Do you, Charles Maurice Latour and Marie Madeleine Fontaine, swear to keep faith and observe conjugal fidelity?" and when they replied that they did, he said, "Pronounce you man and wife. Sign here, citizens," and another Republican wedding was over. They kissed each other; Junot kissed the bride boisterously, and Madame Beauchet kissed her tenderly, whispering when cheek was pressed to cheek, "Father Carrichon will give you his blessing, dear."

They were married at seven in the evening, and went straight to the Luxembourg, where Citizen Barras insisted on giving the wedding reception. When Marie demurred, Joséphine begged her to accept. "Because you know there's no room here," said Joséphine, "and it's *so* important not to upset Paul now. He's very worried about the bill for the new Constitution!" When Marie saw that Charles was flattered by the proposal she gave in at once, and after all it was not an ostentatious evening by the Barras standards. There was no staircase to climb, and the bride and groom stood beside Barras in one of the smaller salons on the ground floor. Marie's hand was kissed by strangers – Charles said later that he had counted six known royalists among them, and three who had voted for the death of King Louis XVI – and the guests she did know seemed to float before her like a dream of her former life. Her tenants the Rocrois were there, nearly as abashed by the palace as the Beauchets, and so was Monsieur Guiart, with Maître Vial, who had once announced her death to Charles. Joséphine, in a new rose pink gauze, was escorted by her son and daughter, on special leave from school. The Talliens were there, with the banker Ouvrard close to Teresa, and Madame Permon came with her boy and girl, Laure clinging possessively to Junot's arm. The health of the bride and groom was drunk in vintage champagne.

It was not until the toasts were drunk that General Buonaparte appeared. He had put on his gold-laced uniform in honour of the occasion, and such was the force of his personality that his entry stopped the noisy conversation of a successful party. White knee breeches, white silk stockings and a gold-hilted sword were so seldom seen in Paris that all eyes were on Napoleon as he made his way to Marie.

"Madame," he said, "now that you're a married lady I may kiss your hand, but with your husband's permission I beg leave to kiss your cheek. After all, it was I who brought the two of you together."

To the applause and laughter of the company he gave the bride the three kisses of ceremony, and it seemed to Marie that she had never felt any lips as cold. Then, with a pleasant greeting to Barras, he shook Latour warmly by the hand. "Be good to her, my friend," he said, "you have a treasure there. And how nice of you to marry on my birthday! Yes, I'm twenty-six! You've given me a happy reason to remember the day."

He bowed, and moved away. When Marie next caught sight of Napoleon in the crowd he was chatting with

Teresa Tallien, who was looking triumphantly at Joséphine, and Charles was whispering in her ear that she had never looked more lovely.

The first wedding at which Marie had ever been present was her own, and she knew nothing of the pretty French custom of sending flowers to the bride. When they returned two hours later to the Quai Voltaire it was a delightful surprise to find the flat filled with blossoms, some fresh and fragrant from the newly fashionable florists, some, already wilting, from the flower-seller's stall on the *quai* and brought by Father Vincent and the nuns. They had all been arranged by Camille Bélard, who with her husband came hurrying across the courtyard to cry *"Vive la mariée!"* and wish them joy.

There were flowers everywhere, pinned to the imitation Bayeux tapestry, filling the stone sink and strewn on the pillows of the bridal bed. To these Charles added, when his wife lay naked on the new linen sheet, the rosebuds from the bouquet he had given her.

"Whiter than the roses!" he said as he embraced her. "My darling Marie! My wife!"

She remembered Napoleon's strange words about a woman's empire and her due. Marie had found her empire in her husband's arms.

25

The women who thought so often, and in such different ways, about Napoleon Buonaparte might have been surprised to know that he seldom thought of them. He was strongly attracted to Joséphine de Beauharnais, who with her graceful submission and Creole allure seemed to personify the warrior's rest, and there had been tentative love passages between them. In her perfumed salon, in the warm silent summer mornings, she had led him from kisses to more intimate caresses which left Napoleon in no doubt that the ultimate favours would soon be his. That would lead to a duel with Barras, and he did not mean that when the inevitable clash of wills with Barras took place it should be about anything as frivolous as a woman.

Frivolity or no, some of the etiquette of the old régime was coming back into favour, and on a chilly evening in late summer Napoleon paid a conventional wedding call on Lieutenant and Madame Latour. Nothing could make the shabby apartment elegant, but Marie had improvised a grate, with bricks instead of fire-dogs, which her husband seemed to regard as one of the engineering feats of the century. Napoleon praised it while he warmed his cold hands at the blazing logs whose light was reflected in the shining marble. The parquet floor was polished too, and Latour poured wine from a crystal decanter into crystal glasses which hid the scars on the old table. Books and flowers and an oil lamp with a rose-coloured shade

329

gave a new glow to the room, repeated in Marie's burnished beauty.

Napoleon told them they were living in a real nest for lovers, and he meant it. When he was out on the dark *quai* where only a wavering lantern lit the approach to the bridge, he wondered what a home of his own would be like. Paid sex, in which he very seldom indulged, was no substitute for a happy marriage.

With an effort he banished such thoughts and walked away in the direction of the Tuileries. He was present nearly every night now to listen to the debates on the new Constitution. He did not think that the proposals for a two-house legislature, with the executive power vested in a Directory of five members, would be successful, even if Barras were to be the most prominent of the Directors. Tallien's name was never mentioned; Tallien had had his day.

He guessed wrong. The Constitution of 1795 was passed by the Convention on 20 August and by plebiscite on 31 August, and the Convention itself prepared to wind up its affairs. There would be an amnesty for all offences against the Republic, and the site of the guillotine, the infamous Place de la Révolution, was to be renamed the Place de la Concorde.

Studying the results, Buonaparte concluded that the new Constitution marked the end of an era in which there was no place for himself. He turned to his old dream, Alexander's dream, of eastern conquest. He had once thought of Egypt as his goal, but Egypt was only a vassal state of the Ottoman Empire, and there was a strong and feminine French influence in Constantinople.

The Sultan Selim III had gone to war with Russia in 1792. He was defeated, and lost the rich province of the Crimea, a disaster which decided him to reorganise his army and navy on modern lines. He started to enlist French officers, and ordered the translation into Turkish of French manuals on mathematics and tactics. A cannon foundry was built at Constantinople, and French instructors in artillery were in special demand. Buonaparte began to think of offering his services.

At twenty-six he was young enough to start a new career, but that career must be continued far from France, where the army had been his whole life. Characteristically, he sought advice from nobody, neither his brothers nor his few intimate friends like Latour or Junot, or Murat, a cavalry officer he had begun to esteem. But indecision racked him when he realised that he must soon apply for a permit to leave France if he were not to find that the Sultan had filled all the artillery posts available. Leave France and all his dreams of glory! He changed his mind from day to day. Then, about the time when the Year Four of the Republic One and Indivisible began on 22 September, he became aware of a new movement of dissent in France.

Gouverneur Morris would have been aware of it much sooner. Gouverneur Morris would have known that What-a-People would not submit to a Constitution which meant the return to power of men of moderate opinions and prosperity, the very opposite of *sans-culottism*. Any technicality would serve as an excuse for rebellion, and the excuse was found in a clause of the new Constitution decreeing that two-thirds of the new Deputies should be chosen from the members of the old Convention. "Down with the Two-Thirds!" soon became as potent a slogan as the "Down with the *aristos*!" of the Terror.

Undemocratic, self-seeking, perjured and contrary to the first principles of the Revolution! The attacks on the Two-Thirds came in a flood from the professional agitators who had harassed France for years, and who poured into Paris from the effervescent south and from the west country torn so long by civil war. Those Parisians who had been enjoying life since Thermidor stayed out of the streets now filled with roving bands shouting, "Down with the Two-Thirds!" and the restaurant and ballroom trade dwindled to nothing. In the early days of the Year

IV the dissidents began to organise themselves better than ever: they had found a leader in General Damican, who had been dismissed from Hoche's command during the Vendée fighting on suspicion of being a secret royalist. Overt royalists, sure that the time had come for a Bourbon restoration, rallied round his headquarters in the Le Peletier Section just north of the boulevards, and with them came Chouans who had escaped from Brittany and émigrés who had evaded Hoche's firing squads, as well as determined *sans-culottes* and renegade National Guards. They were a motley rabble, but they were all armed.

On the evening of the day when General Menou, the commander of the Army of the Interior, was detailed to proceed to Le Peletier with a strong force and order Damican's men to lay down their arms and disband, Marie was waiting anxiously for her husband's return. Citizen Vincent had closed the soup kitchen an hour earlier than usual, though on and beneath the Quai Voltaire everything had been quiet enough except for bursts of shouting. She was at the door as soon as she heard Latour's step, crying, "What happened?" although she read the answer in his face.

"No luck," he said briefly, kissing her before he took off his overcoat. "Come into the warm room and let me tell you . . . That old fool Menou botched the whole thing. He approached the rebels as if they were at a tea party, all apologies and sweet talk, and of course they laughed at him. He came back to the Tuileries and reported failure – "

"*Then* what happened?"

"He was relieved of his command and Barras is the new commander-in-chief."

"Of the Army of the Interior?"

"Exactly."

"I don't believe it."

"It's true, Marie."

"But he hasn't been in the army for years! What does General Buonaparte say?"

"I've no idea. He left the Rue des Capucines before I did, and I only saw him once alone this afternoon. Are *you* all right?" He pulled her down beside him on the day-bed, and began to kiss her.

"Of course I'm all right, darling."

"Listen, I don't want you to go back to that underground place tomorrow."

"A lot may happen before tomorrow, Charles."

"That's what I'm afraid of."

"Let me get dinner." Marie released herself and went to bring a laden tray up the two awkward steps from the kitchen. Neither was very hungry; the shouting on the street took away their appetites. There was only one thought in their minds.

"When the general talked to you, did he know Barras had taken over the Army of the Interior?" asked Marie when their pretence of eating was over.

"Everybody knew it by that time. But when he talked to me alone he only asked if I knew the date."

"Is *he* confused between Vendémiaire and October too?"

"No, he only wanted to know if I remembered tomorrow was the anniversary of the March of the Market Women on Versailles, back in 1789."

"Good heavens, I was just fifteen then, and *he* wasn't here. Were you?"

"You know how superstitious he is about anniversaries. And birthdays, when they coincide with weddings. Smile, darling! I don't suppose he expects another march of the women tomorrow."

"And he can't follow La Fayette's example and save the lives of the king and queen."

"How you remember that! La Fayette did well that day, I grant you, but he only saved them for the guillotine . . . And to answer your question, I was there."

It was seldom that Charles Latour would talk about his service in the National Guard, but Marie drew him out as only she knew how to do, while time passed after the dishes were put away, and in the chilling room they began to put small logs on to the fire one by one. It was the first night they had spent alone together without going early to bed. The street was quiet, and eleven had struck from an old clock on the mantel when Marie became aware of her husband's increasing restlessness. He wanted to be back in a soldier's world and part of whatever might be going forward.

"Have you any idea where the general is now, Charles?"

"Probably at the Convention, listening to Barras speechifying."

"How would you like to join him there?"

"He'd think I was presuming. He doesn't like to be followed. Hark! Can you hear that noise?"

Latour pulled aside the faded curtain and opened the window. Borne on a gust of autumn wind came a steady drumming, the *générale* forbidden by the government, which was the call to arms.

Garchi's and Frascati's and many other places of entertainment had run their shutters down that evening, but the theatres, as always, were full, and Buonaparte took Junot with him to see a performance of *Le Bon Fils*. It was a sentimental piece, *The Good Son*, playing at the Théâtre Feydeau, but for two or three hours it took their minds off armed rebellion, and they were not quite prepared for the scene in the streets. Crowds of people were moving aimlessly this way and that as if driven by fear, and the reason for it was the high reverberation all over Paris of the forbidden *générale*. When the two officers had got no further than the causeway a still more sinister sound was heard: the tocsin, or alarm bell, which had rung for a muster of the populace in the days of the Terror.

"Get on, Junot," snapped Buonaparte. "Make straight for the Tuileries. The Deputies are sure to be in session still."

They were, and to his great surprise they were debating a defeatist motion to delete the Law of Two-Thirds from the Constitution. Giving in to an armed rabble! It was not Napoleon's only surprise, for as he took his place in one of the public galleries he saw Barras seated beneath the president's desk, twisting a bandanna round his wrists like handcuffs to hide their trembling. A commander, and not with his troops! Barras looked fixedly at the Corsican, got up and left the hall.

About ten minutes later the Deputy Fréron, whom Napoleon knew quite well, motioned to him from the entrance to the gallery. "Citizen Barras wants to see you in his office," he said. "Will you follow me?"

"If Junot comes too," said Napoleon. "He can wait in the anteroom."

While Junot remained in the anteroom with Fréron and half a dozen other men, Napoleon was shown into the office without delay. It was the first time he had been in that office since he was offered a little niche in Plans. Barras was not now sitting majestically behind his desk; he was pacing up and down, pale and perspiring, and he gave the newcomer his hand. "Buonaparte," he said, "we are lost. Our spies tell me that Damican will march on the Tuileries at first light with twenty thousand men. How can we defend ourselves against such a force?"

"We attack first, of course; seize the advantage and keep it."

"But we're outnumbered four to one."

"It takes more than man-power to win a battle, it takes will-power too. And we have the will."

"You may have it, I have not," said Barras in a breaking voice. "General, I confess it, the command is too much for me. I haven't got the experience, I haven't got the nerve. Will you take the command of the Army of the Interior from me?"

Napoleon seldom flushed, but now there was colour in his pale face. Here it came – the opportunity so long awaited, so often missed – the chance of a lifetime!

"I accept, citizen general, if you agree to one condition."

"Do you think this is a time to bargain?"

"Yes. If I defeat Damican and his rebels, conclusively, will you give me command of the Army of Italy?"

"Italy?" stammered the shaking man before him. "A campaign in Italy will be for the Directory to decide . . ."

"If we're defeated now there will be no Directory. Nothing but a White Terror or a long civil war. Agreed?"

"Agreed."

"Then I take the field against Damican. Now listen to me. We have five thousand regular troops in the city."

"And three thousand National Guards."

"I can't rely on them. The regulars must be called out and deployed to defend the Tuileries. The enemy won't march at first light; it'll take Damican hours to get that rabble on the road. They're said to be all armed, but with what? Muskets and small arms, while we have cannon. And cannon is my weapon," said Napoleon Buonaparte.

The tocsin had long ceased to ring when there was a thundering knock on the door of the Latours' flat, and when Marie hurried to open it with Charles close behind her they heard the concierge complaining about being roused in the dead of night. A far more cheerful voice called, "*Ici Junot!*" and Charles dragged the heavy door open with an answering shout of, "Andoche! What's the news?"

"Don't make so much noise, you'll rouse the building," complained the concierge, an unappetising figure with his nightshirt billowing over his trousers. "Coming with an urgent message, says he, at this hour of the night!" It was left to Marie, whose hand Junot had kissed as he came in, to apologise to Citizen Bélard and explain that it really was an urgent message from headquarters. She knew without being told that word had come from Buonaparte. When she arrived back in the salon Junot, with a glass of wine in his hand, was ready to blurt out that General Buonaparte had assumed command of the Army of the Interior, and Charles was coming out of the bedroom with a pair of riding boots in his hand.

336

"Have you heard?" he asked in great excitement. "The general's taken charge and he sent Andoche for me. Someone else has gone to fetch Murat, and – and we're all going for a little ride as soon as it's light enough to see!"

"Riding?" said Marie stupidly. "But you're not a cavalryman – "

"I've ridden for Napoleon before," said Charles, dragging on his boots. "D'you remember Mentone, Andoche, and the High Valley of the Roya? A year and a half ago, and the devil of a long wait it's been! But now – now for action at last. Don't worry, darling, go to bed and get some sleep, for I don't know when I'll be back. Come on, Junot!"

He kissed her quickly, so did Junot, who muttered something like, "Sorry, Marie, but it's going to be all right!" and then they were gone. She remembered the High Valley of the Roya better than Junot did, who had not been there, for her husband had told her about his daring reconnaissance of Fort Saorgio and far into Piedmontese territory. The High Valley was a victory of long ago, and here was her husband of six weeks pining for new victories after the boring months in Plans! Marie lay on top of the bed, wrapped in a warm shawl, and buried her face in his pillow. Get some sleep – that was the sort of advice you could expect from a man! When dawn broke over the swollen Seine she got up and coaxed the kitchen stove to light. She could hear the tramp of men in the Quai Voltaire and see the flare of watch fires in the Place du Carrousel; she could hear the jingle of cavalry. Was her husband out there now, on horseback or on foot, ready to fight in the streets of Paris?

It was nearly seven when Charles came home, grimy, sweating and obviously delighted with himself.

"We got the cannon!" was his cheerful greeting. "Those gentry up in Le Peletier haven't got started yet, so the general gave me an hour's leave. 'Tell Marie all's well,' he said. Is there any hot water?"

There was hot water for shaving, there was freshly brewed coffee, there was the hunk of bread which was all Charles wanted. Between bites of truly Napoleonic size he answered his wife's questions about what cannon and where?

The general had ordered him to ride with Murat and a picked troop to Les Sablons beyond Neuilly, where there was a gun park with forty cannon of varying calibres. Damican, blast him, had remembered them too and sent his own troop, but they turned back when they saw Murat and his men. It was a good start to the day.

"They mean to fight, don't they?" said Marie.

"We're ready for them! The general sent to an arms depot for eight hundred muskets and ammunition and had them stored in an anteroom at the Tuileries so that the Deputies can defend themselves if it comes to a last stand. They aren't looking forward to it."

"Do you mean to say the Deputies are still in session?"

"I don't know about a session, but they're all there, locked into their own hall. Best place for them!"

"But what's Barras doing now?" She wondered if the man who was afraid to fight had taken refuge with Joséphine.

"I saw him striking attitudes on horseback. Buonaparte's the effective commander, and when I left he was giving orders to put a field hospital in the old guardroom where I used to sleep. The hospital's going to be a problem, though, for Menou's *Service de Santé* was as sloppy as everything else, and they haven't enough doctors or orderlies. Buonaparte sent to the Hôtel Dieu, but they claim they're shorthanded too. That's what comes of throwing out the Sisters of Charity. Kiss me, darling, I must go."

"Charles, wait!"

"What is it?" he said, impatient to be gone.

"I could help in the hospital."

"You, Marie? Listen, my love, there's going to be a battle, and the battlefield's no place for a woman."

"I'm sick of hearing about a woman's place!" said Marie violently. "I've had a lot of practice in first aid at Citizen Vincent's, and the general knows it."

"This battle won't be fought underground," said Charles. "Come and look."

They had been standing in the dismal kitchen, where there was no room for even one person to sit down, and Charles took Marie by the arm, not tenderly, to lead her back into the salon. It was full daylight now, though cloudy, and across the Seine Marie saw troops marching across the Place du Carrousel to surround the Tuileries, and cavalry riding into the great garden.

"That looks like battle order, doesn't it?" said Charles. "My dear girl, it's out of the question that you should get caught up in it!"

"Nothing's out of the question if Napoleon Buonaparte, who refused the Army of the West, is prepared to start a civil war by firing on Frenchmen."

"This is a different situation, Marie! He has to use every means to defend the elected government."

"Even such means as using a woman's skill? I'm going to the Tuileries to ask the man himself if I can help."

Nothing he could say made her change her mind. Marie was already warmly dressed; she put on a clean white apron under her green overcoat, tied a dark scarf over her hair, and so prepared set off across the Pont Royal with her husband. As they crossed the bridge she told him that on a June day three years earlier Napoleon had said to her uncle and herself that if he were king he would have given the rabble of that time a whiff of grapeshot. "Is that what he means to give them today?" she asked.

"More than grapeshot, judging from what we brought back from Les Sablons," said Charles. "Marie, for God's sake, be careful!" The horses of a new detachment of cavalry were crowding them off the causeway. They were in the middle of an army now, for Buonaparte had stationed foot soldiers at strategic points on the Left Bank, guarding the Seine bridges in case of an attack downhill from the Odéon, but concentrating his forces in the streets around the Tuileries. Provisions were being unloaded from the Quartermaster-General's stores as Marie and Charles made their way to where Napoleon stood with staff officers around him.

"Lieutenant Latour reporting for duty, *mon général*," said Charles, saluting.

"Madame Latour too, I see," said Buonaparte. "Marie, what the devil are you doing here?"

"I told her to stay at home," said Charles, and somebody stifled a laugh.

"I thought I could help in the field hospital," said Marie. "I've had a good deal of practice in first aid."

"I know you have. But amputations and the extraction of bullets can't be called first aid. Can you face up to that?"

"Yes, I can."

"Well – we have one army doctor with us now, and one civilian, and that's all. I can't think of a better training for a medical orderly than the Carmes prison and Citizen Vincent's establishment under the *quai*. Surgeon-Captain Bosquet" (he motioned forward one of the officers in the group) "will you accept the services of Madame Latour? She can make bandages and empty slops."

The army doctor, after a quick assessing glance at Marie, said, "Willingly, *mon général*."

"Remember, madame," said Napoleon, "you are to obey the doctor implicitly, and you are not to leave the shelter of the palace on any pretext whatsoever. Is that clear?"

"*A vos ordres, mon général*."

"*Allez, bonne chance*! Come on, Latour, let's have a look at your old comrades of the Fourth."

With one silent look at his wife Latour strode off with the general to the corner of the Rue Neuve St Roch, where a couple of cannon were trained on the front of St Roch's church. So her old *quartier* was to be in the thick of the fighting! Marie wondered if Louis Rocroi had run down the shutters of the Pharmacie Fontaine, as her uncle would certainly have done on such a day.

"Follow me, madame," said Bosquet. "What kind of bandages can you make – roller?"

"Roller, double-head and single; many-tailed; and triangular."

"Good! We have calico, but nothing prepared. You can start work in here."

'Here' was a side-room no larger than a cupboard, off the *chambrée* where Sergeant Vautour of the National Guard had slept, and where the pallet beds, each covered with two army blankets but no sheets, were now aligned to receive the wounded. In the side-room was one chair, a trestle table, rolls of unbleached calico one metre wide, and a pair of scissors. There was an open window, through which came the sound of wheels and horses, and all the noise of an assembling army. There was also, as Marie took off her coat, the sound of an unmistakable voice saying loudly "Soldiers!" the key word of Napoleon's life.

"You'd like the window left open?" said Bosquet. "Right, but if the firing comes too close get down on the floor. Got everything you need?"

Marie ran a finger along the blunt blades of the scissors. "Have you a pair sharper than these?" she asked.

"We've got two pairs, both sharper, but they'll be needed for cutting through uniform cloth. Just do the best you can."

Suppressing a qualm, Marie set to work. The chair, by good luck, was barred, so that when lengths of calico were cut they could be threaded through the bars and rolled smooth and tight. It was a method Prosper Fontaine had taught her, and Marie reflected sadly that the uncle who made a foolish plan for peace had given his niece some idea of how to prepare for war. He would have deplored the lack of sealed envelopes for the new bandages, but Marie could only leave them on the tables, in rolls and then in piles.

Now and again during that long morning she went to the window for a breath of air, for it was very close in the side-room, and she guessed that fires had been lit in the emergency hospital. She could see very little beyond one of the cannon at the corner of the Rue Neuve St Roch, for the church itself was outside her line of vision, but not outside her memory. She could picture every inch of the façade, with St Roch and his dog over one of the three great doors; she could picture the flight of stone steps up which she had stumbled on a day almost two years ago, through a crowd jeering at the sight of a queen going to the guillotine in a blood-stained dress. She had an illogical feeling that this day, though it was to witness the triumph of the Republic, was in some sort a revenge for that day, with St Roch, locked and silent though it was, still at the beating heart of Paris.

Where was the enemy? Rain had begun to fall, but surely bad weather would not prevent an attack? Marie was glad to hear from a soldier who entered the side-room about midday that Damican's men were on the move at last. Reports announced that they were coming slowly down from Le Peletier, obviously making straight for the Tuileries. The man had brought her some soup with a slice of coarse bread. It was a thick pea soup, served in a soldier's *gamelle*, cleaner by far than the unsavoury mugs of the Carmes prison, but tainted by a peculiar smell which came through the open door of the *chambrée*.

"What's the matter, citizeness?" the soldier asked. "Can't finish your soup?"

"It's very good, but I'm not hungry. What's that funny smell?"

"The Surgeon-Captain's boiling up some pitch."

Pitch, Marie knew, was used to cauterise an amputated limb. The moment of truth was coming closer now. I mustn't weaken, I mustn't be a coward, she told herself, as not long after she was left alone again a faint drumming was heard above the rising wind. Running to the window, she saw a gun-crew gathered round the cannon at the end of the Rue Neuve St Roch, and among them a familiar figure in a grey riding coat and cocked hat. She saw Napoleon stiffen as the sound of drums grew louder – louder still, and Damican's rebels, in a solid phalanx, poured down the Rue St Honoré. He waited, and his gunners waited in a silence broken only by the jingle of harness, until the crucial moment came.

Napoleon shouted "Fire!" in a voice that was the very voice of the cannon, and then came the clap and roar of the shots which tore the leading rebel column apart and sent the survivors up the steps of St Roch's church. There, where an artist had sketched Marie Antoinette on her way to the guillotine, they lay sprawling and screaming in their blood.

Those in the rear ranks wavered, but reformed and came on, while Napoleon ordered a cavalry charge as the cannon were dragged forward to the Rue St Honoré itself. Damican had placed sharpshooters in the forefront of the battle, and for ten minutes the narrow street was filled with a terrible carnage of men and horses until the cannon fired again, east and west to clear the causeway. Then the rebels fled back towards the Rue Royale, and the government wounded began coming into the Tuileries.

As there were no stretcher-bearers or orderlies the troops themselves carried in their helpless comrades, while the walking wounded limped along supporting one another. All Marie's bandages were taken into the *chambrée*, while she listened appalled to the groans, even the cries, which could not be suppressed, and the barked orders of the two doctors and the *sous-officiers* until the call came which she had been waiting for:

"Madame! Come quickly, please!"

Then the bad hours began, when two doctors struggled with the needs of many wounded, and the bucket of pitch was taken off a charcoal brazier and put to its appointed use. The rough surgery of the time did not allow of waiting, and shattered limbs were amputated as a priority, before ball cartridges were extracted with forceps from the bodies of unconscious men. At one point the army doctor was heard shouting, "Get some of those damn Deputies down to help. Why should they sit upstairs on their backsides while we do their work for them?" A few ineffectual civilians made their appearance, but most of the auxiliary orderlies were soldiers, stumbling out, as Marie stumbled, with buckets containing rags of uniforms and dressings rank with blood and pus. No one noticed or cared that one of the orderlies was a woman in a bloodstained apron with her bright hair hidden under a scarf. No one cared about anything but the task in hand.

Marie discovered the use of the sharp shears, for under the civilian doctor's direction she cut off parts of two uniforms, a tunic here and breeches there, and he even allowed her to apply a tourniquet on the upper part of a wounded arm. She was engaged in this task – and earned an approving nod – when a second attempt was made on the Tuileries. This time Damican attacked from the Left Bank, and was met with grapeshot from the Pont Neuf and cannon fire across the river. More wounded were brought to the Tuileries, more bodies taken to an improvised mortuary. But the rebels were in retreat, this time for good, some returning to the Le Peletier Section, others going into hiding in the city or even beyond the Gates. Napoleon was victorious, and the road to Italy lay clear before him.

It was not until all danger of attack was over that General Buonaparte came to visit the wounded men. Sixty lay in the *chambrée*, many drowsy under the influence of such opiates as the Surgeon-Captain had to hand, but all able to smile when the general paused at every bed. He called them his children, praising them, with a tweak of the ear here, a pat on the shoulder there, and Marie saw how even the most helpless followed him with their eyes.

Darkness had fallen, and the emergency hospital was lit by only a few oil lamps, which meant that there were deep pools of shadows in one of which Marie successfully hid herself, nor did Napoleon seek her out. But he must have been aware of her presence, for before he left he had a short quiet talk with Bosquet, who looked more than once in her direction. It was the civilian doctor, whose name she never learned, who told her that the little commotion at the door, where Bosquet was greeting a group of newcomers, marked the arrival of two doctors and four medical orderlies from the Hôtel Dieu. "Some of them were for Damican this morning," he said with a chuckle, "but now they've decided to join the winning side."

"We *have* won, then?" said Marie. Suddenly she felt very tired.

"We have thirty dead and sixty wounded; Damican's claiming three hundred casualties, so the figures speak for themselves. I should think you'll be able to go home now, young lady, you've done well." And as Marie smiled her thanks without speaking, he added, "Who taught you to put on a tourniquet?"

"My uncle," she said, and tears came to her eyes. She brushed them away as Bosquet came up: it would be intolerable if he saw her weakness. But he guessed it, for he said roughly that she must be exhausted.

"You've done a great day's work, madame," he said. "The general told me I was to send you home as soon as the men from the Hôtel Dieu arrived. He meant to tell your husband to fetch you, and I believe he's waiting for you now."

Marie stammered some words of thanks. She rolled up her dreadful apron and threw it into one of the waste buckets before she went into the side-room for her green coat. One long breath of night air through the open window, and then she went to look for Charles, for whom she had been afraid all day long.

He was as dusty and grimy as she had seen him in the morning, but he was standing smiling and unharmed by the great door and Marie wept again when he took her in his arms.

"My darling girl," he said.

"Is it over now?" was all she was able to say.

"The Revolution or the battle?" he said. "Both. Come to the general, Marie, he wants to see you."

Napoleon was not far away. He was standing near one of the watch-fires his men had lit in the courtyard. Night had fallen over Paris and there were no stars in the sky, but in Napoleon's eyes Marie saw the dream of greater victories and a new empire.

He saluted the girl gravely as she came up.

"Well done, Marie," he said, and that was all. Not one of his grandiloquent speeches, just a soldier's brief "Well done."

"The day is yours, *mon général*," said Charles. "This day, and all the days to come."

"Take her home, Latour, and come back immediately," said Napoleon. "We shall have to work all night. I want every Section in Paris disarmed before dawn tomorrow."

Marie knew it would be a dawn of splendour.

She took Napoleon's hand, and kissed it.